true calling series ~ book one

LOVE'S TRUE
Calling

LORI DEJONG

Scrivenings
PRESS
Quench your thirst for story.
www.ScriveningsPress.com

For Eric, who gave me the room to dream, and Michaela, who made me believe it could come true. I love you both with all my heart.

CHAPTER ONE

*H*arper had never felt so ... old.

She fidgeted in her second-row seat as her classmates gathered in groups around the room—the proverbial square peg. The last time she sat in a college classroom, most of these kids were in middle school. Of course, starting her sophomore year of college nine years after her freshman hadn't been the original plan, but then, well ... life. There was no way to see what lay around that next curve.

And hers had seen plenty of curves in her scant twenty-eight years.

She glanced at her watch. Class should have begun five minutes ago. Odd for a professor to be late the first day, especially one with as stellar a reputation as Dr. Marjorie Vance.

A man strode into the room and closed the door behind him. "Okay, everybody, please take your seats, and we'll get things rolling."

Harper froze. She hardly recognized the man, but that voice she knew. The voice she'd witnessed transition from boy to adolescent crackle on the way to its present smooth, deep

1

timbre. The voice she last heard the night she broke his heart. The night he took hers with him when he walked away.

"Wow." The petite blonde next to her stared wide-eyed at their surprise professor. "Who is *that*?"

Harper's heart kicked into an erratic rhythm. Her skin chilled as if the air conditioning had been lowered to arctic temperatures. Was she in the wrong classroom? Or was this a crazy dream from which she'd wake any minute now?

She leaned toward the other girl. "This is Dr. Vance's General Psych class, isn't it?"

The girl kept her eyes trained on the man up front. "I hope so. Although if I'm in the wrong class, I'm stayin'."

Harper's gaze remained focused on the professor digging through the backpack now lying on the desk. Her pulse throbbed in her throat. She hadn't laid eyes on him since he was a boy of eighteen. A bespectacled, lanky boy with a haphazard shock of red hair, whose clothes always appeared a size too large.

But this was no boy. This was a full-grown, filled-out-in-all-the-best-ways man. The eyeglasses were gone, and that curly mop of hair was now more auburn than red, worn short and neat. His physique had caught up to his six-foot-two-inch height, as evidenced by the pullover shirt and jeans that fit as if made for him alone.

He pulled an electronic tablet from his bag and leaned against the whiteboard spanning the front of the room. His brow furrowed much like she remembered from all those years ago as he scrolled through pages on the tablet.

How could this be happening? After all these years? That, of all places, they'd end up in the same classroom at this small Christian university.

How?

He gave the screen a tap. "Let's take a quick roll so I can put names with faces. Anderson, Kathryn."

A girl in the first row and four seats over raised her hand. "Kate."

"Kate." He grinned, then tapped on the screen. "Got it. Barrett, Cody."

Harper's pulse accelerated as he neared the *T's*. Had he already seen her name on the roster before coming to class? Was he more prepared for this unexpected reunion than she was?

"Townsend." He brought the device closer to his face, his jaw falling slack.

Nope. Clearly no time to prepare.

He looked up to scan the room, and when he found her, her breath caught. She didn't know whether it was contacts that made his eyes even bluer than she remembered or his aqua polo shirt with the Dallas Heritage University logo. But that azure gaze communicated with no doubt she was more shock than awe.

"Harper." His eyes locked on hers but with no hint of the grin he'd offered the others.

"Here." A completely unnecessary answer. The silence stretched into awkwardness before he looked back down at the tablet and cleared his throat. "Trent, Shannon."

"Present!" The light-haired girl next to her sang out, and the tightness in Harper's chest reminded her to breathe.

His gaze slid from Shannon back to Harper, then he quickly looked down and rubbed his forehead with his fingers. Another flash from the past raced through her mind. A memory from that night, rubbing his brow with his fingers mere seconds before she shut the door on him, cutting him out of her life forever.

But forever had only lasted eleven years, because here he was. Plain as day. Right in front of her.

Shannon leaned in. "I think our hunky professor might be crushing on you!"

3

Harper shook her head. "Definitely not crushing." Not now, at least.

Her face heated as her hands squeezed together on the desktop. She thought she'd left all of those memories behind. All of that pain. Yet here she sat, face to face with one of her biggest regrets.

He set the tablet on the lectern. "Let's get started." He squared his shoulders, standing at the front with his hands braced on his hips, looking everywhere but at her. "I'm Dr. Wyatt McCowan, Adolescent Psychologist and adjunct professor. I was Dr. Vance's assistant while getting my doctorate here at DHU. Dr. Vance's husband was involved in a serious car accident early this morning, so she asked me to step in for the time being. He's in surgery now, and there will probably be a period of rehabilitation. But, while you're stuck with me for the foreseeable future, you'll likely finish your semester with Dr. Vance, which I know you would all prefer."

"Not all of us," Shannon said under her breath, throwing a grin and a wink at Harper.

Harper tried to smile, but her nerves practically hummed with tension, like static along an electric cable. Looked like he could be their instructor for a while.

She could drop the class, but her parents, who owned and operated the prestigious Townsend Drug and Alcohol Treatment Centers, would think she'd lost her mind. She'd been thrilled to finally have their approval, at least on some level, when she decided to go back to school. To drop the class now —

"Before we go over the syllabus, let's get this semester started right and open in prayer."

He bowed his head and she followed suit. Praying herself still felt awkward, but she loved listening to folks who knew what they were doing. In that regard, Wyatt always had, even as a little boy, praying with his hands folded at the table the many times she'd eaten at his house.

After prayer, they went over the class syllabus, then he pulled a stack of papers out of his bag and handed them to the girl seated at the other end of the first row.

"I'm sure you're all familiar with the Brackett internship. It's one of DHU's most prestigious internships offered to psych students. An amazing opportunity I know from my own experience."

He leaned back against the dry-erase board, crossed his arms over his middle and one ankle over the other, clearly in his element. If she didn't know better, she'd assume he'd always played the part of Big Man on Campus.

"The internship would take place the first semester of your senior year. Competition is fierce and expectations high, so decide now how seriously you take your studies, because that will be a big factor in determining who's awarded the placement. Beginning with this class and your final essay. Take a flyer if you're interested, but it would behoove all of you to think hard about the opportunity. Any questions before we head into the first chapter?"

When the dwindling stack made its way to Harper, she took one and scanned over the contents while Wyatt—that is, *Dr. McCowan*—answered questions. She shook her head. Interning at The Brackett Institute, one of the country's premier mental health research facilities, would be a huge boost to her professional future. And maybe her parents would at last have some hope in her.

Dropping the class now wasn't an option if she wanted to make an impression on Dr. Vance. No, she'd have to stick it out. And pray her hunky professor had let go of the past better than she had.

CHAPTER TWO

*W*yatt dismissed the class and stuffed his textbook and papers into his backpack, hoping to make a quick exit. He would have to face Harper at some point, but he needed to get his wits about him. Seeing her here had shifted his world on its axis. He needed some time to right it before he dealt with this part of his past he had long ago shelved.

Harper. Townsend.

Of all the classrooms in all of Texas ...

It wasn't surprising to run into her here in Arlington, where they'd both grown up, but he would have never expected it to be *here*. In this world he'd built for himself, far from the angst of Conway High School. This place where he'd finally found himself, his purpose, his calling. He hadn't reserved a space for her as he'd moved on. Which had taken some doing, since she'd occupied a large part of his life, and his heart, for years. Before she turned away and never looked back.

Without bothering with the zipper, he tossed the bag over his shoulder and turned, coming to an abrupt stop in front of a foursome of girls. As they introduced themselves, he glanced over their heads to monitor Harper's progress. Good. She appeared to be exchanging numbers with the young lady who'd been seated next to her — Shannon something?

After several giggles and awkward eyelash batting, the girls bid him a good day, and he took off toward the door, hoping to get lost in the shuffle of students.

"Wyatt." The voice behind him halted him, mere steps from making a clean getaway.

He hung his head and closed his eyes for a second before turning to look into the face he'd watched change from little girl to teenager to nearly a woman. "Harper."

"Or I guess I should say Dr. McCowan." She smiled that smile that used to send his heart rate soaring, back when he was a boy in love with a girl way out of his league. Before being kicked back to his place among the see-through kids.

She dipped her head, a curtain of chestnut waves falling over her shoulder, obscuring her face, but not before he noticed the pink blush that suffused her cheeks. When she brought her gaze back to him and swept her hair behind her ear with delicate fingers, she seemed almost ... shy. Uncertain. Nothing like the uber-confident, self-involved girl he remembered.

"Wyatt's fine." Her light fragrance wafted toward him, like wildflowers but with a hint of something ... spicy, if he had to describe it. "It's not like we haven't known each other since we were kids." He looked down at her left hand clutching the strap of her backpack. No wedding ring, and she'd registered for school under her maiden name. Hmm. "So you and Ellison ..."

She shook her head and waved her other hand in front of her. "Long story."

True. A story spanning ten years would, no doubt, be a long one. "I'm sorry. I hadn't heard."

She looked away for a moment, shrugging as she brought those emerald eyes back to his. Eyes he'd lost himself in too many times to count. "No children involved, so a clean break. It's been almost four years now."

He nodded. Divorced four years ago, which meant she and Brett Ellison had been married five years? And no children? That was certainly news.

She glanced around before leaning toward him. "Listen, I know this was unexpected —"

"I'm sorry." He glanced at his watch without really seeing it. "I need to be somewhere. Can we pick this up later?"

Her eyes widened, and she pulled her shoulders back. "Uh, sure. Yes. Of course. No problem."

"Great. See you Wednesday." He took the few steps to the door, escaping into the crowded hallway.

Once outside, he checked his watch again and released a long sigh. What was *that?* Totally not cool, that's what it was. He didn't have anywhere he needed to be until his eleven o'clock Intro to Psych class. But he'd been blindsided by all of those feelings, those memories he thought he'd left behind.

He stopped outside the Jackson Health Sciences building, one hand propped against his hip and the other clutching the strap over his shoulder as he stared down at the sidewalk. The late August sun beating down on him had nothing on the heat flooding his face. Hadn't he just done to Harper what all those kids had done to him? Snubbing her like she wasn't worth his time? That wasn't who he was. Wasn't anywhere near the man he wanted to be.

He spun around to go back the way he'd come and sent up a quick plea for forgiveness. Maybe he could still catch her, to apologize at the very least, and see if perhaps she had time for a coffee or a bottle of water, since the temperature here at mid-morning already topped ninety degrees. At Room 112, he peered inside, but Harper was nowhere in sight.

Disappointment mixed with relief. He wanted to do the right thing, but he also wanted to *say* the right thing. Giving it until Wednesday was probably better all around. At least he'd be ready, unlike today's unexpected, if not unwelcome, reunion.

He slipped on his sunglasses as he exited the building for the short walk to the campus coffee shop. With his usual frappé in hand, he settled himself at a corner table to spend the next forty minutes preparing for his afternoon counseling sessions.

He pulled a file from his bag and read over his notes for a client he'd been seeing about three months. Thankfully, the boy's tuned-in parents had noticed the sometimes-subtle signs of a possible suicide in the making and brought him in for counseling. And not a moment too soon. The eighth-grader had been on the brink but now appeared to be finding his way back.

Wyatt's gut coiled. If only Glen had waited. If only he'd called that night. If only he'd listened …

The *if-onlys* never got any easier. But when his best friend hung himself their senior year of high school, Wyatt swore he would honor Glen by living to make a difference every day. Show kids that their true value in who God made them to be far outweighed any hate or animosity others might have toward them, simply because they didn't look or act like the "cool" kids.

Cool kids like Harper Townsend and Brett Ellison. And the others they surrounded themselves with.

The cool kids who killed his best friend.

CHAPTER THREE

*H*arper sat in her sister's office and released a
weary sigh.

"He really blew you off?" Emery walked around her
French Provincial desk and sat in the other floral-print chair.
For the past four years, Harper had been working at Emery's
family medicine practice, and this was her favorite part of the
day, a few minutes of sister-talk after the last patient left.

"Couldn't get away from me fast enough."

Emery crossed her legs and folded her hands across her
stomach. "High school was a lifetime ago, Harper. Hasn't
enough water passed under that bridge by now?"

"Guess not." Doubtful there was enough water in the world
to cover the pain she'd caused. "You should have seen his
face."

"Little Wyatt McCowan." Emery shook her head, her long,
dark ponytail brushing her back.

"Little? When did you last see Wyatt?"

Her brow furrowed in thought. "I guess when you were
about twelve, thirteen. I wasn't able to make your graduation
because of finals, so I didn't see him give his Salutatorian

address. You guys were the best of friends growing up. What happened in high school?"

Harper hitched a shoulder in a shrug, the old regrets surfacing once again. "What usually happens? A huge change takes place between the ages of nine and fourteen. By the time we got to high school, I was hanging with a completely different group. And he didn't ... I mean, he wasn't ... you know."

"He didn't fit in with your new, popular friends."

Harper stared at her hands clasped in her lap. "I thought I'd found a group I belonged with until I realized they didn't think much of Wyatt or the other uber-smart kids. But by then, I was so afraid of being made fun of that I distanced myself from him."

She looked at Emery, tightness filling her chest. "It's ironic how people perceived me as the girl who had it all together when I was acting out of utter insecurity. Wyatt had much more self-confidence than I ever did, yet I was the one everybody admired. So upside down."

"High school is weird. And hindsight is much clearer than trying to see what's right in front of you at the time." Emery put her hand to her neck and rotated her head from side to side. "It's how we use it that truly defines who we are. I would hope you know now you don't have to live your life to match somebody else's vision of who you should be. Make your own decisions, be who you were meant to be—who God says you are."

"Working on it. Going back to school seems like a good place to start."

Emery nodded and grinned. "Is he still skinny with that curly mop of red hair?"

"Not at all," Harper answered with a chuckle. "Think less Howdy Doody and more Prince Harry. Only more handsome."

Emery stared at her for a moment. "Is the student falling for the teacher?"

"Oh, please." Harper rolled her eyes. "I did have to take a second look, though. I haven't seen him for over ten years."

Ten years and a lifetime ago.

"Let's Google him." Emery jumped up, grabbed her laptop off the desk, and took her seat again. She typed his name and clicked a couple of times before her mouth dropped open. She turned the screen so Harper could see the headshot from his counseling practice website. "*That's* Wyatt?"

"Told ya."

She turned the laptop back around. "'Wyatt J. McCowan, M.S. in Psychology, Ph.D. in Counseling Psychology, private practitioner in Adolescent Psychology, and adjunct Professor of Psychology at Dallas Heritage University.' There's a list of awards and honors he's received longer than my arm. And published in multiple professional journals." She quirked an eyebrow at Harper. "Married?"

"No ring."

"Not that you were looking."

Harper tipped her chin. "Of course not. But his hands weren't exactly in his pockets for the entire class."

"I see. Well, he's quite accomplished for somebody not even thirty."

Harper pulled her arms tight against her middle, but the tidal wave of insecurity crashed over her anyway. "And here's Harper Townsend, college drop-out because she got herself knocked-up, married at nineteen, divorced at twenty-four, working for her sister because she has no discernible skills. A mother with no child. A real success story."

"Oh, honey, that's the enemy talking." Emery set the laptop back on her desk. "Don't believe those lies. The Lord could very well have someone for you out there, and you can still build the family you want so badly."

Regret, all too familiar, blocked Harper's throat. In her heart, she knew God was making her new. But her head still held all of the memories of what she'd been, all she'd done, everything she'd lost, trying to be what she thought would bring her value, affirmation ... love.

Until the truest love she'd ever known came into her life, and she at last felt whole. Then it, too, was taken from her, leaving her broken and searching all over again.

She swallowed hard against the knot of grief that still resided in the deepest recesses of her heart. "Difficult to picture that. Besides, what good, godly man would want me?"

"One who knows a good, godly woman when he sees one. Keep the faith." Emery circled the desk. "Speaking of a good, godly man, I should probably get home to mine."

"Probably."

"Come over. Have dinner with us."

Harper shook her head as she stood. "I need to hit the books, so I'll just throw something together. I have some reading for my World Lit class, and Hunky Professor gave us a heap for Wednesday's General Psych class."

Emery laughed. "Hunky professor? And you're not crushing on the teacher?"

"Not my name for him. Shannon, my new study partner, or so she told me, calls him that."

"She *told* you she's your study partner?"

"Shannon's definitely not shy. Darling little, bouncy, blonde thing. Told me straight up, 'Harper, we're going to be great study partners!' and proceeded to put her number into my phone. I think we're the oldest students in the class, although she's not quite as old as I am. Took three years off after high school and is in her third year at DHU. It's nice to have a friend, though, even if she's probably no more than twenty-three, if a day."

"Age is a number. She sounds like a hoot. And have fun with all that studying. You sure didn't choose an easy field, sister of mine. I hope you know what you're getting yourself into."

Apprehension coiled in Harper's belly. "You don't think I have what it takes?"

"Oh, I have no doubt you can do anything you put your mind to. I just don't want it to be about Mom and Dad. If you want to go into psychology because it's how you think God has wired you, then go for it. But if it's for any other reason, you should ask for the wisdom to find what it is He has for you. Something you're passionate about, that you can't wait to get up and do every day."

"Passionate about," Harper muttered.

"And you know your hours here are flexible. Whatever I can do to help you, I will."

"You always have. But aren't you tired of taking care of your little sister?"

Emery slung her purse over her shoulder and walked over to take Harper in a tight hug. "I will be here for you until my last breath."

Tears welled in Harper's eyes as she clung to her. "And I for you."

How she adored her sister. She considered her and their older brother, Connor, her closest friends. Both of them had walked alongside her during her most desperate of times and still encouraged and loved her without condition.

If only they hadn't been away at college when she'd started dating Brett Ellison. Maybe they would have seen what she hadn't been able to until it was too late.

CHAPTER FOUR

"*Mac*? Earth to Mac. You there?"

Wyatt jerked himself back to the present, his thoughts screeching to a halt as his eyes focused in on his best friend and fellow professor, Mason Carlysle, who stood staring at him with a furrowed brow. "Oh. Yeah. I'm here."

Mason studied him. "You sure? Seemed like you were somewhere else completely."

Wyatt swiped a hand through his hair. How long had he been standing there staring at the wood floor of the community center, his mind meandering to a time he'd spent years trying to forget? "I'm fine. Sorry. Did you say something?"

"Just that we need to start setting up circles." Mason moved around him to the large closet where the folding chairs were stored, pulled out four, and turned back. "Problem with a client?"

Wyatt took the chairs from Mason and walked over to start the first of the four circles for the ConnectUP student ministry meeting held every Wednesday night. "No. Work's been great. In fact, one of my kids reached a major turning point this week. It's times like that I know I'm on the right track."

Wyatt's brother Reed took some chairs from Mason. "No

doubt about that. Not just with your vocation, but look at this ministry." Reed completed the first circle of ten and walked back for more. "What you've accomplished in Glen's memory is astounding."

The ache that always accompanied thoughts of Glen brought the familiar tightness to Wyatt's chest as he started on the second circle. He, Mason, and Reed had spent the last three years helping kids navigate high school's messed-up social hierarchy through this ministry Wyatt had founded for kids at risk of making the same devastating decision Glen had.

"What we've *all* accomplished. Couldn't do any of this without you."

After the circles were complete, Mason closed the storage room door and turned to Wyatt with his hands on his hips. "If it's not work or club keeping you preoccupied, there must be something else going on."

Wyatt released a breath and shrugged. "Dealing with a bit of my own high school angst, I guess."

Another crease appeared between Mason's brows. "How's that?"

"It's nothing." As long as he and Harper kept a professional rapport, that is. He was her professor for the time being, so that alone made it easier to keep a civil distance. They'd exchanged a mere *good morning* before class that day, and he'd been speaking with another student when she left. "Ran into my high school crush. Not a big deal."

"Except you've been distracted and quiet the past couple of days. Has to be more than just an old girlfriend making an appearance."

"I didn't say girlfriend."

"High school crush ..." Reed straightened, his eyes wide as he stared at Wyatt. "Harper? You saw Harper?"

"Right in front of me in my General Psych class."

"You're kidding. Is she still married to the quarterback Neanderthal from high school?"

Wyatt shook his head. "Divorced. Said there were no children involved, which I thought was odd since I'd heard they were expecting when they got married."

"Maybe she lost the baby."

"Yeah. Maybe." His heart caught at the thought of a nineteen-year-old Harper weathering a miscarriage with only the likes of Brett Ellison to offer her support.

"How is she?"

"Fine, I guess. We haven't really had a chance to say much more than *hello*."

The other two exchanged glances before Reed looked at him again. "Haven't had one? Or haven't *made* one?"

Wyatt stuck his hands on his hips and let his head drop, his gaze directed to his tennis shoes. He could never get anything past these two. One was his brother in flesh, his first friend and confidant, the older brother he'd idolized growing up, now a man he deeply respected. The other was his brother of the heart, having connected in an instant as fraternity brothers. He and Mason then went through grad school as roommates and were now both professors at the university they loved. Nobody on the planet knew him better than these two men. Nor held him more accountable.

"Look, little brother." Reed's voice drew his attention. "I know it's difficult for Wyatt—the former science nerd in love with the cheer captain—to think about dredging all of that up again after what she did. But what does Dr. McCowan—the psychologist—say you should do?"

Wyatt chuckled. "Leave it to you to knock me up the side of the head with my own credentials."

Reed flashed him a grin. "That's what big brothers are for."

"I guess I should make the effort. I have to admit, it's been a bit awkward in class."

"Cheer captain?" Mason's dark eyes danced with the broad smile that lit up his ebony-hued skin. "You sure didn't aim low, did you?"

"True. She wasn't on the fringe like I was. She was high school royalty. But growing up, we were best friends. She practically lived at our house, went to church with us on Sundays, even went to one of our family reunions down in Galveston when we were about nine, I think. Then we got to junior high, she made the cheer squad, and you know where there's cheerleaders ..."

Mason nodded. "There's jocks."

"And that was pretty much it. We started hanging out less and less until we weren't at all."

"Until that summer before your senior year," Reed said.

"What happened that summer?" Mason asked as they stood in the middle of the room while Reed's wife Jenny and some other volunteers set up the snack table at the other end.

Wyatt moved his head from side to side. "We ran into each other a few weeks after she'd broken up with her boyfriend. Spent every day together for about a month, I finally worked up the nerve to kiss her, then, *wham*. Back to the boyfriend—literally the next day. Never spoke again. Graduation was the last time I saw her, and then, from a distance."

Mason's eyes widened. "Until she showed up in your class?"

"Yep."

"Son, you really need to have that talk."

"Yo, Dr. Mac!" Carlos, one of their club kids, walked in with four other boys, his big grin lighting up his face. "'Sup?"

Grateful for the opportunity to focus on something other than Harper—and the past coming up on him as if were doing thirty-five in the fast lane—Wyatt fist-bumped the boys of varying skin tones, sizes, and social classes. None of that seemed to matter to these kids, which made him love them more.

"Our score, if you aren't afraid to take us on in hoops," he answered.

"Bring it on!" The challenge came from Ty, a lanky kid

wearing a baseball cap backward over a head full of blond curls.

Several girls trickled in, and before long, the room throbbed with voices, music, and activity. ConnectUP had grown since it began three years ago, and having access to the community center gym for a small monthly fee was a blessing. Two sports courts spanned one half of the room while two ping-pong tables, a foosball table, and an air hockey game sat along the adjacent wall. And a few weeks before, some of the girls had cleared a spot for hip-hop or line dancing.

Mason's girlfriend Rhonda arrived and greeted him with a chaste hug in deference to their current surroundings. Wyatt couldn't be happier for his friends and what they'd found with each other, while a part of him longed for the same.

He hadn't dated much since Allyson, whom he'd been with for a little over two years. But for all the fun they had and the deep respect they held for each other, there'd still been something missing, and they'd parted as friends almost a year ago.

So, while not actively looking, Wyatt hoped God would bring him that one person he was meant to be with, build something with. Something to last a lifetime.

"Hey, looks like we might have a new volunteer." Mason nodded toward the door on the other side of the room.

Wyatt looked over his shoulder before turning all the way around.

"Oh, that's Harper," Rhonda answered. "She came to my service projects table at orientation to see what she could do to get her service scholarship hours. When I mentioned ConnectUP, she was really interested, so I invited her to come tonight."

"She hasn't changed a bit," Reed said.

Mason looked at Wyatt. "That's *your* Harper?"

He gave a small nod. "That's her."

Her gaze raked over the room before settling on him.

When her eyes sparked in recognition, and she sent a smile his way, his pulse did that thing it hadn't in over a decade. Not good.

"Wait." Rhonda's eyes narrowed. "What does that mean —*your* Harper? Are you dating somebody, Wyatt? And how did I not know about this?"

Mason took her hand. "I'll explain later, honey."

"Be right back." Wyatt crossed the cavernous room, noticing several of the boys stood staring. But why wouldn't they? He couldn't tear his own eyes away from the beauty in a pair of modest navy shorts with a red DHU T-shirt and tennis shoes, her long, brown hair in a braid draped over her shoulder.

"Hey," he said as he approached.

"Hey, yourself." Her eyes sparkled in the bright overhead lights. "You work with this group?"

Her soft, flowery scent made him want to step closer. A temptation he resisted. "Something like that."

"Small world that we'd end up in the same place three times in three days."

Almost claustrophobic. "Definitely. Come on over and I'll introduce you."

They crossed the room and joined the others. She already knew Reed, of course, and had met Rhonda at orientation.

"I'm so glad you could make it!" Rhonda's bright smile lit up her eyes. "I didn't know you knew Wyatt, though, or I would have mentioned it."

"Harper and I went to school together," Wyatt explained.

Harper threw him a quick glance and looked back at Rhonda. Maybe she thought he'd tell them more. But getting into their history, no matter how innocently it had all started, wasn't something he relished doing.

"Dr. Mac, you comin'?" shouted Ty from the court, where he twirled a basketball on the tip of his finger.

"Yeah," Wyatt called back. "Give us a minute." He turned

to Harper. "We usually start with recreation before we break for refreshments, then conversation circles."

"No problem." She grinned and waved her hand in the air as if shooing a fly. "Go. I'll be fine."

Rhonda hooked her arm through Harper's. "I'll introduce you to the other volunteers and some of the girls." She blew a kiss to Mason over her shoulder. "Don't let those boys dust you too badly, you guys."

"Oh, we have moves, girl," Mason called after her. "We'll see who dusts who."

The ladies shared a laugh as they walked away.

"We have moves?" Wyatt asked, turning toward the court with the other two men.

"Okay, I have moves, Red. Try to keep up."

Wyatt chuckled as they joined the boys at half-court. Several minutes later, during a break in the action, he spotted Harper with Rhonda and a group of teen girls across the room. Music blared as the students took them through a hip-hop routine. He wasn't sure about Mason, but Harper certainly had moves.

When she tossed her head back and laughed, his pulse gave a little jump. This was the Harper he remembered from that summer, an older, wiser, and even more beautiful version of the girl who'd stolen his teenage heart, then shattered it into a million pieces. It had taken him a while to get over one incredible month spent with her, to leave her behind and move on.

But now she was here. And suddenly that summer didn't seem so far back in his rear view.

CHAPTER FIVE

*H*arper's heart grew another crack as she listened to the girls in Rhonda's little circle of nine share their fears and concerns about the new school year that had started the week before. Fears of emotional or even physical acts of abuse they'd endured in the past. An unkind word hurled at them, pranks meant to humiliate, being snubbed and ignored.

These were the girls she would've given no notice to in high school, so focused was she on keeping her spot at the top, holding on to her perch by her professionally manicured fingernails. Her brother and sister had excelled in academics, the gold standard to their parents. Harper, although smart, was no brainiac, and frankly, her studies bored her to tears.

Socially, however, people gravitated to her. It filled her up inside where the lack of parental affirmation had left its dark void, and she did whatever she could to hold onto her place there. Even if it meant putting a lid on that inner voice telling her to run the other direction.

Her eyes drifted behind Rhonda to the circle of boys at the opposite corner. Wyatt leaned forward, his hands clasped between his knees with his attention focused on a young man sharing something with the group. She'd hurt nobody more than Wyatt on her misguided journey to find acceptance where she shouldn't have.

"Nobody has the right to define you outside of who you already know yourself to be," Rhonda said, pulling Harper's attention back. "You get to pick the voices you listen to, but choose wisely." She picked up the Bible lying on her lap. "This book is chock full of things God Himself says you are. From the very first chapter of Genesis, where He says you're made in His image, to the Gospel of John, where He calls you His friends."

Harper leaned forward in her chair. Every time she found herself with someone who knew the Bible well, she felt like a sponge, soaking up as much as she could hold.

"If you're not sure where to start, go to Ephesians. It's a wealth of information all about *you* and how much you're valued and loved and cared for by the eternal God. A forever God. How long does high school last?"

"Four years," the group answered in unison.

"Exactly. The seasons of our lives are just that—seasons. Don't give value to the opinions of others who won't be a blip on your radar in a very short time." Rhonda looked over at Harper and smiled. "We're so glad you could be with us tonight. Do you have anything you'd like to add as we wrap up?"

Tonya, the girl seated next to Harper, nudged her shoulder. "Yeah. You can come dance with us any time."

Harper returned her smile. "This has been great tonight. More fun than I've had in a while."

She looked around the circle of girls, her heart racing. She so wanted to encourage them, but did she have the right? She'd never walked in the same shoes, but she understood the aching desire to belong. To *fit*. "But if I could share one thing based on my experience, I would tell you to not believe for a second that anybody is better than you. More important than you."

Her voice surprised her, as if she'd begun talking before she'd decided to. She had the attention of every girl in the circle, though, looking at her in expectation. Did she have anything to offer them?

She cleared her throat. "I love what Rhonda said about choosing wisely who you listen to. I didn't, and it cost me." Way too much. "So be real. Be yourself. Choose your own path, your own tribe of people you honestly enjoy and respect and who will always have your back. Be true to you, the way you were made, instead of trying to fit a mold. The world needs more originals, not more copies."

Rhonda smiled and shot her a wink. "Well put, Harper. Thank you."

"I'd say we're all pretty original," Tonya said with a grin, and the girls shared a laugh. "Hey! We should get everybody together after club tonight and divide up by schools so we can walk in together as our own tribe. Sit together at lunch and stuff."

Rhonda nodded. "That sounds great! But don't forget to keep your eyes open for others who look like they need a friend. Invite them here. Or to the barbecue on Saturday." She looked over at Harper. "You should join us. It's our back-to-school shindig."

Harper held out her hands. "I have nothing else on my schedule. I'd love to come."

"Cool!" said Remy, a darling young black girl with braces and the cutest red-rimmed eyeglasses.

"Okay," Rhonda said. "I'm going to repeat what we always say at the end of our conversation circles. Remember, bullying is not acceptable. Ever. If somebody harms you physically or makes a threat, you absolutely have to go to a person of authority. Physical harm or a threat of such is never to be ignored. Got it?"

"Got it," the girls said together as Harper's stomach twisted. How she wished someone had spoken those words into her life when she was fifteen. If she could have trusted someone enough to share her awful truth, she might have avoided a lot of pain. And maybe she and Wyatt wouldn't be just this side of strangers now.

After a final prayer, several of the girls came over to hug Harper and invite her back. Her heart was full to overflowing after spending the last couple of hours with these kids, and she hoped she'd be able to get more involved.

She looked for Rhonda and found her in a circle with Wyatt and Mason, Tonya right in the center, their heads close together to hear the girl over the din of dozens of kids talking at once. Not wanting to interrupt, she walked over to grab her cell phone and keys from the table where she'd placed them earlier. She loved that the group's leadership required everybody to turn in their cell phones on their way in the door. No screen time here, that was for sure. Just a lot of face-to-face community.

When she turned back, she caught Wyatt's glance. He excused himself and walked toward her while Mason called for the kids to huddle up. And once again, she found her pulse picking up speed at the sight of this grown-up version of the boy she used to know. In the long khaki shorts he wore with a navy DHU T-shirt and tennis shoes, she could tell the pounds he'd picked up in the last ten years were nothing but muscle. And those eyes ...

"You're taking off?" he asked.

"Oh, uh, I really need to. I have a paper to finish before New Testament tomorrow, and I have this psych professor who apparently thinks his class is the only one I have."

He gave a low-throated chuckle. "Sounds like a tyrant."

"You don't know the half of it."

He put his hand to the back of her arm for a brief touch she was much too aware of. And although he'd spent a good half hour or so in a hotly contested half-court game of hoops, he smelled of something faintly woodsy. Very masculine but not overpowering. "I'll walk you out."

She kept pace beside him, hoping this would be a slow walk to her car. She hadn't realized until seeing him again how much his absence had left a hole in her soul. These precious few minutes were the most she'd spent with him in over a decade, after their last encounter had left their years-long friendship shattered.

"These kids are incredible, Wyatt."

"They are. And Rhonda said you were pretty incredible too. That you had some good stuff to say."

"I hadn't planned to say anything at all, since I'm only a guest. It all just kind of came out. I'm not even sure from where."

"Ah. I see. *For it is not you who will be speaking—it will be the Spirit of your Father speaking through you.*"

Her brow furrowed as she glanced up at him. "The Spirit speaking?" The Father speaking through her? How could that be? She didn't even pray the right way. Nothing like what she heard from the platform on Sunday mornings, where only the best of the best did the praying in church. No way God would choose her to say what He wanted to say.

"From the Book of Matthew." He pushed the door open, letting her pass in front of him. "Jesus had just chosen his disciples, a ragtag group if there ever was one. None of them experienced in any kind of ministry. They simply trusted and followed. In chapter ten, He's sending them out and tells them when they're questioned about their faith, not to worry, that God will give them the words when they need them."

"You think He does that even with newbies like me? I still have so much to learn."

"We're all learning. God is way too big for anybody to learn everything in a lifetime. Maybe He used you tonight specifically *because* you're a newbie, as you call it."

"Interesting thought. But if only one of them gets something out of what I said—or I guess that the Lord might have said through me—that would be awesome."

"Very."

They stopped much too soon at the driver's door of her little blue Audi Q5, a birthday gift from her parents in July. Nobody could accuse the elder Townsends of not being generous in a material sense. She and her siblings had never wanted for anything, except maybe more of their parents' time. A family vacation once a year, sitting down to dinner together, a family movie or game night.

She shook off the thoughts threatening to dampen the joy of the evening. "Thanks for making me feel so welcome tonight."

"Sure thing." He shifted his weight onto one hip and crossed his arms. "Actually, I wanted to apologize about the other day, for taking off like I did. I felt like a heel. I went back to look for you, but you were gone."

She flipped her hand toward him. "No worries. It wasn't the best time, anyway. I had to get over to the Wentworth building, and it's a bit of a trek from Jackson."

"You have a class after mine, then. I thought maybe you had a job to get to, seeing how well you were dressed." Color suffused his face. "I mean, compared to the others."

She smiled as warmth filled her chest with the compliment. Was she so needy that a simple reference to her attire made her giddy inside? Or was it more about who said it? "World Lit. Then I go to work for the afternoon."

"You work *and* have a full load of classes?"

"Twelve credit hours. But I also need to fulfill my service scholarship hours. Rhonda gave me her number, so I'll call to thank her for the invitation and find out how to get involved here."

He stuffed his hands into his pockets, his gaze directed to the pavement for a long moment. When he looked back up at her with a crease in his brow, her gut clenched. "You understand what our ministry is about, right? That we reach out to kids on the outside looking in, on the fringe, so to speak. I don't mean any offense, but that wasn't exactly where you lived back in the day."

A heaviness settled over her as she studied his face, zeroing in on his eyes narrowed in question. Clearly, he doubted she had anything to offer their ministry. The thought stung, but she understood his reticence. Of course that would be how he remembered her, based on his experience. If only he could see past who she had been to who she was trying to be, now that her heart was in the right place.

"That may be true." She hoped her voice didn't betray the hurt of his rejection, although she believed, as he'd said, he meant no offense. "But that doesn't mean I don't understand how hard it is to be a kid trying to find your place in the world. Your value."

He nodded but appeared unconvinced. "It can be a big commitment. Monday nights for prep and Wednesdays for club. And we try to be available to the kids for weekend activities or to help with homework or be a listening ear during the week. It might be a lot to tack on if you're already working and going to school."

Looking away, she scanned the well-lit parking lot, where several parents waited in cars for their kids. Even though the sun had set, heat still wafted up from the asphalt, bringing the smell of tar with it. "You're probably right."

Except feeling the way she had tonight, being here with these kids, she wouldn't hesitate to make room for them in her life. It would be a blessing.

But Wyatt had been a Christian for years, had been in church since he was a baby, and was much stronger in the faith. If he doubted this was the right place for her, she should probably listen.

With a heavy heart that had moments ago been full of joy,

she pulled open her door and slid behind the wheel. "Guess I'll see you in class on Friday." She'd have to remember to give Rhonda her regrets about not being able to attend the back-to-school barbecue on Saturday. But if Wyatt didn't want her there —

"Drive safely," he told her before shutting her car door.

Once out on the road, she turned down the radio and sighed. "Hi, God, it's me, Harper. I just wanted to say thanks. Spending the evening here with these kids was amazing. And meeting Rhonda, who I think could be a good friend.

"I know my studies need to be my focus right now, and it's clear Wyatt has no desire to see me involved, but something happened in there tonight. Like I found a voice I didn't know I had. If this is something I'm supposed to do, please show me a sign or something. I'd really appreciate it."

She stopped at a red light. "Oh, and, God? Please, please bless these special kids and protect them as they start this new school year. Calm their nerves and help them work together to lift each other up. Okay, that's all I can think of for now. Thank you, as always, for listening. I promise, someday I'm going to get this praying thing down. Amen."

She turned onto another street. "I mean, in Jesus' name, Amen. I'll get it. I promise."

Her phone dinged with an incoming text as she pulled into the garage of her small townhome. Once she'd turned off the ignition, she read the message, smiling to see it was from Rhonda.

> Harper, you were amazing tonight! Please come back any time. In fact, let's do lunch and talk about whether you'd like to get involved. Tomorrow work for you? Let me know!

Yes! Tomorrow would be perfect to talk about how she could get more —

Her smile waned and heart fell. Except Wyatt didn't want her involved. He'd made that crystal clear.

Should she talk it through with Rhonda despite Wyatt's obvious misgivings, or thank her new friend for her kind words and politely pass on the invitation?

She'd asked the Lord for a sign only minutes ago. Was this it? Or was Wyatt's judgment correct?

She shook her head and tapped out a reply.

> Yes, I would love to go to lunch and talk
> about ConnectUP.

Once they'd firmed up their plans, she let out a sigh. Hopefully, she hadn't just added more bricks to the wall that still stood between her and Wyatt.

CHAPTER SIX

"*H*ey, Mac!" Mason's voice reverberated from the foyer of Wyatt's house Saturday afternoon.

"Come on in, Mase!" He looked up from sifting through several days' worth of mail when his friend walked into the kitchen. "So? How'd it go last night?"

Mason's ever-present grin spread into a wide smile as he set two large plastic containers on the countertop. "She said *yes*."

"Never a doubt." Wyatt dropped the stack of mail to grab him in a hug. "Congrats, brother. So happy for you."

"Thanks. It went perfectly, just the way I planned."

"Did she cry?"

"She cried. I cried."

"Wish I could've seen it."

"If you'll be my Best Man, you'll be up close and personal when I more than likely lose it during the wedding."

"You know it, bro." He picked up his mail again. "It would be an honor."

"We're planning for the day after Christmas, with the rehearsal dinner the day before Christmas Eve, since we don't plan to have club that night. That'll give us a good part of winter break to set up house before spring semester."

"Sounds perfect."

"And speaking of setting up house ..."

When the pause lingered, Wyatt looked up from the mail in his hand. "What?"

"My lease expires end of September, and Rhonda signed a new one a month ago, so we plan to move into her place after we're married. I could possibly go month to month, but there's a rent premium for that."

"Just move in here."

"You're sure?"

"Absolutely. I told you when I bought this place you were welcome to move in here instead of staying in the apartment. And don't store your stuff. Move it all in here. You'll be able to save money not paying rent or storage fees."

"I'll pay you rent, bro."

"No, you won't. If you do the cooking, I'm all good. Save your money."

"Thanks, man. That's a huge relief." Mason looked around the family room off the kitchen. "Speaking of stuff, you've lived here, what? Four? Five months?"

"About five."

"You plan to get furniture any time soon? Stuff for the walls, maybe? Something besides that behemoth of a television?"

Wyatt took in his sparsely furnished home. The living and dining rooms at the front of the house, as well as the two spare bedrooms, sat empty, while his study off the foyer was a picture of controlled chaos, skewed more toward chaos than control. And although suitable for the apartment he'd shared with Mason, the hand-me-down bachelor brown chairs and tan couch in the family room didn't do justice to this newly built home.

He loved that behemoth of a television, though, a gift to himself when he had space for a screen fit for quality sports viewing. And tonight, it would be perfect for movie night with the kids.

"I'd like to, if I had any idea where to start."

"You need a girlfriend. Someone to help you make this place feel like a home and not a bachelor pad."

"Oh, okay. Super. I'll just go right out and get me one of those."

Mason laughed on his way to the refrigerator and pulled out a bottle of water. "I can think of at least three great ladies right now who would go out with you in a heartbeat if you'd ask. And Rhonda has this friend—"

"No way. I've been fixed up too many times. Thanks, but I'll pass."

Mason hopped up to sit on the island, baseball cap turned backward, wearing swim shorts, a ConnectUP T-shirt, and flip-flops. "What about the girl who got away? Any sparks still there?"

Wyatt looked up at his friend. "Who? Harper?"

"Yeah, Harper."

"Not even close. It's only been a few days since we saw each other again. Way too much ... stuff ... still sitting there between us to know what kind of relationship we could have."

"Open mind, my friend. Open mind."

He pulled a manila envelope from the pile. "Hmm." It would take more than an open mind to consider getting anywhere close to Harper, much less go on a date. He'd opened his mind *and* his heart to her once and learned the hard way she couldn't be trusted with either.

The name in the return address on the large envelope was familiar, but he couldn't quite place it. He ripped it open and emptied the contents onto the countertop—several brochures, a response card with a self-addressed return envelope, and a three-page printout.

His stomach balled. "My high school reunion." An invitation

to return to the place that had brought him more heartache than joy, despite his numerous successes. Of course, the fact that those successes had come from academic excellence and not because he knew what to do with a ball put a label on him nobody wanted to wear. Geek. Nerd. And others he'd tried to expel from his memory. Not that he'd really cared what those kids thought of him, while Glen had put entirely too much stock in it. Never thought he measured up when he had so much more to him than the gridiron gladiators who'd made his life intolerable. More intelligence, more integrity, more kindness and humanity.

More innocence. An innate naiveté that had blinded him to a pretty girl's evil heart and intentions. Intentions that had driven him to the most desperate act a person could ever carry out.

"Went to mine last year." Mason picked up one of the pamphlets while Wyatt scanned through the cover letter and two-page schedule attached to it. "We didn't have an opportunity to golf at one of Arlington's premier courses, though. You should go for that alone." He picked up the response card. "Not to mention the semi-formal dinner at The Lake House. Fancy."

"Doesn't surprise me. Conway High sits in the middle of some of Arlington's most expensive real estate. A few of us came from the surrounding middle-class neighborhoods, but there were a lot of BMW's, sports cars, and tricked-out trucks in the student parking lot. Right next to my eight-year-old Corolla with the side mirror duct-taped to the door."

"You should go, Red. You're probably more squared away than the vast majority of them."

Shaking his head, Wyatt stuffed the brochures, letter, and schedule back into the packet. "No, thanks."

"You think Harper will go?"

He shrugged. After watching her drive away Wednesday night after club, he'd thought about her too much. It sure wasn't going to help having her in his class three times a week, so it was a relief she hadn't pursued the idea of working with ConnectUP.

"I imagine she would. High school was a pretty heady time for her."

"Maybe you could go together."

What? "Now you're talking nonsense." He threw the packet into a drawer.

"Why is it nonsense?" Mason asked from his perch on top of the island. That was another thing Wyatt needed —barstools.

"For one thing, I'm her professor."

"Come on. It's not like she's an eighteen-year-old freshman. And she'll only be in your class for a few weeks. Marjorie will probably be back before the reunion."

"She's a psych major, so there's a very good chance she'll end up in another one of my courses at some point." Which he hadn't thought about until this minute. It looked like he and Harper could cross paths quite a bit if she stayed on her current track.

"Wes Crandall's wife was in his Christian Apologetics class."

"Oh, so we've gone from possibly going to the reunion together to now she's my wife. Quite the leap."

"Hey, man, just sayin'. There's no harm in asking her out. To the reunion or otherwise. Rhonda really likes her. They had lunch on Thursday, and they're out shopping as we speak. She thinks she'd be good for you. And you for her."

Wyatt, dressed much like his friend in red swim shorts and a T-shirt, leaned a hip against the island and crossed his arms over his chest. "There's a lot of history there that Rhonda's not aware of."

"You're grown-ups now, Mac, not a couple of kids. Rhonda said Harper's seeking hard after God. Almost starving to soak up as much as she can. Rhonda's been pushing ConnectUP, and Harper's really interested in getting involved. Which means you two should have that sit-down and get all of that so-called history straightened out."

Wyatt raised an eyebrow. When Harper hadn't broached the subject yesterday morning after class, he figured she'd decided against volunteering in the ministry. She had a lot on her plate, after all, but Mason was right. If she were to get involved in club, they'd be thrown together even more.

Not wanting to take the time to figure out how he felt about that, he gave his head a shake and looked at his watch. "Speaking of club, we'd better get moving. The kids will be here soon." He glanced at the containers Mason brought in. "Please tell me Rhonda's chocolate caramel brownies are in one of those."

"Yep." Mason hopped off the counter. "And chocolate chip cookies in the other. I'll set up stuff outside for the barbecue."

Mason turned at the door leading to the deck. "I'd think seriously about going to that reunion, Mac. You're a walking testimony of how God can work in a life that's fully surrendered. If not for you, do it for Glen. Because you survived and did something remarkable with your life."

For Glen. Wyatt had nothing he needed to prove to those who'd deemed him insignificant as a teen. But could he do it to honor the friend he'd lost because of the hurt inflicted by a small but powerful few? Could he do it for Glen?

CHAPTER SEVEN

*H*arper glanced at the shopping bags strewn across the backseat of Rhonda's Rav4. "This was exactly what I needed today after my first week back in school—retail therapy. Although I'm probably going to be eating ramen for a month so I can pay off my credit card balance."

Rhonda laughed but kept her attention on the road. "No ramen tonight. My Mason's a master on the grill. Best burger you'll ever eat."

Harper looked over at her new friend. Rhonda was a beauty, with long, straight, jet black hair, flawless dark skin, and willowy figure. The constant light in her hazel eyes gave testimony to her strong faith and the joy she carried in her heart. Joy compounded today by her hours-old engagement to her soulmate.

"Thanks for inviting me tonight. I'm excited to see the girls again."

"They loved you. We're getting more kids all the time, and you'd be an asset to the team."

Rhonda's confidence spread a warmth through Harper's chest. If only Wyatt was of the same opinion. His lackluster response on Wednesday had her wondering if she'd imagined the quickening in her spirit all evening. As if she'd found her place, only to be told it wasn't where she belonged.

She looked out the side window. "Is CU connected to a church or denomination?"

"No. When Wyatt launched ConnectUP three years ago, he wanted to include unchurched, at-risk kids without turning them off with a church-y vibe before they ever came in the door."

Mouth agape, she looked back at Rhonda. "ConnectUP was *Wyatt's* idea?"

"All the way. Mason told me it started when the student pastor from our church approached Wyatt about kids from his group sharing how miserable it was to go to school, knowing Wyatt was working on his doctorate in adolescent psychology. That hit home with him, and he decided these kids needed their own community, their own place to belong."

"That's really something." And made complete sense. Wyatt's high school experience probably weighed heavily in his decision to reach out to the kids who didn't quite fit. If anybody could teach them from example how to embrace who they were meant to be, it would be Wyatt, who had never compromised himself or his values to fit in.

Not like she had.

"Now we're up for a grant from a Christian philanthropic organization that's looking for its next start-up ministry." Rhonda's voice pulled Harper back to the present and out of the unpleasant past before the old regrets could descend on this beautiful day. "Wyatt's up to his neck preparing the proposal for the committee. If we were to get this grant, it could mean branching off into a national organization. Curriculum, retreats, summer camps, college scholarships. That's his dream, anyway."

After pulling off the freeway, they drove a few blocks and meandered through a subdivision still in the midst of building.

"This is beautiful." Harper loved her little townhouse, a

complete but welcome departure from the sprawling, luxurious home she'd been raised in. But she could imagine living in a neighborhood like this, raising a family with a man she could grow old with. If only she'd made better—

"Isn't it?" Rhonda once again pulled her back from meandering too far down a path she'd long ago abandoned. "I love this neighborhood."

Rhonda pulled into a cul-de-sac already lined with several cars and parked in the driveway of a one-story, white limestone home with wooden posts along the front porch and a side-entry, two-car garage.

Harper stepped out of the car, taking in the lush green lawn, rose bushes along the front, and wooden decorative shutters flanking the windows. "Gorgeous." She could definitely be at home in a house like this. Tasteful yet humble. And just big enough for a couple or three kids. "This is where you and Mason are going to live?"

"Not here." Rhonda walked around the front of the car. "We may look into buying in this subdivision, though. Mason's talked about it ever since Wyatt bought this house a few months ago."

Harper's stomach pitched. "We're at Wyatt's?"

"Didn't I tell you the barbecue was at Wyatt's?"

No, she certainly hadn't. Harper would have remembered that. She'd anticipated seeing him tonight, but on neutral territory. It was one thing to be at the university or the community center, or even somebody else's house. Being on his turf was something else altogether. He hadn't appeared all that thrilled to have her back in his life, so horning in on his personal territory seemed like an intrusion.

"He has a really nice house." Oh, how she wished the merry band of butterflies in her stomach would land somewhere.

"It is that, but don't let the outside fool you. Wyatt's great with lawn care, but the inside ... let's just say it needs some inspiration."

They took the flagstone walkway to the porch steps, where the fragrance of roses in full bloom greeted them, their dark pink petals reaching toward the late afternoon sun. Rhonda opened the door and walked into the house bustling with kids, laughter, and voices mixed together. Rich, dark wood floors met them at the entry, continued through the living and dining rooms, and into the study to the left of the foyer. While the other two rooms sat bare, except for the groups on the floor playing games or talking, the office was clearly command central for Wyatt's life. Diplomas hung on the wall in the study, but not one thing adorned any of the other walls she'd seen. Her mind's eye could already see the furnishings and accessories she'd use if this were her house.

She followed Rhonda into a family room with a vaulted ceiling, fireplace flanked by built-in shelves full of books, but not much else, and an enormous television mounted above it. Half a dozen teenage boys surrounded the worn, beige sofa, where two others sat forward with their eyes glued to the screen and thumbs pushing buttons on their hand-held devices. A wood deck sat outside the back window overlooking the yard and the pool, where several kids played water volleyball.

Turning to her left, her eyes widened and mouth dropped open. Her dream kitchen! What she could do with all that counter space—and a gas stove!

Yolanda, one of the leaders Harper had met Wednesday night, spotted them and ran over. "Let me see! Let me see! Let me see!" She grabbed Rhonda's hand to inspect her new engagement ring, then embraced her in a tight hug. "Oh, I'm so happy for you guys!"

Yolanda turned to Harper. "I'm glad you came today! I was hoping we'd see you again."

"Glad to be here." She smiled at the young woman who didn't appear much younger than Harper herself, if at all. Her

English was well-spoken, but her accent, as well as her lush, black locks, brown skin, and dark eyes that shone with an inner light, told Harper that Spanish was probably her first language.

"Hey, ladies."

Harper spun at the sound of Wyatt's voice from behind her, and his eyes widened. "Harper. Hey. I didn't know you were coming."

"Hi." *Hi? Really?* She stared up at him, those belly butterflies multiplying by the second. "Rhonda invited me Wednesday night when I visited club."

She didn't mention how she'd decided to give Rhonda her regrets after he'd discouraged her from getting involved with ConnectUP. But at lunch Thursday, Rhonda had begged her to come, and her newfound friend's enthusiasm had made it impossible to say "no." She only prayed she wouldn't further distance Wyatt by showing up at his house when he clearly hadn't expected her.

A grin softened his features. "I'm glad she did. Welcome."

Her eyes studied him. He sounded sincere, and there was nothing in his tone or facial expression to indicate he was being anything other than genuine. Maybe there was hope he would warm up to the idea of her working with his kids. And perhaps rebuild something from the remains of their fractured friendship in the process.

She returned his smile, then glanced around the room, which was becoming louder by the minute, as more kids arrived or came in from the backyard. "Your house is great. About twice the size of my teeny townhouse."

"It's a lot bigger than I need for now, but I wanted something I would have for a long time. I saved as much as I could of my grad school stipend, as well as my royalties and book advances for a down payment."

Her jaw dropped. "You're a writer too? What *don't* you do?"

His low chuckle did nothing to squelch the fluttering in her mid-section, which she covered with her hand. "Don't be too impressed. Most professors are writers, to some extent, since publishing is a requirement."

Rhonda shook her head. "He's being way too modest, Harper. His dissertation was crazy successful and is now the leading adolescent psychology textbook on Christian campuses across the country. Not to mention his advances on two more books."

His blush brought to mind the boy Harper once knew. "I do enjoy writing, when I actually have the time to devote to it. I've been spread a little thin lately, what with adding another class, my practice, and working with ConnectUP."

"And all the work for your grant too." And he was concerned about how much she had on *her* plate? "Rhonda told me a little about it. Said this was all you."

"It's all God. I had a nugget of an idea and we—Mason, Allyson, and I—started meeting at the apartment Mason and I shared. Had five kids at our first few gatherings, but as word got out, things evolved into ConnectUP. And here we are."

"Here you are." She smiled up at him while wondering who Allyson was. Another volunteer? Just a friend ... or more? "Where did the name ConnectUP come from?"

"We wanted somewhere kids who didn't feel they had a place could connect with each other, and ultimately with God."

"Mac!" Mason called from the back door. "Let's get these burgers started." His dark eyes lit up when he saw Rhonda. "Oh, hey, honey." He closed the door and crossed the distance to his fiancée to take her in a hug. "I didn't know you were here."

"Only a few minutes." Her eyes shone as she looked up at him. "I dragged Harper along."

Mason's gaze traveled to Wyatt and back to Harper. "Glad you could come."

Wyatt looked down at her. "Time for me to assume my *sous-chef* duties. Which means I stand there and hand him things."

She chuckled and turned to Mason. "I hear I'm about to have the best burger ever. Hope your bride-to-be didn't over-promise."

"Oh, you wait," Mason answered. "You will not be disappointed."

"He ain't lyin'." Wyatt gave her a quick grin as he followed his friend. "Talk to you later."

"Later." She watched the two men walk through the back door with several kids following behind. Young people gravitated to Wyatt, like the cool older brother letting them tag along. She'd noticed that Wednesday night. That natural connection.

"Two of the best guys I've ever known." Rhonda stood beside her, watching them through the window as they stood at the grill, laughing with some of the boys who'd joined them. "True men of God."

Harper nodded, unable to tear her gaze from the man she'd last seen as a boy before laying eyes on him again less than a week ago. Every time she was anywhere near him, a little more of her heart came alive. That part he'd claimed over a decade ago, during a stolen island of time, when she'd fallen in love with a boy way out of her league.

That part she suspected still belonged to the man he'd become.

CHAPTER EIGHT

*W*yatt walked the last of the kids out to their cars, then strode into the family room where the ministry team had regrouped after clean-up. These were his favorite people in the world, this close-knit team of seven who came together out of their sheer love for young people who needed an extra dose of hope and encouragement.

His gaze drifted to Harper talking with Yolanda, Steve, and his sister-in-law, Jenny. Her thick mane of hair hung in tousled layers to the middle of her back, her bangs long and swept off her face, and the green top she wore over a pair of flowery shorts set off her emerald eyes.

Her features had changed little, but everything else was new. As if the facade she'd worn all those years ago had fallen away, and what emerged was a million times more fascinating.

He'd watched her interact with their young students throughout the evening, at least three of the girls sticking close to her for the duration. She focused on them when they spoke, laughed with them, and hugged on them. Everything he'd witnessed the other leaders do on a regular basis.

Yet he still found himself hesitant to welcome her involvement. What would she say to a young girl who might come to her after being ostracized or demeaned by a peer group much like the one Harper had been a part of? How could she understand?

Lord, please give me wisdom here. I don't want to get in the way of something You want to do, but I also need to protect my kids. Help me know where the line is.

He grabbed one of the folding chairs they'd borrowed from church and set it in front of the fireplace to face the others. "Hey, everyone. I thought since we're all here, we could knock out our planning meeting and give you guys Monday night off."

Harper looked around as the team took their seats. "Should I go elsewhere? I don't want to get in the way here, but I came with Rhonda."

"Stay," Rhonda said before Wyatt could answer. "You can see how we prepare for the next club meeting and plan activities."

Harper looked over to him, her eyes searching his as if seeking permission.

"Sure," he said. "No problem."

"I'll just plant myself here." She settled on the floor between him and the armchair where Jenny sat.

He nodded and turned his attention to the others. "Matt, you want to open us with prayer?"

After Matt finished his prayer, everybody opened their Bibles, and Wyatt stood to grab another off a shelf next to the fireplace.

He handed it to Harper. "Here you go. In case you want to follow along."

She smiled up at him, and it took him longer than it should have to pull his eyes from her shining face, her very countenance seeming to bear witness of the change in her heart.

He pulled his attention back to the group. "Last week, we focused on what God has to say about who we are in Christ.

This week, we're focusing on the attributes of God, who God says He is, but in a way the kids will understand. Let's pull a few for talking points."

"Can I ask a question?"

He looked back down at Harper. "Sure thing."

"When you say attributes of God but in kid vernacular, what does that mean, exactly?"

"Excellent question. When we speak of the attributes of God, say, from the pulpit or in Bible study, we tend to use church-y words like omnipresent, omniscient, gracious, merciful, and so on. All great things, absolutely true things, but what we want to zero in on for the kids are the things that will resonate. If we talk about God as omniscient, for instance, their eyes will glaze over."

The others laughed as he went on. "But if we talk about God knowing everything about them, that He's always available to them, He's offering a gift they don't have to earn, and He cares about what hurts them, it's easier for them to relate. Does that make sense?"

"Yes!" she answered, her eyes alight. "Perfect sense. Okay, go on."

He chuckled and turned back to the group. "Talking points. Go."

"Refuge, strength," Yolanda said. "Psalm 46."

"Love," Steve offered. "All over the place, but I'm looking specifically at 1 John 4:16."

"Creator. Planner," Rhonda said. "Genesis, obviously, but in 1 Corinthians 12, it talks about how He put everything in the body where He wanted it. Something our girls especially need to hear."

"Good." Wyatt flipped to the passages and jotted down notes. When he looked over at Harper, she had her head bowed over the Bible in her lap, scanning the Table of Contents, then trying to find the scriptures being shared. He winced watching her struggle as the team tossed out more passages. The Bible could be overwhelming to those not familiar with it.

He picked up his cell phone from the coffee table and opened up his Bible app. A gentle tap on her shoulder brought her attention to him, and he showed her how to bring up the book and passage in seconds. The smile she gave him as she took the phone was so full of gratitude, it nearly took the breath out of him. Or maybe it was the fresh, floral fragrance of her hair he'd caught when he bent over to show her the app.

He quickly straightened and turned his attention back to his Bible. As the others kept the suggestions coming, he cast occasional glances her way. His heart clutched watching her read over some of the verses, her face lighting up when she found yet another promise of who God is.

He looked around at the group. "Take some of these you think your circle kids will relate to and go from there. Next on the agenda, we need to work up some fundraising efforts."

They spent the next several minutes talking about how to raise money to cover the Labor Day excursion to Six Flags and other upcoming events.

Wyatt stuck his pen in his notebook and closed it. "Okay, I know this was brief tonight, but I think we can call it, unless there's something else we need to talk about."

"Volunteers," Reed said. "We've grown a lot and need to be praying about and considering who might be a good addition to the team."

"Agreed. I have some folks in mind from my classes I want to approach."

"And maybe someone much closer," Rhonda added.

Everybody looked over at Harper, still focused on the Bible app on Wyatt's phone. When the silence lingered, she looked up, her eyes widening as she straightened and glanced around at the others. "I'm sorry, what?"

"We were talking about our need for volunteers," Rhonda answered, "and wondered if you might still be considering it."

"Oh, most definitely." Her gaze snapped to him. "I mean, if you're ... if you'll have me."

"Yay!" Yolanda exclaimed, the others chiming in with their eager acceptance.

Wyatt nodded, trying to tamp down his own doubt. "We'll get you the application and consent to run a background check, so if you haven't been out knocking over banks recently, you should be in the clear."

"Uh-oh. And I was so close."

He returned her teasing smile, and after Mason closed the group in prayer, they rose to leave, everybody talking at once.

Wyatt walked over to Rhonda and leaned in. "Can I speak with you for a second?"

"Sure." She moved away from where Mason conferred with Jenny and Steve about the Six Flags trip. "What's up?"

He gestured for her to follow him into the kitchen, away from the others. "Can you do Harper's interview?"

Her forehead puckered. "You always do the volunteer interviews."

"I know, but I think I'm a little close to this one, with our history and all. I'm still struggling with separating this Harper from the one who—from the old Harper."

Rhonda stared up at him for a moment. "The Harper who broke your heart."

His face heated. "Yeah. Maybe. I don't know. It's only been a few days since we saw each other again. I'm not entirely sure I can be objective."

"No problem. I'd be happy to do it. I'll be objective, but I do think she has a lot to offer, I don't care what group she belonged to in high school. Maybe she can bring a new voice to the choir."

Wyatt chuckled at her pun. Rhonda had the voice of an angel and had been immersed in choir and drama in high school. Now she used her talents on the church worship team where he played guitar.

"I'm all for new voices, as long as they don't do more harm than good."

"I think she's good to the bone, Wyatt. I hope you can get to know this new Harper and leave the old one behind."

His thoughts spun as Rhonda made her way back to the family room. Leave the old Harper behind. Which one would that be? The Harper she'd put on for everybody else, or the Harper he'd fallen in love with that summer, when she'd let down the mask and let him see who she truly was?

The first one, no problem. But the second? He was afraid that one still had too much of a hold on his heart. And after more than a decade of trying to forget her but only burying her deeper inside, he had no idea how to let her go.

CHAPTER NINE

*H*arper took a deep breath, held it for a count of five, and released it slowly through pursed lips.

The iced coffee she'd picked up on her way to school that morning remained untouched as she sat on the bench outside the Jackson Health Sciences Building. In hindsight, getting coffee hadn't been the best idea. She already couldn't keep still, her crossed legs bouncing up and down while her fingers beat a nervous rhythm against the cup clutched in both hands.

Wyatt's text yesterday asking if she could meet before class this morning had caught her off-guard. Rhonda must have given him her number. Or more likely he'd seen it on the ConnectUP application she'd filled out Saturday night at his house.

She'd started half a dozen texts to him since the ConnectUP meeting last Wednesday, but deleted every one. He'd made it pretty clear he was keeping her at arm's length, although his kindness in showing her the Bible app on his phone the other night gave her reason to hope perhaps they could somehow forge a new friendship from the ashes of their past. So when her phone dinged yesterday with an incoming message, her pulse quickened as she read and re-

read the text he'd sent her. Then read it again for good measure.

> Hey Harper, it's Wyatt. Can you meet me
> before class tomorrow? 8am outside
> health sciences? Let me know.

It had taken her a few minutes and several tries before coming up with a simple,

> I'd be happy to. See you tomorrow.

Now here she sat at 7:55 a.m., worrying her bottom lip between her teeth. What kind of conversation did he want to have after all but fleeing from her a week ago? Had she perhaps trespassed too far into his life in too short a time, first his class, now his ministry? Would he ask her to drop his class because they had a history? Was he declining her application to work with ConnectUP? She wouldn't blame him, not after everything that happened all those years ago. How could she explain, much less ask for forgiveness she didn't deserve?

"Harper."

She sprang to her feet and spun to face the man walking up in a pair of navy slacks and a white collared shirt with blue stripes, his bag thrown over a broad shoulder and holding his own coffee. He carried himself with the same easy confidence he always had. Not arrogance. Just genuinely comfortable in his skin. Unlike her, Wyatt had never jumped through anybody's hoops to be who they thought he should be.

"Wyatt, hi." She ran her free hand down the side of her red capri pants. "How are you?"

"I'm good." He took the last few steps to the bench and picked up her backpack. "Walk with me."

"Whe—okay." She had no choice but to join him as he started down the sidewalk with her bag. They walked together for several seconds in silence, the sounds of the campus coming to life all around them.

She cleared her throat. "Emery and I cyber-stalked you the other day."

He threw her a quick look. "You what?"

"Okay, not stalked, really, in the creepy sense of the word. I told her you were my psych professor and appeared to be quite accomplished. So, we looked you up. I'm happy for you, Wyatt. Really. You should be very proud."

"Nah." He shook his head. "More blessed than proud. I found my passion fairly quickly. Knew by our senior year I wanted to go into psychology. Everything fell into place from there."

Passion. There was that word again. She looked down at the sidewalk. "Something you can't wait to get up and do every day," she said more to herself than him.

He looked down at her as they came to a small table in a secluded alcove outside the library. "Something like that." He gestured to the table. "Is this good, or would you prefer to go inside?"

"This is fine. It's beautiful out here."

He stared at her for a moment. "Agreed."

Like the gentleman he always had been, even as a teenager, he held her chair for her before taking his own. The silence stretched on, so she took a sip from her drink.

"How's your family?" he asked.

Okay, not exactly where she thought this conversation was headed, but she'd go with it, if he needed something to break the ice first. "Really well. Connor's married with two kids I adore. Probate and family lawyer here in Arlington. And Emery's a doctor, family medicine. That's where I work, for Emery and her partners. And her husband is a neurologist in the same building. Met her dream guy in the elevator, of all places."

He chuckled. "Kids?"

She shook her head. "Not yet, but hoping soon. I didn't

have much chance to talk to Reed or Jenny on Saturday, but somebody mentioned they had kids?"

"Two boys and a baby girl. Most awesome kids ever."

"And I bet they love their Uncle Wyatt."

He shrugged but the grin spoke of his pride. "They do love my pool, that's for sure. And Jenny's like the sister I never had. He definitely married up."

They shared a laugh at his brother's expense, but she knew Wyatt had always idolized Reed. She looked down at the cup held between her hands. "So ... why haven't you married?"

His shoulders hitched in a shrug. "I thought I might be headed there once, but as we got further along in the relationship, it didn't feel right. We both knew it, and it ended friendly."

Was that the mysterious Allyson he mentioned Saturday? If so, definitely not in the picture. The thought brought a surprising lilt to her pulse, which was ridiculous. Even if he was available, she'd pretty much put the kibosh on any chance he'd ever ask her out. Again.

"I'm sure God's getting somebody spectacular ready for you."

"As long as she loves God more than she loves me, everything else is gravy."

She nodded and took another sip of her drink. "Emery led me to the Lord almost a year ago. Or I guess I should say back to the Lord. I call myself a newbie Christian, but I believe I was saved back when I walked the aisle at the Vacation Bible School your church held. We were nine, I think."

"*You* were nine. I was ten already." He grinned and she smiled back. Though in the same grade, he'd teased her about the stretch between his January birthday and hers in July making him *so much older*.

"Right. I was nine. But, unfortunately, my faith never grew past childhood. When Emery became a Christian, it was the first time I'd seen it up close and personal as an adult. And something inside of me clamored for what she had. I started asking questions, went to church with her and Tom, and that was it. I was hooked on God."

"That's awesome, Harper. Are Connor and your parents believers too?"

"Connor and Lynne are. My parents believe in God, but we were usually only in church for Easter and Christmas. Their work seems to be their god. Excuse the judgment, but it's taken me a long time to come to terms with the fact I was not an expected child and pretty much just got in the way of their ambition. Looking back, I can see how their lack of approval sent me searching for it in all the wrong places."

He looked down at his coffee. "I'm sorry I couldn't help you more. I just couldn't seem to get your attention."

Her heart contracted with the memory of how often Wyatt had tried to let her know he was still there for her. Then there was that summer, when she thought she might finally be on the right track, with the right guy, only to be dragged back by a past that wouldn't let her go.

"I'm so sorry, Wyatt." Her voice hitched. "For everything."

He stared for a long moment before looking away. "Can I ask what happened with Ellison?"

The trajectory of her thoughts took a hard right. Not the direction she thought the conversation had been headed. "After high school?"

He looked back at her. "I was in my second year here when I heard you got married."

"And you probably heard why."

"I heard ... a rumor."

Her face heated. "Not a rumor."

"I see. Did you have the baby?"

She gazed down at her hands twisting in her lap. "Megan was the most beautiful little girl I'd ever seen." When she looked back up, she tried to focus through the wetness gathering in her eyes. "I was in love from the second I saw her."

His gaze didn't waver as he let her talk. No wonder he was such a successful counselor. His entire countenance allowed one to believe in the absolute safety of confiding in him.

"She'd just turned three when she was diagnosed. Brain tumor. And at twenty-two, my life became about getting my child well. Brett ... he couldn't deal. He didn't want to get married in the first place, but his dad insisted. Having a sick child on top of a marriage that kept him from living the single life to the hilt like so many of his friends only distanced him further."

She took a steadying breath. "I basically moved to Houston so she could be treated at Texas Children's Hospital. Emery was in med school at Texas Tech, Connor had his law practice, and my parents were busy with the treatment centers. I worked full-time for Connor, and he let me take leave to be with her.

"Brett had just started a new job and would come on the weekends. And Mom and Dad would visit when they could. So, it was pretty much just Megan and me. She'd be in the hospital for a few weeks, then out for a while, but we had to stay close for regular labs, tests, and doctor visits. My folks paid for a little studio apartment two blocks from Children's, but when she was in the hospital, I stayed with her there."

When Wyatt swiped at his eye, her tears refused to be kept back. "Harper." His voice was but a soft rasp. "I can't tell you how sorry I am."

She grabbed a tissue from her backpack and dabbed at her cheeks. "She passed away a month after her fourth birthday. Everybody was there — Brett, my family, the Ellisons. She took her last breath lying in my arms as I rocked her. I was the first and last person to ever hold her."

Shaking his head, he looked at her across the small table.

"You were a great mother. Devoted to your little girl. I'm so terribly sorry you lost her."

"Thank you for saying that. I wouldn't have made it if it weren't for Emery. We came back to Dallas to bury Megan, and I could hardly function. Brett lost himself in work and the bottle, so Em took me to Lubbock with her after the funeral. I stayed for a month, and Brett and I talked maybe three times. I knew it was over. We just hadn't put it to words."

He cleared his throat. "It's difficult for even the strongest marriages to survive the loss of a child. Not without help."

"We didn't have a strong one, that's for sure. Still, I didn't make the move to file like I should have, didn't want to fail yet again. So, I stuck it out, even with all the drinking and partying and sleeping around, until he finally left for good eight months after Megan passed. I can't even say I was sorry to see him go. The only pain it left was knowing I'd let my parents down once again. Shotgun wedding at nineteen, divorced at twenty-four, college drop-out. I'm not exactly the child they brag about to their friends."

"Is that why you're back in school? To please your parents?"

Her face blanched. "No. Of course not." Although, she had to admit the delight in their eyes when she told them she planned to get a psych degree was nice to see for a change. "I really admire what they do. What you do. I went through a lot, both as a kid and an adult, and I think I have something to offer. I don't plan to get a doctorate, but with a master's, like my mother, I can be a school counselor, grief counselor, anything."

"No doubt. But you can help people in a lot of ways, not only through counseling."

Her heart fell into her stomach. "Do you want me to drop your class? Or maybe ConnectUP? Is that why you wanted to meet?"

His eyes widened. "Not at all. Not unless you think you're

in it for the wrong reasons. I just thought we should take some time one on one, to catch up, get any awkwardness out of the way. That's why I wanted to meet."

Her shoulders sagged in relief. "I'm glad you got in touch. And I didn't mean to dump all of that on you."

"You didn't. I asked. And I'm glad I know. Thank you for trusting me with it."

The smile she gave him wobbled a bit. "I always trusted you. I only wish I'd made better choices. If I could talk to my younger self, I'd tell her the moment Brett Ellison walked up to her that day in tenth grade English to run and not look back."

Then maybe she wouldn't have lost so much of herself.

"I didn't get my head on straight until I had my daughter. The only good thing to ever come of Brett and me. Being her mom was the greatest thing in the world, as if I'd at last found my purpose. Then she was gone, and I was lost all over again. It wasn't until I came back to God that I had peace. Now I'm ready to take this life and really live it. To honor my Megan. To honor God. And if I can help others find their way, it will have all been worth it. Maybe I ran with a different peer group than your club kids, but there are different forms of bullying. I really believe God can use me with CU. I've been praying about it a lot."

He continued to study her, as if he wanted to say something. But after several silent seconds, he glanced at his watch and stood, retrieving their bags from where they sat next to the table. "We should get to class."

She stood, picked up their cups, and tossed them into a nearby trashcan.

When she turned, he came to a stop in front of her. And something inside her she thought long dead took a breath. A need, a yearning. To be held ... to feel safe. It had been far too long since she'd known the embrace of a man. Except that man hadn't held her the way she'd witnessed Tom wrap his arms around Emery, or the gentle way Connor had with

Lynne. Offering their love with no selfish motive or compulsion.

That's how Wyatt would love the woman fortunate enough to be his. Selfless and all in.

"Thanks for meeting me this morning," he said, breaking into her thoughts.

She nodded, swallowing against the racing of her heart. "Thank you for reaching out. It means a lot to me."

More than he would ever know, although she was surprised he hadn't brought up what happened the night that still broke her heart to remember. Maybe their new fledgling friendship needed stronger legs before they could go there. To that summer. And why she pulled out of his life after the sweetest, most pure and thoughtful kiss she'd ever experienced. Brett was the only other boy she'd kissed, but when he kissed her, it was as if he was staking a claim. Taking, not giving.

Even taking the one thing she could never get back.

CHAPTER TEN

"'The process of transforming information into a form that can be stored in memory.'"

Harper pondered the question posed by Shannon, who sat perched on a stool at the breakfast bar with her textbook open in front of her. While her hands busied themselves tossing a salad, Harper let her thoughts scour her brain for the material she'd spent a good part of the Labor Day weekend reading.

"Encoding."

"Correct! You've got this, girl. I see another *A* in your future."

Harper pulled a pan of lasagna from the oven. "Thanks to you."

"I told you we'd be great study partners."

The study partner Harper was thankful to have now that they'd had a few sessions together over the last couple of weeks. Shannon was whip-smart and a kick to be around, which made studying not only fruitful but fun. "You certainly had that right."

Shannon shook her head. "Not me. God had it right. When I started college three years after high school, I felt a little out of place in my first class. I saw you sitting by yourself with everybody else talking in groups and knew God wanted me to reach out. Guess He knew you and I would have more in common with each other than we would with the young 'uns."

Harper couldn't help chuckling at that. At twenty-three, Shannon was closer in age to those *young 'uns* than she was to Harper, but her life experiences during those three years post-high school had given her a maturity beyond her years. Three years, she'd shared, spent trying to *find herself*, but finding God instead. Something Harper understood all too well.

Shannon pushed up on her crossed arms to look down at the dish sitting on a trivet. "Oh, my stars, that looks amazing."

Harper smiled at her. "I hope you enjoy it. I love cooking, and cooking for one isn't nearly as satisfying. Plus, I figured studying over here would be more comfortable than sitting in the library."

"Definitely." Shannon looked over her shoulder and back at Harper. "Bathroom is that way?"

"Second door on your left."

"Be right back."

While Shannon went down the hall, Harper tidied up the kitchen and carried their meal to the table.

"Could these kids be any cuter!" Shannon said from where she stood in front of a grouping of photos arranged on the living room wall. "Nieces and nephew?"

Harper walked over to join her and looked up at the photographs. "These two here," she said, pointing to a boy and girl laughing into the camera, "are my brother's children, Nicky and Ashlen. He's five, and she's two."

Shannon put her fingers to a picture of a green-eyed tyke with a huge grin, her curly brown hair pulled back with a bow almost as big as her head. "And who's this little doll?"

"That's Megan." Harper's chest filled with the same tangled mix of joy and grief she'd carried the last several years. "My daughter."

Shannon turned to her, mouth agape and eyes wide. "I didn't know you had a child. Where is she? With her father?"

"Her *heavenly* Father. She died four-and-a-half years ago. Brain cancer."

Shannon's face fell. "Oh, Harper. I am so, so sorry."

Harper swallowed the knot of emotion in her throat. "She was the light of my life, although I was very young when I had her. I was a little lost back then and making some awful choices. But once she was here, I absolutely loved being her mom."

Shannon drew her in for a hug. "You're still her mom. And you'll see your baby girl again."

Harper closed her eyes and let herself draw strength from this precious gem of a friend. "Thanks, Shannon." She pulled away and smiled at her. "You're a blessing, you know that?"

"We're kindred spirits." Her gaze went back to Megan's picture as tears filled her eyes. "In more ways than you could ever know."

Harper watched her for a moment, taken aback by the uncustomary sadness playing across her friend's pretty features. "Well, kindred spirit, let's eat. All this quizzing has made me hungry."

Shannon nodded and turned to her, the perky smile back in place. "Do you mind if we quiz while we eat? I have a project for another class I need to finish tonight."

"No problem. I have some prep I need to do for ConnectUP tomorrow night too."

"ConnectUP," Shannon repeated, taking her seat as Harper brought the textbook over to the table. "That's Hunky Professor's thing, isn't it?"

"Yep. The most incredible kids. And you should see Wyatt with them. He's like a magnet and they're metal shavings."

Shannon grinned over at her. "You call him Wyatt?"

Oops. Heat infused Harper's face. She'd forgotten Shannon didn't know their history. "Funny thing, that—"

"I knew it!" Shannon's smile lit up her face. "He asked you out, didn't he?"

"No! No, nothing like that. It's just that we go back a ways. Since kindergarten, actually." She reached for the lasagna and picked up the spatula to cut a generous square to place on Shannon's plate. "But I hadn't seen him in over ten years until that morning he walked into class."

"Oh, *that's* why he looked so thunderstruck. I thought he was just blown away by your classical beauty," she finished with her nose in the air and an English accent.

"Oh, please." Harper laughed as she served herself a piece of lasagna. "He was blown away, all right, but not in a good way. Let's bless this before we eat. You want to lead us?"

Shannon reached over to take Harper's hand. "Dear Father in heaven, thank You so, so much for my friend, Harper, and for this yummy dinner she prepared for us. Bless our efforts in class, and please help us remember all this stuff we're learning so we can ace Hun—uh, Dr. McCowan's test tomorrow. And please, please take good care of little Megan until her mommy can get there. We love You so very much. Amen."

Harper looked at Shannon, her nose and eyes burning. What a sweet prayer. "Thank you."

"You're welcome." Shannon stabbed her fork into her salad. "So, back to you and our good-looking prof."

"There is no me and our good-looking prof. We're just getting reacquainted."

"And you're working in his ministry with him."

She moved her head back and forth as she cut a bite of lasagna off with her fork. "Yes, but there's an entire team working in the ministry. Tomorrow night will be my first as an official leader, although I won't have my own circle yet. I had my interview last week, did my training on Saturday, and we spent the day at Six Flags yesterday with the kids. Best time ever."

"With the kids? Or with *Wyatt*?"

"The kids." Harper's cheeks warmed as a smile spread across her face. "And with Wyatt. It's been fun getting to know each other again."

Shannon took a bite of lasagna then sipped from her glass of sweet tea. "What did you mean he was blown away but not in a good way?"

Harper winced and took a swallow of her own tea. "We didn't run in the same social circles, to put it bluntly. I was too busy trying to stay popular to associate with the brainy kids, which Wyatt was back then."

"Still is. Majorly successful for such a young guy."

"Doesn't surprise me in the least. Super brilliant, very ambitious, even as a kid."

Her cell phone, sitting on the table where she'd forgotten she put it, vibrated with an incoming call.

Shannon giggled when the name popped up on the screen. "His ears must have been burning."

"I can call him back later."

"No, no. I'm good. Go ahead. Take it before it goes to voicemail."

Harper picked up the phone. "Hey, there."

"Hi," Wyatt answered. "Did I catch you at a bad time?"

"Just studying and having a quick dinner with Shannon."

"Oh, well, we can talk later. I just had a question about club tomorrow night."

"No problem. What's up?"

"Yolanda's come down with the flu and won't be able to make it, and Jenny has a PTA thing. Would you be comfortable taking their group tomorrow night? If not, no worries. We can put all the girls together in Rhonda's circle."

"Yes!" Smiling, she looked over at Shannon. "I'd love to take it. Too many in a circle makes it difficult for them to open up. I've been going over all the passages we talked about at the team meeting, so I have several good talking points."

"Great. Just let me know before club tomorrow if you have questions."

"Will do." She resisted the urge to pump her fist. He'd actually *asked* her to take a circle! She couldn't let him down. She *wouldn't*. Wouldn't give him any reason to regret giving her this opportunity to serve in this ministry he loved so much. Not when she knew he'd had misgivings about her ability to commiserate with the club kids. "Thank you so much, Wyatt. I'm really looking forward to it."

"I appreciate your willingness to jump in."

"No problem whatsoever. I'll see you in the morning. Oh, by the way, Shannon and I are going to so ace your test tomorrow."

"Is that right?" he replied with a chuckle. "You both sure did the first one. Oh, and hey, since you're there with Shannon, talk up CU. She's one I'd like to see about volunteering."

"Tell him I'm all over that," Shannon said, having overheard his remark. "I'd love to come see what it's all about."

"She said—"

"Yeah, I heard," he said with a laugh. "If she wants to come tomorrow night, that'd be great."

"I'll be there!" Shannon said, her voice raised to make sure he heard her.

"Super. I'll let you ladies get back to it. Sorry I interrupted your dinner."

"No worries," Harper assured him. "See you later."

"Later."

After disconnecting, Harper looked over and caught Shannon's grin. "What?"

"You are so crushing on the professor. You should have seen your face, talking to him just now. Oh, my stars, what a great couple you'd make!"

Harper's cheeks blazed. "You're quite the romantic,

Shannon dear, but it's not going to happen. Now, we should get back to quizzing, don't you think?"

Sighing, Shannon shook her head, her blonde ponytail swinging behind her. "I'd rather talk about you and Hunky Professor, but okay. What next?"

What next? A very good question.

CHAPTER ELEVEN

a spate of laughter pulled Wyatt's attention to the conversation circle across the room. And not for the first time that evening. He'd let Harper fill in as a leader much sooner than he would have normally done with a new team member. But with Yolanda out sick and Jenny not available to cover, his only other choice was to put all twenty-three girls together.

When Rhonda suggested letting Harper try her hand at leading, he'd balked at first. She'd only completed her training the weekend before. But, whether he admitted it or not, the truth was he had continued uncertainty about her ability to empathize with the CU girls. Rhonda had called his bluff, though, reminding him that twenty or more girls together wouldn't encourage sharing—it would squash it.

Deciding to trust the wisdom of his co-worker in the ministry, he'd made the call to Harper, praying it was the right choice. And watching her off and on throughout the evening had been eye-opening. He knew the girls liked her, but the strength of their connection in the mere two weeks since her first visit surprised him.

Now she sat over there, Bible open on her lap, and every

time he glanced in that direction, she'd been either reading from it or speaking to the girls. And with Shannon sitting in tonight, the students appeared to be having a grand time, if the snippets of giggles and laughter coming from that corner were any indication.

After Mason dismissed their circle in prayer, Wyatt looked over again to find Harper, Shannon, and their girls standing with their arms around each other, heads bowed in a tight huddle. When they finished praying, Harper turned to the girl beside her, a first-timer at CU.

Transfixed, he watched her interact with the young girl. Her gaze never wavered, and her hand held the teen's arm in a loose grip. An attachment, a way of telling her without words *I'm here. I see you. I hear you.*

After a moment, she pulled the girl in for a hug. A bond already formed. A kinship newly forged.

This wasn't practiced behavior. She had a gift. A gift his ministry could benefit from as they worked to reach more at-risk teens. But could he bring down his own defenses and take the chance of letting her in? Would she stick, or run like she had in the past?

Reed came to stand next to him. "She seems to have settled right in."

Wyatt gave a small nod, his eyes still directed to the group across the room. "Seems to have."

Reed looked at him. "You had doubts even after talking things out with her?"

"We didn't really talk things out. Just got ... reacquainted, I guess you could say." He hung his head before looking at his brother. "She told me about her little girl. Passed away from cancer at four years old. Can you imagine?"

Reed's dark eyes clouded with sympathy. "I can't for a second imagine how devastating that had to be. And look at her now."

Wyatt brought his gaze back over to the girls, now talking

all at once, Harper right in the middle of it all. Joy radiated from her, and the love shining in her eyes as she looked each one square in the face brought a tingle to his skin.

"She's a mom," he said, his voice quiet. "With a mother's heart."

"You've been wanting to start a third circle for the girls. I think you've found your new leader."

Wyatt moved his head from side to side. "Yeah, maybe. I can talk to her, see how she felt about it tonight."

"I think that answer's obvious, but you've always had excellent judgment where the ministry is concerned. Don't be afraid to give her a chance. And I don't just mean with ConnectUP."

Wyatt narrowed his eyes at his brother. "What *do* you mean?"

Reed gave his arm a tug, and Wyatt followed him to a quieter corner of the community center. "When did you break up with Allyson?"

"About a year ago, I guess. Why?"

"What happened with you two?"

He shrugged. "Nothing *happened*. The relationship seemed to level off, and we both agreed it wasn't going any further."

"And nobody you've been out with since has interested you, even though you could have your pick out of some top-notch ladies."

"Where is this going, exactly?"

"I just want you to think about why nobody has stuck." He glanced over at Harper, now standing with Rhonda, Shannon, and some of the girls. "Could *that* be why?"

His jaw dropped. "Because of Harper? Reed, that was in high school. Trust me. Ancient history."

Reed cocked his head. "Seriously? I was there, remember? You walked around in a funk for months after she sent you packing. You were just getting back to your old self when Glen died, and all that hurt turned to anger. Everything was about

Harper and her friends and how heartless and mean-spirited they were. That you'd dodged a bullet not getting involved with her. I was concerned about how bitter you became, watching all of that resentment eat away at you before you regained your footing in college. But was Harper even involved in that? Do you *know* she was? Or did your own hurt at her rejection make it easier for you to place blame there?"

Wyatt's gaze flicked to the area around them. He *had* been angry. Angry and bitter and hurt. He left graduation night glad to be done with Conway High and relieved he'd never have to set eyes on Harper Townsend and her lot ever again. He started college with a chip on his shoulder until he met a certain sophomore, who encouraged him to pledge his service-based fraternity that ministered to the area's underprivileged. Mason had seen past the wall Wyatt had erected and helped him realize serving others was the only thing that could heal him. And his life had never been the same.

He looked back at his brother. "I don't think she was directly involved, and maybe I misplaced some blame there. But I was a kid who'd just lost his best friend because he'd been bullied to death by people she ran with. How was I supposed to feel?"

Reed stepped closer, standing directly in front of him. "I get it. I do. I just want to encourage you to try to see past the girl she was to the woman she is. And maybe by healing that old wound, you can finally trust someone enough to build a life with. I'm not saying that's Harper, but I do believe it starts with her. Only the two of you can decide where that road leads."

As usual, his brother was right. He needed to be willing to take out some painful stuff and look at it again. But this time, as a grown man of some intellect who should be able to differentiate between the truth and the assumptions the boy he'd been had accepted as such.

Only the two of you can decide where that road leads. So far, he'd been able to keep Harper at a polite distance. Friendly but not especially close. But to achieve the healing Reed talked about, he had to be willing to get on that road.

No matter where it led.

CHAPTER TWELVE

"Hey, Wyatt," Harper called from the kitchen. "Which one of these hundred drawers has wooden spoons in it?"

Wyatt pulled his attention from his laptop sitting on the second-hand kitchen table and found her next to the stove, her back to him, opening and closing drawers. "Left of the fridge. I think."

She turned and looked at him, hands planted on her hips. "Way over there?"

He couldn't help the grin spreading on his face. Her effort to look stern just looked … cute. "Where should they be?"

"By the stove."

"Oh." He gave her a shrug. "Feel free to move things around where it makes more sense. I just threw it all in drawers when I moved in."

She walked across the kitchen and pulled open the drawer. "How do you do anything with this paltry assemblage?"

"Preach, sister." Mason grinned at Wyatt from his place across the table from Reed. The two laughed when Wyatt shot him a mock stink-eye before walking over to join Harper at the stove, where whatever was cooking smelled like heaven. Or his favorite Mexican restaurant.

The entire team, now totaling twelve, had gathered at his home for their usual planning session this early October Monday evening. ConnectUP had grown to fifty-plus kids, some coming from schools in neighboring cities. And while grateful for their new volunteers, soon they wouldn't have space or the resources for all the kids. Which made acquiring this grant even more imperative.

After planning their topic for conversation circles, he, Mason, and Reed moved to the kitchen table to work on the grant proposal while the others planned the Trunk-or-Treat event for Halloween. Harper had insisted on cooking dinner, going back and forth from the family room to the kitchen.

He leaned against the counter and crossed his arms. "If I don't need it for the microwave or the grill, I probably don't have it."

She dropped a spatula, a couple of wooden spoons, and a pair of tongs into an open drawer next to the stove. He had to admit, that made a lot more sense.

"You don't do a lot of cooking, I take it." She grinned up at him. "You know, in all your spare time."

He chuckled and shook his head. "I wouldn't know what to do even if I had the time."

"I love cooking, although I haven't done as much of it lately as I'd like." She took one of the wooden spoons and stirred the rice concoction simmering in a pot she'd brought with her. The aroma of chilies and spice filtered toward him, and he leaned in to catch more of it. "I'd be happy to arrange your kitchen for you. To make it more user-friendly."

He straightened when she placed the lid on the pot. "Knock yourself out. You're getting more use out of it at the moment than anybody ever has. And I think a hundred drawers is a bit of an exaggeration."

She tilted her chin up. "I would never, ever, in a million years, exaggerate about anything whatsoever."

He laughed outright. "Got it."

She looked around the space. "If you only knew what I could do with a kitchen like this." She opened the oven door a couple of inches and peeked in at two pans of enchiladas with cheese oozing over them. Along with the enchiladas and Spanish rice, she had a slow cooker of charro beans simmering next to the stove.

"My kitchen has never smelled this amazing." His mouth watered in anticipation. Tonight's meal would sure beat his usual sandwich or frozen microwave dinner. Mason had moved in the week before but so far hadn't done any cooking. Even so, as good as Mason was, nothing he made had ever smelled or looked this good. "You know, I think you're the first to ever use that oven."

She shook her head. "I'd kill for a gas range, and here you have one you don't even use."

He looked around his house, humming with people and conversation but which still sat, for the most part, empty and unadorned. At least Mason had taken up residence in one of the spare bedrooms, and all of his earthly belongings sat in the other. But it was time this house looked more like a home, as his friend had told him. If only he knew where to begin.

He looked back down at Harper, now stirring the beans. She'd always had a keen eye for style, not only in the way she dressed, but even decorating her locker to the hilt back in school, complete with a tiny chandelier hanging over the top shelf. He'd only seen it in passing between classes but had chuckled as he walked by. Pure Harper, even making her locker a showpiece. Her *teeny townhouse*, as she'd called it, was no doubt as impeccable.

He watched her give the pot another stir. "I was thinking, would you maybe want to help me —"

73

"Hey, Harper," Shannon called from the family room. "Do you want to use your car for Trunk-or-Treat?"

"Sure thing."

"Count mine in too," he said.

Harper placed the lid back on the beans and looked up at him. "Maybe want to help you ..."

He shook his head. "Nothing. Not important."

"You're sure? I'd be happy to help with whatever you need."

"No, I'm good. But thanks."

Her smile dimmed. "Okay. Well, I should get back over there and do my part."

"I'd say you're doing more than that. Thanks for fixing dinner."

"My pleasure. This will be ready in about fifteen minutes."

"Can't wait."

A couple of hours later, Wyatt closed the front door behind the last of the team members and returned to the kitchen. Harper stood at the sink rinsing dishes before placing them in the dishwasher, another appliance never before used. He hadn't been alone with her since their face-to-face over a month ago, and having her in his kitchen like she belonged there felt too close. Too intimate. He couldn't even count on Mason as a buffer since he left to take Rhonda home and would likely be gone a while.

"Here." He reached for the plate she held. "I'll do this. I'm sure you have more important things to do. Homework or something."

She looked up at him, her brows drawn together as she let go of the plate. He hadn't meant that to sound like a dismissal, but having her in such close proximity reminded him there was still so much unspoken between them, despite the outward friendliness.

"Would you mind if I arranged your kitchen? Not that I

want to get in your business, but it's clear you need some pointers in culinary organization."

He returned her playful grin as he threw forks into the utensil holder of the dishwasher. "That is an accurate statement."

"I'll start over here."

"Have at it."

She moved stuff around while he focused on the dishes with more purpose than necessary to keep his attention elsewhere. When he realized he hadn't heard anything for a while, he looked over his shoulder to where she stood holding a manila folder, staring at it in question.

When she looked up at him, that crease in her brow only deepened. "Are you going to the reunion?"

He grabbed a towel and wiped his hands as he turned to look at her across the island. "Wasn't planning on it. You're going, I take it?"

She set the packet down on the counter. "I haven't had much contact with most of my old friends over the last few years. Two or three from cheer I was close to."

"Yeah. Pretty much the same. Doug, Dan, and Pete are really the only ones I've kept in contact with. I know they're going."

She nodded. "I hadn't decided whether to go or not until Coach Caldwell contacted me."

He tossed the towel onto the island. "The football coach?"

"He's the Athletic Director now. The current cheerleaders asked if the cheerleaders from our class could work up a routine with them for halftime of the Homecoming game, then cheer on the sidelines with them the second half. I called, and all of my girls wanted to do it, so I kind of have to go now. At least to the game."

"What about the dinner Saturday night?"

She looked down and shrugged. "I don't know. A couple of the girls who are single said we could all go together." Her gaze made its way back to him, a wariness in her eyes he didn't expect. "But I'm not that same girl they knew in school. They were talking about going out clubbing after the game, and who they hoped showed up stag to the dinner looking for a good time. I want nothing to do with any of that. I don't even drink anymore. I'm not looking to numb myself the way I did back then."

Numb herself? From what? She'd had the world by the tail —the looks, the status, the star quarterback boyfriend. Everything.

What could have been so awful in her life, she didn't want to feel?

They stared at each other across the expanse of granite before she cleared her throat. "I guess we could … you know … go together. If you'd like. Not like a date. Just friends. That way you could see your buddies, and I wouldn't be stuck with people I have nothing in common with anymore."

He swallowed hard. He still had that packet because he'd contemplated a dozen times asking Harper if she might want to go together, as Mason had suggested. Now here she stood, extending the invitation he'd been too reluctant to offer himself.

When the silence stretched into awkwardness, she bowed her head. "Never mind." She picked up the packet to throw it back in the drawer where she found it. "I shouldn't have put you on the spot. You are still my professor, so probably not a good idea."

"Do you remember Glen Bennett?" His breath stuck in his chest. Where had *that* come from? He certainly hadn't intended to get into this with her now. Maybe not ever, even knowing that to bridge the crevasse between them, he would have to. And now it was out there, where he couldn't pull it back.

She turned and looked at him, her brows pinched together. "Yes. Tragic story. I'm sure that was a hard time for you. I—I'm sorry I never said anything. I wasn't sure what to say."

"And you weren't exactly speaking to me then, anyway."

Pain sparked in her eyes and regret at his ill-chosen words clenched his gut.

"Wyatt, I—"

"Sorry. I shouldn't have said that." He swiped a hand through his hair. This was why he'd avoided being alone with her, because whenever he was, long-buried emotions bubbled to the surface. More proof that he'd never dealt with them, only buried them deep into his psyche. As a kid, that was understandable. But as a grown man, and a psychologist at that, completely unacceptable. Time to get it out there and get it done.

"Is that why you don't want to go?" she asked. "Because of what happened with Glen?"

He released a sigh. "Mostly. If I were to cross paths with Sarah Holmes, even after all these years, it would be very difficult for me to hold my tongue."

Her head jerked back, that wrinkle in her brow making another appearance. "What does Sarah have to do with Glen … doing what he did?"

Wait … *what*? "You don't know?"

"I don't have a clue. I hardly knew Sarah."

Heat traveled up the back of his neck. "What do you mean you hardly knew her? She was as much a part of that group as you were."

"She might have hung with us, but she and I weren't friends. I didn't like the way she treated people, and I certainly didn't trust her."

"You honestly don't know what happened? None of it?"

His chest tightened at the utter confusion he saw in her eyes. Had he been wrong all these years? Assuming Harper had known how Sarah set up Glen? Assuming she'd done nothing to stop it?

Or had he done exactly what Reed had said and placed blame where it didn't belong as a way to legitimize his bitterness at Harper's rejection? To convince himself she'd done him a favor by not letting him into her life?

Had he been wrong all this time?

CHAPTER THIRTEEN

"*A*ll I know is what we were told when it happened, and that was very little."

Harper's answer snapped Wyatt back to the conversation, but he couldn't seem to form any words as he struggled to accept the truth he hadn't allowed himself to believe for over a decade. A truth he should have never doubted, knowing Harper like he had. She might have run with a crowd that included bullies and girls who built themselves up by walking over people they deemed beneath them. But he had to admit, he'd never heard anybody refer to Harper as mean-spirited or cruel, and he'd never witnessed her purposely hurt another.

Except him, that is.

"Are you saying Sarah had something to do with what— wait a minute." Her eyes bored into him. "When did Glen— when did he die?"

"March, our senior year. The twenty-fourth, to be exact."

"Late March ..." Her gaze flitted away, her eyes narrowed for several seconds before she looked back at him. "Something happened with Sarah around that time. I mean, she disappeared. Didn't even finish the year. I heard she had some kind of mental thing, a breakdown or something. I figured it was drugs, because I knew she was using. But I never saw her again."

His jaw dropped. "What?"

His brain flashed back through the end of senior year. He'd never crossed paths with Sarah before she'd dug her hooks into Glen. And after Glen's death, he finished the year in such a fog, it was a wonder he'd held onto his class status long enough to graduate as Salutatorian. It never occurred to him Sarah hadn't walked with their class at graduation. Of course, with eight-hundred-plus graduates, that wasn't altogether surprising.

"Did she do something to Glen?" Harper's voice sounded far away until Wyatt regained his focus. "Something that might have eaten her up with guilt after he killed himself?"

Sighing from a deep, still-hurting place, he took a moment to put his thoughts together. He despised this story, hated that it was part of the framework of his life. Yet it was the catalyst for everything his life was now—his chosen career and his ministry—because he couldn't let another teenager make the same devastating decision. Because he had to protect kids like he had been from kids like—

He studied the woman across the island from him. "She had a class with him." His throat tightened, and his stomach balled into a knot. "They had to find a partner for a project. He was super smart, and she latched onto him right away. He was ecstatic, but I had my suspicions about her motives. Told him to be sure she carried her own weight."

He swallowed against the thickness in his throat. "Turned out I was right, and he ended up doing all the work. Kept making excuses for her—she was busy rehearsing for the dance team's Spring show, so she couldn't work on it after school, that she didn't understand the curriculum as well as he did. He said she told him she liked him, but her ex-boyfriend was super jealous, and she was afraid to be too public with her feelings. I thought it was bunk, but he bought it, hook, line, and sinker."

The corners of Harper's mouth pressed downward. "That sounds like Sarah, unfortunately. She'd use whatever she could to get what she wanted."

"She certainly knew what would work on Glen. And after they turned in their project—or I should say *his* project—she asked him to meet her at the park where they could be alone. He was so excited, he couldn't even think straight. We were good kids, but come on, we were teenage boys. Of course he was ecstatic that this beautiful girl wanted to spend some time alone with him."

He shook his head before continuing. "I knew something wasn't right, but he wouldn't listen to me. Told me I was jealous because things hadn't worked out with you. That ticked me off, so like a jerk, I let him go meet her by himself. Figured he'd see her true colors soon enough. I never imagined—"

"Oh, no," she said with a breath, her eyes wide. "That's what they were talking about."

His eyes narrowed. "Who?"

"Lucas and Evan. Evan was Sarah's boyfriend, not her ex. I overheard them talking to Brett about how they were going to rough someone up for trespassing on Evan's territory. I asked Brett about it later and he told me it wasn't anything, that Evan was just spouting off. But was that—did they hurt Glen?"

"*Hurt* Glen? They didn't just rough him up, Harper. They humiliated him. Beat him to a pulp, stripped him down, and took pictures of him. Sarah was there for the whole thing. They told him if he came near her again, they'd put those pictures out on social media for everybody to see."

Tears fell down her face, and she covered her mouth. "Wyatt ..."

"He hung himself that night." He took a shaky breath and let it out to keep his own tears back. Staring at the floor with his hands on his hips, he pushed his words past the tightness in his throat. "It leveled me knowing the last words we ever exchanged was him telling me I was jealous, and me telling him he was an idiot for believing anything Sarah had to say."

He looked back up at Harper, her image swimming in front of him through the moisture in his eyes. "I had no idea I would never see him again. That all I'd have from him was a note telling me what happened, leaving out names except to say Sarah had set him up, and he was sorry he hadn't listened when I tried to warn him."

With tears streaming, she walked around the island and threw her arms around him. After a moment recovering from the shock, his own came around her, and he couldn't help thinking how well she fit there. In the circle of his arms, her cheek pressed to his shoulder, her face against his neck. Her breath cooled his skin where her tears fell, and he closed his eyes against the onslaught of emotions he'd been avoiding the past six weeks.

"I'm so sorry, Wyatt. I never knew." She pulled back and looked up at him. "I promise. I never knew they did that to him."

He swallowed hard, looking down into her shimmering emerald eyes. "Do you think—could Ellison have been involved?"

Shaking her head, the tears continued to spill. "No. We were together that night. I remember because when we heard about Glen's ... death, I recall thinking that while we were having fun watching a movie and eating pizza with our friends, another boy was ending his life. I couldn't imagine the pain that came with that decision."

Still holding one arm around her, he brought his other hand to her face and brushed tears off her cheek with the backs of his fingers. "I'm sorry I ever thought you knew what was going to happen and didn't say anything. I guess I was still smarting over what happened with us and didn't give you the benefit of the doubt."

She pulled away and swiped her hands across her cheeks. "I know you don't understand what happened that summer. I wish I knew how to—"

"Hi, honey, I'm home!" Mason's voice carried into the kitchen before the sound of the front door closing filtered down the entry hall.

Her eyes widened. "I'm a mess," she whispered.

"Master bath," he whispered back, gesturing toward his room. "In here, Mase!" he called over his shoulder as she turned on her heel and made a beeline for the master suite. He returned to the sink, wishing she could have finished her sentence.

Mason walked into the family room. "I thought Harper was still here. Her car's outside."

"She's here." Wyatt placed another plate in the dishwasher. "In the bathroom. Wanted to rearrange my kitchen, of all things."

"Good for her."

"I'm just finishing up here, and she's getting ready to go."

"Well, I'm hitting the hay." Mason turned and walked through the family room to the hall. "'Night."

"See you in the morning. Honey."

Mason's laugh dissipated as he disappeared into his room, and Wyatt looked over his shoulder when he heard Harper come back into the kitchen.

"Sorry about that." Composed now, her eyes had dried, and her face was devoid of make-up. Few women could look as luminous without that stuff as they did with it, but Harper was one of them. "I didn't want Mason to catch me … like that."

"I understand. And I'm sorry the evening turned into this."

"I know. And I know there's more we need to talk about, but maybe tonight's not the best time."

"Agreed." He wiped his hands again on the towel and tossed it aside. His thoughts tumbled around in his head before he spoke. "If you'd still like to go to the reunion dinner together, let's do it. As for me teaching your class, I heard from Marjorie this afternoon that she'll be back next Monday, so that won't be an issue."

She stared back at him for a long time, and he wondered if she'd reconsidered. "I would like that," she said at last, and he was flooded with equal parts relief and doubt.

"Okay," he said before he could give that much thought. "I'll send in my response with a plus one and give them your name."

"I'll pay you back for my ticket."

"I can cover it."

Every single ounce of him wanted to walk over and take her back in his arms. Those precious few moments he'd held her before Mason walked in hadn't been close to enough. He'd barely touched her in the past several weeks, before she'd all but flown into his arms, because of this very thing. This surge of memories and feelings he'd been trying to hold at bay since that first day of class. When their eyes met, and he was transported to that night on her porch.

The night she pushed him out of her life in the time it took her to close the door.

CHAPTER FOURTEEN

"*A*ir ..." Harper dropped to the wood floor of the gym on her back, welcoming its coolness against her overheated skin through her sweat-dampened tank top. "Need ... air."

Her chest heaved and lungs burned as she strove to pull in the much-needed oxygen, knees raised and arms splayed at her sides. The energetic dance routine she'd spent the last hour of this Saturday morning practicing with the current and former cheer squads would have been a piece of cake ten years ago. Now she couldn't wait to get home to a warm bath and a nap. And ibuprofen. Maybe a heating pad.

Her friend Marney plopped down and crossed her arms on her bent knees, head down as she gulped for air. "Has it really ... been that ... long?"

"Seriously."

"Here you go." A cheery voice came from somewhere above, and Harper opened her eyes to see one of the perky young things standing over her, holding out a bottle of water with a bright smile, looking like she'd hardly broken a sweat.

"Bless you," she told the girl, who'd introduced herself as Libby, the current captain of the Conway varsity cheer team. It had been her idea to invite Harper's squad to perform alongside them. Now Harper wondered if they were being punked.

Once Harper and the six members of the "older" squad could breathe again, the younger girls joined them on the floor. If the current squad needed to raise any money, they'd missed a golden opportunity to clean up, as she was sure her ladies would have dished out fifty bucks a piece for the bottles of water they'd been offered.

"You guys are doing great!" Libby told them, the other girls agreeing.

"You're very kind. But are you sure you aren't reconsidering having us old folks out there with you?"

"Old? I hope I look half as good as you do in ten years."

"You're my new best friend."

They sat for another few minutes, the older ensemble sharing stories of their cheerleading days, when one of the gym doors opened, and a tall, strapping boy in a red letter jacket sauntered in.

"Oh, no." A petite girl with a long blonde braid jumped up when she saw the boy standing inside the door with his arms crossed, his face pulled into a scowl. "What's he doing here?"

"Didn't you check in today, Jilly?" one of the other girls asked, causing Jill's face to redden.

"I'll be right back."

After Jill disappeared into the lobby with the boy, Harper took a sip of water, her eyes coming to rest on a wall-sized work-in-progress banner with the words RUN 'EM DOWN, MUSTANGS! in bold red. A herd of horses had been sketched onto the banner as if running straight out of the wall. What a shame this piece of impeccable artwork would be destroyed at Friday's game when two dozen padded-up and helmeted boys tore through it on their way to their gridiron battle.

"Who's the artist?"

Libby looked over her shoulder at the banner and back

again. "Oh, that's Jill. She's fantastic. Does all the hard stuff and we just paint inside the lines. We're lucky to have her."

"Very talented."

A heavy silence fell over the room as the boy's raised voice drifted in from outside the gym. Harper stood and turned to face the door, her overheated skin chilled as a sense of *déjà vu* descended on her like a cloak.

"That's Dwight," Libby said. "Our star receiver and Jill's boyfriend."

"Boyfriend or handler?" said the girl who'd asked if Jill had checked in.

"Come on, Mags. Give her a chance. I'm sure she'll find a way out."

Find a way out? How many times had Harper tried to *get out* of her situation with Brett, only to assure herself all was well when, in reality, it was nowhere near well?

The boy's voice grew louder, and when Harper heard a *thwack* against one of the doors, she started that direction at a fast clip. Stepping out into the lobby, she found the boy holding Jill up against the next door by the arms.

When he saw her, he let the girl go.

"Jill, we need you back in here," Harper said as if she were in charge, hoping that would give Jill the out she needed.

The stricken-faced girl looked from Harper back to her boyfriend with fear and tears in the big, blue eyes that had been full of laughter mere minutes ago. "Yes, ma'am," Jill said as she turned to go back.

"Jill." Dwight waited until she looked at him. "I'll be here when you're done."

Jill's eyes darted to Harper and back to the boy before she nodded and disappeared into the room. When the door shut, Harper turned to the young man who stood a good half foot taller than her five-foot-eight and probably weighed around two-twenty or so.

"I think it's time you left." She stood her ground, her heart pounding against her ribs, refusing to step back even as he leaned closer.

"And who are you that I should do what you say?"

"Someone who isn't afraid to tell you where to get off."

His eyes squinted in a menacing glare. "Excuse me?"

Sizzling heat spread up her neck to her face. "I'd be happy to. Now leave. Or I'll call the police. Please. Test me on that."

His tightened jaw flexed, his fists clenched. After a tense few seconds that felt much longer, he turned and stalked through the lobby. He was out the door leading to the parking lot before Harper let herself breathe again. If only she'd had a backbone twelve years ago.

Bowing her head, she took a few tremulous breaths as her anger dissipated. Taking on a wide receiver by herself might not have been the wisest idea. But when she'd seen him strong-arming Jill, that mama bear who'd gone into hibernation years ago woke with a start and jumped in with claws bared.

She gave her pulse a minute to return to its normal cadence before she walked back into the gym, where the two squads stood once again in their starting formation. Catching Jill's apprehensive look, she gave her a small nod and took her spot in the front next to Libby.

An hour and many buckets of sweat later, they called it a day and gathered up their things. Harper ran a towel around her neck and over her face as she walked up to Jill, kneeling over a duffel bag in the corner.

"Hey, Jill."

The girl looked up over her shoulder and sprang to her feet. "Harper ... uh, I mean, Miss—"

"Harper's great. After what you've witnessed today, I think we can be on a first-name basis."

That garnered a small grin from the girl. "Harper. I'm really sorry about earlier. He's not always—"

"Never apologize for the actions of another. He's not your

responsibility, nor are you the cause of his behavior. If you're in trouble, there are people who—"

"No! I mean, no, ma'am. Nothing like that. I'm fine."

Harper studied the pretty face in front of her. Jill was a flyer on her squad, tossed around while doing somersaults and splits in mid-air. Harper had been a tumbler, more than happy to let the smaller girls be thrown around while she cartwheeled and backflipped her way down the sidelines or across a basketball court.

Father, help me reach this precious girl.

"Would you mind exchanging phone numbers?" The question came out before she'd even thought about it. But too late to backtrack now. Hopefully, Jill wouldn't think it too out of bounds. "I'm not trying to get into your business, but what I saw today … honey, that's not okay. How he was treating you is not acceptable. Trust me. I've been there. And if I'd had just one person in my corner, things might have turned out differently for me. Let me be that person if you need someone not so close to you. I know we just met, but if it's hard to talk to a friend or a parent, let me be that safe place you can go to."

"He's not always like that." Jill's voice shook with the tears brimming in her eyes. "We've known each other since we were little, and he's really a good guy who's just had some hard knocks. He does care for me. I know he does."

"And it's clear you care for him. But that doesn't mean you have to take the brunt of his frustrations or anger. Please, just take my number, and if you never need it, then you don't have to call me. But if you do ever find yourself needing to talk or someone to help you out of a jam, then you'll have it."

The girl looked at her for a moment, her perfectly trimmed eyebrows crinkled before she bent to dig around in her bag.

Harper released a breath. *Thank You, Lord.*

Jill stood and handed Harper her phone. After pressing the icon to get to Jill's contacts list, she added her name and number, sending herself a quick text so she'd have Jill's number as well. Before handing it back, she noticed several missed calls and even more texts, all from Dwight. This girl was neck-deep in trouble, whether she knew it or not.

"Call or text me anytime," she said as Jill stuck the phone back in her bag. "I mean it. If you need anything, reach out."

If only there'd been someone, anyone, Harper could have turned to all those years ago. But with Connor and Emery both gone, she hadn't known what to do. Who to turn to. Knowing if she said anything to a teacher or school administrator, the situation would only get worse.

So, she'd stuffed it down inside, telling herself it was okay, that it was the only way Brett knew to show her how much he loved her. But it wasn't okay. Nowhere near okay. And if she could help Jill avoid walking in those same footsteps, she'd get between her and her control-freak boyfriend any day.

CHAPTER FIFTEEN

"*W*ere you thinking couch and loveseat, couch with chairs, sectional ..." When no answer came, Harper looked over at the man behind the wheel of the Toyota Sequoia as they exited the gate of her townhome community. "Hay bales, tree stumps, boulders ..."

Chuckling, Wyatt looked over at her. "I like rustic, but maybe not that rustic."

"Oh, good. We're getting somewhere now. The man likes rustic. Since it doesn't appear you have a clear vision for your family room quite yet, let's head to the Home Styles store. I got most of my furniture there."

"You're the expert."

She smiled and settled back into the comfortable light gray leather seat of Wyatt's SUV. He'd surprised her after class on Friday, his last as their interim professor, when he pulled her aside to see if she might be available to help him furniture shop.

I have no clue where to start, he'd told her. *And thought you might have some ideas.*

Boy, did she! His house was a dream and a squeaky-clean slate. Both of them had a full Saturday and decided after church on Sunday would work for shopping. So, here she was with Wyatt for the afternoon. Alone. At his invitation.

She'd hardly been able to enjoy lunch with her family, so giddy was she inside. A shift had taken place after their heart-to-heart last Monday, as if a healing had begun. He'd been handling her with caution, keeping her at a friendly distance, and she'd let him. Some wounds took longer to heal, and many times, deep scars remained. She knew that far too well.

But now he'd taken the first step and reached out. If she could just keep from blowing it.

He pulled the SUV onto the freeway. "You had a rehearsal yesterday with the cheerleaders?"

"We did. So much fun, but I'm definitely feeling it today. I hadn't realized how out of shape I am."

"There's no way you're out of shape."

A grin spread across her face at his compliment, especially when she caught the blush that crept up his neck.

"Well ... you know." He cleared his throat. "It's clear you keep fit."

"I appreciate that, but my morning runs and yoga twice a week were woefully inadequate prep for what those girls put us through. That sweet little cheer captain, who welcomed us all with smiles and gift baskets, morphed into a drill sergeant once rehearsal began."

"Hmm. Now who does that remind me of?"

She looked at him and tipped up her chin. "Why, I can't possibly know what you mean, Wyatt McCowan."

"Ha! Glen and I were installing the new sound equipment in the gym one morning with a couple of other guys when y'all were in there rehearsing for your cheer competition. I remember Glen saying if you'd been coaching the football team, we probably would have won the state championship."

She threw her head back and laughed. "Okay, she did remind me a bit of myself, and Marney actually called her Harper 2.0. But those girls have what it takes, and she's exactly who they need at the helm if they want to go all the way."

They talked away the few minutes it took to arrive, and he chose a parking spot some distance from the entrance before grinning over at her. "Figured a good walk would help you work out the kinks."

"You're too kind." She shot him a saccharine smile, laughing after he'd exited the SUV to come around to her door.

Once inside the store, they meandered through the aisles between pre-arranged *rooms*, taking in the different styles, colors, and fabrics.

"I'm thinking leather for your family room might be the best idea," she said. "That's where you get most of your traffic. It'll hold up better and clean up easier than cloth upholstery."

"Good point. Let's start there and leave the living room for later. I'm still not sure how I want to go with that."

"Just tell me you aren't considering sticking a pool table in there."

His sheepish grin had her rolling her eyes.

"Then you're on your own with that. If you want furniture in there, I'm happy to help. Toys, take Mason." She gave her head a shake. "Bachelors."

He put his hand to the small of her back and stepped close to let another customer pass. When he let her go and moved away, she fought the urge to take his hand. He would no doubt think she'd lost her mind or was making a pass. Neither one the impression she intended to leave this first time testing the waters of their reclaimed friendship.

"This is nice." She pulled up at a brown leather couch with matching love seat. "What do you think?"

He studied it for a moment. "Hmm. Not moving me."

"Not *moving* you? I wasn't aware furniture had a spiritual element."

With a chuckle, he took her elbow and steered her away

from the *faux* room. "It does when it comes with that high a price tag."

She had to give him that one. Wyatt made a comfortable living, with his thriving practice, book royalties, and salary from the university. But she knew from a session they did with the kids on financial responsibility that, besides his mortgage and car payment, he had no other debt, paid a regular tithe, and made it a priority to save. She didn't find it surprising he'd seek the Lord's input before making a large purchase.

"Okay, now *this* is moving me."

They stopped at an *L*-shaped leather sectional upholstered in a rich, dark brick red. "I can see why." She stepped around the large piece to take a seat at the short arm of the *L*.

"Comfortable?" he asked as he walked around the other end.

"Like butter. I love this."

The cushion let out a soft *whoosh* when he sat down at an angle to her, and the smell of new leather wafted in the air. "Oh, yeah. This works."

"It's a sizeable piece, but you have the space for it in that room. And it'll seat at least seven people. Eight or nine of those skinny teenagers. And this color ... hmm. I'm seeing Americana or a Texas motif."

"I like the Texas theme idea."

"Let's look at some rustic oak tables in a medium finish. That would be perfect with this."

He nodded and looked over the sectional, his blue eyes alight.

Everything around her faded into the background as she watched him, her heart beating a staccato rhythm inside her chest. What was happening? She couldn't fall in love with him, because he could never love her that way, not with their history. Not with all her mistakes and bad choices sitting between them. She was lucky he wanted to be her friend again after she'd literally shut the door in his face all those years ago.

She would have to be satisfied with that. And she would be. She would be that friend she should've been all along.

She gave her head a shake to bring the rest of the world into focus and brushed a piece of imaginary lint from her skirt before looking at him again. "I'm going to miss seeing you in class."

He brought his gaze back to her. "You'll see me Monday. I'll be there to introduce Dr. Vance and give my best to the class."

"That's good. I know everybody would like to see you before you turn over the reins. You're an excellent teacher, Wyatt. Highly respected."

That charming boyish grin made her pulse skip. Goodness, this could not be happening. It would only lead to heartbreak. But maybe that's what she deserved after breaking his.

"That's nice of you to say, but you're going to love Marjorie. She's a phenomenal professor. I came away from the first class I had with her knowing I was exactly where God wanted me. Doing what He'd called me to do. Then seeing so many broken people during my internship at Brackett who might have been helped as pre-teens and teenagers solidified my resolve to counsel kids. And that was a few years before ConnectUP was even a thought."

"God has done a great work through you, Wyatt. I'm honored to be a small part of it."

He leaned forward and braced his elbows on his thighs. "I owe you an apology, Harper."

Her eyes widened. "What on earth for?"

"That first night you visited club. You were so excited afterward, and I wasn't very encouraging. In all honesty, I didn't know what you could bring to the table, not having dealt with the same issues as most of our kids. But you've done a fantastic job with your girls. They respect you, and they trust you. That's all I could ask for in a leader. I'm sorry if I discouraged you. You've been a welcome addition."

Tears burned behind her eyes as her very heart seemed to swell. "Thanks, Wyatt," she said, her voice husky with emotion. "That means more than you know."

He held her gaze with his own, rendering her powerless to look away. Her pulse raced. Something had happened. In just those few minutes, with just those few words. As if the gulf between them had narrowed, drawing them ever closer to something ... new. Something not yet defined.

Something she wanted with every heartbeat but knew she didn't deserve.

CHAPTER SIXTEEN

*W*yatt stood at Harper's front door and adjusted his tie, then the coat of his charcoal gray suit. Deep breath in, slow exhale. He shouldn't be nervous. It was just Harper. His old friend. No big deal.

Except it felt like a big deal. Watching her cheer last night alongside girls ten or more years younger, it was hard to tell the difference, and part of him felt like that heartsick kid he used to be. But her natural vivaciousness was even more striking at twenty-eight than it had been at seventeen, as her burgeoning faith filled her with an inner light she hadn't had back then. Sitting there in the bleachers with Mason, Rhonda, and several of the CU kids and leaders, he hardly watched the action on the field that last half as he'd found it hard to tear his eyes from her.

After another quick straightening of his tie, he rang the bell. Then stood there gaping like an idiot when she opened the door, a vision in a light green dress that set off her eyes in all their emerald glory. The skirt swished around her knees and the blingy, sleeveless top accentuated her slender waist. She'd pulled her long hair up, and he wondered how long those impossibly high heels would stay on her feet once they hit the dance floor. She wore more makeup than usual, but it still left her own natural beauty to shine through.

"Wow, Wyatt!" Her smile lit up her face, her vibrant green eyes dancing. "You look fantastic!"

"Um ... thank you. I'm just sorry you got that out ahead of me. I guess I'm a little tongue-tied. You look stunning, Harper."

A blush tinged her cheeks as she gestured him into the house. How was it that a simple compliment could make her blush? Hadn't she been told a million times how beautiful she was? Yet she always looked as if it was news to her. "Thank you, kind sir. Let me grab my sweater and purse, and we can go."

"Take your time." He stepped into the entry and looked around. If truth be told, he wasn't in that big a hurry to get to the dinner, as he wasn't at all sure what to expect. High school was another lifetime that felt a hundred years behind him. And if anybody had told him ten years ago he'd return with the prom queen on his arm, he'd have given them directions to the nearest lake.

She gathered her sweater and small bag from the back of the sofa in her cozy living room furnished in aqua blue and a creamy yellow. Her kitchen was indeed much smaller than his, but she clearly knew how to use it. The collection of cooking utensils sticking out of a canister on her counter put his *paltry assemblage* to shame, as well as the orderly placement of several small appliances, some whose purpose he couldn't have guessed. Everything in her home was tidy yet held such a warmth, he could spend hours there, relaxing with her in front of the fireplace, or sitting at the breakfast bar watching her cook.

He brought his attention back to the present to keep from meandering too far down that path. "Oh, uh, Dan said they would reserve a table for the eight of us, if you're okay hanging with those guys."

"Absolutely." She turned at the door and looked up at him with a smile, her sweater draped over one arm and small pocketbook clutched in her hand. "I'm your plus one, remember? I'd love to visit with your friends and their ... wives? Are they all married?"

"Dan and Pete are. Dan's wife, Sheila, is a paralegal, Pete's wife is a fellow architect at his firm, and Doug's engaged."

Her eyes narrowed. "Wait. I'm going to be sharing a table with an Adolescent Psychologist-slash-college professor, a surgical intern, a paralegal, two architects ... and what does Doug do?"

"Software designer."

"Software designer. Perfect." She laughed. "Am I going to be able to keep up with the conversation tonight? The only one who doesn't have a degree?"

"You're going to be fine. You're both smart and charming. They'll be putty in your hands."

"Oh, that was good. Very slick."

"I'm serious. You'll be fine. No worries. And they're believers, so we all have that in common."

Her eyes shone. "Okay. I'm looking forward to spending the evening with you and your brainy friends."

He laughed and reached for the doorknob. "Then, shall we?"

"We shall." She walked out the door he held open, turning on the porch light on her way.

"I like your house," he said as they stepped outside. When he'd picked her up for shopping last Sunday, she'd met him outside after he called from the gate, so he hadn't seen the inside. "Very nice."

"Oh, thanks. Doesn't have a chef's kitchen," she added with a pointed look his direction. "But I make do."

"Hey, any time you want to get in touch with your inner chef, you can have at it in mine. I certainly wouldn't say no to more of your cooking."

"Be careful what you offer." She dropped her house key into her tiny, sparkly purse. "I'm absolutely in love with that stove, and your island is perfect for all the holiday baking I do. All that space would be a dream!"

"I mean it." He opened the passenger door of the SUV he'd bought two years ago to replace the heap he'd nursed through college and grad school. "I'm a huge fan of holiday baking. Well, not so much the baking part, but the after-the-baking part."

"Maybe we'll do a Christmas cookie-baking day with the girls, then. If you're okay with that."

"Any time."

He'd wondered if the forty-minute drive would be awkward at all, but they had no trouble finding conversation topics. After learning she had no knowledge of what happened to Glen, it seemed as if the dam he'd built between them had sprung a leak, and he found himself seeking out reasons to talk to her during the past week. The furniture hunting trip, talking out on his back deck after Monday's leadership meeting, frozen yogurt after Wednesday's club, walking her to class Thursday afternoon when they ran into each other on campus.

If only they could get past that one last barrier. The conversation he had no clue how to start, the explanation she appeared to have no desire to offer.

"I thought I might feel out of place," she said when he asked about cheering in front of the home crowd again. "It can be disappointing to try to recapture something from your youth and find you should have left it there. But we had a great time, even if it was a challenge keeping up with those youngsters."

He glanced over at her. "You certainly didn't look like you were having a hard time keeping up."

"You should have seen us at the first practice. I thought paramedics might be called in."

They shared a laugh as he turned into the parking lot of the historic building overlooking the city lake and pulled up behind a Mercedes in the valet line. "You definitely looked in your element last night. Keeping up like a pro."

"Thanks, Wyatt. Your encouragement means a lot to me. And thank you for coming with me tonight. I know you weren't thrilled about it, but—"

"I can't think of anywhere right now I'd rather be."

Their gazes held for a few seconds before he realized the vehicle in front of them had moved, and he was holding up the line. He pulled up, put the SUV in park, and got out, coming around to meet Harper on the other side after the valet opened her door. When she took his outstretched hand, he was unprepared for the rush of awareness that passed between them. And from the spark that flashed in her eyes, he wasn't the only one who'd felt it.

Hand-in-hand, they followed several other late-comers into the building. They posed for the obligatory pictures, then walked into the elegantly outfitted room. Guests stood in groups, appetizers or drinks in hand, or sat at tables getting reacquainted, the hum of conversation and the occasional burst of laughter blending with the music pouring from overhead speakers.

Stopping inside the wide doorway, he looked around for Pete, Doug, or Dan, but instead met the glare of another man across the room in a circle of his football cronies.

Brett Ellison. Obviously not pleased to see his ex on the arm of another guy.

"Isn't that Doug?" Harper asked, pulling his attention away from Ellison to look in the direction she pointed.

"That's him." He returned his friend's wave, and they started toward the table where Doug, his fiancée, Kathy, and Pete and his wife, Laurie, already sat.

"Harper!"

She turned at the sound of her name, and Wyatt followed, forced to back up when three squealing women ran up and grabbed her in an exuberant group hug. He recognized one as former cheerleader, Brittney, and he now understood why she hadn't been on the sidelines with the others the night before. It appeared she could deliver any minute.

The other two he thought might have been on the dance team, but he couldn't remember their names. Just that they were all part of the tight group Harper used to run with.

"Oh, my goodness, girl," Brittney said. "Watching you last night, I thought we were right back in high school. I kept expecting you to start doing handsprings and backflips!"

Harper leaned back and laughed. "Oh, no. I would have probably broken my neck."

"You look fantastic," a heavily made-up blonde told her before her gaze floated up to him. "And who's your guy here?"

"Oh, you remember Wyatt McCowan, don't you, Kara?"

Kara's red-painted lips parted in surprise, her eyes raking over him from head to foot. And he suddenly felt like he needed a shower.

"Wyatt McCowan?" She moved from Harper to stand in front of him, offering her hand. "I would have never recognized you."

He took her limp fingers in a quick handshake. "Good to see you."

"And just what are you up to these days, Wyatt?"

"Adolescent Psychologist."

"And professor extraordinaire at Dallas Heritage," Harper added. "That's where I'm attending right now to finish up my degree."

He shot Harper a grin. "I don't know about *extraordinaire*."

The third woman, dark-haired with smiling brown eyes, extended her hand. "I don't know if you remember me. I'm Lorraine used-to-be-Spencer. We had biology together our sophomore year, and you were my lab hero."

"I do remember," he replied, now able to place the woman

he'd last seen as a girl. "We were partners for one of the dissections."

Her mouth twisted in distaste. "Frogs. Don't like them alive, but I really don't care for them opened up on the table in front of me. You were an absolute godsend, doing most of all that cutting stuff."

"Glad to be of service." Had other friends of Harper's been that nice? He recalled that Lorraine had been very friendly in high school, even if they didn't socialize outside of biology. But at least she'd carried her own load on the lab assignment. "And as I recall, you kept the notes because my handwriting is abysmal."

Harper nodded. "True story, there. We practically had to research the meaning of hieroglyphics to know what he wrote on the board in class."

Brittney's brows pinched together. "Wait. He's *your* professor?"

"Just for a few weeks," he explained. "I was subbing for the regular professor who had a family emergency."

"Harper Ellison!" All heads turned to a platinum-blonde holding a colorful drink as she walked up to grab Harper in a one-armed hug. Wyatt's skin crawled. He'd never known her as Harper Ellison, and it didn't sit right with him now.

"Townsend," Harper corrected her friend when she pulled back.

"Oh, you went back to your maiden name. How did Brett feel about that?"

Harper shrugged. "Never asked him."

The woman gave her arm a playful swat. "Well, good for you. So come join us! We have room for one more."

Harper shot a quick look at Wyatt before reaching over to take his hand. "Thanks, Bree, but some of our friends are holding spots for us."

Ice ran the length of Wyatt's spine. Bree Cullen. That's who she was. His eyes narrowed as he studied her, and a tightness in his chest threatened his breathing. Bree Cullen and Sarah Holmes had been joined at the hip in high school. She definitely would have known what her best friend had planned for Glen and had probably shared giggles about it. And if Bree was here, Sarah had to be close by.

Harper must have picked up on the tension because she looked past him and back at the ladies. "Oh, and there they are." Her grip tightened on his hand. "It was great seeing you guys! Catch up later?"

"Sure thing." Brittney smiled up at Wyatt while Bree still stared at him with a questioning wrinkle on her forehead. Did she know who he was? That he'd been Glen's best friend? That he knew what Sarah had done?

Still holding Harper's hand, he turned and led her toward the table where Dan and Sheila had joined the others. Before they got there, she brought her other hand to his arm and pulled him to a stop.

"Don't let that spoil your night, Wyatt." Her quiet voice and shimmering eyes communicated her understanding. "I know how close Bree and Sarah were."

"She had to know what was going to happen."

"Probably. But they have to live with that forever, knowing they played a part in that tragedy. You at least can look at yourself in the mirror, knowing you did everything you could to protect him."

Conjuring up a smile, he linked their fingers together and squeezed her hand. "You're right. I'm not going to let that spoil my night. I'm here with the most beautiful woman in the place, and I plan to simply bask in your light."

With a roll of her eyes, she gave his arm a light slap with her pocketbook. "Stop. Do you honestly have no idea how incredibly handsome you are?"

"I honestly have no idea."

She laughed, and he felt the warmth of it to his core. "Well, I do. I'm going to be the envy of every unattached female here tonight." She leaned in. "I thought Kara was going to eat you up with a spoon."

"Sounds painful," he answered as they started toward their table again, rewarded by another of her bubbling giggles.

"She's one of the girls I mentioned who was hoping to meet someone tonight. I'm just glad you're here with me."

He smiled down at her. "That makes two of us."

CHAPTER SEVENTEEN

*H*arper threw her head back, laughing as Wyatt spun her in a circle before pulling her close when the music changed to something slower. Out on the dance floor a good thirty minutes now, Wyatt's jacket and tie long gone, Harper couldn't remember the last time she'd laughed so much. Or felt so alive. As if her heart was blossoming inside of her.

All because of the man holding her now. He'd given her a dream evening—sharing his friends with her, giving her his focused attention when she spoke, posing for pictures, dancing with her and her only. Who knew Wyatt could dance!

She didn't want the night to end. Didn't want to let go of this rediscovered closeness with the man who'd been her long ago constant companion.

"I never expected tonight to be this much fun." His words pulled her attention to his mouth, almost close enough to— "Did you?"

She swallowed hard and moved her gaze up to his eyes in an effort to rein in her runaway imagination. "No. When I got that packet, I honestly had no plans to come. But now I'm so glad I did."

"Me too. Thanks for being my plus one."

"Hey, anytime you need a plus one, I'm your girl."

When his smile faded, and gaze intensified, she realized she'd spoken from her overflowing heart instead of keeping her head.

"I'll keep that in mind," he said, his voice low and quiet as his gaze lingered on hers before dropping to her mouth.

Her skin tingled. Was he contemplating what she had only moments before?

He tightened his hold and put his chin to her cheek as they swayed to a country ballad. Something about a broken road leading one to their true love. She closed her eyes and let the onslaught of sensation flow over her. A week ago, she'd warned herself to not fall in love with him. But she knew now it was much too late.

Did he feel it too? Could he possibly? Because if he were to only ask, she'd be all in. Ready to dive into something new and exciting and lovely and pure. Something she'd never experienced before.

Moving together, fitting as if made for that purpose, they were as close as two people could get. Yet there was something still there. That barrier. The history that always seemed to be there, from when she'd hurt him in a way she'd never wanted.

Because she'd had to protect him. Had to make sure he didn't become a victim of her devastating, life-altering choices. They were hers, she owned them, so the only life they should affect should be hers.

But it wasn't. That was evident from the moment his eyes found hers that first day in class. For as much as she'd tried to take the hit for him all those years ago, it had still left a mark on him she wasn't sure he would ever give her the chance to erase.

As the music faded away, he pulled back only far enough to put his forehead against hers, appearing as reluctant as she to break contact. Maybe there was something still there of the feelings the boy in him had for the girl she'd been. But the man was too smart, too careful, to let the woman she'd become get too close in case she should hurt him again.

The *thump, thump, thump* from the microphone shattered the moment as the lights came back up. They parted as Neil, their senior class president and evening's emcee, looked out over the crowd. "Okay, ladies and gents. Let's head back to our tables. We have some presentations to make and then a video package we've put together."

Wyatt led her back to their table by the hand, where they joined the three other couples. Thankfully, the ever-efficient wait staff had made sure their water glasses were refilled by the time they got off the floor, and Harper gulped half of it down in one breath.

Over the next several minutes, awards were presented, some humorous, some more sincere. Most Kids, Hardest Person to Locate, Who Traveled the Farthest to Attend.

Neil handed the award to the attendee who'd been married the longest, then consulted the list on the podium. "This next award won't come as a surprise to anybody who attended last night's football game. The award for The Most Timeless Alumnus goes to Harper Townsend."

Harper's face heated as she rose to accept her award for having aged the least of her classmates. Considering the twists and turns of her life over the past ten years, she felt she'd aged plenty, but it was a nice compliment, nonetheless.

On her way down from the stage, her gaze snagged on that of the man sitting with several of the old crowd. A chill cascaded down her body. She hadn't set eyes on Brett Ellison for over four years before tonight. She'd noticed him earlier in the evening, standing in a circle with his football buddies throwing back a beer. But she'd felt nothing other than relief that she was there with a godly man of unquestionable integrity and strength of character. With Wyatt, she wouldn't need a plan of escape should he drink too much and become heavy-handed or short-tempered. She wouldn't have to worry he'd expect certain things and refuse to take no for an answer.

Shaken, she made her way back to the table, working to keep a smile in place as she acknowledged the kind words of folks she passed on the way. She set her trophy on the table and grabbed for her glass, finishing off her water. She didn't realize she was shaking until Wyatt leaned in and put his arm around the back of her chair.

He leaned close. "You okay?"

She nodded.

"Neil's right. That award was a given after seeing you on the field last night."

Looking over at him, she caught his grin and felt her nerves loosen. "You're very kind." Their eyes locked as another round of applause erupted.

"Hey, Mac." They both looked over at Dan, his broad smile directed at Wyatt. "You're up."

"What?" Wyatt glanced around as the applause continued, every eye in their vicinity directed his way. His brow furrowed, and he looked over at Doug, who slapped him on the shoulder. "Me?"

"Yes, you," Pete answered.

"For what?" he asked as he stood reluctantly to his feet.

"Most Transformed."

His face reddened. "For the love ..."

Harper joined in the applause as she watched him walk up and take his trophy.

"Hey, Wyatt, can I have your number?" a woman called out from somewhere in the back, and the room erupted in laughter.

He ignored the request and rolled his eyes as he took his seat again. "Unbelievable."

"Totally believable." She couldn't keep back the giggle that escaped when his face reddened again.

The lights went down as a video came on the screen, and

music popular ten years before accompanied photographs from their high school days. There was plenty of laughter, *oohs*, and *aahs* over various scenes, but in Harper's opinion, there were way too many images of her and Brett together. Riding on the back of a convertible at Homecoming, walking hand in hand down the hall on the way to class, being crowned Prom King and Queen.

Tears filled her eyes when a shot of Wyatt and Glen floated across the screen, their heads bowed as they worked over a project in their junior year robotics class. She glanced over at Wyatt, noticed the hard set of his jaw, and reached to take his hand.

As the music slowed to a somber melody, the words *In Memoriam* preceded images of teachers, administrators, and fellow students they'd lost over the past ten years as they faded in and out of each other. Her heart constricted again when Glen's senior class picture came onto the screen.

But when the last photo came up, her breath caught as pain filled her chest and a tear escaped down her cheek. The face of her beautiful baby girl smiled at them from the screen as *Megan Renee Townsend-Ellison* scrolled under her photo with the dates of her birth and death. Much too close together.

Wyatt let go of her hand and wrapped his arm around her, pulling her close to his side. "She was beautiful, Harper. So much like you."

Laurie took her hand as the lights came back up. "A beautiful girl. I'm so sorry, Harper."

"Thank you. I can't believe it's been nearly five years now."

Several of Harper's friends came over, and she stood to accept their hugs. After a tearful Brittney let her go, she thought she might lose the fight to keep her composure.

Wyatt stood and put his hand on her shoulder. "Harper, is there anything—"

"Um ... I'll be right back." She threw him a glance through eyes filled with tears before she turned away to find an exit.

Any exit, to anywhere, it didn't matter, just to breathe, to think, to get herself together.

The side door leading out to the back deck was the first one she saw and practically jogged to it, pushing it open to let herself out into the night. The cool evening breeze off the water hit her in the face, and she gulped in the fresh air. She gripped the railing overlooking the lake and closed her eyes.

"Hi, God, it's me, Harper. Can You help a girl out here a little and throw some peace on me, please? I wasn't expecting that, but it was so lovely to see my Megan's precious face. Can You give her a kiss for me, please, and tell her Mommy loves her and thinks about her every day? Can You, please? Thank You for being such a good, good Father to my baby girl."

She stood in the stillness of the night, letting the peace she'd prayed for descend on her. Behind her, the door opened, the cacophony of voices and thumping music spilling out before once again fading. Her face raised to the sky, she smiled when she felt a hand touch her shoulder and turned to the man behind her.

Her breath hitched and smile evaporated.

"Brett."

CHAPTER EIGHTEEN

*W*yatt grabbed Harper's sweater off the back of her chair. He'd let her go, understanding she needed some time alone. But she'd been outside for several minutes now and had to be getting cold.

Or maybe that was a simple excuse to check on her. He couldn't get the sorrow he'd seen in her eyes out of his head. Spending the evening with her had been better than he could have imagined, and he didn't want it to end like this. But if she felt she needed to leave, take a walk, jump in the lake in their fancy duds just for kicks, whatever, he'd do anything she wanted if it would dispel the heartbreak he saw on her face for that brief moment before she fled the room.

Someone had propped open the door she disappeared through several minutes ago, probably to let in the cool night air. As he neared, his gait slowed at the sight of the two people standing on the low-lit deck. Harper …

And Brett Ellison.

His dinner turned to stone in his stomach when Brett handed Harper his cell phone, then stepped close, their heads bowed together as she typed into the device. When she gave it back, Brett stuck it in his back pocket and reached for her hand.

Wyatt stopped in his tracks and watched them stand face to face, his breathing shallow with dread. How could this be happening again? Not an hour ago, he'd held Harper close on the dance floor, a current running between them he couldn't deny. He should be the one out there offering comfort and support. Not—

—the father of her child. A man who'd suffered the same loss, understood the same heartbreak. Maybe out of all the people in this room, Brett was exactly who should be with her.

Wyatt caught Harper's eye as the two walked in the door. She smiled when she saw him, but it dimmed a wattage or two when he didn't return it.

He held out her sweater. "I thought you might need this."

"Oh! Thank you!"

She took the sweater and he turned his attention to the other man. "Ellison."

Brett eyed him for a moment before stepping forward to take his hand in a brief shake. "Wyatt McCowan. I hear you're doing some good work. Harper told me a little about it."

"She's a big part of what we do."

Brett turned back to Harper, placing his hand on her arm. "Thanks for the number. You look amazing, Harper. Really. I'm happy to see you doing so well."

"Thank you." Her eyes bored into the other man. "Be sure you call, okay? Please?"

"I will."

Wyatt bowed his head as Brett walked away. Pain seared its way into that part of his heart he'd shuttered all those years ago but had cautiously allowed to open back up over the past couple of weeks.

"Wyatt?"

He looked up and caught the question in eyes now

searching his own. But he was the one with questions. Questions he wasn't sure how to voice, or if he even had the right. "Uh, listen, I think I'll go catch some fresh air for a minute myself." He paused for a moment. "Unless you want to leave."

She pulled her head back, her brow furrowed. "Leave? As in, go home?"

"I thought you might, yeah."

"I'd really like to stay. If you want to, that is."

He nodded. "Sure. I'll be right back."

In an effort to put some space between them, he turned and strode toward the door. He needed someplace quiet to get his thoughts together. He'd enjoyed the past few days, growing closer to her every time they spent more time together. But right now, he needed to reclaim some of the distance he'd allowed to close between them.

The space he wanted wasn't meant to be, however, when she followed him out to the deck. He stopped at the railing and her footsteps silenced somewhere behind him. Concentrating on his breathing, he sent a prayer heavenward for the wisdom to know what to say and, even more important, what not to. When the light fragrance of her perfume wafted his way, he closed his eyes against the avalanche of feelings he hadn't meant to entertain.

She cleared her throat. "Thank you for coming to check on me."

"Are you okay?" He turned around to face her standing a few feet behind him, now wearing her sweater with her arms crossed tightly across her stomach. "After seeing Megan?"

She nodded. "I'm all right. I came out here to get alone with God for a minute, just to catch my breath."

He watched her for a moment, wondering again how much he had a right to know. Deciding he needed all of it, no matter what it might cost him, he took a deep breath and charged on. "And Ellison?"

She cocked her head to the side. "He came out to apologize

for not warning me. When someone from the reunion committee called to ask him if they could honor Megan, I hadn't put in my reservation yet, so he didn't know I would be here."

"And that's it?"

She joined him at the railing, looking up at him with those eyes he could stare into for hours. Eyes that penetrated into his, as if trying to see his deepest thoughts. "We talked about Megan a little. I don't think he's ever dealt with it in a healthy way. Still seems weighted down by how he wasn't there for us. Surprised me, really. He never once apologized after we lost her. But then, we hardly spoke in the months before we split."

"I see. And how do you feel about that? About his apology after all this time?"

Her eyes widened and she took a step back. "Are you asking as my friend or a psychologist? That sounded very clinical, so I'm not sure how I should respond."

"The truth would be a great place to start, regardless of who's asking the question."

"Well, it matters to—"

Several people spilled out onto the deck, drinks in hand, their laughter and loud conversation shattering the quiet.

She turned on her heel and took the steps down to a path below, leaving him no choice but to follow if he wanted her answer. Closing the gap, he walked next to her in silence to a small dock jetting out over the water. The moon cast a wide swath of light over the still surface. A romantic setting in any other context.

After a moment, she looked back up at him. "It matters to me who's asking. I didn't come tonight with Dr. McCowan, Psychologist. I came with Wyatt, my friend. And that's who I'd rather talk to."

"Okay, then. As your friend, all I want is what's best for you. If you don't want to be with me, then don't be with me.

But, please … Harper … don't go back to that guy. He was never good enough for you. Not then, not now."

Her jaw fell. "Go back … to *Brett?* Is that what you think I want?"

"I don't know what you want. Earlier, I thought that we — that maybe — and then I come out here, and there you are with — "

"That we what?"

Shaking his head, he turned to stare out over the water.

She grabbed his sleeve in her fist and forced him to face her. "Wyatt, that we what?" Their gazes locked, her eyes wide and intense. "If I don't want to be with you? You've never said anything about wanting to be with me. But is that a choice I have? To be with you?"

He swallowed hard. "We've been here before, remember? Seemingly on the road to something deeper. Last time, your choice to go back to Ellison gutted me. Yeah, we were just kids, but I was crazy about you, Harper, and it took a long time to get past that. Maybe that's why I want — no. I *need* to know if you're about to walk away again. Before we venture any further down this road."

"I don't want to be with Brett. I didn't even back when — " Her voice caught, and she looked down at the wood planks of the dock. "I was so scared. So confused. I did what I thought I had to do."

Scared? Of what? That she'd lose her spot at the top of the heap? Afraid her friends would never accept him as her choice?

Or was it more than that?

There are different forms of bullying.

Her words from that day sitting outside the library came back to him. Had it been Ellison himself she'd been afraid of?

Apprehension coiled low in his gut, and his skin felt as if ice-cold water flowed over him. How had he not seen it before? As a kid, he wouldn't have recognized it, but after years of education and now a practicing psychologist, how could he have not put it together?

Harper had displayed all the classic signs of abuse. Teenage abuse wasn't altogether uncommon, unfortunately, and girls that young usually weren't equipped to know how to handle it. How to get away from their boyfriend abusers. Had Brett given her an ultimatum? Maybe even threatened her?

All of that anger and bitterness he'd buried inside surged to the surface and dissipated into the evening breeze. It didn't matter what had pulled her back all those years ago. Holding on to past hurts had only kept him stuck there—in the past, wallowing in pain from wounds that had long ago scabbed over.

When she looked back up at him, his heart squeezed as a tear rolled down her cheek. "Can you ever forgive me, Wyatt? Please? So you can let go of anything you might still be carrying and let someone into your heart you can love with all that you are? I want that for you more than anything."

Someone he could love? There was only one someone he could see himself with. Finally.

"Come here." He reached out to pull her close. Her arms came around his waist, and her cheek rested against his neck where he'd opened the top button of his shirt after discarding his tie. Her breath feathered across his throat, and he closed his eyes as longing enveloped him in warmth.

He loved this woman. Had always loved her. Maybe it had started in his five-year-old heart as love for his best friend, that grew into love for the kindred spirit he'd found in her. Then during that too-short month they'd spent together in high school, it had grown into the kind of love a boy had for a girl he wanted to be with forever.

But now ... this feeling he'd been fighting refused to be held back any longer. That she could be *it*. The one his soul had been looking for.

Together they stood there, staring out over the water, the

pulsating music from inside the building a harsh contrast to the frogs croaking and crickets singing around them.

"Please forgive me, Wyatt."

"No need." He laid his cheek to the top of her head and breathed in that mix of floral and spice that was all Harper. "There's nothing to forgive. Although it sounds like maybe you need to forgive yourself rather than asking me to."

She nodded against his neck but made no move to let go. It felt so good to hold her this close, in the moonlight. As if the last remaining bricks had fallen away and nothing stood between them any longer.

"What about now, Harper?" he asked, his voice quiet in the dark. "What do you want now?"

Several heartbeats passed before she looked up at him, her face a mere breath from his. "You. No question, it's you."

His pulse accelerated, but there was still something he needed to know.

"Why did you ask Brett to call you?"

Her forehead pinched in question. "I didn't. He doesn't even have my number."

"But he thanked you for it, and you asked him to call."

She shook her head and pulled away, but he kept hold of her hands, unwilling to let her go far. "I gave him the number of the counselor I saw after he and I broke up. I was grieving hard, not over the marriage—that was done long before the papers were signed. But even two years after Megan died, I was so lost. Surviving, not living.

"Emery encouraged me to see a Christian counselor she knew, and it saved my life. Opened me up to let the Lord in and started me thinking maybe I could do the same for others. That's when I decided to get my psych degree, to go into counseling. But I wanted a more conservative approach, a Christian perspective. That's when I applied to DHU."

"Which brought you right back to me. You can see God's hand all over this. We needed to heal, Harper, if we're going to move forward and try to make something of whatever this is between us."

"You want to make something with me?"

"I'd like to. I know there's something here. It's impossible not to see it, to feel it. Especially tonight, being here with you, sharing all of this with you. It seems like full circle."

She smiled then, and it was as if the moon and stars had brightened. "So kiss me already."

With a grin, he tugged her close and wrapped his arms around her. He stared down at her, his gaze traveling from her sparkling eyes to her full, parted lips, then lowered his mouth to hers.

Fireworks exploding five feet from them couldn't have competed with the combustion of feeling that consumed him. Heat and need and yearning poured through him, and he wasn't alone in it, as she returned the kiss with a fervor that equaled his own.

Her hands slid up his back, pulling herself closer and deepening their contact. If a person could be a home, he'd found his. Kissing Harper again, after all these years, felt like coming home after a long absence. All the barriers had fallen, and all that remained was a pure, unfettered longing to be a part of something. Something genuine and good and full of promise.

The music from inside slowed to a ballad, and they swayed together as the kiss softened. They parted and stood in each other's arms, their foreheads together, still moving side to side in time with the melody.

"Wow," she said on a breath. "I thought our first kiss was the best ever. But *that* ... wow."

"You thought our first was the best ever?"

"It was mine. I'd never been kissed like that before. So respectful, so giving."

"That was my first kiss ever, so it was definitely the best."

She pulled her head back. "You're kidding! It was, really?"

"Really. You were my first, Harper. My first kiss. My first love."

Her smile softened. "You may not have been my first kiss, but you *were* my first love."

He brushed a tendril of loose hair from her face. "A lot of seasons have passed since then. We're not seventeen any longer. We're grownups, with grownup responsibilities, grownup goals. And grownup desires. I want us to go slow and be thoughtful about things. You need to know, I've never been with anybody, in an intimate way. I've always known I'd wait to be married. So let's take it day by day and see where we go. What we want. Does that work?"

"Absolutely! I want something good and godly. If it doesn't honor God, we shouldn't be in it."

"Agreed." He gave her another gentle but lingering kiss.

This was a turn in the evening he hadn't expected, and where this road would take them, he couldn't be sure. But if this new venture was going to work, he had to be all in. He couldn't offer only a part of his heart, but all of it.

And trust this time, she wouldn't tear it apart.

CHAPTER NINETEEN

"*It's* a good thing he didn't go stag." Harper grinned at Mason and Rhonda sitting across from her and Wyatt at the small diner where they met after Monday's team meeting. "Or I'm sure he would have been propositioned a time or two. Or four."

"Okay, wait." Mason looked back and forth between them with a wide smile. "Harper got the award for looking the same as in high school, and you got the one for changing the most?"

Wyatt shook his head. "No words."

"That's hysterical!" Rhonda looked at Harper. "Do you have any photos of him from high school?"

"Oh, honey, I have photos going back to kindergarten. Next time you're over, I'll pull out my albums and yearbooks. Amazing what a haircut and a few extra pounds will do. Oh, and contacts."

The four laughed again before Harper pushed her half-eaten piece of banana cream pie away.

"Are you going to finish that or take it home?" Wyatt asked.

"You want it?"

"I wouldn't say *no*," he replied with that boyish grin that made her pulse skitter.

She pushed it toward him. "Have at it. I don't know how you stay in such great shape, the way you eat. So jealous."

"And I'll be in the gym at six tomorrow morning. Where will you be?" He stuck a forkful of pie in his mouth without taking his eyes from hers. And this after the man had finished his own piece of pumpkin.

"On a three-mile run around my neighborhood."

His teasing grin disappeared. "Oh."

"Yeah, *oh*." She nudged him with her shoulder. "Three miles three times a week and yoga in my living room twice a week."

A crease appeared on his forehead. "Is that safe?"

"Yoga?"

"No. Running in the dark."

She shrugged. "I guess. I've never had any issues. It's gated, the paths are well-lit, and I always have pepper spray with me."

He shook his head. "I don't know, Harper. I don't like the idea of you being out there by yourself. As a student, you can use the fitness center at the college for free."

"But then I'm inside the whole time." Her cell phone vibrated, and she pulled it from her purse. "I like to be outside."

"All right. But I still don't like it."

Her heart swelled to know he was anxious about her safety. So far, he was shaping up to be a top-notch boyfriend, in the two days he'd been one.

"It might be a moot point, anyway." She glanced at the number on her screen. It wasn't one she recognized, although the same number had popped up twice in the past hour. She hit the red icon to ignore it. Couldn't be one of her girls. She already had all their numbers in her phone, so if one of them was calling her, their ID would show.

"Why?"

She slipped the device back into her purse and looked at Wyatt. "Why what?"

"Why might it be a moot point?"

"Oh. I got an interesting call this afternoon. From Coach Caldwell."

"That *is* interesting. What'd he want?"

"Their cheer coach's husband got transferred out of state, so they need a new coach."

He swallowed the last bite of her pie. "And he thought of you?"

"I don't know, but he said he had an office full of cheerleaders first thing this morning begging him to offer me the job."

Rhonda's face lit up. "You'd be a fantastic coach, Harper! And it was obvious Friday night those girls really took to you."

While grateful for Rhonda's encouragement, the frown on Wyatt's face made Harper's stomach roll.

"What kind of commitment would you be looking at?" he asked. "Do you have the time with everything else you have going on?"

"Mostly mornings, three times a week. Which could double as my workout since some of that will be strength training, stretching, and conditioning. Then all the games, of course. They're already working on their routines for the Spirit Championships in January, so some Saturdays."

He shook his head. "It's your decision, but you're carrying twelve credit hours, working thirty hours a week, and you have ConnectUP. Unless you're thinking of stepping down to coach."

"No, I wouldn't do that. I love ConnectUP. But I truly think I can do it. I've been praying about it ever since he called."

"When do you have to let him know?"

"I told him I'd have an answer to him by Wednesday." She

looked at him for a moment. "And it's really not any more than you're doing—teaching two classes, a full-time practice, running ConnectUP, and putting together this grant proposal."

Mason chuckled. "She has you there, Red."

Wyatt stared at her for a moment. "*Touché*. But think long and hard. I'd like to spend some time together when we're not working on something."

She laid her hand on his arm. "It's only for a season. The grant proposal will be submitted in January, and Spirit State Championships will also be done in January. After that, things will slow down."

"Sounds like you're already leaning that way."

"I'm totally open to God closing this door if He chooses to. But this feels divine to me. I don't know how to explain it. If it weren't for those girls inviting us to join them for Homecoming, I'd have never met them. And I'd have never seen ... well ... just that I think I have something to offer these girls. And to think this all happened right when their coach is leaving. I absolutely love working with my girls at ConnectUP, so maybe this is my calling, ministering to girls."

"Except the cheer girls aren't exactly at-risk."

She looked down and brushed a crumb off the table. She knew of one who was very much at risk. And she didn't doubt there were others on the squad dealing with their own demons. "I think you'd be surprised."

His eyes didn't leave hers for a long, silent moment until he nodded. "Okay, we'll all pray about it."

"Definitely." Rhonda reached for her hand across the table. "God will give you the wisdom to know what direction you should go."

Peace flowed over Harper, while at the same time, she found the situation tremendously ironic. A year ago, she'd had no direction at all. Now she found herself pulled in too many. School, work, ConnectUP, cheer coach. And now Wyatt. So many wonderful opportunities.

But even wonderful opportunities could weigh a person down if there wasn't enough time and energy to give to them all. And it would break her heart if she failed at any of them.

Her phone vibrated again, and she let go of Rhonda's hand to pull it out. "Same number. That's four times in the past hour."

Wyatt gestured to the device. "Maybe you should answer it. If it's a robocall, that should make it stop."

She pressed the green phone icon. "Hello?"

"Harper."

Her skin chilled as her eyes darted to Wyatt. "Brett?" Clearly a different number than he used to have, or she would have recognized it.

Wyatt sat up a little straighter, his brows pinched together.

"I need ... help." A sob choked off the voice on the other end. "Please, Harper. Help me. Y-you're the only one."

CHAPTER TWENTY

*W*yatt heaved a sigh. Seriously? He and Harper had been together two days, and here was her ex, insinuating himself between them yet again. It'd been almost four years since the divorce. Why couldn't Brett let her go?

"What's going on?" he asked her.

She shrugged and shook her head. "Brett, I don't know what you mean. Only one who what?" She bent her head, plugging her other ear to block out the diner noises. "Take a breath." She listened a moment longer. "I don't understand."

Wyatt hated that he could only hear one side of the conversation. He tapped her on the arm to get her attention. She looked up and dropped her hand from her ear. "If he's drunk, hang up."

"I don't know." Her eyes narrowed. "Brett? Brett?" She listened for a second. "Brett! Are you there?" She took the phone from her ear. "I heard a thud, and now he's not saying anything."

"Like he fell?"

"More like the phone hitting the floor. I've seen him

intoxicated more times than I care to admit, and this isn't what he sounded like. He's a mean drunk, not an emotional one."

"Tell me exactly what you heard."

"Slurred speech, so he's definitely under the influence of something. He was crying, hard to make out exactly what he was saying. Something about failing everyone. Said Megan's name a couple of times ... and something about shipping out, but that doesn't make sense."

Wyatt's skin crawled. "Checking out?"

Her eyes widened. "That could be it."

"Keep the line open." He pulled his phone out of his back pocket. "Is he still in the same place?"

"He told me at the reunion he never moved out of the house."

"Address." He punched 9-1-1 into his cell phone. She gave him the address, and he recited it to the operator as they scooted out of the booth. Harper apologized to their friends while he informed the operator he thought it might be a possible suicide.

Once in his SUV, and after being assured first responders were on their way, he disconnected. "Anything?"

She shook her head. "Just music in the background. Nothing from Brett."

"I don't get why he called you."

"I have no idea how he even got my number."

They drove in silence for a few minutes before she reached out and grabbed his arm. "Police are there. I can hear pounding and shouting." Her grip tightened. "They just busted in."

"Where do I go from here?" He could use the on-board navigation system in his SUV, but he wanted her mind on something other than what was happening on the other end of the line. If Ellison was dead, she didn't need to overhear that on the phone.

She told him where to turn before stopping mid-sentence. "Yes, sir?" She listened to a voice on the other end. "Harper Townsend. I'm his, um, ex-wife." She paused again. "Yes, sir, we're a few minutes away. Gray Toyota Sequoia. Officer Martinez, okay. I'll ask for you when we get there. Can you tell me — okay. Thank you."

After disconnecting, she took a deep breath and let it out. "One of the officers noticed the phone was live and picked it up. Wants to talk to us when we get there."

"Did he say what Brett's condition is?"

She shook her head, and her eyes filled with tears. "I know things ended ugly, and we hadn't had any contact for years before the reunion, but I don't want him dead."

"Of course not. I get it, Harper. Keep a good thought. And pray."

They turned the corner onto Ellison's street, where red and blue flashing lights from three police cruisers, a fire truck, and an ambulance pierced the dark. Neighbors stood on their porches, peered through windows, and gathered on lawns to watch the drama unfold. He parked a couple of houses down from the one she used to call home back when her name was still Ellison, and they quickly got out.

As they approached the driveway, an officer walked toward them at a determined clip. "Ms. Townsend?"

"Yes," she answered.

"Officer Gabe Martinez. I have a couple of quick questions."

"Can you tell us how he is first?" Wyatt asked.

"He's alive but barely." The policeman looked back at Harper. "Can you tell me if Mr. Ellison has a drug habit?"

Harper shook her head. "Until Saturday, we hadn't spoken in nearly four years, so I don't know about any drugs. But he's been a drinker since high school. It got really bad in college after he lost his football scholarship when he could no longer play due to an injury."

"And that was when?"

"Ten years ago. Our freshman year of college. Then ... well, we lost our daughter not quite five years ago."

"Did he own a gun back then?"

Her hand came to her chest, and her eyes widened. "Oh, no, did he shoot himself?"

"No, ma'am, but there was a gun on the coffee table. One of the officers saw it through the window, which is why we made entry when we did. We didn't know if he had or not at that point."

"Um ... yes." She threw a glance at Wyatt. "He owned a gun."

Movement at the front door drew their attention. Another police officer preceded two EMTs rolling a gurney carrying Ellison while another firefighter held an IV bag over his head.

"Where are they taking him?"

Wyatt shot her a look. Did she intend to go to the hospital? Since he'd picked her up for that evening's team meeting, that meant he would be going too. Not exactly what he'd expected to be doing tonight. Not when two days ago she'd told him her ex was well in her past and she was ready to move forward into something new.

Now, Ellison had yanked Harper right back into his world, as he'd done all those years ago.

"Arlington Med," the officer told her. "If you could both give me your contact information, you can go on."

After giving Officer Martinez their phone numbers, Wyatt took her hand and walked her back to the SUV.

"Are you sure you want to go to the hospital?" he asked as they secured their seat belts.

"I need to know he's all right."

He pulled away from the curb and made a U-turn. "Okay, but it could be hours."

"You can take me home for my car if you don't want to go."

He gave her a quick glance, choosing not to react to the

sharpness of her tone. "I'm not leaving you alone to deal with this. You go, I go."

She nodded but kept her eyes directed out the window. After a couple minutes of silence, she looked over at him. "I'm sorry, Wyatt. I didn't mean to snap at you. You've been great about this whole thing."

Great? Glad she thought so, but he had to admit he didn't feel great about it. If this was the first test of their barely-off-the-ground relationship, however, he would do his best to do and be whatever she needed to get through it.

Two hours later, though, he found his resolve waning as he walked over once again to the bank of windows in the emergency department waiting room, staring out at the inky blackness of the night. A nurse had come to get Harper over half an hour ago, leaving him to cool his heels in this dreary room. He still didn't understand how they ended up here, and a quick glance at his watch told him it was about to be a new day.

The door leading from the treatment area swung open and Harper walked toward him, her gait slow and arms crossed over her stomach.

He met her halfway. "How is he?"

"Conscious. Sort of. Talking but not making a lot of sense." The exhaustion in her eyes cooled his ire as he took her hand to lead her to the chairs. "They're going to admit him to psych for a seventy-two hour hold since it appears this was a suicide attempt and there was a loaded weapon at the scene."

"Have his parents been notified?"

"They're out of the country, but I called his sister, Hannah."

"Is she coming?"

"Went straight to voicemail. She's going to be shocked to hear from me. We used to be close, but we drifted apart after the divorce."

Wyatt studied her for a moment. Her pale skin, slumped posture, and heavy-lidded eyes told him she was done in. But instead of home in bed where she should be right now, she was here for reasons unknown.

"How'd he get your number?"

"Kara," she said with an edge of disdain in her voice. "They hooked up at some point Saturday night, and she asked if it was all right with me if she and Brett, you know … left together. I told her it had nothing to do with me."

"Why would she give him your number, then?"

"I asked him about that, and he laughed. Said she didn't know she'd given it to him. I think he went through her phone when she wasn't aware of it." She gave her head a shake. "Who does that?"

A man on a mission, Wyatt suspected but kept to himself. "So, what now?"

She yawned, then released a deep sigh. He wasn't sure how she was even still on her feet. They'd danced into the wee hours Saturday night before joining several others for breakfast at an all-night diner. He dropped her at home a little after four yesterday morning, they'd both still somehow made it to their respective church services, then spent the day with her siblings at Emery's house. Exhausted, he'd fallen into bed a little before ten, but when he called to say good night, she was doing homework. Now here it was midnight Monday night, and she looked about to drop.

"We can go," she said. "I know you and Mason have an early workout, and I need to be at work by eight. I'll come by after my afternoon class to see how he's doing."

He looked away for a moment and back again. "Harper, don't let him pull you back in. It's not a coincidence that you saw each other two days ago after four years, and now he's reaching out after all but stealing your phone number."

Tears filled her eyes. "I can't just walk away," she said, her voice quiet and tight. "This is about Megan. It's as if he's finally catching up to what's happened, and, like he said, I'm the only one in his life who understands this particular grief."

"Except you didn't choose to lose yourself in the bottle. Or in whatever drug he's graduated to. Don't take this on yourself. This is on him. To recover, if he chooses to, he has to own that. You can't make it easier for him. If people are propping him up, he'll never do it on his own. You know your parents would tell you the same thing."

"But he's dealing with both addiction *and* grief. I can't help him through addiction recovery, but maybe I can help him find his way through the pain of losing Megan. I don't know how I can turn my back on him now. Is that what Christ would do? Would He walk away from someone asking for His help?"

He shook his head and released a sigh. "No. He wouldn't. But Jesus wasn't a doormat, either. Even going to the cross was *His* plan. He wasn't manipulated into sacrificing Himself."

Her face fell. "You think Brett's manipulating me?"

He took a moment to measure his response. She would always hurt in that place where Megan would forever live in her heart. And Brett laying all this on her only made it worse.

"I'm saying he knows what buttons to push with you. I don't know what he used before to get you back, but if that's his end game here, he's playing right to what matters to you most."

Her gaze went to her hands in her lap, but she didn't respond.

He reached over and smoothed a lock of hair behind her ear. "If he's sincere in wanting help, he needs to understand it doesn't involve pulling you back through all of that. To help him doesn't mean going into the mud with him."

She reached for his hand and nodded. "Can we go now? I'm so tired, I don't know what to think."

"Sure thing." He stood and drew her up in front of him.

"Just know I'm here for you no matter what. I'll do anything and everything I can to make this easier for you."

As long as that didn't mean letting her go. He walked away once without a fight. He wouldn't make that mistake again.

CHAPTER TWENTY-ONE

*H*arper paced in the hospital corridor, her head pounding as she clutched a Bible to her chest. She needed sleep in the worst way. Yet every time she closed her eyes, Wyatt's words from three days ago came back to her. *He knows what buttons to push with you. I don't know what he used before to get you back, but if that's his end game here, he's playing right to what matters to you most.*

If that was true, Brett sure had it right eleven years ago.

Wyatt. Her heart sat heavy in her chest. Since that first night, he hadn't pressed her about how much time she'd spent here the past three days. Hadn't forced her to make a decision, even after she canceled their Tuesday dinner plans. But the concern and questions she saw in his eyes at last night's ConnectUP club pricked at her conscience.

Because she was in love with him. No doubt about it. Even before Saturday night's decision to take their relationship to the next level, she knew her heart was his should he ever want it. Yet here she was, spending part of her already full days with the man who had never valued her instead of the one who treated her with nothing but respect and dignity. The one she hoped to build a life with, Lord willing.

The brand-new leather fragrance of the Bible she clutched alleviated the antiseptic smell of the sparkling clean hospital corridor. Her own Bible had lost its new book smell, now that it had been well-used, marked up, and dog-eared. She'd had it only a year, but it bore the marks of a much-read, long-owned, beloved treasure. She'd even memorized the order of the books inside it in the nearly two months since that first evening at Wyatt's when he showed her his Bible app.

Her pacing ceased when a nurse exited the room.

"You can see him now. I'll warn you, though. He's not a happy camper."

Not that he ever had been the over past three days. "Thank you. I won't be long."

After drawing in a deep breath and letting it out, Harper knocked and pushed open the door.

"Finally. Someone I actually want to see." Brett sat up in the bed, television remote in hand. A definite improvement over the last two days when she'd found him curled up in a fetal position or bent over a bowl throwing up. "What's with these people? Treating me like I'm a basket case. I don't belong here."

"Hello to you too." She stopped beside the bed and studied him. Although still handsome, booze and drugs had taken their toll. And the throes of detox hadn't helped any, leaving dark circles under his brown eyes and a gray pallor to his skin. At least his hair was clean and face shaved, so he'd been able to make it to the shower.

"Sorry." He clicked the television off and laid the remote on the bed. "It's good to see you. As always."

She pulled up a chair to sit and set the Bible on the bedside table. "Your family wants to see you."

"Right," he said with a humorless chuckle. "You mean my mom and sister." He shook his head, then winced, his hand coming to his temple to give it a rub. "Last thing my mom needs to see is me in here, like this."

"She doesn't care what state you're in or what department, for that matter. You're her son. She wants to be here for you."

"My seventy-two-hour hold is up tomorrow morning, and then I can ditch this place. She can see me at home."

She stared at him hard. The next few minutes could set the trajectory for the rest of his life. She could offer him a plan, but he would need the courage to work it. *Lord, give me the words. Give him the strength.* She took another cleansing breath. "What do you want, Brett?"

His brow furrowed. "What do you mean, what do I want?"

"What do you want? For your life? Your future? When you walk out of here tomorrow, what will you do differently so you don't end up here again?"

"I won't mix scotch with Oxy, for starters."

"And the loaded gun they found right next to you?"

He swallowed and looked away. "I didn't plan to use it, if that's what you mean."

"Brett, you called me four times within an hour. What was that about if you don't really want help?"

His hardened gaze snapped back to her. "Yeah, four times, Harper," he said, side-stepping her question. "Why'd it take you so long to pick up?"

"I didn't know the number. It's not the one you used to have."

His mouth opened, then closed as a red flush crept up his face. "Oh. Right. I forgot about that. I got messed up with some chi—woman I picked up in a bar a couple of years ago. Went all *Fatal Attraction* on me. She wouldn't stop calling and texting, so I finally just got a new number. Thankfully I never took her to my house."

"Didn't answer my question. If you don't want my help, why call me?"

His countenance darkened again. "I was drunk, okay? I'm not proud of it, but I'm having a hard time here. You of all people should understand. Ever since the reunion ... and that picture." He dropped his head back against the pillows behind him and stared at the ceiling. "Why'd I give them that picture?"

"Because you loved your little girl, and it's an honor to have her remembered like that."

"All I remember is how I was never there for you. You were moving heaven and earth to get her well, and where was I? Going to happy hour every night after work and home with whoever was willing to help me forget for a little while."

He pulled his head up to look at her. "I'm sorry. I didn't mean to drop that on you."

"Trust me, I'm not shocked by the admission. If it weren't for your dad insisting you marry me, you would have had the life you wanted."

"*Pfft.* I was never going to have the life I wanted as long as my dad was breathing, with or without you and Megan."

Harper couldn't argue with that. She knew how demanding the senior Ellison could be. "You're a grown man now. If your dad isn't respectful of your wishes for your own life, you don't have to let him in. Your mom and sister love you and want to support you. You have friends who want to be there for you. They're not scattering because you're in here. They're lining up, asking how they can help.

"So instead of sitting here counting the hours until you can *ditch this place*, think about what you want. Do you like having to drink every day? Do you honestly not want to remember your daughter? She never felt you weren't there for her. She loved you like crazy and would tell anybody who would listen how handsome and funny and smart her daddy was."

A tear started down his face. "I didn't deserve that. Didn't deserve *her.* When you told me you were pregnant, I kept hoping you would — "

He put his hands to his face as a sob tore from his throat, his shoulders shaking from the outpouring of grief he'd never let himself feel.

She moved to the side of the bed and took him in her arms, letting him cling to her until his tears were spent. She pulled back and looked him in the eye. "You need to decide where to go from here. Are you going to fight for your life, or go back to doing everything you can so you don't have to feel?"

He brought his hands to her face and ran his thumbs along her cheeks. The intimate gesture brought none of the warmth it did when Wyatt touched her like this. Before Brett could act on what she saw in his eyes, she pulled his hands away and moved back to the chair.

"I need you, Harper," he said, his voice hoarse. "If I'm going to fight this, I need you."

She shook her head. "No. You don't. You have to do this for you, not to be with me. Not to please your dad or make your mom happy. You have to want it badly enough to face what you've been running from."

He looked away, a muscle working in his jaw as he stared out the window. She let the silence linger while he worked through his thoughts, praying he would find the strength to enter the fight of his life. The fight *for* his life.

"You love him?"

The out-of-the-blue question startled her.

He looked back at her when she didn't answer. "McCowan. You love him?"

"We're just starting out, he and I. But, yes. I think I've loved him all my life."

"So that summer when I—"

"You tore my heart out."

A wince crossed his face. "Yeah, I think I knew that. But I just told myself you'd chosen me and pretended everything was okay. I think I finally accepted in college that wasn't true, that I'd given you an impossible choice. Then that weekend … and everything changed."

"When Megan was conceived. Shouldn't have happened, but how can I be sorry I had our precious girl for four years? My only regret is how she suffered in the end. Otherwise, I wouldn't change it. I can't imagine not being her mother."

"You were a stellar mom. I'm sorry I never said so."

Fresh tears sprang to her eyes. "You're saying it now. Thank you."

"Will I not see you again?"

She brushed a finger under her eye. "Brett, you have a decision to make. If you want to recover, I have an opportunity for you. But you have to be all in or forget it. They won't give you another chance."

"They?"

She nodded and cleared her throat. "I talked to my parents, and they can get you into one of their programs. It's intense, and it's long. In-patient for sixty days, then a transition home for another sixty. You'll have to take a leave from work for at least the first sixty. You can work during the second, but you have to test every day when you get back. One slip-up and you're out."

"Sounds harsh."

"It's all or nothing. No second chances. My mom was steadfast against it when I talked to them, but Dad was willing to give you a chance, and she's come around."

She pulled a pamphlet from her purse and handed it to him. "A Townsend program director will be here in an hour to go over all of this with you. You can either be transferred directly there when you're released tomorrow, or you can go home and get on with your life. But either way, I won't be back. You and I aren't an *us* anymore and haven't been for many years, even before we made it official."

She stared at him until he looked up from the pamphlet. "I'll be praying for you, and if there's anything required of me during your recovery, I'll do it. But this is *your* journey. I've already taken mine, and God's done a great healing in me. He can do the same for you if you'll let Him."

He nodded but said nothing, giving her no indication which way he would go.

She picked up the Bible. "I know this has never been a part of your life, but your sister and I want you to have it. Everything you need to know about love and healing and grace is in these pages. If you're not sure where to start, talk to Hannah. She'd love to share this with you."

After placing the Bible back on the table, she stood. "Take care of yourself, Brett."

He offered no more than another small nod of his head before she turned and walked out of the room.

Outside the door, she stopped and took a deep breath. Peace enveloped her like a silken cloud. Just as Wyatt had told her, she couldn't walk Brett down this path, not if he was to beat back his demons once and for all. She'd done all she could, and she prayed he'd make the choice that would take him down a new path.

Because it was time she got back on her own.

CHAPTER TWENTY-TWO

*W*yatt rocked back and forth in one of Harper's porch chairs and glanced at his watch for the umpteenth time since he arrived. He'd come straight from the office after his last appointment and had been waiting now over thirty minutes. She was probably working late—again—due to the time she'd been spending with Ellison every day.

He'd held his tongue since their talk in the emergency room Monday night, praying she'd take his words to heart. If not as her boyfriend, at least as a professional in the field. But instead, she'd worked herself to a frazzle trying to keep up with school, work, ConnectUP, and daily hospital visits.

When she canceled their Tuesday dinner plans to spend the evening with her parents, a part of him wondered why she hadn't invited him along. They were a couple, right? This Sunday after church would be spent with his family, including his parents, but she wasn't ready for him to be with hers? She hadn't offered any explanation after last night's club, and he hadn't asked, instead hoping she'd open up on her own.

Looking up at the sound of an approaching vehicle, he saw her blue Audi turn the corner that led to the rear-entry garage. Hers was the end unit, so after returning her wave, he walked around the side of the building and met her as she stepped out of the car.

"Hey, there," she said, her smile wide. "This is a pleasant surprise."

He ignored the impulse to take her in his arms and kiss her as if the last few days hadn't happened. Like he had at the reunion, at her door the next morning, and when he'd left her Sunday night. But there were things he needed to know first. Then, hopefully, they could get back on track.

"Yeah. I was hoping we could talk."

Her smile disappeared. "Okay. Come in. I can fix us something to eat if you're hungry."

"Not really."

Her brow furrowed, but she didn't say anything as she turned to walk into the townhouse, pressing the button to lower the garage door on her way in. She dropped her purse and backpack on a barstool and turned to him.

"Would you like something to drink?"

"I just need to know what's happening. Because I really can't do this again."

Her eyes narrowed. "Do what again?"

"Watch you make this mistake."

She gave her head a shake. "I'm sorry. What are we talking about?"

"Seriously?"

"Yes, seriously." She took a step toward him. "Wyatt—"

"I thought you were past this, past *him*. But here we are, and once again, you're getting sucked back in by Brett Ellison. Whatever hold he has over you—"

"Okay, stop." Her voice wavered and eyes sparked. "I'm not getting sucked back into anything. Brett does not have any kind of *hold* over me, and I take exception to the insinuation I can't think for myself."

"Then tell me what *I'm* supposed to think. You went

running back to him so fast that summer, and here you are again, letting him back in. History repeating itself. We were just kids, I know, but I thought we had something. Then all it took was a crook of his finger, and you went running right back."

"We *did* have something! I *did* care about you! Wyatt—" Her voice broke, and her eyes filled with tears. "I didn't go back to Brett because I loved *him*. I went back because I loved *you*!"

His head jerked back as his brain tried to catch up to what she'd said. "That doesn't make sense."

"It did when I was seventeen and forced to make a decision nobody should ever have to. But I was terrified I was going to lose you, so I felt like I had no choice."

"And yet that's exactly what happened. For eleven years, we never spoke. Not since that night when I stood on your porch, and you told me in no uncertain terms it was better for me not to come around anymore. Right before you shut the door in my face. You remember that?"

"Vividly. And what you didn't see was how I crumpled on the other side of that door when you left."

He took a step toward her, his hands held out in front of him. "Then explain it to me. Why put us both through that? If you loved me, how could you walk away from me without a backward glance?"

"Because Brett said he was going to kill you!" Her breath hitched, and she swallowed hard. "And I believed him, Wyatt. He was beyond livid. Out of control. When he got home from his trip with his family, somebody told him you and I had been spending a lot of time together. He was waiting, saw you kiss me, and came back later, drunk out of his mind, with a gun. Told me he would take you out if I didn't get my head on straight. If he'd just threatened me, maybe I'd have handled it differently. But if he hurt you ..."

His head spun. He'd wondered if perhaps Brett had

threatened *her*, but had never once considered the threat had been about *him*.

"I couldn't take that chance. Don't you see?" Her voice faltered as a tear escaped. "How could I know for sure what he was capable of? I wasn't willing to risk your life or well-being because of my poor choices.

"So I had to tell him—make him believe—that I had only gone out with you to get back at him for cheating on me. Every word was a complete lie that made me sick to my stomach, but I would have stood in fire if it meant keeping you safe."

"Harper ..." His anger withered away in the face of her honesty. He hated the pain he saw in her eyes and etched into her face, but he'd had to know. He couldn't fight for her if he didn't know what he was up against. "Why didn't you talk to me? We could have gone to the authorities, our parents. The school. We had options."

"I didn't see any options. If we or our parents had gone to the authorities, and Brett got kicked out or arrested, we would have had the entire school coming down on us. Everybody knew he was Conway's best hope for a state championship that year. Football is king in Texas. And you don't mess with the head that wears the crown."

He sighed and stuck his hands on his hips. She was right. It would have been a nightmare for both of them if anything they did had prevented Ellison from playing that year. Even though, as it turned out, they missed the state championship one game out.

"And that was if anybody even believed me. I couldn't win, Wyatt. It didn't matter which way I went, I was going to lose. I just needed to know you were safe, and that was anywhere *not* near me."

Deflated and ashamed he'd put her through this, his shoulders slumped as he rubbed his brow with his fingers. "I am so sorry, Harper." He walked over and wrapped his arms around her. "That you weathered all of that by yourself. I wish we could have worked it through together."

"I know." She pulled back to look up at him. "But I couldn't take that chance. Even if he just roughed you up, I don't know how I could have lived with it. Especially now, knowing what those other guys did to Glen. If that had been you …"

She pulled away and walked over to sit on the other barstool across the counter from him. His heart went out to her. She looked wrung out, emotionally as well as physically, and he hated that he'd contributed to it.

"I didn't know how to tell you at the time, and now it's been so long ago, I didn't want to bring it all back out. Up until I lost Megan, that was the most awful time of my life, knowing how I'd hurt you."

He planted his hands on the countertop and leaned against it. "I honestly don't know what to say. I never imagined this. I'm sorry I blamed you all those years, assuming you weren't willing to be seen with the geek. Shows who the real jerk is."

Her eyes widened. "Not you. It wasn't your fault any more than it was mine. It was all Brett. But I let him keep me a victim for too long." She released a deep sigh. "Speaking of which, I told him today I wouldn't be back. That he needed to decide for himself if he wanted to fight for his life or not. That I couldn't do that for him."

Remorse washed through him. He'd sat on that porch, waiting for her, letting his temper rise. If he'd only let her explain before opening his mouth, he wouldn't have put her through all of this.

"I'm so sorry, Harper. This is what comes of not checking in with God before letting my tongue get ahead of me. I'm not jealous. I'm committed. And I told myself this time I wasn't walking away without a fight. I just didn't handle that very well."

"No apology needed. This week has been confusing, and I

know it didn't help that I felt like I needed to be there for him. I sat down with my folks Tuesday night to talk about getting him into treatment, if he would agree. Either way, today was going to be it. I knew it was time to make that break."

"And Brett?"

"Thinking about it. I told him this was a one-shot deal, that there wouldn't be a second chance. Not at Townsend Rehab Centers, which, in my opinion, are the best in the country."

"You're not alone in that. Your parents have built an outstanding reputation."

But at what cost? Harper had spent a good part of her life trying to win their approval. And he wasn't sure she was past that even now. If her going into psychology truly was her calling, she didn't appear all that zealous about it. Not like she was about the ministry.

Her phone chirped with an incoming text, and she pulled it out of her bag. She read it and pushed the phone across the bar to him. "Brett."

> I'm in. Thank you for talking to your folks for me. I'll take those prayers you offered. I know this fight won't be an easy one.

Wyatt slid the phone back over to her. "You okay?"

She stuck her chin in her hand. "I will be after a pizza with everything. As long as I get to eat it in front of a movie with you. I actually have no homework for a change."

He smiled and leaned across the bar to kiss her. "I'm not going anywhere."

CHAPTER TWENTY-THREE

*W*yatt stood at the kitchen sink in the house he'd been raised in, washed and rinsed a salad bowl, and handed it to Harper to dry. "This brings back memories."

She returned his grin. "It does. I think we started doing dishes here when we had to stand on stepstools to reach the sink."

He glanced over his shoulder. "Mom, why haven't you ever had a dishwasher?"

His mother set the last of the dinner dishes by the sink and smiled up at him. "I had two of them until you boys left home. Now it's something your dad and I like doing together." She gave him a pat on the shoulder. "Tell me you aren't enjoying standing here with your lady, working side by side."

"You've got a point there."

She took a rag and wiped down the counter. "I remember the two of you sitting here at the table, eating homemade ice cream after school, back when your feet dangled a good six inches from the floor."

Wyatt shot a wink at Harper. He too had many happy memories of her here with his family, from the first time her nanny dropped her off for a play date when they were five.

His mom had fallen instantly in love with the little girl with the huge green eyes and chestnut hair. Usually in a ponytail with a bow that matched her outfit. From that day on, Harper came home with him after school more often than not.

"I think I ate dinner here more than at my house, Arlene." Harper took the plate Wyatt held out to her and glanced back at his mother as Reed walked into the kitchen with three-year-old Aaron skipping along at his heels. "Your cooking was a whole lot better than Greta's. She was a great *au pair*, no question. We adored her. But she was a lousy cook."

They shared a laugh at poor Greta's expense, but it was true. The few times Wyatt had been over at Harper's for the dinner hour on a weekday, they'd usually been fed boxed mac and cheese or mushy spaghetti with jarred sauce. And most evenings, by the time his dad picked him up, her parents weren't even home from work yet. He couldn't imagine being raised by a nanny, but the Townsend kids had known nothing else.

Which, looking back, was probably why Harper wanted to spend as much time with his mom as she did with him. His mother was so different from her own, and she'd been starved for some maternal attention. Something Mom had been all too happy to give her.

"Emery started doing the cooking when she was in high school," Harper continued. "I enjoyed helping her, and that's how I discovered my love for it."

Wyatt nudged her with his shoulder. "You're good at it, that's for sure. I think I've gained five pounds just in the past three weeks."

"Not that I've noticed." Her gaze held his, and his insides did that fluttery thing it did every time she walked into a room, or their eyes met, or when he thought about her in the middle of his workday or at night lying in bed. He was falling fast and hard and couldn't do a thing about it.

"Remember backyard camping when our cousins would

come visit from Houston?" Reed's question popped him back to the conversation.

"Do I!" Harper answered. "Your dad would scare the wits out of us with his fireside ghost stories, just before we were supposed to go to sleep."

"Which is why you usually ended up with your sleeping bag right up next to mine," Wyatt said. "Scaredy cat."

"Oh, like you were so brave. What was that bear's name you always slept with? Barney?"

He laughed as he pulled the plug to let the water drain. "Bernie. He was a monkey and a great comfort."

"I'm quite sure." She stacked the last of the plates and lifted them up into the cabinet.

This was the second Sunday dinner over the past three weeks they'd spent with his family, and she fit like she'd been there forever. As if those eleven years of silence had never happened.

"Juice!" Aaron said, looking at up at his dad. "Papa, juice!"

"You want some juice, buddy?" Reed asked.

"Seemed pretty clear to me," Wyatt teased his brother. "His communication skills are on point."

Reed shot him a look, then pulled out a juice box from the fridge. "You wait, little brother. When you're a dad, I'm so going to be all up in your business."

Wyatt's laughter joined the others, but for the first time, he could actually see that day happening. Only three weeks with Harper, but he had no trouble picturing a future with her. A long one. A forever one.

Jenny walked into the kitchen with eighteen-month-old Mandy on her hip, and Jamie, their kindergartner, following behind. "I don't know how it can be possible after that amazing dinner, Mom, but these kids want ice cream."

"S'cream!" Aaron echoed, no longer interested in the juice.

Mom shared a grin with Harper. "We were just talking about ice cream. We made a batch of peach yesterday and still have some of the strawberry from last week out in the freezer."

"I'll get it, Grams!" Jamie dashed to the door to the garage.

Jenny looked at Harper. "Strawberry's his favorite."

"Mine, too, but I couldn't eat another bite." Harper looked up at Wyatt. "In fact, I really need to get to my homework. I'm sorry to cut this short."

"No problem." He looked at his watch. "It's almost three. Head to my house or yours?"

"I don't have my backpack with me, so mine, if that works for you."

"Sure thing. We'll drop by my house on the way to pick up my laptop so I can get some work done while you're studying."

After the kids were seated at the table with their ice cream, the adults made their way to the door. His dad pulled Harper in for a bear hug, then pulled Wyatt in for the same while his mother took her turn with Harper.

Dad gave him a hard squeeze. "You take care of this pretty girl, son, you hear?"

He gave his father a pat on the back before releasing him. "My plan exactly, Dad."

After he hugged his mother, he and Harper walked out hand-in-hand to his SUV. After letting her in on her side, he looked back, gave his parents a final wave and climbed into the driver's seat.

"I love these Sundays with your family," Harper said once they were on the road.

"They love having you here. Did I tell you Mom actually cried when I told her we were dating? She was beyond happy."

"No!" She looked at him, her face alight. "You didn't tell me that. I've always adored your parents. They treated me like one of their own back in the day."

"You practically were."

"Well, maybe one of these Sundays we spend with my

family, my parents will put in an appearance. They've been out of town so much, but I know they'd love to get to know you better."

"Hmm." Wyatt wasn't as sure. They'd met the elder Townsends for a late dinner at a high-end restaurant earlier in the week, but it felt more like an interview than a visit. He must have passed, because Harper would have surely heard about it by now if they'd had reservations about him.

After a quick stop at his house, they drove to Harper's, where he started a fire in the fireplace to dispel a bit of the early November chill, then joined her at the kitchen table with his laptop. It would be nice if they each didn't have so much to do, but he'd take all the alone time with her he could get, regardless of how they spent it.

"Ugh!" Her groan from the other side of the table pulled his attention from the manuscript on his screen after more than an hour of working in relative silence.

He looked at her over his computer, where she sat with her head face down on her arm. "Problem, dear?"

"Dr. Vance is going to think I'm a complete dunce," came her muffled reply before she sat up, shaking her head as she gestured to her computer. "I've been drafting this essay for a week, and it's the worst thing I've ever put to paper."

Probably an over-exaggeration, but his heart went out to her, nonetheless. This essay was a big percentage of their semester grade, so it was important for anybody considering the Brackett internship to turn in their best work. But for all of Harper's A-plus work in the class, he couldn't say he saw a strong passion for the subject-matter. As if her head had all the right answers, but her heart wasn't in it.

He stood and held his hand out across the table. "Let's take a break."

After she took his hand, he led her to the sofa in front of the fire. He pulled her close and laid his cheek on the top of her head as she snuggled into his side.

Except for the crackle of the flames, quiet surrounded them. Taking in the scent of her rosy shampoo and the warmth of her body pressed to his, he didn't know the last time he'd felt so content. If only he could help Harper find her own peace. Watching her these past few months had shown him one thing — she had a gift for ministry to students. He didn't want her to miss it while looking in another direction.

He cleared his throat. "Are you sure psychology is where you want to be?"

She stiffened under his arm. "You don't think I'm up to it? That I couldn't do it?"

"I'm not saying that at all. But I never hear you say much about it. Not like you do about your CU girls or coaching the cheer squad. I guess I'm just wondering if you're that passionate about it."

The flames flickered and crackled in the silence that lingered. "I do love working with the girls, that's for sure. It's like I found my place at ConnectUP. My purpose. And it's just spilled over into my coaching."

Several more ticks of the wall clock went by before he ventured ahead. "Maybe psychology isn't where you should be putting your energies. Maybe you're being called into ministry."

She sat up and turned to look him in the eye, leaving his arm draped along the back of the sofa. "You mean, don't get my degree?"

"Or get one in religious studies." He brought his hand to her shoulder, picked up a long lock of silky hair and ran it through his fingers. "But if God's calling you to ministry, you don't have to have a degree."

"My parents would disown me if I changed my major again, or dropped out of school ... again. Mom's already on my case about ConnectUP and coaching being hindrances to my studies. She even told me having a relationship would be a distraction."

Her face broke into a grin. "Until you won her over with your considerable charms at dinner the other night. Now she thinks having a boyfriend who's a practicing psychologist is just what I need." Her smile waned, and a crinkle appeared between her brows. "Whatever that means."

Chuckling, he gave his head a shake. "I doubt my charms, considerable or otherwise, had anything to do with it. I got the distinct impression it was more about my resume than anything else. I would have passed muster if I'd sat there like a brick."

"I don't mean any disrespect. Please don't misunderstand. I'm looking forward to spending more time with your parents. But you have to admit, their measuring stick for success is a little skewed."

A cloud of sorrow crossed her features. "You're right. Which is why I've never measured up. Coming along behind Connor, Salutatorian of his class, and Emery, Valedictorian of hers, and here I was, the cheer captain ... well, let's just say I didn't stack up. Now Connor's a lawyer, Emery's a physician, and I'm a twenty-eight-year-old divorcée college sophomore who can't seem to stay on course and keeps taking on more *distractions*."

"Harper ..." He took her hand, his heart hurting at the sadness in her eyes. Even as a kid, he could see her parents' disconnect with her. She was smart, no question, but her pursuits ran more toward the physical than the cerebral.

Without a day spent in gymnastics or competitive cheerleading, she'd taught herself how to cartwheel, do handsprings and backflips, the splits, and cheer jumps. He'd lost track of how many hours he sat in his or her backyard in fourth and fifth grade, he with a Game Boy or book in hand while she cartwheeled and flipped back and forth across the lawn.

"Thing is, those distractions bring me the most joy. Yes, of course I want to succeed in school, get my degree, and do something with my life that matters. But does that mean I can't do the rest too?"

"And how does getting your degree make your life matter more than what you're doing with these kids whose lives you're already impacting? You've led five girls to the Lord in two months. That's incredible. Don't undervalue what God can do through you, degree or no degree. It's been amazing to watch you minister to your kids."

Her eyes glistened with unshed tears as she slipped her arms around his neck and kissed him. "I love you."

She sat up and put a hand to her chest, her face flaming. "I'm sorry, Wyatt. That just—I didn't—I mean, I know you said you wanted to go slow, but that just slipped out and—"

"I love you too."

Her eyes widened. "You do? Honestly?"

He stroked a finger down her cheek. "Honestly. I've loved you forever."

"I think I've loved you forever too. It's just taken me a while to find my way. To God. Back to you. Finally."

"Finally and forever, if that's what the Lord has for us."

"I want that, too, Wyatt. But—" She chewed her lip for a second. "I'm divorced. And you're a good, godly man. Aren't you concerned—"

"Not for a second." Which was true. He hadn't given it a moment's thought or energy, but she apparently had. "Your divorce was the result of infidelity on the part of your husband. If the Lord should grow us toward marriage, I wouldn't have the slightest hesitation about that."

"I just don't want to do anything that would tarnish your reputation or make others question your relationship with God."

"Anybody who would judge me for being involved with you would need to focus more on their own relationship with God than mine. I'm very at peace with the Lord. No conviction whatsoever that I'm out of His will being with you. Okay?"

She smiled, and his heart puddled in his chest. "I only ever want to be a blessing to you."

He swept a lock of hair behind her ear. "You already are, Harper. In so many ways. But I'm serious when I say you should examine what it is you feel compelled to do. What you feel passionate about. Don't spin your wheels trying to be something you think will make someone else happy."

She nodded, but he could see the conflict in her eyes. Follow God's leading knowing her parents might once and for all give up on her? Or stay the course to earn their approval?

He took her hand and threaded their fingers together. "If you were to change direction, it wouldn't be a failure if you were to do so to follow His leading, regardless of how others might question your decision. And I'll be here to support you, whichever way you decide to go."

"That's good to know." Her smile wobbled. "Because if I change my major, to religious studies, of all things, my parents will have plenty to say about that. If they speak to me at all."

CHAPTER TWENTY-FOUR

*H*arper watched the flames dance in the fireplace, tucked in close to Wyatt on her aqua-blue couch. This was her favorite place to be, next to him, touching him, inhaling the woodsy fragrance of his aftershave. Only three weeks, and she already dreamed of a day when they wouldn't have to part at the end of the evening. Of waking in the morning with his face being the first thing she saw.

It was much too soon for such lofty ideas. But he'd told her he loved her, and with Wyatt, that wouldn't be halfway. How was she so blessed to have him in her life again? That he would open up his heart to her again?

When the cell phone she'd placed on the coffee table rang, she considered ignoring it. She wanted to stay there, pressed close to Wyatt for a little longer, before letting the world back in. With a sigh, she left the warmth of his body to pick it up and check the Caller ID, in case it was her sister or one of the girls.

She threw him a quick glance over her shoulder before accepting the call. "Hey, Mom, what's up?"

"Did Brett ever hit you?"

The abrupt question punched her in the gut with as much

force as Brett's fist had on more than one occasion, momentarily leaving her unable to speak.

"Harper Renee, I need to know. Was he abusive to you?"

She lifted herself from the couch and gulped in a breath as she walked back to the kitchen table. "Um ... Mom, this really isn't a good time."

"You're with Wyatt?"

"Yes." She sank into a chair. "And this is a conversation that should be had face to face, don't you think?"

A heavy sigh reached her from the other end of the line. "I think you've answered my question. I was just—I mean, I know I shouldn't have looked because we have a history with him, but I was curious how he was doing."

Wyatt joined her at the table, his brow creased as he stared at her.

"You're right, Mom. You shouldn't have been going through his records."

"I can go through any patient record I want since it's my clinic. And I have to say, Harper, I'm stunned by some of this. I can't believe you never told us these things."

And just when would she have done that? When they'd walk in the door at eight or nine o'clock after a long day working out other people's problems? Over the phone when they'd call from a speaking engagement at a conference or mental health symposium?

Her throat tightened. "I went over all of this with Leslie. I really don't want to rehash it."

"Leslie was that counselor Emery had you see?"

"Yes. She was amazing. Helped me a lot." Although there were some things even Leslie didn't know. Things Harper had never put to words because she wouldn't let herself go back there.

Mom released a shuddering breath, and Harper's eyes filled with tears. Was Mom emotional because of something Brett might have admitted to doing during their tumultuous relationship? That would be new. She knew her parents loved her. Loved them all. But theirs wasn't a touchy-feely, warm-and-fuzzy family dynamic. Rarely did a hug or some other form of emotional connection happen. Except between her and her siblings. The three of them never had trouble showing affection for one another, even if they weren't as comfortable doing so with their parents.

"I'm glad to hear that, at least," Mom said. "I just wish you'd told us this before we let his father talk you kids into getting married. We would have stepped in had we known."

"Really?" The question was out before she could stop it. But the statement caught her by surprise. Would they truly have helped her if she'd been able to confide?

"Of course. We would have never let you continue dating that boy, much less marry him. Please tell me he never raised a hand to Megan."

"Never." Of that, she was sure. "Brett was very good to Megan."

"Except he let you go through that whole nightmare alone."

Harper laid her forehead in her hand. "I really don't want to hash this out right now, Mom. Can you understand?"

"Yes, honey. I understand. I didn't mean to upset you. I was just going through his counselor's notes on my laptop and couldn't believe what I was reading."

No surprise to know Mom was working on a Sunday. No doubt Dad was also holed up in his study, going through charts or preparing his next keynote address. "I'm honestly shocked he admitted to any of it."

"Yes, he seems to be coming along well in his program so far. Working through the Twelve Steps. Only two weeks and he's already at Step Four—soul searching. Guess he's finally seeing his behavior for what it was."

"I'm glad for him. I truly am. But I've already worked through all of it. I really don't want to bring it all out again. Just suffice it to say, I'm fine. Did I go through some stuff with

Brett? Yes. I did." Major understatement. "But God has healed me from the inside out, and my life is better than it's ever been. I'm at peace. I'm finding my way and my purpose. I'm with a good man. I don't need to go back there, so please don't ask me to."

The silence stretched so long, Harper pulled the phone from her ear to see if the call had dropped.

She put it back to her ear. "Mom?"

"I'm here," came her quivering voice. "I'm just so ... I don't know ..."

"Angry?"

More silence. Then, "No. Sorry. Harper, honey, I'm so very sorry. That we didn't know. That you didn't think you could tell us. That we missed all the signs. I can see it in a patient two minutes into a session, and I didn't see it in you under my own roof. I don't know that I'll ever be able to forgive myself."

The lump in Harper's throat grew, making it difficult to find her voice. She never expected this from her mother. Never. It touched her to her soul, bringing out that little girl who so wanted to curl up into her mom like she'd seen Wyatt do with his when they were small.

"Mom, it's okay. I'm okay. And if Brett needs to bring all of that out in order to heal, more power to him. But it's not about me anymore."

"You know he may ask you to come in so he can make amends."

Her stomach pitched. "I know. I'll deal with that if or when the time comes."

Because right now, the last thing she wanted to do was sit across from Brett and have him confess all the ways he'd done her wrong. That list was much too long. And some of it ...

She gave her head a shake. No, he wouldn't want to go back there any more than she did. It was too ugly. Too raw. Nothing good could possibly come from revisiting it. Remembering all that pain, all that ... shame.

"I hope you know I'm proud of you, Harper, honey." Her mother's voice brought her back to the present before she could venture too far into the darkness. "For going back to school, setting out to get your degree. Sounds like you've experienced some things that will make you a top-notch counselor."

Harper's eyes widened as she met Wyatt's gaze across from her.

"And we'll be happy to offer you an internship or anything else you need. Even a job when you get your degree, if you'd like to work for us. It would be wonderful to have you as part of Townsend Treatment Centers."

The furrow in Wyatt's brow deepened as she stared at him. Ten minutes before, they'd discussed her changing course in her education. About whose approval she should seek. She at last had what she'd sought her entire life—her mother's encouragement, her support. Her approval.

How could she let her down now?

CHAPTER TWENTY-FIVE

$\mathcal{W}$yatt's front door opened and closed, but it was a few seconds before Mason appeared at the end of the entry hall as he walked into the family room, his eyes wide. "Am I in the right house?"

Wyatt smiled from where he sat at his new oak plank kitchen table, updating client notes on his laptop. "Hey, Mase. Welcome back."

"This place looks completely transformed."

"It was all delivered yesterday, and we spent the evening putting everything together with some of the kids. Looks pretty good, doesn't it?"

"It looks amazing." Mason dropped his bag next to the island. "I go away for a weekend and come back to a whole new house. That living room is stunning, but this ..." He drew his arm out toward the family room. "This is fantastic."

Wyatt looked over the newly furnished room, with its rich, leather sectional and rustic coffee table. Texas-themed artwork adorned the walls, complete with a Texas flag made from wood planks, and photos Harper and her girls had put in frames. The house looked, and felt, more like a home than it ever had.

He and Harper had finished up the last of the furniture

shopping the weekend before, and his new dining room table and chairs should arrive on Tuesday, just in time for Thanksgiving. He had to admit, he would kind of miss those furniture-hunting excursions with Harper. She made everything a grand adventure.

And praying with her was a joy. Her *Hi, God, it's me* intros made him grin every time, but he wouldn't change a thing about the way she prayed. Like her faith, it was so real, so authentic. She never tried to mimic what she heard from the pulpit or from others who'd been longer in the faith. She went to the Lord as pure Harper, self-described newbie Christian, soaking up everything she could, as fast as she could, about this God she'd fallen for head over heels.

Over the years, when praying for the unknown woman who would someday share his life and his name, he'd asked that she love God more than she did him. And Harper was desperately in love with God. There was no doubt her heart's priorities were aligned right, and Wyatt had no problem coming in second.

He looked back at Mason with a grin. "You told me to get a girlfriend to help me spruce up the place. Just following your advice, my friend."

"She's done a phenomenal job." Mason looked around. "Where is this girlfriend of yours?"

"In bed." His eyes widened. "Wait. That didn't sound right. We came back here after church, and she kept nodding off on her homework. I told her to go take a nap in my bed, and she's been out cold for over an hour."

"No worries, bro. I know you too well to assume anything else. But let me tell you, I can't wait to get through the next—" he looked at his watch "—four weeks, six days, and two hours until I'm a married man."

"I can imagine." He was a red-blooded, young, healthy male, after all, exactly the way God made him. Loving Harper the way he did, his body reacted to hers in all the ways it was designed to do. But both of them being committed to wait for marriage, they were careful to treat each other with integrity and respect so they wouldn't be tempted to go somewhere they shouldn't.

"Hey, Wyatt?" came Harper's voice from the hall to the master suite.

He looked over his shoulder as she walked into the kitchen, her head bowed over her phone and thumbs racing over its face. "Yeah?"

"Can I borrow your SUV?" She looked up, her eyes widening when she saw he wasn't alone. "Mason! Hi!"

"Hi, yourself."

Wyatt grinned at the pink flush infusing her cheeks. "Relax, sweetheart. He's cool."

Relief flooded her face. "Can I borrow your car, please? I have a kid in tears."

Concern erased his smile. "One of your CU girls?"

She shook her head. "One of my cheerleaders."

He stood and walked over to the door leading to the garage, removing his fob from the hook beside it. "Which one?"

"Jill."

He splayed his hands at his waist. "Harper, if it's the boyfriend, I'm coming with you. You are not getting in the middle of those two again when he outweighs you by a hundred pounds."

"It's not Dwight. Her parents are going through an ugly split, and her dad showed up at the house. She just needs to get away from all the drama, and her dad's car is blocking hers in."

"Okay, but call if you need me." He looked at Mason. "You'll be here for a bit, right? If I need your car?"

Mason nodded. "Absolutely."

She grabbed her purse and denim jacket, pulling it on over the long-sleeved white shirt she wore with a pair of jeans and knee-high black boots before she walked over and wrapped her arms around him. "I love you."

"Love you back." He kissed her and let her go.

Once she left through the garage door, he turned to his friend. "I'm worried about her, Mase. She's doing so much, I honestly don't know how she's still on her feet. The kids don't seem to understand she works full-time and carries a full load at school. She would never tell one of her girls she didn't have time for them, whether they're from CU or the cheer squad. Add all the other stuff on top of it, and she's doing the work of three people. No way she can keep this up indefinitely."

Mason leaned against the island. "You two seem pretty serious. Rhonda and I didn't use the *L* word until we'd been together a few months."

Moving his head back and forth, Wyatt mirrored his friend's stance, leaning against the island, his arms crossed over the front of his navy Dallas Cowboys sweatshirt. "I guess things are going faster than we intended at the beginning, but I don't know how to slow it down. Not even sure I want to. I like where we're heading."

"And where's that?"

"Honestly? I hope where you are." He shook his head. "I don't know, Mase. I feel like she's it for me. Ally and I dated for two years, and I never felt what I already feel for Harper. What I think I've always felt for her, even though we spent a lot of years apart."

His phone beeped from where it sat on the table and he walked over to pick it up.

Have Jill. Going for coffee. Love you.

"Man, that Jill," he said as he texted a quick response. "She's going through a lot."

"What's the deal with the boyfriend? And Harper getting between them?"

He released a heavy sigh. "Harper's pretty sure Jill's in an abusive relationship with her wide receiver boyfriend but hasn't been able to get her to open up. The first day she met this girl, she intervened when the boy got a bit rough."

The corners of Mason's mouth tipped downward. "Wow, what these kids go through. Even kids everybody else looks up to are dealing with things they shouldn't have to at such a young age, if ever."

"Yeah." Mason's words took Wyatt's thoughts back to a troubled and searching Harper.

What would have happened if God had brought somebody into her life like He'd brought Harper into Jill's? Would she have escaped a lot of the pain she'd endured?

She'd told him once if she could help any of her girls because of all she'd been through, then it would have all been worth it.

But where was the line? She pushed herself so hard to meet the needs of everybody else, as if on a mission to make up for her own history, her own choices. But how much did she have to give before her body gave out? He could only pray she would find that balance soon.

Before she had nothing left.

CHAPTER TWENTY-SIX

"*Y*ou can take me back now." A still tearful Jill sat across the small coffee shop table from Harper. "Daddy's probably gone. That's what he does these days. Storms in, does his damage, then leaves Mom a wreck for me to deal with."

Harper's heart grew another crack. The story Jill had shared was one of a family splintered due to neglect, then finally shattered by infidelity, with this precious girl left churning in the wake of its devastation.

Her own may not have been the most attentive parents, but she'd never worried they would split up. Still devoted to each other, and their work, after thirty-seven years of marriage, she was confident they would be together until death should part them.

"I'm in no hurry," Harper assured her, although she'd be up half the night finishing her homework after taking that impromptu nap and now the last hour spent with Jill. But there was no way she was going to rush the girl back to a place of chaos. "Unless you think your mom will worry about you."

Jill's mouth twisted before she looked down. "I doubt she's given me a thought."

A heaviness filled Harper's chest. How she wished she could take away Jill's pain. "Oh, honey, I'm sure that's not true. She just has a lot going on right now. Divorce is never easy, and it sounds like there's a lot of stuff they're having to work through."

"Yeah, but that's just it. It's all *stuff*, nothing important. Who gets the beach house, who gets the horses? I can't wait to graduate next year and get out of there, wherever *there* ends up being, if we have to sell the house so each of them can get their half."

Harper nodded. At least her divorce had been pretty cut and dried. It wasn't as if she and Brett had accumulated that much in their brief union, and all their discretionary income had gone to medical bills.

But here Jill was stuck in the middle of her well-to-do physician parents, feuding over *stuff* that didn't matter. All of that wealth, the accumulation of years of material possessions, when the one thing that should mean the most, this daughter they were blessed to still have with them, felt as if she wasn't even spared a thought.

Is that why Jill felt she couldn't live without Dwight? Because he at least showed an interest? Made her somehow feel she was important?

"We're not even doing Thanksgiving this year."

"What?" Harper stared at her with eyes widened. "Not at all?"

Jill shook her head. "Mom took the holiday shift to work labor and delivery at the hospital, and Dad's spending it with his girlfriend and her kids. He invited me, but no way am I spending the day with them."

"Then plan to spend the day with us. We'll be eating twice, which means we'll have to work extra hard at practice Saturday morning to burn it all off."

Jill's face lifted. "Really? I can spend the day with you?"

"Absolutely! We'd love to have you. Why don't I pick you

up around eleven Thursday morning, and you can help us cook? We're going to my sister's, then Wyatt's family is coming to his house. He said they always eat later because his parents work the line at a mission their church sponsors earlier in the day. Fingers crossed his dining room furniture gets there when it's supposed to, or we'll all be eating off our laps."

Jill giggled, the first smile Harper had seen on her pretty face since she picked her up from the house that was more estate than home, it was so grand. "I'd really like that, Harper. Thanks. But I can drive over. Just let me know where."

"I'll text you my sister's address. But would you like to come over now, to Wyatt's? I have homework, so if you'd like to bring yours, we could have an unofficial study hall."

"My homework's all done, but we're supposed to hang the playoff banners this week, and I need to finish the drawing, which always takes time. Mustangs are hard."

"I remember that well. I never could draw those horses." A thought struck, and she cocked her head to the side. "Do you know Tonya Atwater at school? She's a junior like you."

Jill's brow puckered in thought. "Tonya Atwater. Yeah, I think we might have been in art together our freshman year."

"She's a fantastic artist. Maybe we could get her to help. I'm sure she'd love it."

Jill shrugged. "Sure. I'll take all the help I can get."

"Let me see what she's up to right now." Harper pulled out her phone and sent a quick text to Tonya, grinned when she got a response, and sent a quick one back.

"She said she's free and bored. So why don't we go by your house, pick up all the stuff, then go get Tonya and take everything back to Wyatt's? You can spread out in the garage."

"Perfect!"

Jill was in much better spirits by the time they picked up the half-completed banners from her house and drove to Tonya's in a much more modest townhome complex. Tonya ran out the front door with a bright smile, shrugging into her jacket before she turned to wave at her mom standing at the front door.

Harper lowered her window. "Hi, Marta!" she called to Tonya's mother. "Thanks for letting us borrow her for a while!"

"No problem!" she answered. "Have fun!"

Tonya climbed into the backseat. "Hi, Harper!"

"Hey, Tonya. This is Jill Denison. Jill, Tonya Atwater."

"Hi, Jill. I've seen you cheer. I don't think I could ever let anybody throw me around like that. Aren't you ever afraid they'll drop you?"

Jill laughed and turned in her seat to see the girl in the back. "Not really, but then I'm used to it. I've been in cheer since I was about six."

"Like me and soccer. Only I quit playing when I got into high school. Knee injury."

"That's a bummer."

Harper listened to the girls talk to each other with an ease that surprised even her. Hope, like the first flicker of a candle, gave breath to the idea this could be the start of something more. Something bigger than they'd ever imagined.

Life and all its cruelties made no distinction between groups, color, socioeconomic level, or educational boundaries. It came for everyone in individual ways. Like Jill staying with an abusive boyfriend in her desperation to be loved, to belong to someone, because she felt overlooked at home. Like Tonya and other CU kids who had been snubbed, belittled, or even victimized for circumstances outside their control.

Like Glen, who so wanted to belong, to feel important, he believed the lies of a pretty girl over the truth his best friend tried to instill. And paid dearly for his choice.

These kids needed to see that. Needed to know they were all on equal ground. Perhaps ConnectUP could be the bridge between groups that appeared to have little to nothing in common. If they expanded the scope of the ministry, they could reach even more teens at risk of making life-altering choices in their quest for acceptance. Kids exactly like she had been.

Would Wyatt be open to that idea? He had an affinity for fringe kids because he empathized with them from his own experience. But she understood the other side, how kids who looked like they had it all together on the outside could be a complete mess on the inside. Maybe they could work together to erase those labels. Fringe kids, top-tier kids, popular, outcast.

And save even more lives.

CHAPTER TWENTY-SEVEN

*H*arper parked in the driveway and raised the garage door so she and the girls could spread out the banners on the concrete floor. When Wyatt stepped out into the garage, her heart danced like it did every time she set eyes on him. Even in the baggy sweatshirt and loose-fitting jeans he wore with tennis shoes, he couldn't be more handsome in her eyes.

His gaze beneath a furrowed brow moved from the girls unrolling an eight-foot-long banner back to Harper. "Hey, there. What's going on?"

"The girls are going to work on the spirit banners to be put up at school this week for the start of playoffs."

"Hi, Wyatt!" Tonya said as she took a seat on the garage floor across from Jill.

"Hey, Tonya. Good to see you." His gaze moved to the other girl. "And you must be Jill."

Jill shot him a grin. "Put that together pretty quick, didn'cha?"

"That's why they gave me a doctorate," he teased back. "Cuz I'm smart that way."

She giggled, then turned her attention back to Tonya, who

sat with a pencil at the ready. "Okay, so we want a Mustang head coming out of the *O* in *GO*, and then we'll work on the herd running off the end. Sound good?"

"Sounds awesome!" Tonya answered. "I love that idea!"

"Hey, girls," Harper said. "I'm going to close the garage door so it doesn't get so cold in here. I have a ton of homework, but I'll be right inside if you need anything. Oh, and there's water and sodas in the fridge inside. Just help yourselves."

"And we're ordering up some dinner." Wyatt looked from the teenagers back to Harper. "Mason went to get Rhonda, and they're coming back here."

"Sounds great."

Harper followed when he turned and walked back into the utility room.

Once in the kitchen, he faced her, that furrow returning to his forehead. "What's going on?"

"With what?"

"Jill. And Tonya? How'd that come about?"

"Oh. Well, Jill was a little overwhelmed with all this work she still needed to do on the banners, and I instantly thought that she and Tonya might be able to work on it together."

"And you think this is a good idea?"

Sensing a change in the vibe of the conversation, her grin slowly disappeared as apprehension crawled along her spine. "Why wouldn't it be?"

"I just don't think you've thought this through. What happens when Jill's back with her posse tomorrow and meets up with Tonya in the hall at school and completely snubs her?"

Startled, she could only stare back at him, her eyes wide, and a deep chill locking her in place, like it had whenever she'd been in trouble as a kid.

"You've done a good job keeping your work with CU and your cheer girls separate, so I'm a little shocked."

"Why would I have to keep them separate?" Her question

somehow squeezed through the tightness in her throat. Was he mad at her? Had she missed something? Misjudged the situation?

He shook his head. "I just feel like you're setting Tonya up for a fall, and it doesn't seem fair. She trusts you implicitly."

Her face blanched as if he'd thrown cold water on her. "Set her up? I adore Tonya! I'd never do anything I thought would hurt her."

With a shrug, he turned back to the table where his laptop still sat. "I guess we'll see." After taking his seat, he looked back up at her. "We've worked really hard to make ConnectUP a safe place for those who fight off the biases and judgments of kids like Jill every single day they're at school. And we've helped them discover who they are without buying into the superficiality of popularity."

"*Kids like Jill?*" Heat slowly replaced the chill in her chest. "Isn't that being judgmental, assuming you know everything about Jill because she's a ... what? A *top-tier* kid? To be honest, I've never liked that term, as if our CU kids are *beneath* the top-tier kids, and we need to help them be okay with that."

"That's not what we do. We don't consider them beneath anybody, and we don't teach them to be *okay* with unfair labels. My hope is that they understand they don't have to meet the standards elitist kids have set in order to feel valuable."

"Elitist kids. Like my cheer girls. Girls you don't even know."

He waved his hand in the air and turned his attention to his laptop. "I didn't mean to get into this. I'm worried about Tonya, and what'll happen when her new *friend* acts like she never met her next time they pass each other at school. Or whenever Jill doesn't need Tonya's help any longer."

She studied him for a moment. So that was it. When he saw Jill, he saw Sarah. A so-called *top-tier* kid who would only associate with a fringe kid for whatever they could get out of it, then toss them aside. Just like Sarah had done to Glen.

Her indignation faded away. This man she loved still carried so much pain and guilt because he hadn't been able to save his best friend, so he put all his energies into saving other kids. But was that same guilt blinding him to the wounds of teens who might otherwise be judged as having it all together?

She swallowed hard. "Wyatt, Jill isn't Sarah Holmes. She's nothing like Sarah."

He looked back at her, his scowl deepening. "I didn't say she was."

"No, but you're measuring her against Sarah, assuming she'll use Tonya for what she needs, then dump her. I'd be stunned if that happened." Her stomach roiled. How could he possibly think she would ever put one of her CU girls in a position where they could get hurt? Especially when, between the two girls, Jill was by far the most in need of some direction.

"Like I said. Guess we'll see. I just hope this doesn't come back to bite you."

Funny. Felt like it just did.

The spark of hope she experienced earlier died away in the face of Wyatt's obvious doubt. How could he find no good in a situation where that's all she saw?

She walked around the island and picked up her World History textbook before turning back to him. "Oh … uh, I guess I should tell you I invited Jill to spend Thanksgiving with us. She didn't have anywhere else to go, and I can't stand the thought of her spending the holiday alone. I hope that's not a problem."

He looked up at her. "Of course she can spend the day with us. And I'm sorry if I offended you. I'm very protective of our kids and don't want to see any of them hurt because of something we, as their leaders, do. That's all I was trying to say."

When the front door opened before she could reply, she picked up her laptop and walked over to the new sectional.

"Hey, you two," said Mason as he and Rhonda came into the family room.

"Hi," Harper responded, unable to match the note of cheerfulness in his voice.

"Hey," Wyatt answered, his tone as flat as hers.

Harper looked over her shoulder at the man typing client notes into his laptop. Her eyes filled with tears, and her throat burned. She hadn't felt this distant from him since before their discussion about Glen in this very room, and it had nothing to do with the several feet between them.

Rhonda let go of Mason's hand and walked over to sit on the couch, facing Harper while Mason took a seat at the table with Wyatt. "Everything okay?" she asked quietly.

Harper shook her head. "I messed up," she whispered.

Turning to stare into the fire in the fireplace, her thoughts ran amok. Had she overstepped by bringing Jill and Tonya together? Had she inadvertently set Tonya up for a fall? Her heart clutched at the thought.

"I really need to get this done," she said to Rhonda as she gathered up her book, laptop, and backpack. She was about to lose it and didn't want to do it with an audience. "Oh, if you want to say hi, Tonya's in the garage working on spirit banners with Jill."

Rhonda stood when Harper did, her face lit with her smile. "Really? That's cool!"

Surprised, Harper looked from her to Wyatt talking to Mason at the table about ConnectUP's upcoming Thanksgiving dinner deliveries and back to her friend. "You think so?"

"Yes! What could be wrong with that?"

"I—I'm not sure." Shooting another glance at Wyatt, she turned and started toward the front of the house.

In the study, she set her book and laptop down on his now organized desk, then sat and buried her face in her hands. "Hi Lord, it's me. I know I've been asking for guidance a lot lately, but please don't let me have hurt Tonya, however innocently. I hope I didn't get ahead of You here. Please forgive me if I did."

Harper dropped her hands and looked across the room at the cross mounted on the wall, a reminder of the sacrifice Christ had made for all of humanity. Who were they to place boundaries on who heard the message and who didn't?

She would never question Wyatt's heart or his motives. They were pure and loving and thoughtful, like the man himself. But could she help him see how much further their ministry could go? Or would she push him away if he felt unsupported by the one person he should be able to count on above all others?

"Father," she whispered. "Please help me know how to reach these kids with Your love and not lose Wyatt in the process."

CHAPTER TWENTY-EIGHT

*W*yatt watched Harper leave the room, then rested his elbow on the table and put his forehead in it, plunging his fingers into his hair.

"Anything you wanna talk about?" Mason asked. "Other than the Thanksgiving food drive, that is."

He shrugged, staring at but not really seeing the words on his screen. "I don't know. First major disagreement, I guess you could say."

And maybe he could have measured his words with more grace, but what had she been thinking? Was she more concerned with her cheer girls than she was her ConnectUP girls? Maybe because she related to them better, having been a top-tier kid herself? She probably hated that term because it hit too close to home.

He looked over at Mason and sat up in the chair with a heavy sigh. "Harper got it into her head that somehow putting Jill and Tonya together was a great idea. They're out there working on cheer banners, of all things."

Mason's brow puckered. "So, you're concerned about ..." He gave his head a shake. "I'm sorry. What are you worried about?"

Really? Was he the only one who could see the train wreck coming? "Tonya? And Jill? Yeah, today they're getting along great, and Tonya's probably thinking she made a new friend, while Jill's just happy to have the help and tomorrow won't even acknowledge Tonya. That's exactly what we try to protect our kids from, and Harper stuck them together without even thinking."

"Oh. This Jill's not a nice girl?"

Wyatt shrugged. "I don't know her."

"Hmm. I see." Mason studied him for a moment. "I guess you said as much to Harper? That this was a bad idea?"

"Well ... yeah. I think all this time spent with her cheerleaders has her more concerned with their needs than her CU girls. She may have to choose at some point which side she's going to come down on."

"And if she chooses her cheer girls, how will that affect your relationship?"

Wyatt had to think about that. He cherished working side by side in the ministry with Harper, but if she decided in the long run to go another direction ...

His gut clenched. "I don't know. She has to do what she believes is best for her, and I have to do what I feel is best for ConnectUP."

"Yeah, bro, I totally see your point. But consider for a second that Harper has always acted from the heart. Dare I say a *mother's* heart. Maybe you can cut her a little slack?"

Rhonda walked back in from the garage. "Those banners. Two very talented young ladies."

Wyatt and Mason exchanged a glance as she joined them at the table. Her smile faded as she looked back and forth between them. "Am I interrupting?"

"No, honey. It's fine. Wyatt's just concerned about Tonya."

Her eyes widened. "What's wrong with Tonya?"

"Just that this thing with Jill could backfire."

"Oh. Well, obviously there's no way to tell how these things will go, especially with girls whose moods can change with the wind. But I think we should give Harper the benefit of the doubt."

"Wait, really?" came Jill's voice as the girls walked into the kitchen. "It's just you and your mom?"

"And my sister, yeah." Tonya opened the fridge to pull out two bottles of water. "My dad left about three years ago. Mom was a mess at first, but she's doing great now. I bet your mom will be okay too. Just stick with her so she knows you have her back, and you might even find you'll be closer than ever."

"Yeah." Jill took the bottle Tonya offered her and opened it before taking a long drink, her eyes coming to rest on the adults sitting at the table.

Tonya turned and looked their direction. "Oh, hey. Sorry. Hope we're not intruding. We were just thirsty."

"No problem," Wyatt replied. "How's the progress?"

"Great!" Jill answered. "I was going to be up all night working on these, so this is awesome, having Tonya to help."

Wyatt nodded, his stomach in knots. That's exactly what he'd been afraid of. Jill needed Tonya's help. Today. But what about tomorrow, when Tonya had outlived her usefulness?

Rhonda stood. "Hey, girls, we're going to order up some dinner from Wong's China Bowl. What would you like?"

Wyatt got up when Rhonda walked over to get the girls' orders. "I'll go see what Harper wants for dinner."

He stopped at the open French doors to the study and watched her for a moment, sitting at the desk, periodically checking her textbook before typing in her next answer. Love and guilt fought for equal space in his chest. She worked so hard, and he'd only added to her burden.

As if sensing his presence, she lifted her head and looked at him. "Hi."

"Hey. Rhonda's putting in our dinner order."

"Oh. Um ... I'm not really hungry."

He walked over and knelt beside her. "I'm sorry that I hurt

your feelings. That wasn't my intent. This is just a line we've never crossed before, and I'm not sure what to expect."

She nodded and the uncertainty in her eyes brought an ache to his heart that he'd caused it. "If Tonya is hurt in any way, I'll never forgive myself. I'm not any more committed to my cheer girls than I am to ConnectUP. I don't have favorites." Her eyes flooded. "Except you. You're my favorite. And I'm so sorry if you believe I undermined you or did anything to hurt the ministry."

"Come here." He stood and pulled her up into his arms. "I apologize that I made you feel that way." He pulled back and looked down at her. "And you're my favorite too." They shared a gentle kiss before he let her go. "We're having Wong's, and I know you've never been able to pass up their sweet and sour chicken."

Her smile lit up her face. "Okay, you talked me into it."

That was easy. If only he had a simple answer for the questions he knew she had. Questions he'd never before pondered.

Questions that could pull them apart.

CHAPTER TWENTY-NINE

*H*arper closed her eyes, took a deep breath through her nose, held it for a count of five, then released it through pursed lips.

Leslie had taught her the centering technique during counseling, to employ whenever she became overwhelmed or when her thoughts meandered back through darker times. It occurred to her now she hadn't used it much in the past few months, only when it pertained to her parents or Brett. All of whom surrounded her in this place.

She opened her eyes and looked around. She could be with Wyatt right now, putting up his Christmas tree and stringing lights on the house. Instead, here she sat in the waiting room of a Townsend drug treatment facility while an instrumental version of "Silver Bells" wafted from speakers in the ceiling. Gave a whole new meaning to *Black Friday*.

To take her mind off wondering what awaited her this afternoon, Wyatt had taken her tree shopping that morning, returning with two strapped to the top of the SUV. Tonight, they planned to decorate his massive eight-footer with Mason and Rhonda, and tomorrow they would put up her more modest six-foot fir after cheer practice. Hopefully, after this meeting she'd been dreading, she'd be free to enjoy the rest of her holiday weekend without the anxiety that had hung over her the past couple of days.

The door from the hall opened, and a tall, lanky man walked into the room. "Ms. Townsend?"

She stood and shook the hand he offered. "Please, call me Harper."

"Harper. I'm Mark, Brett's counselor." He stuck his hands on his hips. "Clearly, I know you're David and Camille's daughter. Do I need to do any kind of prep for you? Do you have any questions before we meet with Brett?"

"No. I can't think of any."

"Okay, then. Follow me."

He punched a code into a keypad on the door and held it open for her to pass through ahead of him. The *click-clack* of the boots she wore with her mid-calf-length skirt and loose sweater was the only sound in the wood-floored hall lined with art and photographs. Her parents had worked hard to make their centers comfortable and homey, not sterile and depressing. A place for healing and hope.

Mark stopped at another door with a keypad, and when she entered the small conference room, Brett turned from where he stood at the window overlooking the grounds outside. He'd lost weight in the month since she last saw him, but his color was good and eyes clear.

"Harper." He smiled and started toward her. "It's good to see you. Thank you for coming."

She clutched the strap of her purse with both hands when she realized she was shaking. "Of course."

They stood in awkward silence until Mark gestured to three chairs placed in a circle.

Once seated, Mark spoke first. "As you're aware, Brett's completed his first month of in-patient therapy —"

"Thirty-four days, to be exact," Brett said.

"But who's counting, right?" Mark chuckled and looked back at Harper. "Anyway, we offer various types of programs, depending on the patient, and Brett chose the Twelve Step program."

"Not that I was a big believer in God. But I was so far gone, I decided if I was going to succeed here, I would need all the help I could get."

She nodded. "I see."

"I'm not sure you do." Brett looked down at his hands clasped between his legs before looking back up at her with tears in his eyes. "You literally saved my life, Harper. The ER doctor told me if you hadn't called 9-1-1 when you did, I more than likely wouldn't have made it. The alcohol and Oxy had nearly shut down my breathing."

"What were you planning to do with the gun?"

He put his hands palms up out in front of him and dropped them again. "Honestly, I don't know. I was in so much pain, I just wanted it to stop. When we lost Megan, I shut myself off. From you. From acknowledging how I'd abandoned my little girl when she needed me most."

He looked at the floor in front of her for a long moment before meeting her eyes again. "Watching you that morning … holding her … rocking her and singing to her as she slipped away. You were a stranger to me then. A grownup, responsible-beyond-her-years woman, ushering her child from this life into the next with such grace."

Harper swiped at the tears that started down her face. That day had been the worst of her life. Holding her precious daughter, Megan's breaths coming farther and farther apart until …

She still remembered the utter stillness. The deafening quiet. Knowing the life that was her daughter had left. Sitting in that chair, holding Megan's small form tight against her as the tears spilled unheeded, she felt as if her own life had drained from her, leaving her empty, spent. Numb, yet in the most intense pain she'd ever known.

Mark rose and moved to the other side of the room, leaving them as alone as the rules would allow.

Brett took a deep breath and let it out. "But instead of stepping up to be the man you needed after she was gone, I did everything I could to push you out of my life. You see, I needed to be free. Free to live the life I'd been robbed of. Or that's what I told myself, anyway. Looking back now, I can see it was because I was ashamed of who I was, that I couldn't be all you needed me to be. Which drove me deeper into work, into alcohol, and dead-end relationships.

"Then the reunion committee called, wanted to honor Megan, and I dug her picture out. Seeing her on that screen, then talking to you after ... everything came rushing back, and I couldn't escape it. Even two days of drinking couldn't make it go away."

"I'm so sorry, Brett." Her voice barely pushed through the emotion blocking her throat.

His brow furrowed. "No, Harper, *I'm* sorry. Sorry for all I put you through. When I think back to the things I did—" His voice caught, and he looked over at Mark. "This is when I really want a drink, you know?"

Mark nodded. "I know. But you'd have to face it at some point, right? And maybe she needs to hear it as much as you need to say it."

Her heart beat faster with that sense of doom one must get when they see the car coming at them but have no way to escape.

Brett bowed his head and closed his eyes, as if he were ... praying? Or maybe just preparing himself. But for what? What was it she needed to hear?

Several silent seconds passed before he looked up at her, the bleakness in his eyes causing her pulse to skitter. "Harper, I was nuts about you in high school. But I was also arrogant and self-centered. Wanted what I wanted, and I wanted you. I know I hurt you. I know I—I took something—stole something ... that didn't belong to me. That I had no right to."

No, no, no!

She doubled over against the pain in her belly and covered her face with her hands as sobs tore from the deepest part of her. She wasn't ready. Didn't want to go back there.

But it was too late. Memories of that night enveloped her, a roar in her ears, a searing fire in her gut. The fear, the pain, the humiliation. The betrayal of trust. The guilt for letting it happen. The shame that had kept her tethered to him, convincing herself it wasn't what it was. That they'd simply gone too far, and it was just guilt she would eventually get over.

But she couldn't lie to herself any longer, not with Brett facing her, confessing his part in it. Defining it for what it was.

"Harper, I'm so sorry." His desperate whisper feathered across her ear, and she realized he was kneeling in front of her with his hands on her shoulders. "I'm so, so sorry. Please forgive me. Not for me, but for your own healing."

She brought her head up and looked him in the face. His eyes overflowed with tears as they stared at each other. Mark set a box of tissues at her feet without a word and returned to the other side of the room. Brett pulled out several and handed them to her.

"Thank you." Her lips formed the words, but little sound came out. She dabbed at her face with the tissues, and Brett moved back to his chair, giving her space to collect herself.

He swiped at his eyes. "I don't deserve for you to give me another second of your life. I hope you know how much it means that you'd even come here today."

She nodded and blew her nose. "I wanted to come. Maybe I needed to come." Her gaze rested on him for a long moment. "I—I thought it was my fault, what happened that night."

His dark eyes widened. "How could it be your fault? Harper, don't do that to yourself. That shame isn't yours. It's mine."

She looked down at the tissue torn to pieces in her hands. In her counseling sessions with Leslie, she'd talked about the physical abuse, the verbal barbs, and the psychological games she'd endured with Brett. But she'd said nothing about that night. Hadn't wanted to take it out and look at it because the shame and humiliation were all-consuming.

Her gaze drifted back to the man across from her. His courage in facing the truth, in accepting full responsibility for the act that could never be undone, had somehow freed her. Like a thorn stuck deep into flesh, the pain increased as it slipped from the skin, leaving nothing but a tender spot where it had been.

Only God could bring such healing.

She cleared her throat. "I do forgive you. I hope that will help you forgive yourself."

"I'm trying. You being here is a big step toward that."

She nodded, pulled another tissue from the box, and blew her nose again. "Why did you call me? The night this all started?"

He gave his head a shake. "I'm not sure. The night of the homecoming game, I saw you out there, cheering and looking so much like you did in high school. Back when I last felt valued and confident. All because I could throw a football with a decent amount of accuracy."

"It was more than that. You were a star."

"Until I blew out my shoulder two days before my first college start. That's when my life tanked. I had no idea who I was without football.

"That night at Homecoming, I saw the girl I fell for all those years ago, and something inside me wanted to recapture that feeling. Then at dinner the next night, you walked in with McCowan."

Tingling raced up her spine, remembering that magical night, out on the dock with Wyatt, tearing down the wall between them to walk into something new. "It took us a while to get to that point. For him to trust me again."

"Which is my fault too." He sighed. "Harper, if we were to go back through every way I hurt you in the years we were together, we'd be here all day. You deserved so much better than you got from me, and I want nothing more than for you to live your life happy and free of anything you might be walking around with that I caused."

She watched him for a long moment, this man whose name she used to wear. The father of her child. A man who'd been so lost only a month ago, now grabbing hold of his life with both hands and doing the hard work. "I want you to be happy too. You have so much ahead of you if you can embrace who you are."

"You're right. And I think I'm finally seeing that. When we talked at the dinner and then the times you visited me in the hospital, I could see how you'd changed. That you had a peace and a confidence you hadn't had before. The Bible you gave me got packed in with my things when they sent me here, and one day I just started reading. Hannah comes to visit twice a week, and we've been going through it together. I gave my life to Christ last weekend and knew I needed to make things right with you. As much as I could, anyway."

Her heart swelled in her chest. She'd prayed for him every day since she'd given him that Bible, that he'd find his way to the truths within its pages. Even with the damage he'd left in his wake, she had loved him once. Or thought she had. When she was a lost girl seeking someone to belong to.

"Five minutes," Mark said. "Sorry, but we have group at 3:30."

"No problem." Brett looked from Mark back to Harper. "Do you have anything you want to talk about? We can schedule another time, if you need it."

She shook her head. "I think I'm okay."

He stood and offered his hand. She took it and stood to face him before he drew her in for a hug. "Thank you, Harper. For Megan. And helping me find my way to God. You'll always have a place in my heart."

CHAPTER THIRTY

"That should do it." Wyatt clipped the last string of lights to the roof and descended the ladder.

"I like it," Mason said from behind him.

Wyatt turned to his friend standing at the curb, looking back at the house they'd been decorating the past hour. "How can you tell? You won't be able to see anything until it's dark."

"Not the lights." Mason spread his arms in front of him. "What do you think?"

Wyatt looked at the family of white reindeer Mason had erected around the front yard. They, too, would light up when plugged in tonight. "Oh. Yeah. They look great."

Mason walked over the grass to join him. "What next?"

"I think we're done." Wyatt collapsed the ladder and picked it up. "I'm going to try to get a little time in on the proposal until Harper gets here."

Inside the house several minutes later, Mason set a can of soda next to Wyatt and peered over his shoulder at the revamped ConnectUP website open on the laptop in front of him. "That's impressive."

"Yeah. Reed's been working hard on it. And this logo

Tonya created is epic. You'd think we paid someone big money for it."

"Tonya's amazing."

"And the very picture of a ConnectUP kid. It astounds me to see how far she's come the past two years. Her testimony video is one we're putting on the website. Brought Harper and me both to tears when we watched it."

"Things are really coming together." Mason's smile spread across his face. "Man, when I think about what we could do with that grant money."

"I hear ya."

Wyatt stared at the screen, but his mind wandered to a building he'd never been to on the other side of Dallas. Harper was probably with Ellison right this minute, hearing whatever it was he needed to say to her. To further his own healing, his own recovery.

But what about hers? Had Brett given any consideration to how his reappearance had disrupted her life, just when she'd found her way after years of searching? Would this meeting help Ellison but hurt Harper?

"Mac? Mac."

He looked over at Mason, now seated at the table. "Sorry. What?"

"You okay? You looked a million miles away."

"Not quite that far."

Mason sat back in his chair. "Harper's with Brett right now?"

"Probably."

"You think this is about making amends? Or about working through the death of their daughter?"

"Could be either. Or neither. His counselor just called and asked if she'd be willing to meet. I'm not altogether surprised by the request, but I didn't figure it would be this soon. It's only been a month since he went in."

He sighed, sat up, and crossed his arms on the table in

front of the computer. "I just don't want him hurting her anymore. She's finally found her footing, found some peace. But since the call on Wednesday, she's been nervous. Stressed out. Even yesterday, with all the cooking and family time, all the stuff she loves so much, she would get quiet and pensive, and I knew she was thinking about this meeting. Jill had dinner with us at Emory's, then took some food to the hospital to meet her mom. That was the only time Harper seemed truly herself, when she was focused on Jill."

"Y'all prayed about it, right? Before she went today?"

"Absolutely. I wanted to go with her, but she felt like she needed to do this on her own."

"Leave it there, with God. He'll take care of her. And her wanting to go on her own shows some real grit. She's facing her past head-on, I would imagine, so she can wash her hands of it once and for all."

Wyatt nodded. Mason was right, but he still wished he could protect her from whatever she might have to face today.

"Hey, man. She's crazy about you. Anyone around you two for any length of time can see she's all in with you. You can take that to the bank."

"I sure hope so, Mase, because it's getting to where I can't see my life without her." The doorbell rang, and he rose from the table. "If the past would leave us alone for five minutes, maybe we could start thinking about the future."

Mason's laugh followed him to the door. But when he opened it, his breath hitched.

Seemed the past wasn't quite done with them yet.

CHAPTER THIRTY-ONE

*a*fter changing into jeans and a DHU sweatshirt at home, Harper headed to Wyatt's and parked in the driveway behind his Sequoia. Mason's car was gone, and the garage door left open, so he'd probably left to pick up Rhonda for their tree-decorating double date. Her spirits lifted as she got out of her car, and she smiled for the first time in what felt like hours. After her emotional roller coaster afternoon, she needed to be with Wyatt as much as she needed to breathe.

An unfamiliar white Honda CRV sitting at the curb caught her attention as she closed her car door. Maybe one of the kids got an early Christmas present and stopped by to show off their new wheels.

She walked into the kitchen, surprised to find it empty. That was usually the natural gathering place whenever anybody came by. Wyatt's voice carried from the front of the house, and she walked that direction, curious to discover the owner of the car.

"Oh, I agree wholeheartedly." A woman's voice she didn't know stopped Harper in her tracks. That wasn't one of the kids.

"Really?" Wyatt said. "You don't think we're being short-sighted or limiting our reach?"

Harper stood, barely breathing, in the hall, where she could hear but couldn't be seen.

"Of course not," the mystery woman answered. "Your goal from the beginning has been to foster a safe environment for your kids. And you've had enormous success. Why change course now?"

Harper leaned forward only far enough to see Wyatt seated at the desk with his laptop open, a statuesque blonde standing to his side with her hand on his shoulder, her back to Harper while they studied the screen. Harper's pulse thrummed in her ears. Who was this woman, and why did she and Wyatt appear so familiar with each other?

"Hmm," he said. "I just don't want to miss reaching other kids who need to hear our message."

"Wyatt, you've built an amazing outreach here. Don't second-guess yourself now. Not with this grant so close. Think of what all you could do with that!"

"You're right. We could do some amazing things with that grant money. I guess we should stay the course, then."

"Absolutely."

"Thanks, Ally. I appreciate the input."

Harper pulled back out of sight, her breath catching in her chest.

Ally.

That had to be *the* Allyson. The one who'd stood alongside Wyatt when he founded ConnectUP. Who'd helped lay the foundation of this ministry he loved.

Who agreed *wholeheartedly* with his vision.

Before anyone noticed her presence, she made an about-face and returned to the kitchen, thankful the new rug they'd bought for the foyer muffled the sound of her sneakers. She needed to breathe. Get her heart rate under control and act like nothing was amiss. How she could use Rhonda's theatrical skills right now.

Wyatt and Allyson's combined laughter reached her ears before they appeared in the doorway from the entry hall.

"Harper!" Wyatt smiled like it was completely normal for him to be standing there with the stunning woman he once thought he might marry. "I didn't know you were here."

Obviously. "Uh … yeah. Just got here." With more control than she knew she possessed, she returned his smile before looking at the woman by his side.

"Oh, Harper, this is Allyson. Ally, this is Harper."

"Nice to meet you, Harper." Allyson's own smile didn't quite meet her eyes.

"Good to meet you too." Harper returned her gaze to Wyatt, the awkwardness thick in the air. Had he mentioned they were dating? Had he mentioned her at all? "I can leave you alone if you want to visit. It's no problem." Wow, that lie came too easily off her lips, and she prayed for forgiveness.

"Oh, I was just leaving." Allyson turned to Wyatt. "Sorry for dropping in on you out of the blue, but it was great to see you. Tell Mason I look forward to seeing him and Rhonda soon."

"Sure thing," he answered. "Glad you stopped by. Let me walk you out." He turned to Harper. "I'll be right back. Mase ran to get Rhonda and pick up barbecue."

She could only nod as they turned and disappeared back down the entry hall. And for the second time that day, she closed her eyes, drew in a breath, counted to five, and let it out. Then once more, for good measure. By the time Wyatt returned, her heart had almost regained its normal rhythm.

He came over and pulled her in for a hug. "I'm glad you're here."

"Me too." She closed her eyes and grasped him tight around the waist, reveling in the feel of his arms around her.

He pulled back and looked down at her. "So, how'd it go?" he asked as if the elephant hadn't just walked out of the room.

She pulled out of his arms. "It went ... good. Maybe we can talk about it later."

His brow creased. "Okay. Whatever you need."

Whatever she needed? She needed to know they were on the same side, that nothing had changed.

Except things had changed. From the moment she put Jill and Tonya together, she'd felt an ever-growing pull to do what she could to bring kids together, not keep them apart. But if Wyatt put more stock in Allyson's opinion than hers, where did that leave them?

"How long has it been since you've seen Allyson?"

He leaned back against the island and braced his hands on either side of him. "About a year, I guess. Just before she left for Central America."

"What was in Central America?"

"Her dad is a medical missionary in Guatemala. In fact, that's where she met Yolanda. They've been best friends since they were teenagers and came to the States together for college. Both got nursing degrees. Still joined at the hip, those two."

"Her dad? What about her mom?"

"Passed away when Al was about twelve, I think. On the mission field. Very sudden."

Harper couldn't help the swell of sympathy for the other woman. How awful to have lost her mother at such a young age. And Harper knowing Wyatt's mom, Arlene, the way she did, there was no doubt Ally had found a mother figure in her while with Wyatt. Just as Harper had when she was little.

"That's awful. It's nice she's still close to her dad, though."

He moved his head from side to side. "Pretty close. As much as they can be with sixteen hundred miles between them. She has an older brother up in Colorado, though, and they see each other a few times a year. They're super close."

"How'd she know where you lived?"

"I'm one of their mission's financial supporters, so they have my address to send out periodic updates about what they're doing. I got a couple of notes from her, as well, just letting me know what she was doing out there."

"That's nice, that you could still be friends."

He shrugged. "Like I said, we both knew the relationship had lost its steam." He sighed and straightened, holding his hands out in front of him. "This is what you want to talk about right now?"

"You know all about Brett, but I don't know anything about Allyson."

"I only know about Brett because I was there, remember? I had to watch you guys together for three years. Drove me crazy. And don't worry. I told her about us."

"I wasn't worried. Just curious, I guess, about what would have her dropping in on you after a year away."

He reached for her hand and led her into the family room to sit on the sectional. "She asked about ConnectUP and if there might be a place for her to get involved again."

A tingling sensation invaded her midsection, as if in warning. "She's back for good?"

"Sounds like it. Said she's working freelance nursing jobs until something permanent comes up."

The knot in Harper's stomach tightened. "We always need more volunteers." Of course, Allyson could have found that information on their website. Or with a phone call. Email. Smoke signal. Instead of just *dropping in* on her ex-boyfriend. Harper suspected it was more of a reconnaissance visit of the romantic sort than gathering information on ConnectUP. A checking-in, of sorts, to get a pulse on whether or not the relationship could be restored.

"That's what I told her. Guess we'll see."

"Guess we will."

His eyes narrowed. "Would that be a problem?"

She shook her head. "Not for me. We all need to be where God's leading us. If she believes that's where she should be, I would never stand in the way."

"Yeah, she loved ConnectUP, so it surprised me when she left so abruptly. She never talked about going back to the field while we were together. In fact, just the opposite. She was raised on the mission field and always said she wanted to make her life stateside."

"And she was with the club from the very beginning?"

"Pretty much. At the time we met, our student pastor had already approached me about how to help some of his kids he feared might be on the verge of making some devastating decisions. One in particular, and you actually know him."

"Who?"

"Matt."

Her eyes widened. "Team leader Matt?"

He nodded. "He was having a tough time with a group of kids bullying him at school, online. You name it, he went through it. Pastor Tim introduced us, and I started spending some time with him. Man, I could see Glen all over that kid. He was a mess."

"And that was only three years ago? I would've never imagined. He's walking so close to God and is amazing with the CU kids."

"Because he gets them. He told me last year, when he applied to become a leader, how close he'd come to literally pulling the trigger. Had the gun, the place he would do it, was just getting his *affairs* in order, was how he put it. He didn't want to leave a bunch of stuff behind for his folks to deal with. Said I stepped in probably within days of when he—" His voice broke, and his eyes filled with tears.

Harper slipped her arm around his shoulders. "You saved his life, Wyatt. And probably more because of the kids he's been able to help. ConnectUP is your legacy." Her own eyes welled up. "Glen would be so proud of you. Of the man you've grown to be. As proud as I am of what you've accomplished."

"I hope so."

"I know so. I always knew you were destined for great things. Even before I truly understood your faith, I knew you would change the world."

He put a hand along her face. "You're so easy on me, Harper."

"Just telling you what I see. What I always have."

Still cupping her face, he leaned in and kissed her. A soft, lingering kiss, gentle but intense. Whenever Wyatt kissed her, it wasn't a physical act with no thought. She felt love and care in his kiss, sometimes desire, sometimes playfulness, and other times comfort. Something he sought from or gave to only her.

He pulled back and swept her hair behind her ear. "I love having you with me in the ministry. It means everything to me to know we're on this journey together."

She nodded, but her stomach clenched. She wanted nothing more than to travel this road with him. Through all the twists and turns, ups and downs. But what if they came to a fork in that road? Would they choose the same direction?

CHAPTER THIRTY-TWO

"*W*ait. Let me catch up here." Wyatt's stomach pitched, as if punched by an unseen fist. He turned his head to stare into the brightly lit Christmas tree he and Harper sat in front of, facing each other on the living room rug.

"Wyatt." His name was but a whisper on her lips. "I don't —I don't want this to change things with us. Before this afternoon, I'd never talked about it with another soul, but I don't want there to be secrets between us."

Drawing on all his psychologist skills to remain calm and detached—a Herculean effort after what he'd just heard—he looked back at her. Knowing she and Ellison were intimate in high school hadn't come as a shock. But this ...

He wanted to hit something, or a particular some*one*, but needed to rein in his baser instincts if he was going to be any good to Harper in the here and now. And *now* was all that mattered.

After a deep breath in and out to calm his pulse rate, he took both of her trembling hands in his. "Sweetheart, there's nothing you can tell me that's going to change how I feel about you. I'm your safe place."

Her throat worked as she fought the tears he knew threatened below the surface.

"I held him off for a year." Her gaze moved to the front of his shirt. "By then my mom had insisted I go on the pill. I told her nothing had happened, and all she said was, 'It will'."

Fire exploded in his chest anew. Her own mother hadn't told her she had every right to say no? That no meant no, and if some stupid boy couldn't accept it, he wasn't worth it?

"I told myself it was my fault. That it was too much to ask of a guy to stop once you let him go past a certain point."

Her eyes came back to his face, the blinking white lights of the tree reflected in their depths. "I was in such a state of shock when it was over, I couldn't even cry anymore. He even thanked me, as if I'd willingly given him something precious, when I had bruises on my arms for days from him holding me down."

Unshed tears burned behind Wyatt's eyes, his skin crawled, and his heart beat hard in his chest. He didn't want to hear this. Didn't want to know it. But this wasn't about him. He needed to be here for Harper, to help her heal. Help her move on from the trauma she'd experienced at the hands of another who had claimed to love her.

"Sweetheart, I'm so sorry." As tears slipped down her face, he battled to keep his own in check.

"It took him confessing his part in it for me to acknowledge I didn't *give* him anything. He took it. I felt such shame for putting myself in that position to begin with, knowing what he expected and somehow believing he loved me enough to respect my wishes."

Unable to find any words, Wyatt reached out and swept the backs of his fingers down her cheek.

"You must think I'm terrible for staying with him after that. I'm not sure I even know why."

"Because you needed to legitimize it." His rough voice

raked against his throat. "By staying with him, you changed the narrative."

She cocked her head and looked at him with a crease on her forehead.

He cleared his throat against the emotion collecting there. "Your mind had to change the story so you weren't a victim. I see it all the time in counseling. Girls unable to leave their boyfriend abusers, so they change their thinking. It's how they survive. And most of the time, it's because they don't think they have anybody to turn to."

"Change the story," she muttered. "I was changing the story."

"What happened to you wasn't your fault. Staying with him was your coping mechanism. Your parents weren't there for you, Emery was at college, and your friends would have probably told you it gets better.

"You need to go back and tell that girl she did nothing wrong, that she survived because she's strong and courageous, that what happened to her then has no bearing on who she is now. If you and I are destined to be together forever, our first time will be *our* first time. And it will be special and pure and exactly the way God intended it to be. I won't ever give you reason to be afraid of me."

"I've never been afraid with you. And if I could go back, there are so many things I would do differently."

"We all wish that from time to time. But it's how we use what happened that counts. We can let it continue to push us down the wrong path, or learn from it and chart a new course."

"If only I'd understood that sooner, I would've never agreed to marry him. I would've never been in the position where I felt I had to."

He looked down at their joined hands resting between them. "Can I ask how that happened?" He brought his gaze back up to meet her eyes. "If you were protected?"

She let go to swipe at her cheeks with both hands, then clasped them against her chest. "I was having a hard time adjusting to college. Couldn't sleep, fighting depression. I didn't want to go back down the way I went after what happened with you and me, and no way was I asking my mom for help. When I read that St. John's Wort could help minor depression and that I could get it over the counter, I thought it was perfect. I wanted something natural. Not addictive."

Wait ... what? "Back up. What do you mean the way you went after what happened with us?"

She bowed her head. "I hurt my knee in cheer practice right before the first game our senior year." She looked back up at him. "I mentioned it at lunch one day, and one of the guys gave me about three days' worth of Percocet. I found it not only relieved my knee pain but helped me cope with all the other stuff as well. More or less numbed me. He kept me supplied, until I realized I was taking it every day even though my knee pain was long gone. I missed three days of school because I took myself off the stuff cold turkey while my parents were away for a week at a conference. I just told the attendance lady it was the flu."

His jaw dropped. "Home by yourself, coming off of opioid dependence? Harper, you have no idea how dangerous that was. Your parents are two of the most successful drug treatment specialists in the country, and you had to go through detox alone?"

"I researched it, covertly asked my dad some questions. And I wasn't necessarily addicted. I'd only been on them about five months. Detox scared me to death, though, and I knew I never wanted to go through that again. When I heard about this natural supplement, I thought I'd try it, and three months later, the stick came up positive."

"That'll do it."

"The irony of it all was Brett and I were practically done,

we just hadn't said the final words yet. But we'd made plans to go camping over Memorial Day weekend with some friends. We were drinking, one thing led to another, and that was it. I thought that was the last time, and we'd go our separate ways once we got back."

"You'd actually broken up?"

She nodded. "We hadn't seen or spoken to each other in almost a month when I took the test. Brett was not happy when I told him, wanted me to end it, but I refused. My parents were disappointed but not angry, while his dad was furious and wouldn't hear of anything less than us getting married.

"And there I was, right back with Brett again. Only this time, he didn't want to be with me either, because he couldn't live the college frat boy life with a wife and a child on the way. We didn't get our footing until Megan was about eighteen months old. Brett was in his last year of school, his parents bought us that house, and it was almost as if he enjoyed being home with us. He paid a lot of attention to Megan, and she was crazy about her dad."

Pain sparked in her eyes. "Then she got sick, and he retreated again." She took a breath, held it and let it out, a coping mechanism he often taught his young clients. Had she learned that in therapy herself? "I can't be sorry about having her, though, except for her getting sick. Having her in my life opened up a part of me I never knew was there. Until I got my life straight with the Lord, she was the only thing I ever felt I did right."

"You've done a lot of things right." He took her hands in his again. "And all the fire you've passed through won't return void. If given to the Lord to use as He sees fit, He'll turn all of that ugliness into something beautiful."

In fact, He already had. Restoring their friendship, then turning it into something more. Hopefully something permanent. And giving her two groups of girls who needed all the wisdom, grace, and love she had to offer.

If only she could reach both of them without compromising what he'd worked so long and hard to build.

CHAPTER THIRTY-THREE

*H*arper applauded the sixteen girls standing in front of her Saturday morning. "Awesome job today, ladies! Now go do something fun. I have a date with a very handsome man and a Christmas tree."

"Your professor boyfriend?" Kendra's smile lit up her ebony face as the girls made their way to the bags stashed along the wall.

"Yes, ma'am. Although, he's not my professor anymore."

"He's super nice," Jill said.

"You've met him?" Maggie asked.

"Yeah. Tonya and I worked on last week's banners over there on Sunday."

"He's the bomb!" Tonya called from where she stood in front of another barn-door-sized banner, painting a Mustang running straight at them, nostrils flaring, mane billowing. Another work of art to be destroyed in seconds.

"We want to meet him!" Libby and Maggie said in unison.

"Okay." Harper laughed, but she didn't mind showing off Wyatt anytime, anywhere. Being *his* was one of her favorite things to be. "I'll have him come down to the sidelines and meet you guys after next week's game."

As the girls pulled their sweats on over their shorts and T-shirts, she made her way over to Tonya and threw her arm around the girl's shoulders. "Absolutely gorgeous."

Tonya's pleased grin beamed up at her. "You think so?"

"Oh, honey, it's fabulous. You are so gifted. It just kills me to think of it being torn to shreds."

Tonya looked back at the banner and shrugged. "I guess that's the point. I do have several paintings at home, though, if you'd, you know, ever like to see them."

Harper's jaw dropped and she pulled back to look at her. "Yes, ma'am! Of course I would! In fact, that sounds like a perfect Christmas gift for Wyatt, if you'll let me buy one."

A pink blush infused Tonya's face. "Cool. Come by anytime."

"I'll do that."

"I'd better get this stuff gathered up. I came with Jill."

"Talk to you later." She gave Tonya a hug and ambled over to where she'd left her own bag. She'd been delighted to see Jill and Tonya already working when she arrived for that morning's cheer practice. Jill introduced Tonya to the rest of the squad as they came in, and everybody had been effusive in their praise of the girls' work.

Ever since Wyatt had shared his misgivings, and knowing Allyson backed him one hundred percent, Harper had battled with doubts in her judgment. But witnessing how easily the cheerleaders had accepted Tonya into their midst renewed her conviction that if more kids from different social circles actually interacted, they would see how similar they were. How even the things they didn't share in common could enrich a relationship between them.

Her eyes narrowed when Jill threw her bag over her shoulder and winced, holding her hand over her ribs. Concerned, she took the teen aside as the other girls filtered out.

"You okay, Jill? You didn't get hurt, did you?"

"Uh, no. I'm fine."

Harper studied her face for a moment. "It's not healthy or wise to push through an injury. If you're hurt, we can address it and take measures to make sure you don't overdo before it's resolved."

Jill nodded, glancing at the floor before looking back up at Harper. "I—I ran into something and hurt my ribs, but I'm fine. Really. Just a little sore."

Except Jill's gaze kept moving away. Something wasn't right.

"You ran into something? Or something ran into you?" Harper's stomach coiled. "Did you see Dwight last night?"

The girl nodded but still didn't look at her.

"Jill, did he hurt you?"

Those azure eyes darted back to her, wide and alarmed.

Harper stepped toward her to keep their conversation private while Tonya gathered up their art supplies. "Sweetie, if he's hurting you, we can get you some help. You don't have to put up with that."

"He doesn't mean to hurt me. He's just bigger than me."

"Yes, he is, and he should know better. Jill, let me help you."

"I don't need help." Tonya glanced their way at Jill's forceful tone, her brow furrowed. "Honestly," Jill said in a quieter voice. "I'll wrap for Monday's practice, and it'll be fine."

"Okay." Harper reached out and drew her in for a hug. "I'm praying for you, Jill, honey. You're so incredibly special and deserve to be treated like a princess. Don't settle for less." She pulled back and looked into Jill's tear-filled eyes. "I meant it when I said I'd been there. Trust me, it doesn't just stop. You have to walk away."

Jill backed up a step. "I need to go help Tonya."

Harper watched her go, her heart aching, wishing she knew what to do to reach her. For now, she would continue to pray about the situation and let God provide the opening she needed. Jill's life could depend on it.

CHAPTER THIRTY-FOUR

*H*arper pulled her hair into a ponytail on her way down the stairs to meet Wyatt. He walked through her front door with a bag of tacos from their favorite food truck in one hand and a bouquet of flowers in the other.

"Hey, beautiful." He stopped long enough to give her a heart-melting kiss. His hands full, he couldn't hold her, but she made up for it by clutching his jacket and pulling herself to him. She loved kissing this man, knowing he was hers, and she was his. Forever, God willing. If she could be so blessed, she looked forward to the time she would greet him coming in the door at the end of the day. Coming home. To her.

He pulled back and smiled down into her face. "Wow. I love how you say *hello*."

She pulled him back for another quick buss. "Hello."

When she let him go, he held out the flowers. "For you."

"These are gorgeous." She brought the soft petals to her face and inhaled. "And they smell incredible. Thank you!"

After closing the door behind him, she followed him into her kitchen, enjoying the view, as usual. The man looked as amazing in jeans, long-sleeved shirt, and brown leather jacket as he had in the tux he'd tried on last Saturday at his fitting for Mason's wedding.

He pulled plates down from the cabinet while she put her flowers in water and poured sodas for them both. They settled at the table, prayed a blessing over their meal, and dug in.

Wyatt poured a generous stream of spicy salsa onto his chicken taco. "How was practice?"

"Great!" She applied a milder version to her barbacoa in a corn tortilla. "I definitely worked up an appetite."

"Good thing I got extras, then."

"Good thing."

He wolfed down his taco in three bites, wiped his mouth, and reached for a second.

Only halfway done with her first, she lowered it to her plate. "I have some interesting news."

One eyebrow shot up as he looked at her. "Do tell."

"Remember the conversation we had about three weeks ago about me possibly changing my major? When my mom called and pretty much offered me a job once I had my psych degree?"

He nodded as he chewed.

"Well ... I've thought a lot—and prayed a lot—about what you said. About where God may be calling me, and that He's the only one I should be living my life for. Making decisions to please Him and Him only. Which has been a learning curve for me, since I've lived most of my life trying to please my parents or my friends or whoever I was trying to get validation from."

Silent, he nodded again, but in his eyes she found what she always had. Encouragement, acceptance, love. She never needed to jump through hoops to get his attention or affection. He loved her for no other reason than she was who she was.

She swallowed the lump in her throat. "I want to live wholly surrendered to Christ, whatever the cost. So, I've decided to change my major to Biblical Studies with an emphasis in student ministry."

His eyes widened. "Harper, that's fantastic!"

"You think so?" She leaned forward, her belly fluttering at his enthusiastic response. "I mean, of course *I* think so, because I prayed so hard that God would show me it was the right decision, and I was beyond excited when I checked the course catalog and saw that all the classes lined up perfectly, then the advisor I spoke with on the phone could get me in right away, so everything seems to be falling into place like it was all meant to—"

"Harper." He reached out to grab her hand, laughter in his eyes and a smile on his face. "I absolutely think so. I'm really excited for you. But you don't need mine or anybody else's approval. You only answer to One. And how could He not be pleased with your decision?"

She returned his grin. "You're right. I know you are. Although, I'm sure my parents are going to disown me when I tell them I'm going into ministry instead of what they consider a *real* career."

He let go of her hand and picked up his taco. "I know you don't want to disappoint them, but you have to be true to yourself, to where God's leading you. All they need to know is you're following your own path, and you would appreciate their support. Period. You're not asking their permission, and hopefully they'll see what all the rest of us see—a woman passionate about kids."

She nodded but despite her confidence in the decision she'd made, apprehension still coiled inside of her knowing her parents would likely distance themselves further from her. "I know. I'd love their acceptance, but it may take a while for them to see how real this is to me. And it is, Wyatt. I'm in it, heart and soul. If only Mom and Dad could share the joy of faith with me instead of me having to choose between them and God.

"But this all started when Rhonda invited me to ConnectUP. Like everything settling into place. I hadn't felt that since the moment they placed Megan in my arms the day she was born, like my life had a purpose, had *meaning*. I love these kids so much, and watching Jesus work in them is like witnessing miracles every day."

"You're amazing with those girls. And they adore you. But then, I know just how they feel."

Oh, could she love this man any more than she did right this minute? She leaned in and gave him a quick kiss, the spicy oil from the salsa leaving her lips tingling. At least, she assumed it was the salsa. "Thank you. These last few months have been a whirlwind of change for me. First, going back to school, getting involved in CU, then coaching cheer. And falling in love with you all over again. Sometimes it leaves my head spinning."

"A lot of changes, that's for certain. All good things."

"All wonderful things." She picked up her taco and took a bite.

"You said practice went well?"

"Really well. The girls are killing it. Oh! And guess who was there?"

"I wouldn't know where to begin."

"Tonya! Jill asked her the other day if she'd like to come work with her on new banners. She introduced her to the others, and they were super enthusiastic about her helping out."

He said nothing for a moment, his brow furrowed as he again doused his taco with salsa. "You don't think they're using her, do you?"

Her spirits deflated with his assessment. "Not for a second. I wish you knew them like I do. These girls are hard-working, sweet-spirited, and smart. Do they venture outside their circle very much? Probably not. But do most kids?" She studied him for a long moment. "Is that how you thought of me back in high school, that I was mean-spirited and hateful?"

His sigh filled the space between them. "I never thought of

you as mean-spirited. Self-involved?" He shrugged. "After that summer, when you chose Brett over me, I figured it was because he was Mr. Everything and I was Mr. Nobody."

Her heart splintered. "You weren't a nobody to me, Wyatt. And I envied how authentic you always were when I felt like I had to keep up appearances at all times. I loved cheerleading, and that was the one thing that made me feel like me."

"Maybe that's why you relate so much better to your cheer girls, then."

Her jaw dropped and mind whirled in confusion. Two minutes ago, he'd told her she was *amazing* with her CU girls. So, which was it? "Relate better? How am I not relating to my CU girls?"

"I didn't mean that. Bad choice of words. I just meant that it seems like you're pushing these girls together. I don't want those cheerleaders taking advantage of Tonya and her talents, then dropping her when they don't need her any longer."

Just like Sarah did with Glen. He hadn't said the words, but she heard them all the same. That devastating incident and its beyond-tragic end seemed to color everything Wyatt did with regard to the ministry. She understood it, but she also saw how it limited their reach. That couldn't be what he'd intended. Could it?

Her appetite gone, she pushed her plate away. "I wish we could get past this. My cheer girls aren't going to use Tonya and then dump her. And Tonya's not thinking she has a whole new peer group. Her best friend is Tish, and she's not leaving her behind just because she and Jill have gotten to know each other. She's already had such a positive influence on Jill, because Tonya's been through the trauma of divorce and has been able to encourage her."

"I see what you're saying. But what I also see is Jill seems to be benefiting more from this association than Tonya. She's getting help with her banners, help with her mother. What's Tonya getting out of it?"

"A chance to minister to another kid, which is what she prays for all the time in our conversation circles. She's getting affirmation of her talents. She's making new friends. I see both girls benefiting from their *association,* as you call it. I call it a friendship."

"Okay." He put his hands out in defense. "I'll trust your judgment on this. I guess time will tell what comes of it."

"I guess it will. But fringe kids aren't the only kids who need what we offer. Jill's probably more lost and broken than any of my CU girls. I just wish there was a way ConnectUP could help her and kids like her."

"She'd hate ConnectUP, I'm sure, since our kids are the ones her circle deems non-entities."

She sighed, her pulse picking up speed as frustration tightened her chest. "There you go again, making these assumptions with no grounds."

His eyes narrowed. "No grounds? I lived that life, Harper. And it killed Glen." He placed his napkin next to his plate. "Look, sweetheart. I know we disagree about this. I don't like arguing with you, especially about the ministry. There's nothing the enemy would like more than to hurt ConnectUP by bringing division in the leadership."

She fought the lump forming again in her throat. "That wasn't my intent. I just thought we could talk about it."

"About what? ConnectUP has always been about providing a safe environment for kids who feel they don't have a voice. I won't have them feeling like that at club too. I'm sorry Jill's having a tough time. I've been praying for her, and I'll be happy to come alongside you any way you see fit to help her. We would never turn a kid away, but ConnectUP isn't the place for Jill. I can't imagine she'd be comfortable there."

Her heart sank at his refusal to even discuss it. Because she felt ConnectUP was exactly the place for Jill and others like her. CU was a thriving ministry with a valuable message. But somewhere along the way, an undercurrent of *us against them* had seeped in, which she'd become increasingly uncomfortable with. Probably because she lived in both camps.

But what would happen if they took it from *us against them* to *we're all in this together*? Would they alienate their CU kids, as Wyatt feared, or show even more young people the way to the cross?

CHAPTER THIRTY-FIVE

*W*yatt scanned the community center, making sure everything was set for the evening's club. Thoughts swirled around in his head, as they had the past several days whenever he wasn't counseling, teaching, or writing.

The afternoon spent decorating Harper's tree on Saturday, followed by an evening snuggling in front of a Christmas movie, had been ... nice. Maybe a little too nice, as if neither wanted to venture into precarious territory. A circumstance that had carried over into the week.

He didn't like it. They'd never had to walk on eggshells with each other, and he missed the easy camaraderie they'd enjoyed. Before she appeared to lose confidence in what he was trying to achieve with ConnectUP.

"Hey, Dr. Mac!"

Several boys came in the door and sauntered in his direction, their faces red from the December cold. The sight of them warmed him from the heart.

"Hey, guys! Go grab some basketballs, and we'll shoot around."

"You got it, Doc."

Yolanda hit the stereo, and music blasted through the room as more kids arrived. Harper had texted him earlier that she would be a little later than normal but would make it in plenty of time to take her circle.

He couldn't wait to see her, eager to close the distance growing between them. There had to be a middle ground, a way for ConnectUP to stay on track as well as for her to minister to girls like Jill, who desperately needed to hear a message of hope.

His gaze strayed to the far end of the room where Yolanda, Jenny, and Allyson set out refreshments. Jenny had been excited when Ally walked in earlier with Yolanda, but he wasn't at all sure how Harper would feel about it.

Reed walked up and stopped beside him. "How do you think that's going to go?"

Wyatt looked at his brother. "You mean Allyson?"

"Allyson and Harper. Have you given Harper a heads-up she would be here?"

"I didn't even know she would be here, although I knew it was a possibility she'd want to get involved again. And, yes, Harper's aware of that. Also, I told you before, Allyson was as on-board as I was about the breakup. No hard feelings, I can assure you."

"Hmm. If you say so."

Wyatt was saved from answering when a couple of girls came in the door.

Tonya ... and Jill.

His heart fell. Middle ground? How could he and Harper find middle ground when she kept going around him?

Tonya spotted him and waved, Jill following suit, although she looked uncertain. He moved in their direction, but none of the girls had made any effort to greet them. Even Tish, Tonya's best friend, turned her back, speaking instead to a circle of others gathered in the dance area across the room.

"Hi, Wyatt." Tonya's usual cheery countenance faded as

her gaze moved from him to the girls in the far corner and back.

"Ladies. Great to see you. Jill, welcome."

"Uh, yeah." The petite girl's expression turned wary as she looked around the large room. She looked uncomfortable, exactly as he'd thought she would. "Thanks."

"Where's Harper?" Tonya asked.

"Should be here any minute," he answered.

"Okay." Tonya looked back at the other girls, but her smile had yet to reappear. "I'll go introduce Jill around."

The two walked across the room and up to the group that included Tish, Remy, and Beth. Remy turned toward them until Tish reached out and pulled her back around, leaving the new arrivals standing on the outside of the circle.

His gut clenched. While he wasn't sure this was the right place for Jill, he still sympathized with her. Being snubbed hurt no matter what social tier you might be on. Hadn't his kids learned the hard way how it felt to be excluded?

He turned his attention to the woman walking toward him with a smile. "Hey, Ally, welcome back."

"Good to be here. It's grown in the last year." She looked around the room, bustling already with fifty-plus kids, her perusal stopping at the group in the corner. "What's the story there?"

He shook his head. "I have no idea. It's not what I expected. I was worried about the cheerleader snubbing our CU girl. It never entered my mind our own girls would snub the cheerleader."

She looked at him with eyes widened. "Oh, this is that situation you told me about when I came by your house. Guess that proves your point."

Proved his point? Not by a long shot. This wasn't how he wanted his kids to be treated, but even more so, it wasn't the way he wanted them to treat others.

Out of the corner of his eye, he caught sight of Harper

coming in the door looking a bit harried, as if she'd been rushing. Probably because she'd intended to be there when Jill arrived.

"Excuse me." He gave Ally's arm a quick squeeze and headed toward Harper. He wanted to get to her before she got too far inside. At the door, he turned her around the way she'd come. "We need to talk."

She threw him a confused glance over her shoulder on their way back outside. "What's going on?"

"I was hoping you could tell me." They stopped around the corner from the entrance, the blast of cold air making him wish he'd grabbed his jacket on the way out. "You know I care about Jill and what happens to her, but did you really think I would change my mind when she walked in the door?"

"Who? Jill? She's here?"

He stared down at her face illuminated by the lights outside the community center, her brows pinched in confusion, her cheeks and nose pink from the chill. "You didn't invite her?"

"Of course not. I may not wholly agree that ConnectUP isn't the place for her, but I respect you enough to do as you ask. I would never—" She looked away, shaking her head. "Seems that respect only runs one way. That you'd ever think I could do that to you. Put you in that position."

His sigh released a cloud of breath as he reached out and took her gloved hand. "I'm sorry. They just walked in a couple of minutes ago. I didn't know what to think."

"And you automatically assumed I would go around you to get my way?" The eyes that looked up at him held the same hurt he'd seen that night at the reunion dinner. When he'd accused her of being drawn back into the clutches of Brett Ellison without giving her the benefit of the doubt.

She shook her head again. "I hate this, being at odds with you. I'm going to say this once more, and I want you to hear me. I love ConnectUP. I'm committed to this ministry. I will not stand in the way of the direction you believe in your heart is right, and I would never, ever undermine you by intentionally going against you."

The chill of the evening paled in comparison to the sting of her words. He'd jumped to the wrong conclusion, again, and made an accusation instead of looking for the truth. He pulled her close and held her against him. "I hate being at odds with you too. I'm sorry I didn't check with you first."

"I love you."

"I love you too." He pulled back and took her by the hand to head back toward the entrance. "I'm not sure what kind of group you're going to have tonight."

"Because of Jill? I don't think she'll cause any problems."

"Maybe not intentionally, but it's almost as chilly in there as it is out here. I have to say, I'm a bit disappointed in our girls. Even Tonya got the cold shoulder."

She pulled up before they got to the door. "Really? That is disappointing."

"Oh, and Allyson's here."

A couple of seconds ticked by in silence. "So ... she's back?"

"It would appear so. Are you okay with that?"

Her gaze darted away. "Of course. I just don't want things to be awkward for you."

He started to reply when the door opened, and Tonya and Jill walked outside.

"Hey, girls," Harper called.

"Harper." Tonya's tear-filled eyes held hurt and confusion while Jill continued to her car without responding. "Um, we're going to go."

"What happened?"

"Let's just say my friends really let me down."

After exchanging a quick hug with Harper, she ran over to Jill's BMW and climbed in.

As they pulled away, Harper looked up at him. "I don't even know what to say to that. I didn't know Tonya had invited Jill, but I'm not surprised. She probably felt CU had a lot to offer her. But I'm disappointed our own girls would turn around and treat someone else the way they hate to be treated. How did I mess that up?"

He shook his head. "You didn't. I don't know what happened, but this isn't what we've taught them. Just tread lightly in circle tonight, okay?"

"Of course. But we'll need to address this at some point."

"Agreed. But let's pray over it first."

Because something was broken, and he had no idea how to fix it.

CHAPTER THIRTY-SIX

*H*arper pulled her backpack and jacket from her Audi and strode through the garage into Wyatt's kitchen. It had been a long day, and she was weary to the bone. Tonya's text asking if they could meet last night after club had prevented any alone time with Wyatt. He'd understood Tonya needed her, and she'd done her best to console the distraught girl who felt torn between two friends, unsure how to be loyal to both of them without losing someone she cared about.

Although common sense told Harper to go home and get some sleep, she needed to be with Wyatt. There had been entirely too much distance between them over the past several days, and she was desperate to bridge it.

He looked over his shoulder from where he sat on the sofa. "Hey, sweetheart."

"Hi."

He turned off the news and met her in the kitchen. "Rough day?" He lifted her backpack from her shoulder to set it on the island, then wrapped his arms around her.

"Not too bad." She pressed her cheek against his neck as her arms grasped him around the waist. The simple act of breathing in the familiar woodsy scent of him relaxed her. Yes, this was much better than going home to a lonely house. "Just tired. I was with Tonya until almost midnight, finished up some homework when I got home, and was at cheer practice at 6:30 this morning."

He pulled back and shook his head. "I don't know how you do it all."

"I'll be fine. Winter break is almost here, and I'll be able to breathe a little easier. I'm more concerned about what's going on with Tonya and the girls. She was a mess last night."

"We can talk about it if it would help."

"I'd like that. But I have so much to do for my classes tomorrow."

"Okay, let's order pizza, get some work done, and if you want to talk, I'm here."

She nodded. "Sounds good."

They shared a slow kiss that worked itself into the depths of her, like a balm to her soul. The love she had for this man deepened with each passing day, so the distance growing between them hurt all the more. He let her go to order their pizza, and she settled into her favorite corner of the sectional with her laptop.

When Wyatt finished his call, she looked over at him. "Do we have everything in place for the CU Christmas party on Saturday?"

"Pretty much." He pulled two bottles of water from the refrigerator. "Yolanda and Shannon have taken that on with gusto. I'm just supplying the house."

She chuckled. "Shannon could lead a coup in a small country if she had a mind to."

They spent the next half hour working in relative silence until their pizza arrived. She hadn't realized how hungry she was until he placed the box on the coffee table, and the aroma of cheese, tomato sauce, pepperoni, and Italian spices assailed her.

Wyatt pulled a piece from the box. "How did your circle go last night?"

Tossing her head from side to side, she put her half-eaten piece of pizza on her plate and brushed her mouth with a napkin. "It was … awkward. I let them talk, but I had to keep reining it in from becoming a gripe-fest about the popular kids and how Tonya was buying into all of that just because a cheerleader was being nice to her. Tish especially was angry, although it was coming from a place of hurt. She thinks Tonya's chosen someone over her, and nothing could be further from the truth. Tonya's broken-hearted that Tish is upset with her. If only …"

She shook her head. This wasn't where she'd intended the evening to head. She'd treaded carefully the past few days to not push Wyatt into a conversation she knew made him uncomfortable. But her time spent with the girls last night, then with Tonya afterward, only deepened her convictions that they were missing the big picture.

"If only what?"

She set the plate on the coffee table. "I just wish they could see past the social divide so they could understand how Jill's so much like them. She wants to be loved, accepted, valued. Just like they do."

"Except in their eyes, Jill already has it, so her showing up at ConnectUP made them feel like she was infringing on their turf."

"But don't you see a problem with that, Wyatt? *Their turf?* How is that any different than what they think so-called *top-tier* kids have done to them?"

He sighed and put his plate next to hers. "I'm not saying they're right, but do you see where they're coming from? Or are you only looking at it from Jill's point of view?"

Taken aback, she stared at him for a moment. "What's that supposed to mean?"

"Just that you were the girl with everything, like Jill. You've never been in the same place as your CU group."

Her stomach balled up. "But I was a kid. A teenage girl. I may have been in a different circle, but I still wanted the same things my girls want and looked for it in all the wrong places. If somebody had shown me early on how to find my identity in Christ, my life would have been drastically different."

He shook his head. "You're asking a lot of these young girls. You see it from your perspective as a lost girl looking for her place, same as Jill. But these kids see someone who, in their eyes, has everything she could want but now wants what they have. I can understand it."

Heat traveled up her back, like hackles on an animal defending its territory. "If by everything, you mean parents who are so wrapped up in their own stuff, they have no idea what's happening with their kid. Or the boyfriend who treats her like an object for his own gratification, and that's when he's not using her for a punching bag, then, yeah, I guess she has everything. Just like I did."

"They don't know that." He kept his tone gentle, clearly employing his counselor tactics, which annoyed her even more. She didn't want to be *handled*. She wanted to be *heard*. "They see the cheerleader who has the football star boyfriend, wears designer clothes, drives a BMW, and runs in the popular circle. Again, I'm not saying they're right. I'm just saying that's what they see."

Turning her face to the fire crackling in the fireplace, she counted to ten in her head. She didn't want to be defensive, so she decided to meet him halfway. "I can understand that." She looked at him again. "I guess I'm still reeling at how they treated both Jill *and* Tonya last night, as if Tonya had chosen a side and was no longer welcome. I don't want to instill an *us-against-them* mindset in our kids. A belief that there's no way to bridge the gap."

"I don't think that's what we're doing. Despite their

reaction last night—which didn't please me either—I don't believe we're teaching them to be intolerant. We're just encouraging them not to put their value in a label placed on them by a group they consider higher than they are in the hierarchy."

"I get that. And I agree with it. But I think it's a mistake to limit who we reach."

His head jerked back. "Oh, I see. Everything I've grounded this ministry on is a mistake."

Her eyes widened at the sudden shift in his demeanor. If she'd wanted to be heard, he'd certainly heard *that*. "No! Wyatt, that's not what I'm saying at all. Maybe *mistake* was the wrong word, but I think we're limiting our reach by focusing solely on fringe kids. Doesn't that mean we're being exclusive?"

"Harper, I'm in the middle of trying to get a major grant to launch this ministry to even more cities. Hopefully, even nationwide. And *now* you're telling me we're too *exclusive*? That we're doing it wrong?"

"That's not what—"

"This is exactly why I was hesitant when you first expressed an interest in working with us. Because you've never been where these kids are. You've been straddling two worlds, Harper. Maybe it's time you came down on one or the other. Decide where your commitment is going to be—with me, or with your cheer girls."

Her mouth dropped open as her heart jumped in her chest. "You mean my commitment to ConnectUP, right? Or did you really mean to you?"

"Take your pick. This is my calling, Harper. My practice is my way of earning a living, but ConnectUP is what I *do*. It's who I am. You know my goal is to someday be in full-time ministry, as is yours. But how can we do that together if we don't agree on how it's being done?"

The world suddenly seemed to spin faster, making her head

swim and stomach lurch as if she were on a roller coaster. What just happened? He wanted her ... to *choose*?

The past month had been a whirlwind—working with her ConnectUP girls, coaching the cheer squad, spending time with Wyatt however they could fit it in ... trying to be there for all of them and still keep up with school while working a full-time job.

But it had also been the happiest time in her life. These six weeks with Wyatt, working together, praying together, *being* together, had been a treasure. Her only wish was to come alongside him as a helpmate in the ministry he'd built. But she couldn't turn her back on the others who needed her. Needed what she felt ConnectUP could give them.

"Wyatt—" Her voice broke as weariness settled over her. This was a mistake, coming here as exhausted and confused as she was. "I'm ... sorry. I didn't mean ..." She closed her textbook and stood. "I should go."

He jumped to his feet. "Are you continuing with club? Or are you done?"

Shaking her head, she hitched her shoulders in a shrug. "I —I don't want to be done. I love working with CU, and I certainly don't want to leave my girls. My intent isn't to limit the ministry, Wyatt. I want to grow it. With you."

He splayed his hands on his hips. "I thought that's what we were doing. Until ... all this other stuff."

Tears burned her throat and eyes as she grabbed her backpack and slung it over her shoulder. "I can't ignore the burden the Lord's given me for other girls who need the same thing we're teaching our CU kids. I'm sorry if you think I'm the enemy again, siding with one group over the other. But that's exactly my point. My cheer girls and my CU girls should not be enemies. That's not even biblical. And it kills me to have to differentiate between them when, of all people, I should be helping them bridge that gap. Not play both sides of it."

He bowed his head and rubbed his forehead with his

fingers, a gesture she recognized as one he went to, consciously or not, when tense, stressed, or upset. None of which she'd wanted to cause him. She was supposed to be his safe place, the one person he could depend on when he felt the rest of the world coming down on him. That's what she wanted to be. Forever.

"Harper ..." He looked up, and the confusion and pain in his eyes tore her heart open. "I don't know what to say. I don't know what you want. Change the whole direction of ConnectUP a month before we're to be considered for a huge grant? Rework a proposal we've already spent weeks on? Bring the kids our clubbers fend off every day into the very environment we've spent three years building for them? And what if it doesn't work? Then we've lost everything. Not just the grant, but the trust of our kids. I don't know that I can do that. I don't know how you can expect it."

Nodding, she backed away. "You're right. Absolutely." She turned and walked around the sectional. "I'm sorry. I'm exhausted. I'm going to call it a night."

"Harper." He started after her. "Harper, wait."

At the door, she stopped but didn't turn around. If she looked at him, she wouldn't be able to keep back the tears, and she didn't want him to see how much his rejection of her convictions felt like a personal one.

"I'll see you Saturday night ... at the party." Her effort to keep her voice from betraying the state of her emotions failed. "Good night."

She pulled open the door and was halfway through it before he took her gently by the arm, turning her back to him. Despair filled his eyes, and it was clear neither felt like they'd won anything.

"Why did that sound more like goodbye than good night?"

"I would never tell you goodbye." Her voice could barely get past the emotion blocking her throat. "No matter what happens with us. But I don't know where to go from here. I feel strongly about where I believe God is leading me. And you know where He's leading you. I thought it was together, but tonight ... I don't know. You're a stronger Christian than I am. You've been at this longer than I have, so maybe you're right, and I'm wrong. I can certainly live with that if God can give me peace with it. But I don't have peace right now. So maybe it's best we give each other some space."

His eyebrows shot up. "Space."

"I love you, Wyatt. And I know you love me. But if we're being led in different directions, maybe loving each other isn't enough."

His face blanched. "What does *space* look like? Are we not seeing each other? Are we not ... us?"

She bowed her head, and the tears finally came. "I don't know." Her voice hitched, and she cleared her throat as she looked back up at the man she loved with all she was. "All I know is we've said from the beginning, if this relationship didn't honor God, we shouldn't be in it. I don't see how arguing about our ministry ... our calling ... whenever we're together for any length of time brings Him honor. This all happened really fast with us. I think we need to take some time ... separately ... get in the Word and pray about where He wants us to go, whether it's together or not."

"I don't want to be without you, Harper."

"I don't want to be without you, either. But we need clarity, Wyatt. *I* need clarity. I'm willing to be wrong, but I need some time to get alone with God so He can show me if I've misunderstood His leading. I'm confident in my call to work with kids. I just need some clear direction as to what that means, boots to the ground. And fighting with you about it only confuses me. That's of the enemy, and we need to thwart that, however we can."

"Even if it means being apart?"

Pain filled her chest, as if her very heart split in two. "Even if it means being apart."

CHAPTER THIRTY-SEVEN

*T*he scent of fresh pine surrounded Wyatt as he stood in front of the well-lit Christmas tree centered in his front window. The perfect spot, according to Harper, when they put it up the day after Thanksgiving. An evening filled with fun, laughter, and sweet kisses.

Now, a mere six days later, an ache that knotted him up inside had replaced that joy. He hadn't seen nor spoken to her since she left here two nights ago, the chasm between them widening with each silent hour.

How had it all come apart in so short a time, especially with them both following hard after God? When all either of them wanted was to be in the center of His will, to do His work?

When they loved each other so much?

He'd tried to pray over the past couple of days, but never got very far, always ending up asking *why*. Why bring her back into his life, his heart, only to yank her out again? He'd been so sure — so at peace — they were on the right road, he'd made a decision two weeks ago, and a diamond solitaire now sat in a black velvet box in his bedside table drawer. A ring he'd bought with so much promise now sitting with no purpose.

When headlights swept across the window, he peered

around the tree. Yolanda parked her car behind the others already there, and a minute later, she, Ally, and Shannon started up the walk with shopping bags hanging from their arms and each carrying a slow cooker.

He went to the door and opened it before they got there. "Hey, ladies, need some help?"

"Nope," Yolanda answered. "We got it."

"Okay. Make yourselves at home."

"When don't we?" Shannon shot him a playful wink over her shoulder as they turned the corner into the kitchen to join the other leaders there early to prep for the CU Christmas party. A party he didn't feel up to, for the first time ever.

Ally stopped a few feet away and turned back, her brow creased in question. "You okay, Wyatt?"

"Uh, sure. Yeah. All good."

She stared at him for a few seconds longer before she nodded and turned to follow the others into the kitchen. Maybe she'd been gone for a year, but Ally still knew him too well. He'd have to try harder to put aside his heaviness of spirit tonight, at least until his guests left.

With a weary sigh, he started to close the door.

"Wait, wait, wait!"

His heart hammered against his sternum at the sound of the voice he'd only heard in his dreams the past two days. He yanked back on the door to find Harper rushing up the walk from the driveway, carrying another slow cooker and even more bags. The partygoers wouldn't starve, that was for sure.

Once inside, her gaze latched onto his. All he wanted to do was drink in the sight of her, like a man stuck in the desert for days finding a stream of pristine water.

"Sorry. I didn't see you." He reached for the pot. "I'll take that."

"Oh, that's okay." Her voice quivered, and her throat worked as she swallowed. "I have another one in my backseat with some platters of cookies, if you wouldn't mind grabbing those."

"On it."

Neither of them moved. For a long silent moment, he stood there staring at her, memorizing her—her wind-kissed cheeks accentuated by the red sweater she wore under a white jacket with a pair of white jeans, red boots, and a red, green, and white scarf around her neck. The very picture of Christmas.

"Harper—"

"Wyatt—" she said at the same time. "Sorry. You go."

But what was it he wanted to say? That he loved her with every part of him? That he was sorry? And for what, exactly? For standing up for the ministry? For being true to his calling? Protecting his kids?

"I guess I just wanted to see how you are."

Her green eyes pooled. "Taking it a day at a time. You?"

"Same." A day ... an hour ... a minute. "I—"

"Whatever that is smells amazing." Mason's voice preceded him into the foyer.

Harper glanced down at the pot and over to their friend. "Your favorite."

His eyes widened. "Pulled pork?"

Her grin took a bit of the chill off Wyatt's insides, even if it wasn't directed his way. "For sliders."

"Can't wait!"

Wyatt's gaze snagged with hers for another moment before she made her way down the hall to disappear into the kitchen amid happy greetings from her fellow leaders.

Once she was out of sight, he caught Mason's quizzical expression before he turned and walked out into the night, avoiding the unvoiced question. "Mase, help me get the rest out of her car, will ya?"

Thirty minutes into the party, with a hip-hop version of "Santa Claus is Coming to Town" booming throughout the house, Harper emerged from the master suite with her purse and jacket. She stopped long enough to say something to Rhonda, who nodded her head before Harper made her way through the crowded kitchen.

He intercepted her at the entry hall. "Are you leaving?"

She stopped mid-stride and looked up at him in surprise. "Um, yes. No. I mean, yes, I'm going to go get Tonya. I texted her a few minutes ago to see where she was, and she said she hadn't planned to come because she didn't want to mess up the party for the other girls."

"Yeah, I noticed she wasn't here. I can't remember Tonya ever missing an event."

"I told her several of the kids had asked about her and that I'd come get her so she wouldn't have to walk in on her own. Please pray everything will go well with the girls tonight."

"You got it. Drive safe."

He followed her to the living room, where she knelt next to Tish sitting on the floor with some other girls. Harper spoke in her ear and waited while the teen gave thought to whatever she'd said. Tish finally nodded, stood, and pulled on her jacket. That looked promising.

They disappeared through the door, and he said a quick prayer in his head on the way back to the family room, taking in all the activity he hadn't been able to enjoy as fully as he had in years past. Leaders and kids laughed and talked, played games, or stood around the island covered with food. Several slow cookers sat on the counter in front of various electrical outlets, a pot of apple cider bubbled on the stovetop in a gigantic pot, and some kind of spice cake Harper had whipped up baked in the oven.

Rich aromas of cinnamon, ginger, spicy meat, and fresh-baked cookies wafted throughout the house. It smelled like a *home*, one he'd imagined sharing with the woman who still filled his heart. A few days ago, he could imagine them living here together, filling the spare rooms with a couple or three children, hosting Bible studies, game nights, and swim parties, praying over one of her delicious meals at the dining table. Her imprint was everywhere in the new furnishings, artwork, knick-knacks, and even kitchen equipment and accessories.

But now ...

His gaze caught Allyson's across the room. She knew. Or at least suspected. He could see it in her eyes. Unless Harper had said something, nobody yet knew what had transpired between them. But they hadn't spent a minute near each other since she arrived, and the others were sure to notice at some point.

Another wave of grief washed over him, and he pulled his shoulders back to keep from being swept away in its pull. This was a celebration, and there were people here who needed him to be present. These kids he loved and had sacrificed for, even letting go of the love of his life so he could be all they needed him to be.

"Hey, bro." Mason nudged him in the arm. "Great turnout this year."

Wyatt pulled his attention to his friend. "Yeah. Club's grown a lot."

Mason looked around before leaning toward him. "Am I picking up on some tension between you and your lady?"

Wyatt hesitated, then gestured for Mason to follow him down the entry hall to the study, where they could talk in relative privacy behind the closed French doors. "We didn't want you guys worrying about us, not with everything else you have going on. That's the only reason we haven't said anything."

Mason's brow puckered. "Said anything about what?"

"We're taking a break, I guess you could say. She called it *space*. Whatever that means."

Mason's dark eyes widened. "So you're ...?"

Wyatt shrugged. "I'm not sure what we are. We love each other, no question. But she has a different vision for the ministry, and I'm hesitant to make changes that could alienate our kids."

"And she asked for space?"

"Just to get a better sense of where God is leading her. And I get it. She needs to know for herself which direction He wants her to go. Even if it's away from ConnectUP. Or from me."

Just saying the words cut like a knife to the chest. If God intended him to live without Harper, he would need an abundance of peace about it. Because right now, he had precious little.

"That's amazingly astute for someone so new to her faith."

Wyatt leaned back against the edge of the desk. "Growing by leaps and bounds, and it's been a blessing to witness it front and center. She's on fire for the Lord, Mase. Absorbed in the Word, absolutely in love with God. I have to be willing to let her go if it turns out His plans for her and His plans for me don't mesh."

He chuckled, but it held no humor. "When Ellison suddenly reappeared, I thought no way was I going to stand by and lose her to him again. It never entered my mind I could lose her to God. But how can I be angry she made that choice?"

No matter how it gutted him.

Mason's eyes narrowed in thought. "You said she asked for space to figure out where God's leading her?"

"Pretty much."

"Are you doing the same?"

Wyatt cocked his head. "The same?"

"Are you taking this time to ask God where He's leading *you*? ConnectUP is three years strong now, but that doesn't mean it can't grow and change. Are you willing to ask God if it's time for your baby, this ministry you conceived, to spread its wings?"

Wyatt stared at this man he loved like a brother. This man who never hesitated to hold his feet to the fire.

I'm willing to be wrong, but I need some time to get alone with God so He can show me if I've misunderstood His leading. Harper's words in his head were so clear, she may as well have been standing in the room. He'd heard her the other night, but had he *listened?*

"And you know you aren't alone in any of this, brother." Mason's voice pulled him back. "We have the best set of leaders we've ever had, and more volunteers all the time. You don't have to carry this thing by yourself. If you have questions about what direction we may need to go, talk to us about it. We've got your back."

Mason pulled open the door. "Now, I'm going to go get some more of those pot-stickers before they're gone."

Wyatt nodded but didn't follow when Mason left the study.

I'm willing to be wrong ...

But was *he* willing to be wrong?

CHAPTER THIRTY-EIGHT

*H*arper leaned against the family room window, her back to the brightly lit deck outside the glass, watching the four girls seated by the fireplace huddled close in conversation. The laughter and restored camaraderie warmed her heart, a welcome change from the frozen barrenness of the past two days.

Rhonda came to stand beside her. "That's good to see."

She nodded. "I wasn't sure what to expect when I asked Tish to come with me to get Tonya."

"How'd you get them talking?"

Harper turned to face her friend, but her eyes instead fell on Wyatt standing at the island with a plate of food in his hand. With Allyson. The other woman's face glowed, and her free hand gestured in the air as she shared what must be a humorous story. And when that hand landed on Wyatt's forearm, pain seared through Harper's chest when the two shared a laugh.

I agree wholeheartedly … Your goal from the beginning has been to foster a safe environment for your kids.

Allyson's words rang in Harper's ears. Would Wyatt find

Allyson a more suitable partner in ministry? Because she didn't question him, didn't push him?

Harper peered down at her folded hands. Maybe she'd pushed him too far. Maybe if she apologized, put aside her convictions —

"Harper?"

Her head snapped up. "I'm sorry, what?"

Rhonda's furrowed brow softened. "Are you okay, sweetie?"

She glanced over at the two in the kitchen and back at her friend. "Um ... yes. I'm fine. Maybe a little tired. I'm sorry. What did you say?"

"I asked how you got the girls to talk."

"Oh. Uh, I just told Tish how upset Tonya was. That bringing Jill to CU wasn't about showing off, but about hoping Jill would find some direction, like they had. When we got to Tonya's, Tish was out of the car and running up the walk faster than I could unbuckle my seat belt. It was hard not to cry myself when I saw them holding on to each other in tears."

"I would've been a puddle."

"It was a sweet moment. When Remy and Beth saw Tish and Tonya were back on good terms, they were eager to welcome her back. I think they felt caught between them." She shook her head and turned to stand next to Rhonda, putting her back to the scene in the kitchen. "All that drama, and it's my fault. I really thought bridging that gap was the right way to go."

"Honey, it's not your fault. Your instincts were spot on."

Harper's pulse skipped with hope, as if she'd been thrown a lifeline in the sea of doubt she'd been treading since leaving here Thursday night. "You think so?"

"Absolutely! The girls' response was a shock to us all, and it's something we need to address. I know Mason—" Rhonda stopped as Tonya and Remy walked up. "Hey, girls. What's up?"

Tonya and Remy exchanged a quick glance. "We've been talking," Tonya said. "And we wanted to ask y'all's opinion on something."

"Sure." Harper looked around the room buzzing with activity, a myriad of voices, and a trio of chipmunks singing "It's Beginning to Look a Lot Like Christmas" blaring from the speakers in the ceiling.

Rhonda gestured to the hallway. "Let's go to Mason's room where it's quieter."

Harper followed Rhonda and the girls, glancing at Wyatt over her shoulder, still engrossed in conversation with Ally. In Mason's room, she looked around the tidy space. He'd only put his bed and a dresser in the room, nothing to decorate the walls or spruce it up since he was only here temporarily. She and Wyatt had discussed what to do with it once Mason moved out, and although she hadn't voiced it to Wyatt, her mind had gone directly to *nursery*. Two days ago, that seemed like a not-so-out-there possibility for the future.

But now ...

"Like I said, we've been talking," Tonya said. "About inviting Jill and Kendra to our next meeting. I think I can talk Jill into coming back. She was asking a lot of questions about it before ... well, the first time."

Harper snapped back to the conversation. "Wait. Kendra? From the cheer squad?"

Remy nodded. "She's my cousin. My uncle got hurt last year and can't work. They lost their house, and they're on government assistance. They don't know it, but my parents paid all of her cheer expenses anonymously so she could stay on the squad. But she's really scared and isn't sure who she can trust, so she hasn't confided in anybody."

"And you want to invite her to club?"

"I think she'd like CU. We used to be really close before high school. Then she was top-tier, and I was ... well, me." She pushed her red glasses up on her nose. "Since they're living with my grandparents, we see each other a lot more and have been hanging out and stuff."

The spark in Tonya's eyes matched her smile. "Can we invite them?"

Harper bit her lip, uneasy making these decisions about ConnectUP without Wyatt's input. She certainly didn't assume she was right and he was wrong. God had given her a heart for girls who needed to find their way in a world sending them all kinds of erroneous messages about their worth. And Wyatt empathized with kids who felt socially ostracized.

If only they could merge their convictions without constantly being at odds. The past couple of days had been difficult, not seeing him, not speaking with him. Many tears had fallen, and prayers had been lifted, but the yearning that flowed through her at seeing him the second she'd come in the door tonight had almost taken her breath away. The longing to drop everything and walk into his arms had asserted itself as a physical ache, no matter how hard she'd tried to prepare herself on the drive over.

"Maybe start with an outing," she suggested, not wanting Wyatt to feel backed into a corner if some of her cheerleaders suddenly showed up at club. "Christmas shopping or something. Jill may not be comfortable coming back yet, and we also have to consider how the other kids would feel."

Tonya's eyes brightened. "That's a good idea. But there's no way we'll talk Beth into Christmas shopping."

"A movie?" Remy offered.

Tonya nodded. "Or drive around to see Christmas lights."

Remy's dark eyes lit up. "I love that idea! Maybe next Saturday?"

"That sounds like fun," Harper said. "If you'd like for me to come along, I could ask Wyatt if we can borrow his SUV."

"Yes, absolutely!" Tonya turned to Rhonda. "And you, too, if you can."

"I'd love to," Rhonda answered, smiling. "But I have this little wedding coming up and a million things yet to do."

Harper looked back at the girls. "See if the others can do next Saturday, and we'll make a plan." Assuming Wyatt would be okay with her borrowing his vehicle once he knew why. She shouldn't have volunteered that until she knew. If he couldn't do it, then maybe she could get Connor and Lynne's van.

Excitement laced the girls' voices as they left the room with Rhonda, and Harper sank down onto the side of the bed. Mental and physical exhaustion pulled at her limbs, and her insides felt as if everything had been moved around, and none of it liked its new location.

But that had nothing on the jumble that was her brain. The girls wanting to reach out to be the imprint of Jesus on two others outside their own peer group was exactly what she'd believed could happen.

Yet she knew Wyatt didn't agree. He saw nothing but potential disaster putting the two groups together, and the drama that unfolded on Wednesday only cemented his resolve. She couldn't blame him. All he could see was what happened to his best friend when Glen put too much stock in the attention of someone he considered greater than himself.

Crossing her arms over her middle, she doubled over in an effort to hold back the tears she'd been fighting all evening. But when a pair of gentle arms wrapped around her shoulders, she lost the battle.

"Mason told me, sweetie," Rhonda said in a quiet voice. "I could sense something wasn't right, but I had no idea."

Harper sat up and leaned into her friend's embrace. "This is *your* time, and you shouldn't think about anything else but starting your lives together."

"But we're family. And family sticks together."

"Rhonda, I miss him. It's only been two days, but we're already so far apart in spirit. And my heart—" She swiped at her cheek. "I've lived most of my life trying to do and be what would please the people I love. My parents, my friends. Even Brett. It's Wyatt who encouraged me to be me, the way God made me, and to go where He leads, despite who it might disappoint. Ironic that when I finally get it, the person it's taking me away from is Wyatt."

"Oh, honey, don't give up on the two of you yet. Keep seeking God, and pray for Wyatt to have wisdom in how he leads the ministry."

"I do every day and have from the beginning. I love him so much. But if God should take me another direction, I have to walk that road. No matter what it might cost."

CHAPTER THIRTY-NINE

*W*yatt walked his young client out to his parents sitting in the counseling practice waiting room, then returned to his office. His next appointment had canceled, so he planned to take advantage of the free time to work on the grant proposal. But ten minutes later, his fingers still rested on the keys of his laptop, waiting for instructions his brain had yet to send. If only he could string together a cohesive thought.

He stifled a yawn and stretched, letting his elbows come to rest on the arms of his office chair. Sleep had been in short supply the past few days, and he'd worked at keeping himself busy so he wouldn't have time to think about Harper.

Seeing her at the Christmas party and again last night at the Monday team meeting was nowhere near enough when what he longed to do was wrap her in his arms and not let go. Last night's only one-on-one conversation between them consisted of her asking if she could borrow his SUV for an outing with some of her girls on Saturday. At least she'd been up front about it and explained it would be both CU girls with a couple of her cheerleaders, at the request of Tonya and Remy.

Surprised delight at his agreement had dispelled the

uncertainty in her eyes upon asking her favor. How he wished he could give her the answer that would keep that light in her eyes, and fix the widening fissure between them.

Are you willing to ask God if it's time for your baby, this ministry you conceived, to spread its wings?

Mason's exhortation had hung over Wyatt's head since his friend delivered it Saturday night. But the courage to do so hadn't shown up until this morning's quiet time, when he'd hit his knees to ask God to show him if there was something more CU should be doing. Something he'd missed by placing his sole focus on kids like Glen.

A knock sounded on the frame of his open office door, and he looked up where one of his partners stood in the doorway. "Hey, Jim. What can I do for you?"

Jim strode into the office. "You know I'm one of the crisis counselors at Conway High, on call whenever there's a tragic event or a kid they determine needs intervention."

"Right."

"They've asked if I could come see one of their kids this afternoon, but I have a packed schedule. Thought I'd check in with you, since I know you went to school there."

"What's the story?"

Jim sat in one of the chairs in front of the desk. "Finn Colter. Football player. Junior. Doing in-school suspension as we speak." He handed Wyatt a USB flash drive. "I downloaded the file the school sent me in case you wanted to take a look. Short version is he beat up a kid after the game Friday. Put this kid in the hospital overnight. Lucky he's not eighteen, or he could be looking at time. The other boy's family already has an attorney."

Wyatt plugged the drive into the side of his laptop. "Suing him or the school district?"

"Everybody. I doubt they'll get very far with the district, since it happened off-campus after school hours, but Finn comes from deep pockets. I'm sure there'll be a substantial financial settlement to keep it out of juvenile court."

Wyatt opened the file named *Colter* and scrolled through it. "What about the parents?"

"Dad's not in the picture at all, according to Dr. Anders, the principal. Mom's remarried, corporate attorney, and the stepfather is CEO of a large tech company. Both very career-oriented and mostly absent."

Wyatt skimmed through the file. He remembered Finn from the football games he'd attended with Harper. Outstanding player. And according to the file, popular among his peers. Homecoming Court this year, class rep his sophomore year, football awards, varsity baseball since his freshman year. From outward appearances, a kid with everything, but upon a deeper dive, carrying the weight of circumstances outside his control. Starting with aloof parents not dialed in to what was going on with their own child.

Just like Jill.

And just like Harper.

He pushed the unbidden comparison aside and scanned through the rest of the report. "School's out at what time?"

"Three-forty-five, but he's supposed to stay until four-thirty. I'd have to cancel two appointments to get over there, so I wanted to see if you might be able to take it."

"My three o'clock canceled, so I'm actually free." And grateful for the opportunity to fill his time, and his thoughts.

"Thanks, man. Dr. Anders is concerned for this kid and doesn't want him getting expelled. Or worse."

Wyatt nodded. *Worse* could be anything from running away to bringing an act of violence on the school or anything in between.

He stood and grabbed his keys off his desk. "I'll head over there now."

Twenty minutes later, he checked in at the school reception

desk and picked up his guest badge. He hadn't even made it to a chair when the principal walked out to greet him.

"Dr. Anders." Wyatt shook the man's hand. "It's been a long time."

"It certainly has. Not that we ever saw much of you in here." Dr. Anders led the way into his office. "Your name only came across my desk if you were getting another award for something. Have a seat."

"Thank you." Wyatt took a chair at a small round table in a corner of the office while Dr. Anders took one across from him.

"I can't say I'm surprised to see all you've accomplished. And knowing how the Glen Bennett tragedy affected you, I can understand why Adolescent Psychology would be your chosen vocation."

"Yes, sir. That's been the driving force behind a lot of what I've done."

The older man sighed. "Unfortunately, he isn't the last one we've lost to suicide. We've had two more since your class graduated. I did a quick check on you when Jim called to say you'd be coming in his stead, and I see you're involved in a ministry for kids who might otherwise choose a bad path. As a believer myself, and one who's worked with teens his entire career, I can't say how happy I am to see something like that out there."

"Yes, sir. We started ConnectUP to reach at-risk kids, on the fringe, as it were, to show them there's a better voice they should listen to."

Something akin to weariness settled into Dr. Anders' features. "I wish there was something like that for these kids who think they have to push and bully their way through life to find their value. Like this kid you're here to see. If there was ever an at-risk kid, Finn's your guy, even though he's not on the fringe."

Wyatt's pulse spiked as he studied the man across from him, a man who'd spent his entire career on the front lines of this battlefield called high school. A man with a wealth of wisdom and experience. A man who'd just described a top-tier kid—a bully—as at-risk. Too bad Wyatt didn't put stock in coincidences. Sometimes that would be more convenient to accept than divine purpose. Was God already answering his morning's plea?

He rose from the table. "Okay. Let's go meet Finn."

Dr. Anders led him down the hall and into a room where a boy the size of a grown man looked up from his textbook when they walked in. Wyatt caught a hint of apprehension in the teen's dark eyes before he masked it with an air of annoyance.

"Finn," Dr. Anders said. "This is Dr. Wyatt McCowan. Dr. McCowan, this is Finn Colter."

"Doctor?" The boy shook a lock of brown hair out of his eyes. "I don't need no doctor."

"Dr. McCowan's a psychologist. And it's a mandatory part of your suspension to meet with a counselor."

Finn huffed and leaned back in his chair, crossing his arms over his chest. "Nobody said nothin' about me needin' a head doctor."

"I'm not a shrink." Wyatt sat down across the table from the young man sending him a glare. "I just listen. Or not. Whatever you want."

"So, if I don't wanna say nothin', you'll just sit there starin' at me?"

"Something like that."

Dr. Anders walked to the door. "I'll leave you be. Let me know if you need anything, Doctor."

"Yes, sir." The principal closed the door behind him, and Wyatt turned back to Finn. "Can't say as I've been in this room before."

"You haven't met with any other prisoners here?" Anger rolled off the kid like steam across a hot spring. "I thought it was *mandatory*."

Wyatt shook his head. "Nope. You're my first. I actually went to school here. Just had my ten-year reunion."

"And you came back willingly? Man, once I'm out of here, I'm never comin' back."

"Seriously? I thought you had a lot of friends here, that you're a star football player. I've seen you play. Good stuff."

"Yeah, but we're out now."

"You play baseball, don't you?"

"Yep. It's doubtful I'll get to play college football, but maybe I can get on somewhere with baseball."

"That's a great goal. What are you doing to achieve it?"

Finn's forehead crinkled. "What's that supposed to mean?"

"That's quite an undertaking. It'll require a lot of work, more than just showing up for your games this year, and this is the year you need to catch the attention of college scouts. If you have a goal, you need a plan to achieve it."

Finn peered at him for a long moment, but at least the granite stare had dissipated into inquisitiveness. "I dunno. Maybe batting cages or something."

"That's a good start. I know regular workouts are part of your football regimen, so don't let them fall off. Keep up the work, but look into what kind of program you need to implement to pinpoint your specific position. Which is ...?"

"Outfield. Center."

"Then you need to be fast, with a good throwing arm. You're a tight end in football, right?"

"Mostly."

"Keep up your running. Don't add any time to your sprints. A lot of ground to cover in center field."

"Yeah. Okay, that makes sense." His eyes narrowed. "You played baseball?"

"Not really. Little League but not high school ball. Just a rabid sports fan." The bell sounded, and he looked at his watch. "If I can clear it with the principal, you wanna head out and hit a few in the cages out back? Just to help you get into the swing. Pun completely intended."

The barest hint of a grin almost softened the boy's scowl. "We can do that? I'm supposed to be in solitary confinement until four-thirty."

Wyatt leaned forward and crossed his arms on the table. "Now, see, there you go again, thinking of this as something negative."

Finn's right eyebrow disappeared into his bangs. "You do know why I'm here, right?"

"I do. But everything in life is a matter of perspective. You made a choice—not a smart one—but then I think you already know that." The boy's face colored. "Think of this as an opportunity to figure out why you made that choice and how you can make a better one next time. This is good chill time. You don't have to be *on* for anybody. You can be just Finn, in here getting to know Finn. Yeah, for the school, it's punishment. But for you, it's whatever you make of it.

"As for getting out of here, I'll check with Dr. Anders. But as long as you're on campus under supervision, it should be fine."

Finn gestured toward the door. "Have at it, then. I'm sick of these four walls."

After getting an eager thumbs up from Dr. Anders, Wyatt took Finn out to the cages set up next to the high school baseball field where they spent almost an hour hitting balls flung at them from a pitching machine. He let the boy give him tips on how to anticipate the pitch and power through his swing, and even had him laughing a few times. A big departure from the sullen kid he'd met not two hours before.

Finn stuck their bats back into the slots they came out of. "So, uh, are you gonna come back, or was this a one-time deal?"

"I'm happy to come back if you'd like."

Finn looked around, then down at his feet, toeing a stone

on the ground with his tennis shoe for a moment before bringing his eyes back to Wyatt. "Yeah, like, if you wanna, that would be all right with me."

"Sure thing. I'll come by tomorrow after my appointments. We can even hit a few again if you want."

For the briefest of moments, Finn's face lit up more like the boy he should be rather than the big man on campus he was trying to be. And in that moment, Wyatt saw a kid who just wanted someone to value him. To *see* him. Not because of what he could do on an athletic field, but just because he *was*.

Just like the ConnectUP kids.

CHAPTER FORTY

*H*arper set her salad down on Emery's dining room table Thursday evening and took her place between Tom at the head and her mother beside her.

"Your young man couldn't join us tonight?" Mom asked.

Harper shook her head. With everything she was about to drop on her unsuspecting parents, telling them she and Wyatt were taking some time apart could wait. "He had plans to go hit baseballs with one of the kids."

Which she found out from Rhonda when they'd spoken that afternoon, not Wyatt himself. Except for a brief hello at last night's club, her last conversation with him had occurred on Monday when she'd asked if she could borrow his SUV this Saturday.

"Does he do things like that often? Spend his off hours with kids?"

"All the time. He's very dedicated." One of the things she loved most about him.

Her eyes burned, and she looked down at her plate. Today marked one week since that awful night she realized God could be leading them down separate paths. But if anything, her love for him had grown. As had the pain of being apart.

Tom took Emery's hand and reached for Harper's. "Let's pray."

The family joined hands around the table. While Tom prayed aloud, Harper prayed silently for the strength and the words she would need tonight. When she told Emery two days ago that she'd changed her major, Emery couldn't contain her excitement.

Knowing she needed to share her decision with her parents, Harper had gratefully accepted when Emery suggested they get together for dinner, offering her home as neutral territory. If only Connor and Lynne could be here, as well, but they had another obligation.

After Tom finished his prayer, Dad reached for the platter of roast while Emery picked up the salad to start it around the table. Harper wasn't sure if it was the aroma of beef cooked with carrots, potatoes, and onions that had her stomach rumbling or if it was her nerves. But she was determined to enjoy this time with her family, in case the evening should end less than favorably.

Over dinner, she did a lot of listening and nodding, unable to contribute much more with her thoughts in a jumble and stomach in knots. Before long, they cleared the table and settled in the living room with coffee. For her part, she decided to forgo the caffeine rush as her adrenaline level had her heart racing already.

Mom, seated on the loveseat next to their father, took a sip and placed the cup back on the saucer she held in her lap. "How are your finals going, Harper, honey?"

"I feel good about the ones I've taken so far. I have my last one Monday, then I'm done."

"You've worked very hard this semester. I don't know how you do it all, with school and work, your cheerleaders, and your other kids, but I've also never seen you so ... happy. So content. It makes me glad, after all you've been through."

"Thanks, Mom." How she wished she could bask in her

mother's uncharacteristic encouragement before she burst her bubble. "I am happy. And I've learned a lot over the past few months."

"Oh? About what?"

Harper looked from her mother to her father, both of them watching her intently, as if truly interested in what she had to say.

"About me. And God. About who He is and how He can take everything from my past and use it to help others find their way, hopefully sooner than I did.

"But even though I made some atrocious decisions, I can see how God is using all of that in our ministry, and with my cheer girls. Aside from being Megan's mother, I've honestly never felt as passionate about anything as I do about these kids. I feel—I *know* God is calling me into student ministry. I've prayed about it a lot, then I met with an advisor in the Christian Studies Department about changing my major."

Her mother exchanged a quick look with Dad. "Student ministry. And what would that be, exactly?"

Harper kept her chin up while her heart sank. Her head had told her to expect push-back, but her heart hoped for acceptance. "Any number of things. But my burden has been to bridge the gap between kids who live on both sides of the social divide. I found an organization in Atlanta that's planning to launch a ministry with this objective, and they've invited me to meet with them over my winter break."

Dad studied her. He rarely spoke without thought, and she could practically see the wheels turning behind his eyes. "Honey, can you make a decent living in ... religious work? With a psychology degree, you have numerous options, including working with young people."

Her mother gave her head a shake. "I can't imagine Wyatt would be on board with this. Not with having such a successful practice of his own."

"Wyatt fully supports my decision," Harper answered.

"He's the one who encouraged me to pray about what I wanted to do with my future. He could see I wasn't all that excited about my studies, but how invested I was in the kids. I feel alive when I'm with them. I've never experienced that with anything, except with Megan."

Mom placed her cup and saucer on the coffee table and sat forward, her hands folded in her lap. Her psychologist-about-to-get-to-the-crux-of-the-matter posture. "Sweetie, I think what's happening here is a bit of transference. That's not altogether a bad thing, in the right context. But Megan would be nine now. The students in your club thing are just a few years older. I believe what you're experiencing is a place to put all of those maternal instincts that have nowhere else to go. It's certainly not a sound foundation upon which to build your entire career. Your future. I'm shocked Wyatt can't see that."

Harper's throat tightened, and she stared down at her hands clasped in a tight grip. She wouldn't cry. Not now. Maybe later, when she once again lay in bed trying to sleep. The dark and the quiet of night only compounded the loneliness—the deep pang of missing Wyatt. She could pile on the knowledge that she'd once again fallen in her parents' estimation and have one, big cry.

After several seconds, she looked back at her parents. "I can understand why you would believe that. I love these kids, and I do feel maternal toward them, no question. But it's the Lord who gave me that instinct. Entrusted me with a child He knew would need a mother to walk her through her short but traumatic life. He gave her to me, knowing I would move every mountain I could to make her happy and comfortable in her four years on this earth. He gave her to *me*, because He'd already entrusted me with the instinct and love and zeal to meet her needs as much as was within my ability."

She paused to take a steadying breath. "Even though I wasn't following Him at the time, He gave me everything I needed to be a good mother. Everything I need to be a good minister to kids."

Emery sniffled and brushed a tear from her cheek. "You were a spectacular mother to Megan. With an abundance of grace and wisdom beyond your years. If you can give that to kids who need to find their way, then I know God chose you specifically for that purpose."

Tom nodded. "You have our unwavering support, Harper. Prayer, finances, resources. Whatever you need, we're here for you."

So much for waiting until later to cry. "Thank you." Her voice was a whisper, the only sound she could push through the emotion clogging her throat. "That means the world to me."

She looked at her mother, who stared back with a deep *V* between her brows. "If this is transference, Mom, then it's God-ordained. That's all I can offer to help you accept my decision."

Her parents exchanged a grim look before her mother turned back. "I don't know what to say if this is your final decision. But we can't support you in it." She stood, and Dad followed. "I only hope you come to your senses before you find yourself floundering again because you have no career foundation."

Harper stood and faced them, pulled her shoulders back, and willed calmness into her voice. "I understand. But I have to do what I believe with all my soul God is calling me to do."

And at that moment, every last shred of unease and doubt fell away. As if she'd only needed to confess it out loud, in the face of objection from the two people she most wanted to please on this earth, for the truth to take root. For her courage to show up.

Standing here now, with her parents' disapproval once again hanging over her, without Wyatt bolstering her with his love and faith, she felt strong, free. Steadfast even though her path ahead still lay unknown in front of her.

In the past, when she had no sure direction, no clear picture of her future, she felt lost, afraid, and in turmoil.

Today, having no sure direction, no clear picture of her future, all she felt was ... peace.

So much so, she decided her parents needed to know everything.

"Before you leave, there's one more thing I need to tell you. About Wyatt."

CHAPTER FORTY-ONE

*W*yatt pulled into the lot of the popular local diner, parked, and glanced at his watch. Five minutes early, but he spotted the Townsends' black Mercedes sedan already parked in the next row. Dr. Townsend's call yesterday afternoon had been a surprise, but no more than his invitation to meet with him and Harper's mother this Saturday morning. Wyatt had wondered why they wanted to go to breakfast during the time Harper had cheer practice, until her father had asked him to keep it confidential.

He'd reserved judgment on that, however. After he heard what they had to say, he'd determine if he could follow through on that request.

Inside the diner, David Townsend waved him over to a corner booth, where he stood with his unsmiling wife.

"Good morning, Wyatt." Harper's dad reached out to shake his hand.

"Dr. Townsend." He looked at the woman staring up at him, her face a mask that told him nothing of what might transpire during this visit. "Mrs. Townsend."

"Wyatt." She gestured to the opposite side of the table. "Please, have a seat."

He slid into the booth across from the older couple. Older but still striking in appearance. Camille Townsend, like her daughters, was the very essence of class. Even dressed casually in jeans and a sweater with high-heeled brown boots, and with every chin-length dark hair in place, she exuded confidence and status.

Her husband, the highly esteemed physician, had grayed more than his wife—although she may have had help in that regard—but was himself a picture of health and fitness.

Once they'd placed their orders and coffee had been poured, Dr. Townsend clasped his hands on the table. "Thank you again for meeting us this morning."

"Sure thing. Although I don't know if you're aware—"

"That you and Harper are no longer seeing each other?" Mrs. Townsend finished for him. "Yes, we're aware."

He could only nod, wondering what they'd been told. Did they blame him for the breakup? If so, he'd gladly take it on himself, preferring they find fault with him rather than Harper. Not that there was any fault to assign. Not in his opinion. It simply was … what it was.

"But she said you were still close," Dr. Townsend said. "That her decision had nothing to do with how she felt about you but with her trying to find her way."

Wyatt looked down into his coffee. "I've loved Harper my entire life, it seems." He looked back up at the couple across from him. "But I can't fault her for making the decision she did. Maybe we'll find our way back to each other, and maybe we won't. We have to wait on God to provide that answer."

"Then it's true that you support her claim that she feels a *calling* from God?"

"One hundred percent."

Mrs. Townsend took a sip of coffee and placed her cup back on the table. "And you believe you have a calling to ministry as well? Even with your practice being so successful?"

"Yes, ma'am. I've been called to ministry since grad school.

My ultimate goal is to grow ConnectUP into a national organization and work it full-time once it can support salaries. That's the vision God has given me."

"And Harper shares this vision?"

He shook his head, trying to keep his disappointment from showing on his face. "Not entirely. She sees a niche that ConnectUP isn't addressing, and it's been heavy on her heart. Heavy on mine that I can't seem to figure out how to fix that without hurting the kids we're already working with."

Although this afternoon might shed some light on that, if his plan to have Finn over to spend some time with a few of the CU guys didn't backfire like the Jill fiasco.

Their breakfast came, and the young waitress topped off their coffee. She responded to his "thank you" with a wink, looking him up and down before she walked away. His face heated when Dr. Townsend gave him a knowing grin. Great. Being hit on right in front of Harper's folks.

"May I bless this real quick?" he asked, hoping they could see that he in no way returned the young woman's interest.

"Uh ... sure." Dr. Townsend put down his fork. "Please do."

Wyatt prayed over their meal, and all was silent while they salted and peppered eggs, poured syrup over pancakes, and sipped from tall glasses of orange juice.

Mrs. Townsend poked at her eggs with a fork, studying her plate with a crease in her brow. Without taking a bite of her breakfast, she set her fork back down and looked at him. "How does one decipher a *calling* from God? How do you know it's not simply your own aspirations?"

He took the time to chew and swallow a bite of pancake to formulate his answer. "First, you need to know God. Not just believe in Him but *know* Him. Know His attributes, what's true, and what would go against His character.

"Second, pray for wisdom, knowledge, direction. Then ... listen. Meditate. And I don't mean in a Zen, mystical kind of way. I mean in a focused, quiet way. Away from the clamor of life and the noise of other voices so you can hear Him."

Mrs. Townsend's eyes widened. "You can't tell me you actually hear God."

He swallowed a bite of eggs and followed it with a sip of OJ. "I can't say that I've ever audibly heard God's voice, but I have had very clear stirrings, for want of a better word, that I knew were from God. A sudden urge to call somebody only to find they needed that call right then. Or an impulse to help a perfect stranger that sometimes turns into a conversation where I can introduce Christ. I've had many occasions like that. ConnectUP is a result of a very strong conviction I'd had for a while but didn't have the opportunity for until about three years ago. And God's blessed us beyond my wildest imaginings."

"And you knew that how?" Dr. Townsend asked. "A stirring, an impulse. We all have those. How do you attribute that to God?"

"That's a great question. And the truth is, not every idea or impulse I've followed has been Spirit-led. But God can't steer us if we're not moving. When I get a sense He might be trying to lead me somewhere, I at least move in the direction I believe He's taking me. Sometimes I find a closed door and understand that perhaps I made a wrong turn or misunderstood. And sometimes, He wants to teach me more from the journey than the destination. It's not always about arriving. It's about the willingness to follow."

Dr. Townsend nodded, his eyes narrowed in thought. Mrs. Townsend finally took a bite of her omelet, staring out the window as she chewed. The silence stretched for several seconds, and Wyatt prayed something, anything, he might have said would help them understand Harper's faith a little better.

The doctor cleared his throat. "You're a bright young man, Wyatt. Highly educated. In science, even. Psychology. How do you reconcile faith in something—some*one*—you can't see or hear with the facts you know about how the brain works? How we make the choices we make?"

Wyatt swiped his napkin across his mouth and placed it next to his plate. "Dr. Townsend, I can't look at how intricately we're made, how complex our brains are, how our bodies function with all of these moving parts, and *not* have faith.

"You asked me if I believed Harper was truly following a calling from God, and I said a hundred percent. The reason I believe that is because she's poured herself, heart and soul, into her relationship with Him. Her faith is much deeper than some people who have been Christians for years. People who have a lot of head knowledge but they haven't experienced God. Harper has. She's always seeking, always in learning mode, and always willing to do the hard thing if it's the right thing."

Even if it meant walking away from him ... again.

"Then you're on board with her traipsing all over the country for research?"

Wyatt looked at the man across from him, his mind blank. "I'm sorry?"

Mrs. Townsend waved her hand back and forth. "Oh, you know. This trip to Atlanta she's taking later this month. To meet with some ministry people who supposedly think they can help bullied kids and their aggressors come to some kind of understanding. Or something like that."

His thoughts spun and gut twisted. Harper had been researching other ministries? Ministries she felt were succeeding where he had ... failed?

Disappointment and confusion pulled at his spirit, but he needed to keep his head in the game. Right now, this moment, it was more important to help the Townsends understand their daughter's faith.

A faith that appeared to be pulling her farther away by the day.

CHAPTER FORTY-TWO

*H*arper parked Wyatt's SUV in his garage at a quarter to midnight and turned off the ignition, torn between hoping he might still be awake so they could spend a few minutes together and doubting the wisdom of it. It was hard to be alone together, almost awkward, as they navigated this new ... whatever it was.

She wished she knew where their middle ground was, because one thing was clear. God hadn't moved her away from her conviction that ConnectUP should broaden its scope, and it didn't appear Wyatt had moved from his position that nothing should change.

If only he could have seen the girls that evening. Six girls from different peer groups, laughing, talking, sharing snacks, exchanging phone numbers. It couldn't have gone any better.

She gathered up her purse and jacket and climbed down from the Sequoia. In the kitchen, the light over the stove had been left on and the fob to her Audi sat on the island. Seeing no other signs of life, she picked up her fob and hung Wyatt's on the hook by the door to the garage.

"Harper?"

She spun to find him sitting up from where he'd been

lying on the sectional. He ran a hand through his sleep-tousled hair, and her heart almost combusted as he walked toward her.

"Hi." She clutched her bag and jacket to keep from throwing her arms around his neck. "I'm sorry it's so late."

"No problem." He stopped in front of her, wearing a navy DHU sweatshirt, loose jeans, and thick socks. Not much different from her attire, except she wore tennis shoes. "How'd it go tonight?"

"Really great. And I promise, no spills or crumbs in your car."

He swiped a hand through his hair again, and she so wanted to reach up to brush an errant lock off his forehead. "I wasn't worried. I'm glad you had a good time."

"You should get some sleep. You look done in. Long week?"

His gaze bored into hers for a moment, as if assessing her, but he finally just shrugged. "I guess. Finals, three new clients, finishing up my book, and ConnectUP stuff."

"The semester's almost done, then maybe we'll both have some more time to decompress."

"Hopefully." The furrow in his brow deepened.

"Um, well, I guess I should go. Thanks again for letting me use your car. Oh, and it's all gassed up."

"You didn't have to do that."

"No problem." Their gazes locked for several more seconds, and she couldn't deny the pull that still existed between them. She wanted to walk into his arms and stay there for days. Did he feel it too? Was his struggle as agonizing as hers?

Did he want to reach for her as much as she wanted him to?

Disappointment cascaded over her when, instead of pulling her to him, he crossed his arms tightly over his chest. Of course it was for the best. But right now, her heart, her mind, and her body didn't want best. All of her just wanted *him*. Even if only for a moment.

"Listen," he said, drawing her out of her ruminations. "I wanted to talk to you about some things, but it's so late now, and I'm half out of it. Can we do lunch after church tomorrow?"

Her heart jumped, but she wasn't sure if it was excitement that he wanted to spend some time with her, or dread of what he might have to say.

"I'd love to, but I'm actually going back to my old church tomorrow and have dinner plans after."

His face blanched. "You're going back? I thought you loved our church. Please don't leave because of ... this."

"Oh, I'm not. I do love our church. It's just for tomorrow. So much has happened that I haven't told you. I wish we..." She sighed and shook her head.

"Me too. I hate this distance. I understand it, though, Harper, and it's actually been good for me. I've spent hours in the Word and praying ... and missing you. Missing *us*."

"I miss us too." Her voice felt tight with the pain in her chest.

"Well, tomorrow night, you're hosting Rhonda's shower, so I won't really get to talk to you before Monday's planning meeting."

"I guess not. Was there something in particular that you ... you wanted to talk to me about?"

His jaw worked for a moment as he stared at her, and her stomach rolled into a ball. "Were you going to let me know about Atlanta?"

A chill scrolled down her spine. "Atlanta? How did you—how do you know about that?"

"Your parents told me."

Her jaw fell slack. "My parents? When did—"

"This morning. They asked me to breakfast."

She pulled her shoulders back, that chill turning to heat. "To what? Talk about *me*? About what a mistake I'm making? And what was the general consensus? That Harper's lost her mind?"

"Of course not. They had some misgivings, some questions. I should have told you I met with them. I thought about it when you came by this afternoon, but the guys were here, and you were on your way to spend the evening with the girls. Not the best time."

"I can understand that, but what I don't get is why you didn't let me know immediately after being issued the invitation. Did you not think I had a right to know what was going on behind my back?"

"Like you researching other ministries behind mine? To see how wrong I've been?"

Her cheeks warmed. "I wasn't doing that behind your back, Wyatt. I was trying to find out if I was even on the right track. I didn't start researching until after you and I—after we decided to take some time. That was the whole point, to see where God might be leading each of us. I've never once thought you've been wrong in the way you minister to our kids. I just wondered if we could do *more*. But you've been dead set against making any changes, so I wasn't sure if you'd even want to know what I found."

"Well, I do. I'd love to know." He sighed and bowed his head to rub his brow with his fingers.

She bit her lip, wishing she could take back the last two minutes of this conversation. She could have done a better job of controlling her tongue. But finding out her parents had reached out to Wyatt rankled. As if they hoped he would somehow intervene to keep her on the road *they* felt she should be on.

Which made Mom's phone call that afternoon even more confusing.

He looked back up at her, his eyes hooded with exhaustion.

"I'm sorry, Harper. I didn't mean that to sound so snarky. I'm struggling with my own frus —"

Her phone chirped with an incoming call and she reached for it in her purse. "It's Jill."

"*Now*? It's midnight."

She pressed the icon to answer. "Hey, Jill, what's up?"

"Hi, Harper. I'm sorry to bother you so late after you spent the whole evening with us, but I'm not sure what to do."

"No apology needed, honey. What's going on?" Road noises sounded through the phone, so Jill must be in her car. But where could the girl be going at this time of night when Harper dropped her off at her front door not even a half hour ago? "Are you driving somewhere?"

"I need to find Dwight."

Harper's stomach dropped and her gaze flew to Wyatt. "Why do you need to find Dwight? Does your mom know you're out?"

"She's at the hospital. She's been taking a lot of extra shifts lately. And I really need to find him. He sent me a bunch of texts the whole time we were out tonight, even though he knew I was with the girls. But his last few … I don't know. He sounds … weird. I'm worried."

So was Harper, but not so much for Dwight as she was for Jill and what might happen if, or when, she found her over-domineering boyfriend. Especially if he was angry she'd spent the night out with her friends instead of with him.

When Wyatt gestured to his ear, Harper put the phone on speaker. "Okay. I'm with Wyatt right now. Tell us what you're worried about."

"I'm not sure, exactly. Just some things he said in his last few texts. And he left me a couple of voicemails where it sounds like maybe he's been drinking or took something."

Wyatt stepped closer. "Jill, honey, listen to me. If he's under the influence or angry, you don't want to be with him by yourself. Do you know where he is?"

"I'm pretty sure at the swings in Sherman Park, over by his house. His last text said if he meant anything to me at all, to meet him where we first kissed or I would never see him again. I don't know what that means."

Harper's gaze locked with Wyatt's. The boy might only be trying to get Jill's attention. Or he might have something more serious in mind. Either way, it couldn't be ignored.

Wyatt looked at the phone on the counter. "We're on our way to you but stop and wait for me before you approach him. Got it? I mean it, Jill. Do not go try to find him on your own."

"Okay. I—I got it. But please hurry."

CHAPTER FORTY-THREE

*W*yatt grabbed his fob off the hook and ran out to the Sequoia, Harper right behind him. His gut twisted. Had Dwight been drinking? Had he taken something? Was he making empty threats, or did he have more serious intentions? Maybe they should call the police, but what would he tell them? There's a kid who's mad because his girlfriend isn't paying him enough attention? Doubtful that call would be high on the priority list.

"Stay on the line with me," Harper told Jill as they climbed into the SUV.

She braced herself against the dash with her free hand as he backed out of the garage and onto the street faster than he ever had. He couldn't help the comparison to that night ten-and-a-half years ago, when he'd had a bad feeling about letting his best friend go down to the park alone. He hadn't gone with his gut that night, but tonight, he'd break every road rule he needed to if it meant he could prevent a potential tragedy. Just as he would have if he'd known Glen—

"I shouldn't have ignored his texts all evening." Jill's tension-filled voice continued from Harper's phone.

"Sweetie, this is not your fault in any way. And more than

268

likely, he's just being dramatic to get your attention." She looked over at Wyatt and crossed her fingers.

"Hopefully," he said under his breath as he took a quick turn onto the road that would take them to the upscale subdivision and neighboring park. After a four-minute drive that felt like twenty, and with Harper doing a remarkable job keeping the girl calm, they pulled around a curve where Jill's BMW sat parked next to a black Jeep in the otherwise empty lot.

They were barely out of the car before Jill started into the park at a near jog. Wyatt went after her and pulled her up by the arm.

"Whoa. I'll go."

"No, I need—"

"Just until we know what condition he's in. Okay? Just let me check it out." He gestured to Harper as she ran up to them and took the girl in her arms. "You both stay in the SUV where it's warm."

He took off toward the playground. A cold wind swiped at his face as he ran headlong into the darkness under a canopy of oak trees.

Please use me, Lord, to help this boy. If only I'd had the chance to go after Glen.

He slowed when the trees thinned, and he could make out the playground in the light of the moon. A boy sat slumped on one of the bowed rubber swings, his large frame incongruous with the innocence of his surroundings. Before he could gently alert the boy to his presence, Dwight sprang to his feet and whirled to face him. Wyatt put his hands out in defense against the gun now pointed square at him, suddenly regretting his choice to not call the cops.

"Easy now, son."

"Who are you?"

"Wyatt. A friend of Jill's cheer coach. Jill was worried about you and asked us for help."

"I don't need your help. I just need Jill. Is she here?"

Wyatt let his gaze fall to the gun in the boy's shaking hand before looking back up into his eyes. "Put the gun down on the ground and we can talk."

Dwight looked at the gun as if only just realizing he had it before lowering it to his side.

"All the way to the ground, please."

The boy stared down at his feet for so long, Wyatt wasn't sure whether to wait him out or tackle him. If he saw one twitch—

"Did she even bother to come?" Dwight's quiet voice barely sounded over the chilled breeze.

"She did. But I didn't know what she would find so I wouldn't let her come over here."

Finally, the gun dropped to the ground with a soft thud and the boy sank back down on the swing, burying his face in his hands.

With slow steps, Wyatt walked over, picked up the gun, checked the safety, and emptied it of its ammunition. He put the bullets in his pocket and tucked the gun into his waistband, then took a seat in the swing next to the teen. "Dwight, I need to know what your intentions were with the gun. Why you asked Jill to meet you here and brought a weapon."

"It wasn't for Jill. I would never hurt Jill."

Except he had. Harper had witnessed it firsthand.

"I brought it … in case she didn't come."

Wyatt nodded. "I see. So, you wanted to end it here tonight?"

The boy shrugged. "I dunno. Maybe." He released a heavy sigh. "I just want it to stop hurting. It's been so long, I just want it to stop."

That simple statement told Wyatt more than the boy had probably meant to. Whatever had driven him to this point started before Jill ever entered the picture.

"How long?"

The silence stretched, and Wyatt crossed his arms over his sweatshirt, wishing he'd grabbed his jacket on the way out the door. Didn't matter how cold he got, though. He'd wait it out with this troubled young man. That was his mission, right? The calling God had placed on his heart?

Except he'd never once reached out to kids like Dwight. Like Jill and Kendra and Finn. Not before Harper had shown him how deeply wounded many of these kids were. That couldn't have been a coincidence, her showing up at the small college where he taught part-time, in the department that would guarantee she would be in one of his classes at some point. That it was her first day back in school after a decade's absence couldn't have been anything but God.

"My mom …" The broken whisper had Wyatt straining to hear over the freezing wind that cut to the bone. "When I was twelve. I didn't even get to say goodbye."

"She left?"

Dwight shook his head. "She … died. Brain aneurysm. I was at school. My aunt … came to get me." He reached up and swiped at his face with the cuff of his letter jacket. "She was fine that morning, but I never saw her again after she dropped me off at school." He looked back up at Wyatt, the pain darkening his eyes and pinching his features. "I never understood how she could … that she was just … gone. And my dad …"

Dwight looked out at the trees surrounding the playground. "He's married again. Living life as if my mom never existed. And playing dad to his wife's two little kids, like they have as much right to him as I do."

"Doesn't seem fair, does it?"

"It's not fair. They get a mom *and* a dad, and I don't have anybody. Now I'm losing Jill. It's like nobody wants me."

"Like your mom did."

The boy nodded. "Yeah. She was always there for me. Until she wasn't."

Which wasn't his mother's fault, and deep-down, Dwight probably knew that.

"Dwight, I can help you, if you'll let me. I work with kids every day who need help getting past events in their lives that keep them from moving forward. I don't think your issue is with Jill at all."

Dwight looked back at him with a deep furrow in his brow. "It isn't?"

Wyatt shook his head. "I think this is about being left. Your mom didn't leave you on purpose, but as a twelve-year-old kid, that's more than likely how your psyche dealt with it. Now the fear of being left makes you over-possessive. Trying to keep someone else you love from leaving you."

The boy stared at him for a long moment before his face crumpled and he crossed his arms over his knees, put his head down, and sobbed.

Wyatt laid his hand on Dwight's back and let him cry it out. He was the boy's safe place, somebody he'd never laid eyes on before. Which was probably why he'd confided, why he felt secure letting down his guard and giving in to the grief he'd pent up for years.

A few minutes later, Dwight sat up and swiped at his face with his sleeves again. "You really think you can help me? Not to feel this way anymore?"

"I do. But you have to commit. You would need to come in to counsel with me, and I would expect your honesty and openness. The more you're willing to share, the better and faster you'll heal. I see nothing but good things in your future, Dwight. Even being able to have a healthy, secure relationship based on love and respect, not possessiveness. If that sounds good, I'd be happy to talk to your dad about it."

Dwight looked away again, clearly in thought for several long seconds before he nodded. "I think I'd like to try. I don't want to be like this anymore."

"Of course you don't. And making this decision is a huge step toward healing."

Dwight looked back at Wyatt. "I know it's late, but can we talk to my dad now? I've … uh … well, I've kind of been drinking, so if you could drive me home, that would probably be the best idea."

"Absolutely. I'd be happy to drive you home and talk to your dad."

Wyatt stood and offered his hand to help the boy from the swing. Like Finn, Dwight was a boy in a man's body, a child dealing with adult problems. *Thank You, Father, for getting me here in time.* Saving this boy didn't change anything about what happened to Glen, but at least it was one less tic mark on a statistical chart nobody wanted to see.

Without another word spoken, the two returned to the parking lot. In the pool of light around the SUV, he saw Jill reach for the back door until Harper stopped her. He didn't know what was said, but it was Harper who emerged from the other side. A wise decision. Jill didn't need to see Dwight in his current condition, and Dwight didn't need the added burden of putting on a good face for her.

Wyatt turned to the boy. "Give me your keys and go wait for me in your car. Don't approach Jill right now, okay?"

Dwight nodded and handed him the keys. "Can I apologize?"

"There'll be a time for that. Let me speak with Miss Townsend, and we'll get you home."

Dwight walked to his car with his head bowed and shoulders slumped, with Wyatt watching until he was safely ensconced in the front passenger seat of the Jeep.

Harper walked up to him, her arms crossed over her middle. "Thank the Lord."

"A good place to start." He bowed his head before looking back up at her. "He was going to kill himself if she didn't show up. Or at least was thinking about it. I took a gun off him."

Her eyes widened. "Oh, no, Wyatt. You could've been—"

"But I wasn't. We actually had a really good conversation. He's going to be okay."

"What happens now?"

"I'm going to talk with the parents. See if they'll let him counsel with me. He's really raw right now but also under the influence, so I'm going to drive him home. Can you follow Jill to make sure she gets home okay, then come get me? I'll text you the address."

"Sure. Thanks, Wyatt. I can't believe all of this."

"*This* should have never happened."

"It could have been so much worse. Thank the Lord you both walked out of there."

With a sigh, he rubbed his brow with his fingers. Speaking of raw, he wasn't sure how much more blistered his own psyche could be. "I'm so sorry, Harper. If only I'd done something sooner."

She cocked her head and stared at him for a moment before reaching out to place her hand on his arm. "We got here as fast as we could. You did good, Wyatt. This is a save."

His heart clutched at the absolute trust he saw in her eyes. A trust he wasn't sure he deserved. "Not a great place to talk about this." He looked at her for a moment before giving in to what he'd wanted to do from the moment she'd walked in his door earlier. When he reached out and pulled her close, she held on tight. Maybe she'd been wanting this, needing this, as much as he had.

He stood with her in his arms, soaking up the precious seconds of being so close to her when they hadn't touched for over a week. Even in the tension-filled environment, her gentle floral-spice fragrance enveloped him, her soft hair blew around him in the wind.

"Wyatt ..." Her gentle whisper against his neck spilled warmth over his skin even in the frigid night air.

"I know." Much sooner than he wanted, he let her go, the chill overtaking him once more.

"I'll see you after I know Jill's home okay."

"Be safe." He started toward the Jeep but stopped and turned back. "Harper."

She looked back at him.

"I—" The air between them crackled with the force of the unspoken words, like an electric current finding connection between two poles. A connection his heart, his soul, had been desperate to find since the night she walked away from him.

Tears filled her eyes and she nodded. "Me too."

CHAPTER FORTY-FOUR

*W*yatt climbed into the passenger seat of his SUV idling in the Perkins' driveway, laid his head back on the headrest, and released a sigh. "What a night."

Harper looked over at him from where she sat behind the wheel. Bone weary, he was happy to let her drive.

"How were the parents?" she asked.

"Shocked. Sad. Scared. I believe strongly this is all connected to the sudden death of his mother four years ago, but I'm encouraged they appear motivated to get him the help he needs."

"Oh, how awful for him."

"Yeah, he's hurting, confused, terrified of abandonment. Which explains why he's so possessive with Jill. Why he felt he had to resort to bullying, to assert control over her so she wouldn't leave him."

Just like Finn beating up a kid he felt had disrespected him, to assert his dominance over someone to feel superior. Wyatt's gut clenched. How many others had he missed while trying to help the kids he identified with? Had he, like Jonah, only been willing to minister to those *he* deemed worthy but refused to go and show a better way to those he didn't understand?

Harper pulled around the driveway and onto the street. "Where's he stuck?"

Wyatt glanced over at her. "Sorry?"

"You said you think it's related to the death of his mother, so I assume he's stuck in one of the stages."

"Oh. Anger. Definitely anger."

She nodded. "I can understand that, since he was so young when she died. For me, it was a mixture of denial and depression." She looked both directions, then pulled out onto the main road. "I understood at some point Megan's diagnosis was terminal, yet once she was gone, I went numb. Denial stage. That's when Emory took me back to Lubbock with her. She was in med school, but she could see I was barely functioning, and she didn't think Mom and Dad would take the time I needed. And Brett ... he was so far down his own dark hole, he hardly acknowledged me. I don't know how she did everything that month, but she was my rock. Single-handedly kept me alive."

Tears burned his eyes. Harper would always carry that ache deep inside, yet somehow lived her life with such grace and peace and joy. The way she'd reached out to the kids with all of that mother's love she came by naturally, even though her own childhood had been devoid of that same warmth, was a testament to her strength of spirit.

"Once I was back home, I pretty much climbed into myself and concentrated on breathing. Didn't socialize or make an effort to see anybody. Depression stage."

He swiped at his face. "Where was Brett during this time?"

"Your guess is as good as mine."

His pulse hitched, chest tightening as he fought back anger. How could any man see her in that much pain and not do everything in his power to protect her? To care for her? He would never understand that.

He cleared his throat. "You said he hit the bottle pretty hard after she died. Did that exacerbate the abuse?"

"No, surprisingly. He was hardly home, which I didn't mind, to tell you the truth. I was pretty much going through the motions. Would go to work at Connor's law firm, come home, pull something together for dinner, usually a bowl of soup or cereal, and sit in front of the TV until I couldn't stay awake, go to bed in the spare room, then do it all again the next day."

"I'm so sorry you had to go through that alone," he said as she turned into his subdivision. "Grieving for Megan with nobody there."

"So much of it is a blur." Her voice was quiet inside the confines of the vehicle. "Except for the pain. That I remember like it was yesterday." She hit the remote to open the garage, pulled in, and killed the engine, but made no move to get out. "I've been through some hard things, for certain. But if any of that helps me help kids, then it wasn't in vain. If I can use all of that to honor God, that's a gift."

He nodded and turned his attention to his hands clasped between his thighs before looking back at her. "Look, I'm sorry. You were absolutely right. I should have let you know your dad called me on Friday inviting me to breakfast. He asked me not to tell you, but I should have let him know right off I didn't feel right about that."

"No, I'm sorry. I shouldn't have taken such offense. I know they're not on board with my decision, but knowing they tried to pull you to their side stung."

With a shake of his head, he released his seat belt and shifted to face her. "That wasn't it at all. They never once asked me to talk to you or bring you over to a certain way of thinking. Whatever you said Thursday must have struck a chord, Harper, because they both seemed to be trying to figure some things out. Spiritual things. I only hope I gave them good answers."

Her eyes widened. "Seriously? Huh." She looked away with a shake of her head. "I guess that explains my mom's call."

"What call?"

She looked back over at him. "That's why I'm going back to my old church tomorrow. My parents are meeting us kids there for the service, then we're going to Connor and Lynne's for dinner. I was shocked, to say the least. But now I get it. You must have given them some very good answers."

"I think it definitely started with you. Often our mission field includes our own families." He stared out the windshield at the wall festooned with various tools hanging from pegs. He might not know what to do with kitchen stuff, but tools, he understood.

He thought he also understood troubled teens. Kids who lived in the circle he had, who struggled like Glen did. But this week had been eye-opening. Mind-opening. *Heart*-opening. Jill. Kendra. Finn. Dwight. All kids he would have never crossed paths with in high school. Kids who avoided him, and he avoided right back.

But he couldn't avoid them now. God had placed them directly in his path, like the beaten man on the road to Samaria. He couldn't walk around them like they didn't matter, like he had a higher purpose because he was already helping teens who felt unseen, brushed aside, discounted.

"Wyatt?"

His head snapped around at her voice.

"You okay?"

He stared at her for a moment. "This research you've been doing, what have you found, exactly?"

Her brow crinkled. "Mostly secular anti-bullying groups, until I happened upon this ministry in Atlanta. By chance, really. I've been outlining a Bible study I thought I might test with some of my girls at some point, alongside of ConnectUP, not in place of it. So, I just searched for ministries to bridge teenage social circles, and this one came up. Reach Over

Ministries. A new start-up under the umbrella of Becker Ministries. I emailed the guy on the website, we had a video call Wednesday afternoon, and he invited me to come out there over my winter break to see what they were doing."

He couldn't stop the smile that spread across his face. "You're writing a Bible study? That's fantastic."

Color suffused her cheeks with her shy grin. "I just felt this tug and started writing, studying scripture and other books on teenage self-esteem. Aside from being a mom, working in CU has been the most amazing thing I've ever done. I can only hope to honor God like you have in following what He's asked you to do."

He reached across the console to take her hand. "Everything you do honors God, Harper. And it's been a privilege to watch it happen."

The irony wasn't lost on him. This *newbie Christian* hadn't hesitated to reach out to any and every girl she felt needed the truth of the gospel. She hadn't limited herself to only those who were *like her,* but had opened her heart without hesitation to the CU girls she fell in love with that first night. And here he was, a Christian since childhood, called to ministry, committed to ConnectUP, but limited in sight to only those within his social periphery.

How many more had he missed?

CHAPTER FORTY-FIVE

*H*arper placed the last of Rhonda's shower gifts in the trunk and closed it. "I was a little worried it wouldn't all fit."

Rhonda reached out to hug her. "Everybody was so generous." She pulled back but held on. "And thank you for hosting. Y'all made me feel so special."

"Well, that's easy. Because you are."

They shared another embrace. "I love you, sweet sister."

"I love you back."

Rhonda climbed into her car and backed out of the driveway. Harper gave her one last wave, closed the garage, and walked back into the house. How could her heart feel so many things at one time?

Joy for her friends who had found love and a place of belonging with each other. The pain of being parted from Wyatt that never seemed to go away.

And yet ... hope. A spark of something new. A flicker that had ignited overnight. They'd spent the wee hours of the morning helping a troubled teen. Together. Of the same mind, with the same goal.

But would there be more? For the first time, she'd sensed a

shift in Wyatt, as if he finally understood how wide and far and deep his ministry—*their* ministry—could go. He'd asked about the Atlanta group, about her research. Had been authentic in his excitement about the Bible study she wanted to write.

Could they be on the verge of taking ConnectUP to new heights? Or was it too much to hope for with the grant proposal deadline looming on the horizon?

She checked the clock on the wall. Last night he'd said he wanted to get together and talk. But with her family plans, then the shower this afternoon, that hadn't been feasible. She'd hoped maybe after the ladies' left, they might find time. But it was already seven-thirty, and she still needed to study for a final exam tomorrow morning.

Besides, if he'd been available, he would've called or texted her. A look at her phone showed nothing from Wyatt at all, so she settled in with her World Lit book and class notes.

When her phone rang thirty minutes later, she tried to set aside her disappointment that it wasn't Wyatt but an Atlanta number she recognized. She hadn't spoken with Reach Over's director since their video chat earlier in the week, although he'd emailed her several times with additional information about their ministry. His missives were always friendly, and his passion for his mission transmitted clearly, even through the ethernet. He lived to help kids.

Just like Wyatt.

She tapped her screen to answer. "Zane. Hi. How's it going?"

"Any better and I'd be in heaven. How about you?"

"Things are good here. One more exam, and I'm done with school for the semester. Then I can focus on Christmas."

"And your trip out here, I hope. You're still coming, right?"

"Booked my flight up for Friday and returning Monday. I want to be here to help my friend get ready for her wedding the day after Christmas, and we have the ConnectUP girls doing their Christmas cookies that Tuesday."

"Oh, sure. I can understand that. Although I'd hoped we'd have you a bit longer. From all I hear, you have a lot to offer, and I'd like to have a few days to pick your brain."

She cocked her head. "How's that?" Heard what from whom? She didn't know a soul in Atlanta.

"I had an interesting conversation today with the leader of your ministry there."

Her skin erupted in tingles. "You spoke to Wyatt?"

"I got an email from him overnight, so I called and spoke with him at length this afternoon. He had nothing but great things to say about you."

"Oh. Well, that's nice." Overnight? That meant Wyatt must have looked up Reach Over as soon as she left in the wee hours this morning and emailed Zane.

"Which brings me to why I called. Is this a good time? I was too excited to wait."

She glanced down at the textbook in her lap before setting it aside. "Sure. What's on your mind?"

"Have you already registered for classes next semester?"

"Uh, yeah. I've changed my major so I'm a little behind on the required courses. I'll be making some of that up online and in summer school. Why?"

"Can you attend school full-time online at DHU?"

"Yes, they have their courses online, as well."

"And you work full-time?"

"Thirty hours a week." Where on earth was this going?

"What if I could offer you a full-time position with Becker Ministries? Full benefit package, including one hundred percent tuition paid for your continuing education as long as it's ministry oriented. Would that interest you?"

Harper's heart rate doubled in time. "You're offering me a job? In Atlanta?"

"I know it's a little sudden, but an opening at Becker just came up, and since it's directly involved in the startup of Reach Over, I thought I could put it on the table for you to think about and pray over. Then when you're here in a few days, hopefully we could go ahead and onboard you. To start whenever you could relocate here, of course. I know that would take some time, and it would mean taking your courses online. But you'd be at the forefront of a brand-new ministry."

A spike in adrenaline made it impossible to sit, so she stood and paced in front of the fireplace. "Wait. Go back. Wyatt told you I'd be a good fit for your ministry there?"

"That was the gist of it, yeah. He said you had a heart for kids from opposite sides of the social divide and wanted to bridge the gulf between them. You shared a bit of your story with me when we video chatted a few days ago, and I felt then you would be an excellent addition to our staff. But after speaking with Wyatt, there's no doubt. We'd love to have you."

The warmth emanating from the fireplace did nothing to slow the ice forming around her heart. That flicker of hope that perhaps she and Wyatt could work together to widen CU's reach and find their way back to each other died without so much as a wisp of smoke to show it was ever there.

Wyatt hadn't wanted to change the direction of CU. All of those questions about Reach Over had been about finding out if it would be a good place for *her*. And he hadn't hesitated a moment to contact Zane to let him know she could be a valuable asset to his team.

He probably intended it to be a grand gesture, showing her that he supported her ideas, even if he had no intention of going along with them. Showing her there was a place for her to minister to kids and bring them together, regardless of their social tier. A place other than ConnectUP.

"Harper? You there?"

She swallowed the knot of emotion in her throat. "I'm here. Sorry. Just thinking."

"I know it's a lot to process, but please consider it. You're everything our ministry needs."

Everything except local. Yet how could she leave

Arlington, the only place she'd ever called home? Leave Emory and Connor? Leave her parents, to whom she felt closer than ever after only one morning spent in church with them? Leave her CU kids? Her cheer girls?

Leave Wyatt?

Because relocating would mean giving up any hope of a future with him. A life with him.

But wasn't that exactly what she was supposed to do? Surrender her all to follow the path God intended? Had she truly surrendered her dreams of a life with Wyatt, or just put them aside for a while in hopes he would change his mind about CU?

She closed her eyes and took a deep breath as realization hit her like a jab to the middle. She hadn't released to the Lord the part of her heart that held onto Wyatt. She'd shuttered it off, not allowing God access to it in case He should want to renovate it, make it something else. Something new.

Her heart wanted to cling to the hope she and Wyatt could build a future together. But her head reminded her that if she surrendered one hundred percent of herself, including her heart, God would fill her life with good things. Even if Wyatt wasn't that good thing.

Zane's offer was a wide-open door into a ministry to help kids understand each other, find their value in God. To heal the hurts that too many teenagers lived with through no fault of their own. Everything she felt God calling her to do.

Was this her good thing? Her true calling?

CHAPTER FORTY-SIX

*W*yatt stared out his third-floor office window, his thoughts tumbling over each other. Harper, ConnectUP, Reach Over, and his nearly three-hour conversation with Zane Carpenter Sunday afternoon.

Harper.

He hadn't seen nor spoken to her since Saturday night's drama, due to their schedules not meshing long enough for them to have a decent conversation. This being Tuesday afternoon, that was way too long, in his opinion.

A rap on his open office door was a welcome interruption to the wrestling match in his head.

"Hey, Jim," he said to his co-worker. "She here?"

"Yep. You still good to meet?"

"I have about an hour before I need to leave for class." He stood and joined Jim on the other side of the desk. "This is the woman who called you last week?"

"Right. She founded an organization to prevent teenage suicides and wanted to meet with us about aligning our services. I was going to meet with her myself, but she was adamant about seeing us both."

Wyatt shrugged. "Always happy to meet others wanting to help kids stay alive."

He followed Jim down the hall to the reception area, where a woman in a tailored navy suit stood at their approach, her red hair falling straight to her shoulders and eyes locked on his.

All the oxygen left the room as he was transported back to his senior year of high school. When his best friend fell for the beautiful, red-haired, lab partner whose only goal was to use him for her own purposes, then kick him to the curb. Only that wasn't enough. She had to completely annihilate him.

"Wyatt McCowan." The woman offered her hand, her smile timid in a face that had matured but was still striking. He might even think she was pretty, if he didn't know the ugliness that lived inside her. "It's ... good to see you."

Unable to return the sentiment, he stared at her hand before accepting it for a brief handshake. "Sarah Holmes."

Jim looked back and forth between them, his pursed brow a sign he'd already cued in to the tension. "Clearly not the first time you've met each other."

Wyatt pulled his gaze to his co-worker and friend. "Um, no. Sarah and I went to high school to—went to the same high school."

"Hmm." Jim had no doubt picked up on Wyatt's quick change of phrase. He and Sarah had never done anything *together*. Not in high school or otherwise.

"Jim. Would you mind if I met with Ms. ..." He looked at the woman in front of him. "Is it still Holmes?"

She shook her head. "Thompson. But, please. Call me Sarah."

He'd called her many things in his head over the years, but rarely by name. He looked back at Jim. "Do you mind if we speak alone?"

"Not at all. You two catch up." He looked between them. "I

don't have anything scheduled until after lunch, so let me know if you need me."

They just might.

Wyatt gestured for Sarah to precede him down the hall. "Second door on the right." Once inside, he closed the door and offered her a seat. He contemplated sitting behind the desk but realized that came from a need to assert control. Probably not the best posture to take, so he took the seat adjacent to hers, folded his hands in his lap, and stared down at them.

"Your body language tells me what I've always wondered."

He looked up at her. "And that's?"

"If you knew."

"If I knew what?"

Pain sparked in her eyes. He wasn't trying to be cruel, but he needed to hear her own her actions.

Her throat worked for a moment before she cleared it. "That I'm responsible for what happened to Glen Bennett. You have no idea how deeply ingrained that is in me. As if I'd tied that rope myself."

He stared at her through narrowed eyes, anger that had been percolating for over a decade bubbling to the surface. "We were like brothers, Glen and me. We'd known each other since we were eight years old. Other than Harper, he was the closest friend I'd ever had."

Her forehead creased. "Harper Townsend?"

"Yes."

"I didn't know you were close."

He took a cleansing breath and let it out. Spewing his long-festering grief would only do more harm than good, and disrespect the memory of his friend. For Glen, he'd do his best to rein in his tongue. "We were very close, until junior high. But then she was who she was, and I was ... like Glen. Science geek, too smart for our own good."

She winced. "To the girl I was back then, Glen was an easy

mark. It was obvious he liked me, and I took full advantage. Evan got a big kick out of it, and when he and Lucas started talking about how they could teach Glen a lesson for trespassing on Evan's territory, can you believe I actually felt valued?"

A humorless chuckle accompanied a shake of her head. "I was so needy that being considered a possession made me feel important. I wonder if that's how Harper felt with Brett. Like she was his trophy. That's how he treated her, anyway. I wonder whatever became of them."

Wyatt studied her for a moment. "You weren't at the reunion."

"No way. I have no desire whatsoever to go back in time, revisit that girl I was, or that group of people I thought were the be-all and end-all if you wanted to be somebody."

He crossed his arms over his stomach, and a bit of his wrath cooled in the face of her obvious self-deprecation. "Brett and Harper married after their first year of college. They had a little girl who passed away at four years old, and they divorced a year later."

Her jaw fell. "How tragic. I'm so sorry to hear that."

"Harper and I reconnected a few months ago and have been working together in a ministry to help kids like Glen. Help them find their value in who God says they are, instead of putting stock in the opinions of kids like—"

When he didn't finish, she nodded. "Kids like me." She ran a finger under her eye to remove the moisture gathered there. "Not Harper, though. Now, there was a class act. I can't tell you how many times Brett did a verbal slap-down on that girl when she'd stick up for somebody they were dissing."

Her eyes narrowed, and she cocked her head to the side. "Are you two … together?"

He uncrossed his arms and rubbed the middle of his chest, where an unseen knife seemed to pierce him through. "We were. But we had a difference of opinion about what direction ConnectUP needed to go, so we're taking a break to get a better perspective as to where God might be leading each of us."

Her eyes widened. "ConnectUP is you? A young lady on my team was one of your kids about two years ago. Shelly Pasternack. She'd been contemplating suicide until she got involved with your group and met the Lord. You do some very important work."

"Shelly was one of our first." He studied her for a moment. "Are you a Christian, Sarah?"

"About eight years now. I was such a mess in high school, and after what happened with Glen, well, let's just say I finally saw myself for who I truly was. That I could take part in such an atrocious act on a sweet-spirited, completely innocent soul—"

Sarah rose quickly and turned to walk to the window, staring out over the courtyard below. He let the silence linger. A counselor tactic to allow the client to find their own words.

But this was no client. This was somebody he'd labeled the enemy. Not somebody he would have ever wanted to help find their way. Not after what she did. How did God expect him to deal with this? Why now, when he was already questioning everything about his ministry, his purpose?

"I'm so sorry." Her broken whisper barely crossed the room before she turned to face him. "Wyatt, I'm so very sorry for what I did to your friend. I've had years of counseling, hours spent in the Word and on my knees begging for forgiveness, and praying for God to somehow make my life mean something. There are nights I still wake up in a sweat from another nightmare about that night. And hearing the next day that he had—"

A sob caught in her throat.

Wyatt hung his head. He would know what to do for any client standing in this office about to fall apart. Would know the right words, the right action to take. But this ... this was too much. Too hard.

Lord, help me know what to do here. Help me get outside of myself, my own pain, to be Your hands. Your voice.

Because he knew he couldn't do it alone.

CHAPTER FORTY-SEVEN

*W*yatt grabbed the box of tissues from his desk and held it out to Sarah.

"Thank you." She pulled a couple from the box and blew her nose before she looked up at him. "We heard about his death at lunch, and I had to run to go throw up in the restroom. When I came out, Evan was waiting for me. He grabbed me by the arm and told me I needed to get myself together and not say a word to anybody about what had happened."

She took a shuddering breath. "And I did. I kept it all inside, and it tore me to shreds. I couldn't eat, I couldn't sleep. Never left the house, even for school, after that day. My mom thought something had happened to me, something I couldn't talk about, and it was easier letting her assume that than tell her I'd been the aggressor, not the victim."

Wyatt swallowed against the thickness in his throat. He'd been in such a fog of grief, anger, and guilt, he hadn't even noticed Sarah's disappearance. Never knew how her own actions had not only taken one life but had upended hers. If he had, would it have changed his feelings toward her? Would he have felt sympathy or vindication? How did he feel *now?*

She twisted the tissue in her fingers. "Ten days after it happened, I had a complete breakdown and ended up in a psychiatric facility. I didn't want to stay in Arlington after they released me, so I moved down to my dad's in San Antonio, got my GED, went to community college, found a local church. I kept waiting for a cop to show up at our door to arrest me. I kept thinking Glen's friend certainly had to know he was coming down to the park to meet me. Why hadn't he said anything to anybody? Why wasn't somebody coming after me?"

Wyatt nodded. "I did know. Then in the note he left me, he didn't mention Evan and Lucas, just that you had set him up. That if I saw photos of him stripped down, he wanted me to know he didn't have sex with you. That's not why he was going there to begin with. He didn't want to sleep with you, he was just excited to spend some time with you. He was a good guy, who actually respected you. You weren't an object to him, but a person. A person he cared about."

More tears spilled down her cheeks as she walked back to her chair. "If only I could have understood that kind of care. It wasn't until I was in counseling that I saw it all started after my dad left when I was eleven. The parade of men through our house followed soon after. Mom had no idea who she was without a man, somebody who would take care of her, make her feel wanted. As I got older, a couple of them actually came on to me, so I thought that's how it was done. Look good, and somebody would validate you."

Her watery brown eyes bored into his as he again took his seat. "I honestly didn't realize how rough Evan and Lucas were going to get until it started." She swallowed hard. "I knew they'd gone too far, but I was afraid to jump in. To help him. Harper would have. She would have at least tried to intervene. But I was a coward. Stood there and watched them demean Glen in every way they could."

Wyatt leaned forward, bracing his elbows on his legs and

holding his head in his hands as he fought the emotion that burned his eyes and throat. Why hadn't he gone that night? He may have fallen victim to the same treatment, but at least he would've been there. He and Glen could've maneuvered through the humiliation and derision together. He could've kept his friend alive if he'd been alongside him, because Wyatt would have never contemplated taking his own life. Those kids weren't worth it.

"He never cried." Sarah's quiet voice quivered. "He resisted, but he never begged, never threw a punch. At one point, lying on the ground, beaten to a pulp, he looked over at me, and the question in his eyes is what I still see in my nightmares. He saw me for who I truly was in that moment, and I was never the same."

Wyatt sat up and looked at her then. Really looked at her. Until this day, he'd never exchanged one word with Sarah Holmes. Had never given her a thought until Glen had fallen for her.

Yet he'd spent the past eleven years hating her with a deep-seated passion he was only now aware he'd never let go. What a hypocrite he was, expecting ... *teaching* his kids to forgive those who hurt them, walk away with their heads held high and a prayer in their hearts for the kids who dissed them, abused them, victimized them. All the while nurturing this root of bitterness inside him.

As a broken-hearted, angry teenager, he'd hoped she'd suffer as much as Glen had. And with maturity, unfortunately, that thought hadn't changed much. He'd wanted her to pay for what she'd done. Hoped it would haunt her the rest of her days.

And here she sat, guilt etched into her features, confessing outright her part in the tragedy that had charted the course of his life. Sharing how it had destroyed the rest of her teenage years and still woke her in the middle of the night.

So, where was the feeling of vindication? That sense of

victory? Why was the ache in his own heart compounded by the knowledge of hers?

The tragedy that had charted the course of his life. His mind reeled with realization. The same tragedy that had given him his life's purpose had also charted the course of hers. And they both now shared the same passion to help kids make a different decision than Glen had.

He bowed his head for a moment. "Sarah ... I—I don't—I—"

She leaned forward to grab his hand. "I can see how affected you are by it still. How raw the hurt is. I hope my showing up here wasn't the wrong thing. I was given Jim's name as a psychologist we might use as a referral, and when I looked up his practice, there you were. And I felt this immediate stirring, like I needed to see you. It wasn't something I relished doing because I felt in my gut you had to know what I'd done."

Tears fell down her cheeks. "I just—I needed to ask ... I know I don't deserve it, but I hope, for your own sake, you can forgive me."

The dam he'd built from bricks of sorrow collapsed inside of him, letting loose all of that hate, the bitterness he'd buried under layers of doing the right thing, the veneer of having it all together, and tears spilled down his face. Sarah took his hands in hers and bowed her head, saying nothing. Was she ... praying for him? When he'd never uttered one word in prayer for her, except in anger, asking God to punish her for what she'd done?

"Sarah." His voice came out a broken rasp, and he waited for her to look at him so she could see the truth in his eyes. "I do forgive you. And God forgave you long ago, the day you gave your life to Him. You don't have to keep begging His forgiveness, because it's done. Just as you needed me to forgive you so I could heal, you need to forgive yourself so you can do the same."

She nodded. "Thank you for that. My husband knows how I struggle with the guilt and has told me many times that I need to stop looking back and keep looking forward to all we can do for other kids considering the option Glen chose."

He cleared his throat and swiped the last of the wetness from his face. "Your husband sounds like a wise man." His watch beeped, and he glanced down at it. "I'm so sorry, Sarah. I have a class in thirty minutes."

She picked up her bag and they both stood. "No problem. I want to speak with Jim for a bit." She looked around the office. "Is there somewhere I can freshen up?"

"Sure." He pointed to a door at the side. "Restroom right through there. Give Jim all of your information, and I'll let him know I'm on board. Any way we can help, please let us know."

"Oh, thank you! Thank you so much. That means the world to me."

"You're welcome." He released a deep breath, surprised at how much lighter he felt, how the tightness in his chest had loosened. He'd carried that load of resentment for so long, he'd simply become accustomed to it. But now that it was gone, he felt ... free. At peace. "And thank you for listening to that voice telling you to see me. I think we both needed it."

Now he needed to get to Harper. To tell her all that had happened over the last week. All that God had shown him. Maybe they could meet after his class, since she'd be off work by then and was done with her finals.

On his way out to the parking lot, he checked his phone and found a voicemail she'd left while he'd been with Sarah. His pulse quickened when he heard her voice, then nearly stopped when he listened to her message. Not sure he'd heard it right, he played it again.

Hey, Wyatt, it's me. I wanted to let you know I moved up my plans to go to Atlanta. Emery gave me the next few days off, and I'm getting ready to board my flight. I'll be back next

Monday, but don't worry about club tomorrow. Ally said she could take my circle. I —I'll talk to you when I get back.

Inside the vehicle, he put his head against the headrest with a sigh. He had so much he needed to tell her, but by now, she was no doubt thousands of feet in the air, putting even more distance between them. Distance he was desperate to close.

But was he too late?

CHAPTER FORTY-EIGHT

*H*arper dropped her jacket and leather tote in the chair inside her hotel room and collapsed onto the bed. Her sigh seemed to come from her very soul as she stared up at the ceiling. The last two days had been equal parts exciting and taxing, and all she wanted to do was curl up under the covers and sleep for the next twenty-four hours. She didn't want to talk, didn't want to think ... didn't want to make this decision.

After Zane's surprising job offer, and the knowledge it came with Wyatt's glowing endorsement, she'd done a video call with Zane and Becker Ministries' vice president on Monday morning. As with Zane, she'd had an instant rapport with Maggie Watson, and it was determined that if Harper were to consider coming on staff, she would need to be there during the work week. She thought about waiting until after the holidays, and the wedding, but decided to come now in case she needed to change her class schedule and arrange her relocation before the new semester began mid-January.

Rescheduling her flight out of Dallas had been easy, but yesterday's journey had been fraught with one obstacle after another. And to make matters worse, she'd somehow arrived in

Atlanta without her cell phone. The last time she remembered having it was when she'd called and left a message for Wyatt before boarding her first flight. The first of three, as it turned out, since they'd been returned to the terminal after a problem was found with one of the engines. While she was thankful they'd found it before they were airborne, it meant waiting it out in the airport for a healthier plane.

The delay also meant a missed connection in New Orleans. It was when she wanted to call her sister with an update on her status that she realized her phone was gone. Sitting on the last plane to Atlanta out of New Orleans, exhausted and near tears, she wondered if the enemy was working against her because this was the right call, or if God was trying to tell her she'd gotten ahead of Him.

She tried her number during breaks today, but nobody ever answered. Calls to the airline and the customer service desk at Dallas Love Field yielded no good news, either. So, after work, she and Zane went to her carrier store to buy a new phone. Then he insisted on taking her to dinner to talk about her first impressions of Becker Ministries. His enthusiasm for the work they did was infectious, and she knew she could fit in well with their team.

Speaking of team.

She sat up and crossed the room to take her new phone from her bag. The salesperson had set it up with the same number, but without her old phone's SIM card, she'd lost almost everything. It being an hour earlier back home, ConnectUP was set to start in twenty minutes. Maybe she could catch Rhonda beforehand.

She plugged in the charger and tapped in the number.

"Harper!" came her friend's voice after one ring. "Goodness, girl, have you fallen off the face of the earth?"

"Not quite, although I think my phone has. I had to get a new one today."

"You don't have any of our texts or messages, then?"

The clamor of voices and laughter, basketballs bouncing against wood floor, and the *thump-thump* of hip-hop music filtered through the phone. Harper's chest filled with the yearning to be there. "No. And what do you mean by *our*?"

"Mine, Shannon's, Yolanda's. Wyatt's."

Her pulse hitched. "Didn't he get my message yesterday?"

"He did. But he called me this afternoon to see if I'd heard from you since he hadn't been able to reach you."

"I'm sorry. There was a problem with the plane out of Love Field, so I didn't get to the hotel until well after midnight and hit the ground running to make my eight o'clock breakfast meeting with Maggie and Zane. This is the first minute I've had to myself all day."

She looked over at the leather bag with her laptop and spiral-bound book Zane had given her. Reach Over's ministry plan. "All I have the energy to do now is get into my jammies and go to bed."

"And Maggie is who again?"

"Vice President of Operations. She's amazing. Met with me for about two hours when she only had a day's notice I was coming. I'm actually going to Becker's semi-formal Christmas party at her house Friday night. I didn't bring anything that dressy, so I'm going to have to go shopping at some point."

"Hmm." Silence hung in the air for a moment. "Is this really a thing, Harper? You're considering their offer?"

Harper plucked at the wool skirt she wore with a sweater, leggings, and knee-high boots. "I've been praying for God to show me where He wants me to go. And then this just dropped into my lap. Doesn't seem like a coincidence to me, especially when it was Wyatt who told them I'd be a good fit for their ministry."

"Wait, say that again? Wyatt what?"

"Zane told me himself." She stood and walked over to the window overlooking downtown Atlanta, wrapping one arm around her middle as she watched the Christmas lights below sparkle in the dark. "Said Wyatt told him how much I wanted to help bridge the gap between teenage social circles. That's what Reach Over will be all about once they get up and running. I could be instrumental in getting that ministry off the ground, and have school paid for at the same time. How can I not consider it ... considering?"

"I guess that's true. I just can't stand the thought of you moving that far away."

Harper's vision blurred as tears pooled in her eyes, and she put her forehead to the cool glass. "I can't, either. But God often asks hard things of us to bring about His purposes." And this would be walking-on-hot-coals hard.

"That He does. Just promise me you'll think and pray long and hard before you give them your answer. Please? I know I'm being selfish, but I feel like there's still so much here for you to do. With us. With Wyatt."

She closed her eyes tight. "I was beginning to hope so, after everything that happened Saturday night."

"Is there anything you'd like for me to tell him?"

That I love him. That I miss him with an ache that still doubles me over.

"Just tell him hi. Tell everybody hi." Her head came up off the glass. "Do you know why he was trying to reach me?"

"He said something happened at work he wanted to tell you about."

Her spirits fell. "Oh. Probably an update on Dwight. I know he was meeting him and his parents Monday evening. I guess just let him know about my phone and that he can call if he needs anything. Otherwise, I'll see him next week. The girls and I are taking over his kitchen Tuesday afternoon for cookie baking, so I'll see him then for sure when he and the boys come later to sample the fruits of our labor."

Rhonda chuckled. "I'll tell him. Wish I could be there for the baking, but with our rehearsal dinner the next night, I don't see how I could."

"You have plenty on your plate right now, and there's always next year." Her breath hitched. No doubt cookies would indeed be baked next year, but would she be there? "Um, I'm gonna call it a night and hit the hay. I'm exhausted." She swallowed the lump in her throat as she returned to sit on the edge of the bed. "I'll really miss being at club tonight."

"You'll be missed, as well. Love you, girlfriend."

"Love you too."

After hanging up, Harper put on her flannel pajamas, scrubbed her face, pulled out her laptop and Reach Over ministry plan, and planted herself in the middle of the king-sized bed. But the numbers and graphs and pie charts swam in front of her. Zane had certainly done his homework, but she couldn't help but compare it to the grant proposal Wyatt had put so much time and effort into.

Looking at the CU proposal, one got a vision of who the ministry was about. It too contained the necessary statistical information and financials. But the story of its inception, as well as the pictures and testimonies from leaders and clubbers past and present, lent a warmth and sense of family to the work. Becker's proposal read more like a business, as if crafted by a board of directors of a large corporation.

With a sigh, she sank back against the pillows. Family. If she took this position, it would be her first job not working for one of her siblings. In a mere year and two months since she'd recommitted her life to the Lord, it would appear He wanted to strip her of all her earthly support. Her crutches, as it were. Her job with Emery, her plan to get a psych degree. Her relationship with Wyatt.

And now her home. Is that what He was trying to teach her? That she needed no one and nothing but Himself?

She closed her eyes. "Hi, God, it's me. Again. Seems I've been praying non-stop for days. I just need to know for sure if this is where You want me. Right now, I'm terrified to think about being so far away from everything I love so much. But I love You more, and I trust in Your peace and provision. I surrender all of myself to You. Just please, please, show me clearly which way to go. Give me the strength to stay on the right road, no matter what I leave behind. Show me Your way."

Her new phone beeped with an incoming text. She recognized Shannon's number.

> Don't worry about your girls tonight. We'll take good care of them for you. XO.

Of that, Harper had no worries. And maybe that was the sign she'd been waiting for. The assurance that all would be well, even without her.

CHAPTER FORTY-NINE

*W*yatt looked at the leaders he'd called into a quick huddle. To not see Harper's face among them brought a pang to his chest, but he hoped they could take some time when she returned to see where they were. Where they could be. Over the past few days, his hope in the possibility they could fix things between them had sparked to life.

Until she left.

He gave himself a mental shake. One thing at a time. "Hey, everybody. Just a quick word before tonight's club. Mason, Reed, and I have been talking and praying about the future of ConnectUP and decided since this is the last club until after the holidays, we should meet with the kids in one group. To let them know how we want to move forward in the new year."

Mason nodded. "We'd hoped to talk to y'all at Monday night's leadership meeting, but Wyatt had to meet with a new client and his parents. Since this is really his vision, I felt he should present it."

Wyatt looked down at his feet. *His vision*. Maybe now, but only because God had done some powerful work in him over the past week. If only Harper were here ...

"Please, everybody," Reed said, looking around the circle.

"Keep an open mind and pray that our kids will embrace this opportunity to grow our reach."

"Absolutely!" Yolanda said, with several other leaders nodding.

"All right, let's get everybody together."

Wyatt turned from the group, but before he could take a step, Allyson grabbed him by the arm. "Hey, Ally." He took in the downward turn of her mouth and deep crease in her brow. "What's up?"

"Are you giving in?"

He drew his head back. "To what?"

"Not to *what*, to *who*. Is this to win Harper back?"

He looked around before taking her by the elbow to steer her to the community center kitchen. Once alone, he faced her again. "Did Rhonda tell you we broke up?"

"Nobody said anything, but it's obvious. Or maybe it's because I know you so well."

He looked away and sighed before turning back to her. "Okay, to answer your first question, yes, you could say I'm giving in. I'm finally listening to what the Lord has been trying to tell me. After fighting it for weeks, I finally asked God to show me if we needed to be doing something more. And boy, did He.

"To answer your second question, no. I'm not making changes to a well-established organization that's growing by leaps and bounds, asserting my will onto a group of unsuspecting teenagers who just want to feel valuable and safe, and making my team adjust to a new mission statement, not to mention rewrite a major portion of our grant proposal, all in an effort to get Harper back. Do I hope we can work things out? Absolutely. But we have to know what God has for us, whether together or separate, and I haven't had a chance to talk to her since Saturday."

Tears gathered in her eyes. "Then there's really no chance for us again?"

His jaw fell slack and face heated. Had she just asked …?

Her gaze held his, imploring, seeking. "I thought … maybe … since you and Harper weren't together, that we could see if there's a future here. Between us. It's only been a little over a year since we ended things. I guess I was hoping, after some time apart, that we could maybe try again."

Okay, he'd definitely heard her right. He swallowed hard and took her hand. "Al, I—I'm sorry. I had no idea you still felt that way. When we broke up, we both thought it was for the best."

Her smile wobbled as a tear fell. "No, that's what *you* thought. I was completely blindsided when you broke up with me. I thought I was going to be proposed to that night, and instead, you left me at my door with no ring and a kiss on the cheek."

Guilt swirled in his gut. How had he misread her so badly? After two years together? "I don't know what to say. I thought we were in complete agreement. You said you felt the same way."

"Of course that's what I said. I didn't want to dissolve into tears in front of you. I was at a complete loss, so when my dad told me his head nurse had to leave suddenly and they couldn't get a replacement for three months, I thought it was a sign. That getting away would help me move on and get over you."

She pulled her hand from his, took a step back, and crossed her arms over her stomach. "I never expected to be there a year, but here I am, fourteen months after we broke up and still dealing with all of this. I tried putting it behind me once and for all after you told me about Harper, but when I realized you weren't together any longer, I thought that maybe—"

"Mac." Mason stood at the doorway. "We're ready out here." He looked at Allyson and back again. "Or I can start if you need some time."

Ally stared hard into Wyatt's eyes. "No, it's okay." She nodded and reached out to give him a hug. "Really, it's okay," she whispered before pulling back. She gave him a shaky grin, but her eyes still brimmed with tears. "I just want you to be happy."

"That's all I want for you too. I'm so sorry."

"No need." She glanced at Mason and back again. "Guess we'd better get out there."

Mason moved aside to let her out the door, following her with his eyes before looking back again. "That looked intense."

"You have no idea." Wyatt took a deep breath and let it out before moving toward the door. "Let's do this."

He took his place in front of the group of kids while Mason stood to the side.

"Hey, guys, it's great to see y'all. I know we're ramping up to Christmas, but we're glad you took the time to come out. Tonight, we wanted to meet with you all together to talk about what ConnectUP will look like in the coming months."

He glanced at Mason and found encouragement in his friend's broad smile. "ConnectUP's growing. But just as it's grown in numbers, we believe ConnectUP has grown in purpose. Mason, Reed, and I have been praying and talking about how ConnectUP can reach more kids. And, guys, that means we need to expand our borders."

He opened his Bible and laid it open on his palm. "ConnectUP cannot become the very thing it was created to fight. We can't be exclusive, shutting out anybody who doesn't fit *our* definition of what a clubber should be. We don't have that right.

"Guys, we have something special. Something powerful. Keeping it to ourselves not only goes against everything God teaches us right here, in His Word, but it stunts our growth as Christ-followers. We can't just choose to follow him along pristine paths. We have to be willing to follow Him into the trenches. Into other circles, as it were."

His gaze met Rhonda's, but the furrow in her brow on her usually cheerful face surprised him. He knew Mason hadn't yet told her of the changes they wanted to make, but he'd expected her to be on board. Maybe he could talk to her later about any reservations she had.

He looked back at the kids. "We want to challenge you to move outside your comfort zone. To close the gap between peer groups. Build bridges, not walls."

He flipped through the Bible in his hand. "Romans 15:7 says, *Accept each other just as Christ has accepted you so that God will be given glory*. And Romans twelve tells us, starting in verse fourteen, *Bless those who persecute you. Don't curse them; pray that God will bless them*. Verses seventeen and eighteen, *Never pay back evil with more evil. Do things in such a way that everyone can see you are honorable. Do all that you can to live in peace with everyone*."

Scanning the group facing him, he sent a prayer heavenward that the kids would hear what he was saying and open their minds and hearts.

He closed his Bible and set it down on a chair. "Y'all, I've seen some things this past week or so that brought me to my knees. Kids in pain, with deep wounds, trying to find their value and looking in all the wrong places. These kids need God. Desperately. And we can help them. *You* can help them. ConnectUP is about connection. Connection with each other, connection with God. And connecting with others we may not understand, may not even *like* in some respects."

He looked around at the teens sitting in silence, their eyes fixed on him.

"What do you think? Do you have it in you to reach past your own circle, your own tribe, so to speak, to help someone you might consider a part of a different peer group but who is really just another kid looking for something to give their life meaning? Do you think ConnectUP can expand its borders, let in others you may have thought of in the past, or maybe even now, as the enemy?"

"Yes, definitely," Ty answered right away.

"That sounds awesome!" said Tonya, and Tish agreed with an enthusiastic nod of her head.

"We're on it, Dr. Mac," Carlos said.

Wyatt returned his smile. "I believe you are. So, over the break, be aware of anybody the Lord might put in your path who needs a message of hope and acceptance. Any kid, from any group, clique, or social circle. Step out in faith, and God will meet you there. Let's pray, then head over for some snacks."

After prayer, the kids took advantage of the early dismissal to play some more and devour the refreshments the ladies had set up. Mason slapped him on the shoulder and gave it a squeeze. "Nicely done."

He looked at his friend. "Thanks for all your encouragement and wisdom. I just wish Harper could have been here."

"Speaking of Harper," Rhonda said as she walked up. "Why on earth would you recommend her for a job at Becker if you planned to integrate her ideas into CU?"

Mason's smile left as he looked from his fiancée to Wyatt and back again.

"What job?" he and Wyatt asked at the same time.

Rhonda sighed and crossed her arms. "Harper said you told that Zane guy she'd be a perfect fit for their new ministry there in Atlanta, and he offered her a full-time position with benefits and the whole shebang. They'll even pay her college tuition."

Wyatt's jaw dropped along with his stomach. That explained Rhonda's less-than-enthusiastic expression during his talk. "That's not what I said." He put his hand out. "Wait. When did you talk to Harper? I've been trying to reach her for two days."

"Right before club. She lost her phone at the airport yesterday and just got a replacement today, so she doesn't have any of our texts or messages."

"Is that why she went out there earlier than she planned, because of this job offer?"

"That's what she said."

"Oh, man. I messed that up."

"What happened, then, if that's not what you said?"

He shifted his weight to one leg and stuck his hands on his hips. "Harper told me about Becker on Saturday night. I was kind of wound up when I got home after the incident with Dwight and couldn't sleep, so I looked them up online, liked what I saw, and sent an email to the ministry coordinator listed as the contact. He FaceTimed me Sunday afternoon, and we talked for almost three hours. He asked a bunch of questions about ConnectUP, told me about Reach Over, and then asked about Harper. I just told him the truth, that she has a passion for kids from all social tiers and wants to bridge the gaps between them. I honestly don't know how he took that to mean I was recommending her for a job. A job, mind you, he never even mentioned to me."

"Call her now," Mason said. "Before she accepts that offer."

Rhonda shook her head. "She was completely done in and going to bed early. Not that she wouldn't want to hear from you, but maybe you can call her in the morning."

His thoughts in a whirl, he nodded. If he couldn't talk to Harper right now, maybe there was someone else he could. He looked at Mason. "It's an hour later in Atlanta, right?"

"Right. A little after nine there now."

"Do you mind if I take off? I need to check into a couple of things."

"Go. Let us know if you need anything."

"Just prayer." He grabbed his jacket off the back of a chair. "And a lot of coffee," he added under his breath.

On his way to his SUV, he pulled out his phone, scrolled through his recent calls, and pressed the one with the Georgia area code.

"Zane here."

"Zane. Wyatt McCowan. I hope I'm not catching you too late."

"Hey, man! Not at all. Always good to hear from a fellow soldier. You still planning to come out here after the holidays? We've been hearing a lot of really good things about ConnectUP from Harper. Can't wait to meet in person and see how we can help each other."

"Uh, yeah. About that ..."

CHAPTER FIFTY

*H*arper peered through the passenger side window of Zane's immaculately restored vintage Ford Bronco as they pulled through a gate to a large home adorned with what had to be a thousand Christmas lights. "Oh, wow, this house is magnificent."

Her nerves sat in a bundle in the pit of her stomach as they made their way up the drive to the Becker Christmas party at the Watsons' home in one of suburban Atlanta's wealthier neighborhoods.

"I hope you don't get the wrong impression about Maggie." Zane pulled up behind several other vehicles waiting for the valet. "Becker doesn't pay this well. Her husband's a prominent cardiologist from a wealthy family, but they're very generous with their time and resources."

She looked over at him. "No judgment here. I've been really impressed with Maggie and what y'all are doing at Becker."

The silence stretched for a moment as she watched the elegantly dressed guests emerge from their vehicles and walk up the steps to the massive front door festooned by garland glittering with white lights.

Zane cleared his throat. "I wanted to apologize again that I wasn't able to meet with you today. I hope you enjoyed your tour of Atlanta with Phoebe, though. I thought it would be a good way for you to see our fair city, since Maggie and I had back-to-back meetings all day."

"I enjoyed it very much. And I'll never pass up a chance to shop."

"Speaking of that, that dress is really nice. Green looks good on you."

She glanced down at the Christmasy-hued dress she'd found that day at one of Phoebe's favorite boutiques. It cost more than she should have spent, but it would also be perfect for Mason and Rhonda's Christmas-themed wedding next weekend. The velvety material of the bodice and three-quarter-length sleeves felt like a whisper against her skin, and the filmy, full, tea-length skirt swished around her legs like sea foam.

"Thank you. You clean up pretty good yourself."

"Every now and then." He grimaced as he once again adjusted his tie. "I hate these things."

Once he'd turned his vehicle over to a young man in black pants and a red jacket, he helped her into her coat, and they walked up the stone steps to the open front door.

He pulled her aside before they entered. "I just wanted to say something before we go in."

Uh-oh. Had Zane taken her friendliness as a sign of something else?

"Sure."

"I know we've come on strong this week in hopes you would accept our offer. But bottom line is, we only want you if this is where God is leading you."

Okay, that she didn't expect. "Have you changed your minds or had second thoughts about me?"

"Not even close. We'd love to have you if it's meant to be. I just ... well, I want you to know that if you choose to stay with your current ministry, we certainly understand and wish you only the best."

Relief mixed with added uncertainty in that knot that only grew in her midsection. She'd been in constant prayer about what direction she should go, but no burning bushes or writing on the wall had appeared to give her a clear answer.

"I appreciate that, Zane. Please know how inspired I am by your vision for Reach Over, and it would be amazing to be part of that team. I'm praying hard about where God wants me, and I'll try to have my answer for you by the time we meet on Monday, before I go back to Dallas."

"Sounds good." He glanced at the door and back at her. "I hope you have a good time tonight. No matter what happens."

No matter what happens? "I'm sure I will."

He held his hand out toward the entrance. "Shall we?"

She preceded him in the door behind another dressed-to-the-nines couple, handed her coat to a young man Zane greeted with a high five, and waited to say hello to Maggie and her husband, who stood in the marble-floored foyer to accept their guests.

"That's Maggie's son," Zane explained. "A senior at Yale, home for the holidays."

"Harper!" Maggie smiled brightly, the red of her gown bringing a healthy glow to her cheeks. Light from the chandelier above twinkled from her diamond drop earrings. "You look lovely." She gestured to the handsome man beside her. "This is my husband, Oliver. Oliver, this is Harper Townsend, the young woman I've been telling you about."

"Oh, yes." His smile left crinkles around his eyes. "Not so much talking about as extolling your virtues. It's nice to put a face with all the accolades."

Harper's face warmed. "That's nice of you to say, although I'm sure she exaggerates."

He leaned in close. "My wife never exaggerates." He

straightened to shake Zane's hand. "Zane, my good fellow, nice to see you all gussied up."

"Once a year is my limit."

"Zane," Maggie said as he leaned in to kiss her cheek. "I'm so happy to see you. Oh, and your guest is here somewhere. Arrived about ten minutes ago."

He glanced at Harper and back at their hostess. "Okay, great. Thank you."

Zane took Harper by the elbow and steered her through the foyer toward a large sunken living room. Well-dressed guests mingled and laughed, holding small crystal plates of *hors d'oeuvres* and cups of red punch while a three-piece string ensemble played "Carol of the Bells," their bows moving at warp speed.

She looked over at her escort for the evening. "Zane, if you had a date lined up for tonight, you should have brought her. I could have driven here on my own."

"Date?" He chuckled. "Not really my type." They came to the top of the steps leading down into the vast but elegant living room and stopped. "I was thinking maybe more yours?"

When he gestured with a crook of his head, she followed his line a sight and gasped when a man standing with his hands in his pockets talking to several of the Reach Over team members looked up, his gaze locking on hers.

"Wyatt," she said on a breath.

Zane laughed from beside her. "Yeah, that's what I thought. The way you two light up when you talk about each other, I knew there had to be something there."

She looked over at Zane and shook her head. "No, we're not—"

"Come on, Harper." He gave her that dimpled smile that probably sent many a woman's pulse all a-twitter. But her heart beat only for one man. "It's all over your face. And his, for that matter."

Her insides seemed to liquefy as Wyatt excused himself

and started toward her, wearing the same charcoal suit he wore to the reunion dinner. Would she ever be able to walk into a room and not have a physical reaction when she saw him? "But what's he doing here?"

"I'd wager a guess he's here for you. But I'll let him explain. Just let me know if it turns out you don't need a ride back to the hotel later."

"Thanks, Zane."

He gave her a nudge to the small of her back. "Go. I have lots of five-star food to devour and you're holding me up."

She nodded but couldn't take her eyes off the man coming closer as she took the three steps down into the room quickly fading into the background.

What was Wyatt doing in Atlanta? Was he really here for her? To bring her home, or ease her transition into a new ministry, a new life? A life that didn't include him.

CHAPTER FIFTY-ONE

*H*arper put her hand to her stomach, a futile effort to stop the fluttering there that had nothing to do with the fact she hadn't eaten since lunch.

Wyatt stopped in front of her. "You look stunning, Harper. I mean, really. Do you always have to outshine every woman in the room?"

Her face heated even more than when Oliver had complimented her at the door. "You're very kind, Dr. McCowan. You look quite handsome yourself."

He took her hand and leaned in to brush a kiss on her cheek. "It's great to see you. I've missed you. No matter what's happened between us, I don't like going days without talking to you."

Her skin tingled at his touch. "I don't either. If I hadn't lost my phone—"

"Oh!" He let go of her hand and reached into his inside coat pocket, bringing out a cell phone in a hot pink case. "I almost forgot."

Her eyes widened. "My phone! How do you have my phone?"

"I got a call from a guy who said he found it lying under a

seat on a plane they were working on. He stuck it in his toolbox and forgot about it until he found it yesterday morning. I picked it up at the airport before catching my flight."

"So it did get on the plane in Dallas with me. It just didn't get off with me."

"Apparently not. The phone was disabled since you'd purchased a new one, but he was able to go through your contacts. Guess I'm still in there as your emergency contact."

"Oh. Right. I never changed that."

He shrugged as he placed the phone back in his pocket. "I don't mind being your person."

Their gazes locked and held, and all she wanted to do was launch herself into his arms and kiss him silly. Probably not a good move, considering their present location. "Wyatt, I don't understand why you're here. Not that I'm not really happy to see you, but what's going on?"

He glanced around the room. "Let's go somewhere more private." He took her hand to pull her out of the flow of guests arriving or making their way to the dining room, where the massive table sat covered with an array of appetizers and dessert offerings. It looked wonderful, but she wouldn't be able to eat a bite of it in her current state.

After entering the study off the living room, they walked over to a window overlooking the terrace, lined with Christmas trees twinkling with white lights.

He turned to face her. "I came out here to clear up a misunderstanding, I guess you could say."

"A misunderstanding? Wi—with me?"

He moved his head side to side. "Yes. But more so with Zane."

"I don't understand."

"Harper, I never told him you would be great for their ministry here. I just told him you were great. Period. Because you are. Wherever God calls you to be, you're going to do big things for Him, and I'll support you one hundred percent. But I need you to know I never wanted you away from Arlington or ConnectUP." His gaze softened. "Or me."

"Wyatt—"

"Have you accepted their offer?"

She shook her head. "Not yet. But I can't stay in Arlington just because it's home and it's comfortable. I have to be where God can use me the best."

"I couldn't agree more. But give me a chance to plead my case, if I may."

Her mind reeling, she gestured with one hand. "Yes. Of course. Plead away."

With that boyish grin that made her heart race, he reached into the other side pocket of his suit coat and pulled out his phone. "I want you to see something."

Confused, she stared at him as he tapped a couple of times on the screen. He handed her the phone as a video played of their CU kids sitting in a large semi-circle. She looked up at him in question.

"Club. Wednesday night. Reed took that."

She nodded and looked back down at the phone as his voice came through the device's speaker. Everything around her fell away as the impact of his words hit her.

... we need to expand our borders.

ConnectUP cannot become the very thing it was created to fight.

We have to be willing to follow Him into the trenches.

We want to challenge you to move outside your comfort zone. Build bridges, not walls.

Tears filled her eyes. She glanced up at him and he nodded, a smile spreading across his face she couldn't help but return before looking back down at the screen.

I've seen some things ... that brought me to my knees.

These kids need God. Desperately.

ConnectUP is about connection. Connection with each other, connection with God. And connecting with others we may not understand.

She laughed at the kids' enthusiastic responses and put her hand on her chest as if to capture the warmth spreading there. And when the Wyatt on screen began praying, she reached up to wrap her arm around the neck of the Wyatt standing in front of her.

"Harper." His soft voice so near her ear caused ripples across her skin. "There's so much I want to tell you. So much that's happened."

She let him go and handed him his phone. With a sniffle, she looked up at the coffered ceiling of the study, placing her index fingers under her eyes to keep her tears from leaving tracks in her makeup. "Ugh. I think this is a losing battle. I blame you if I end up with mascara streaks down my face the rest of the evening."

He laughed and handed her a handkerchief he'd pulled from his shirt pocket. Why couldn't women's clothing come with such convenient hidey-holes so they wouldn't have to carry a pocketbook just to have a place for a lipstick and cell phone?

"I'd hoped to talk to you before I told the kids," he said as she dabbed at her eyes along her lower lashes. "But you left before I had the chance. Harper, I finally had the guts to ask God to show me if we needed to be doing more, and he kept putting people in my path that I would have never thought ConnectUP could reach—Finn, Jill, Dwight. Sarah Holmes."

Her jaw dropped. "You saw Sarah?"

"A long story I'll tell you later. Bottom line is, I was finally able to deal with all that anger I was still carrying. And it was like releasing a bag of bricks from my back. Instantly."

"Wyatt! That's amazing!"

"I had to finally surrender and be willing to be wrong. To take a step beyond myself, beyond what I know, to what God wants to teach me. To where He wants to take ConnectUP."

"I'm so happy for you. Truly. This is tremendous."

"And it gets tremendous-er." He shrugged. "Okay, I just made up that word, but you know what I mean. Zane and I had a marathon talk last Sunday about our visions for ministry, and I knew I needed to find out more. I worked it out with him to come out here week after next to talk about ConnectUP and how we might be able to work with Reach Over.

"But when Rhonda told me you thought I had pawned you off on Zane—my words, not hers—I knew I had to fix it. I called him after club and moved up my plans. I worked almost all night revamping the grant proposal into a ministry plan, slept on the plane, got in yesterday afternoon, then went straight to Becker. I spent the late afternoon into the evening with Maggie and all day today with Zane and his team."

"*You're* the reason he canceled on me today." She leaned in. "Thank you for that, by the way. It's been amazing to see all they do here, but I am completely overwhelmed. Shopping today was just what I needed."

He leaned back and laughed, and she let the sound wash over her like a cool breeze on a July afternoon in Texas. How she'd missed this man and all things Wyatt, from his laugh to his auburn hair, his sparkling eyes to his king-sized heart for God.

She cocked her head. "Hold on. You've been here since yesterday and didn't call me?"

He grimaced. "I told Zane not to mention it until I met with the Becker folks, to see if the ideas he and I were throwing around during our call on Sunday were even feasible."

"Ideas?"

His smile warmed her from the inside out. "What if I told you Becker is considering sponsoring ConnectUP?"

Her eyes rounded. "Are you? Telling me that, I mean?"

"Yep. We, as in you and I, meet with their board of directors Monday morning. If they agree, which Maggie believes they will, they'll take our name since we're an established organization with name recognition, non-profit tax status, and a ready-made stable of volunteers from which we can hire our first staffers."

He looked up and tapped his chin. "In fact, I can think of one who's highly sought-after in the youth ministry biz. I wonder if she'd even give us the time of day, considering her caliber?"

She swatted at his arm. "Stop it. Besides, I couldn't be your first staffer. Not when some of the others have been with you longer."

"We're considering bringing Matt on as well until he's out of school, so you both would work part-time until you're ready to take on full-time status. If Emery can do without you, that is."

"She'd be beyond happy for me. But what about the grant? Will you have to rewrite the entire proposal?"

He shook his head. "That's the beauty of it. With Becker on board, we don't need it. That money can go to another deserving ministry. And the icing on the cake is that they would allow ConnectUP to headquarter in Arlington."

She couldn't stop smiling. "Oh, Wyatt, I am so ... so ..." She threw her arms up in a shrug. "I can't find the words. Your dream, your vision, it's all coming to fruition."

He stepped close and took her hands in his. "*Our* vision. I couldn't do any of this without you. You were the one, Harper. The one who opened my eyes to what we could do. To what could be accomplished for God if we expanded our focus. Just be warned, though. We have a lot of work to do to get our ministry plan into motion, starting with off-shoots from the Arlington club. I'm counting on your help, if you can do it with all of your school commitments."

"It'd be an honor."

"And you'll be my plus one for the rehearsal dinner and wedding next week?"

She dropped his hands, walked into his arms, and grasped

him around the neck. "I told you. If you ever need a plus one, I'm your girl."

His hands slid around her waist. "Forever?"

Her eyes widened as her pulse accelerated. "For as long as you'll have me."

He let her go, reached into his pants pocket, and pulled out a small, velvet box. After bending to one knee, he opened the box to reveal the most perfect diamond ring she could have ever imagined, and she gave up the fight to keep her tears from falling.

"I have no doubts, Harper. About where I want to go with you. The life I want us to build together. I know it's only been a couple of months, but I'm sure, sweetheart. Will you marry me? Be my wife and my family? Walk alongside me and grow old with me?"

"Absolutely. Yes, yes, a jillion times, yes!"

He stood, slipped the ring onto her finger, and took her in his arms, covering her mouth in a kiss she'd been craving since the last one they'd shared in his kitchen, before the conversation that had sent her world toppling.

But once she'd been willing to surrender all of her own wants and dreams to follow God only, He'd led her back to Wyatt. To a ministry they could build together. Dreams they could realize ... together.

He pulled back and brushed a tear from her cheek with his thumb. "I love you, Harper Townsend. Always have, always will."

"I love you back, Wyatt McCowan."

"How about from now on, it's you and me, with God as our Plus One?"

EPILOGUE

*W*yatt held Harper close on the dance floor, drowning in her eyes while swaying to the love song that had nothing on what he felt in his heart. "Most amazing wedding ever."

"The wedding of my dreams." Her smile beamed up at him as it had from the second their eyes met when she started down the aisle toward him, on the arm of her proud father.

"And you're the bride of mine."

He let go of her long enough to spin her around and back into his arms before leaning in for a lingering kiss, to the delight of their many guests watching them take their first dance as husband and wife. He couldn't remember ever seeing a more beautiful woman in his life, in her white, strapless, flowing dress, her hair curled and cascading down her back. And his ring on her finger.

After accepting his surprise proposal in December, Harper had spent the last seven months planning their wedding with Emery and both of their mothers. It had been a pure joy watching her and her mother grow closer as the elder Townsends immersed themselves in their newfound faith. As if making up for all those lost years.

"I'm crazy about you, Dr. McCowan."

"I'm pretty nuts about you, too, Mrs. McCowan. Have been most of my life. My first crush. Cutest girl in the whole kindergarten class."

"And I loved your red curls. I can't wait to have little red-haired babies."

"With your gorgeous green eyes."

He pulled her close and she rested her head against his shoulder as they moved in time with the music. Too soon, their chosen song ended, and the DJ invited their guests to join them.

Still swaying in his arms, Harper looked around the elegant ballroom. "I think every one of our kids is here with us tonight."

"They've all been very excited."

A young couple moved past them, their gazes glued to each other as Dwight took Jill around the waist, her arms reaching up to wrap around his neck. Jill had been a believer coming on four months now, Dwight not far behind. The two had found their way back to a close friendship over the past few months but had recently started dating again. Wyatt knew from his sessions with Dwight that the boy had made great strides in releasing his need to control and now wanted a healthy relationship, based on trust and mutual respect.

Wyatt spotted several of the ConnectUP kids gathered in a group and laughing it up as they always did when together. Four of the guys had acted as ushers, and Harper had enlisted Jill and Tish to cover the guest book and gift table while Tonya and Remy lit the candles on the altar at the start of the ceremony. The kids loved taking part in their special day, and it meant just as much to him and Harper to have them there.

"Hey there, Dr. and Mrs. Mac!" Tonya beamed as she and her date walked by hand-in-hand onto the dance floor.

Harper smiled at them. "Hey, girl."

She brought her sparkling eyes back to him once the teens

were out of earshot. "Tonya and Finn. I didn't see that coming."

He looked over to the young couple dancing close together and back to his bride. "I'm not surprised. He told me a few months ago he was done dating for what he could get out of it. That he'd wait until he could find a girl like Tonya, someone sold out to God."

"She certainly is that. Plans to get her degree in Biblical Studies at DHU and go into missions. Only a senior in high school and already knows what she wants to do with her life. I was twenty-eight when I finally figured it out."

"I could see them going that same direction. Especially if he ends up at DHU to play baseball."

"You think they'll consider him?"

He shrugged. "His school record is a disaster. But he's taking summer classes to get his GPA up, is doing volunteer work, serving at church. If they see he's committed to service and to his classwork, they may be willing to take a chance on him. They were beyond impressed with his skills on the field." He grinned down at her. "Doesn't hurt that one of the admissions counselors is a frat brother of mine and is taking my recommendation under advisement."

"Doesn't hurt."

"Finn reminds me of you when you were a newbie Christian. On fire for the Lord and soaking up everything he can. When I think about how angry he was when I first met him, to see the young man he is today, only seven months later, it's astonishing."

"God's like that, isn't He? In the business of total transformation. Of taking something broken and making it more beautiful than it ever had been before."

Wyatt stared down at the woman in his arms. Only eleven months ago, upon his first sight of her over a decade after she literally shut her front door in his face, he'd wanted to do nothing but flee. Now here they were, husband and wife a full two hours now, and he couldn't imagine not being right here. With her. Planning a future. Building a ministry. Becoming a family. The healing of their bond that had begun as children was nothing short of a divine act, leaving him humbled and, oh, so very grateful.

Tears filled his eyes as he swept the backs of his fingers down her cheek. "Like the miracle of us. Which is what I feel when I see you. A miracle He brought you back to me, and now here we are. The two of us. Forever."

She reached up and gave him a gentle kiss. "The two of us. Plus One. Forever and always."

ACKNOWLEDGMENTS

Building a house, birthing a baby ... writing a novel. All of these ventures involve planning, time, patience, a lot of prayer, and even some pain. And none of them are solitary endeavors. It takes a crew to build a house, a medical team to help a momma bring a baby into the world, and an army of prayer warriors, critique partners, beta readers, editors, conference teachers, and the support and encouragement of family, friends, and fellow writers to bring a novel to fruition, from story concept to plotting to writing to finally ... hopefully ... publishing.

This is not my first novel. It's my *debut* novel, but there were many before it that helped me cut my teeth and hone my skills as a writer. Most will never see the light of day but are no less vital because they brought me to this place. This goal achieved. This dream realized.

But I would not be here without my amazing writer posse, with their support, encouragement, brainstorming help, critiques, and so much more. Thank you from the bottom of my heart to Lori Altebaumer and Kristi Woods, my sisters in Christ and writers-in-arms, for your hours of time spent brainstorming, critiquing, advising, and just plain listening. You ladies are my heroes. To my WOWG critique group— Brenda O'Bannion, Wendi Threlkeld, Bruce Hammock, Teresa Lynn—your insight, feedback and encouragement are so appreciated. To my FHL critique group— Jennifer Looft,

Betsy Iler, Laura Schad. Thank you so much for your excellent critiques and the support you've shown for this manuscript.

And I can't forget all of the amazing conferences, workshops, and writers' groups that have helped me hone my skills as a wordcrafter—ACFW National Conference, ACFW Virginia Royal Writers Conference, Kentucky Christian Writers Conference, Flourish Writers Conference, ACFW Dallas/Ft Worth, Novel Academy, 540 Writers, Faith, Hope, and Love Christian Writers, South Central FHLCW regional group, and CenTex Christian Writers Group. Thank you to the contest coordinators and judges for the 2022 ACFW Genesis contest, for your time and excellent feedback. A huge thank you to Laurie Schnebly for your amazing classes (where the concept for this novel was born!) and retreats. What I've learned from you over the years could never be put to words. I am so blessed by your friendship. And to Liana George and Teresa Wells, my Novel Academy huddle-mates. You ladies are extraordinary, and your wisdom, encouragement, and friendship mean so much to me. And thank you to my beta readers—Jennifer Petter, Leslie Foster, and Jen Meitzen—for your time and excellent feedback.

I am so honored to be a part of the Scrivenings Press family and so appreciate the support and insight of Linda Fulkerson and Amy Anguish, editors extraordinaire! I can't tell you how much I appreciate you and your investment in me. It means everything.

And to my family, for the years you've encouraged and supported this dream of mine and for sharing my joy when it was finally realized. To Eric, my husband and best friend. For your listening ear when I needed to work through a plot or character problem when you probably would have preferred scrolling through Netflix. And to Michaela, my precious daughter, for your belief in me and encouraging me to keep going when it would've been tempting to throw in the towel. Also, for helping me with all the techy things my brain just wasn't made to understand. And to my mom and dad, who have cheered me on throughout the years. I love you all so much!

Finally, but most importantly, none of this could have been achieved without the constant presence, guidance, love, and grace of my Creator, Counselor, Father, King, and Confidant. I would have no words, no message, no calling if not for the precious gift of His Son who came to give life to all. My sincerest prayer is that everybody who picks up this humble story of mine will find it pointing to the Greatest Story ever written, a *true* story. To a God who loves us without condition and offers joy, hope, redemption, and forgiveness. To Him alone goes all the glory.

ABOUT THE AUTHOR

Hey there, y'all! I find writing about my fictional characters much more fun and exciting than writing about myself, but here goes.

First of all, I love Jesus and the Bible and writing stories full of grace and the redemptive power of God's love that inspire hope, joy, laughter, and that maybe even touch a soul or two to get to know Him better. I couldn't ask for any more than that from the words I put to paper. Nothing else matters.

I was born and raised in Phoenix, Arizona, but arrived in Texas in 2005, and dug those roots right in. I do love me some Texas, especially here in beautiful Georgetown, where my husband and I live in our empty next (except for our two fur-babies, Buddy and Lily). We have one daughter, Michaela, who is living and thriving in the Dallas area and is the absolute joy of my life.

I love to write about love and romance and all that fun stuff, with a firm foundation of faith. Clean but sassy, sparkly, and even goose-bumpy romance is a *thing*, y'all! With God in the middle, and with characters seeking and learning and changing, nothing could be more heartwarming or spine-tingly.

My debut novel, *Love's True Calling*, was the 2020 winner of the Scrivenings Press Novel Starts Contest, the 2022 winner of the ACFW Genesis Award for Romance, and a 2022 Maggie finalist. Watch for *Love's True Home,* coming in 2024, and *Love's True Measure* in 2025.

Lone Star Sweetheart

by Shannon Sue Dunlap

Katherine Bruno's passionate, unfiltered temper makes her the shrew of small-town Sweetheart, Texas. When she's drafted to help the mayor's wife run against her own husband, Katherine meets opposing big city political consultant Ryan Park. The good-looking, flirtatious campaign manager gets under her skin, but fraternizing with the enemy is off-limits.

Katherine must battle her lack of experience, campaign sabotage, and her growing feelings for Ryan as she strives to succeed. His unprejudiced acceptance of her strong-willed character beckons her heart, but his jaded rejection of God is an insurmountable barrier. Will Ryan return to his faith and stay with her in Sweetheart or leave when the election ends?

Get your copy here:

https://scrivenings.link/lonestarsweetheart

~

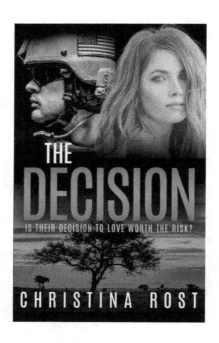

The Decision

by Christina Rost

Running from her grief, interior designer Ava Stewart makes a hasty decision to join a missionary group heading to Uganda. She's in the country only a few days before tragedy strikes, and a mistaken identity leaves her with an uncertain outcome.

Special Operator Blake Martin is assigned to a humanitarian mission when he's captured by a group of armed men. Wounded and miles away from his team, Blake's brought to Ava, and she's ordered to care for him.

Thrown together in chaos, with the threat of danger pressing in from all sides, Ava and Blake are forced to rely on each other—and God—to escape. An undeniable bond is formed during their flight to safety, but opening their hearts to love carries its own risk. A risk they aren't sure they're willing to take.

Now, miles apart and living separate lives, they need to decide if the connection they shared in the untamed, wilds of Uganda is strong enough to confront the future. A future where Ava's fragile heart and Blake's hazardous job collide, and only God knows the outcome.

Get your copy here:

https://scrivenings.link/thedecision

∿

Operation Find a ~~Job~~ Guy

by Amy R. Anguish

Skye Jones has one goal for the summer—keep her father from taking away her convertible. That's the *only* reason she agrees to work at her sister's bridal shop in Boulder, Colorado, while she searches for a non-boring job. Why else would she have anything to do with weddings when she has no interest in marriage?

Benjamin Smith somehow ended up as a groomsman in two weddings over the summer, so he's spending a lot of time at Happily Ever After events. Falling for a blonde with no dreams of settling down wasn't in his five-year plan, yet the more he sees Skye, the more he wants to figure her out.

But all she sees him as is a boring attorney-her complete opposite.

Besides, romance is supposed to be for Skye's friends, not her. And she's in Colorado to get a job, not a guy. Right?

Get your copy here:

https://scrivenings.link/operationfindaguy

Stay up-to-date on your favorite books and authors with our free e-newsletters.

ScriveningsPress.com